THE
FOOTBALL
MANAGER
MURDERS

THE
FOOTBALL
MANAGER
MURDERS

CHRIS TOOKEY

The Book Guild Ltd

First published in Great Britain in 2018 by
The Book Guild Ltd
9 Priory Business Park
Wistow Road, Kibworth
Leicestershire, LE8 0RX
Freephone: 0800 999 2982
www.bookguild.co.uk
Email: info@bookguild.co.uk
Twitter: @bookguild

Typeset in Garamond

Printed and bound in Great Britain by CPI Group (UK) Ltd, Croydon, CR0 4YY

ISBN 978 1912362 516

British Library Cataloguing in Publication Data.
A catalogue record for this book is available from the British Library.

Dedicated to Frances and Dan

1

THE LADY VANISHES

Monday, 1st August, 2011

"Boss? Boss! There's someone to see you, boss," said Marti, coming in, the way she always does when she's buzzed me and I have failed to buzz back.

Marti always calls me "boss" but with a weird tone to her voice, as though she's sending me up. She's our receptionist until her singing career takes off, or she gets an acting job. Neither of these appears to be imminent.

"A client?" I asked.

"Clients," she said. "Two of them. Arrived together. It's like Noah's ark out there."

"Wonders will never cease," I replied, hurriedly firing up a Word document on the screen.

"Oh no," she said. "You're not playing that computer game, are you?"

She came to peek over my shoulder There was no point denying it. The top of the Football Manager window was showing, just above the Word document.

Football Manager is addictive, especially to blokes. It's been cited in thirty-five divorce cases, one of them mine. The appeal lies in the detail. It's amazingly well researched, and as pitiless as real life. The first time I was fired from managing the Arsenal, it took me a week to get over it. I started all over again with a non-League club to hone my skills. But somehow I always drift back to old haunts.

"Just whiling away the idle hour," I said. "I'll have you know, I'm on the brink of leading the England team to glory in the European Cup."

"How thrilling," said Marti, in a voice that suggested the opposite. "I thought you were managing Arsenal."

"I was, but I got so successful, they offered me the England managership as well."

"You must be very proud."

"I know it's only a game, but…"

Marti crossed back to the door.

"So, what shall I do, boss? Send them away and tell them you're too busy playing computer games?"

"Spare me the sarcasm, Marti. Is it anyone I know?"

"I recognise the bloke, but I can't place him," she said. "Sorry. The other's a woman. Foreign. They wouldn't give me their names. The bloke just said you'd be glad to see him."

"Mysterious," I said.

I looked around the office. It was in its usual state. Unlikely to impress.

"So shall I send them in?" asked Marti.

"Better not. It looks like a tip in here, for which I hold you personally responsible."

"Charming," she said. "It's you who won't let me clear anything away."

"Is it hot in here?" I asked her.

"It certainly is," she said. "I take it the window won't open."

"The sash is broken," I said. "I don't suppose the air con is working?"

"No way," she said. "Nor are the lifts."

"No sign of anyone repairing them yet?"

"They're not going to do that on the hottest day of the year," she said, fanning herself with her fingers, the way she does when she's trying to dry her nail varnish.

"Maybe you'd better send our visitors into the conference room," I said.

Marti gave me her mock military salute.

"Anything you say, boss."

Even in normal weather, my office gets too stuffy to accommodate more than one client at a time. It could also do with a lick of paint. The ceiling tiles are a disgrace. Some time before we moved in, there must have been a flood from the floor above, and the landlords never got round to replacing the tiles, which are stained and cracked. I expect they're waiting for the whole lot to cave in, and claim on the insurance.

By contrast, the conference room is double the size of my office. It has a decent fitted carpet, apart from a few coffee stains, and a high ceiling, which makes it the least sordid area of what estate agents might laughingly describe as our suite. It has a good view of Soho Square, right across to where the Football Association haul people in to give them a dressing down. I nearly chose it as my personal space, but then thought I'd never get any work done. I've always enjoyed people-watching, and I'd spend my entire life peeking out the window, hoping for a glimpse of Wayne Rooney squaring up to some unfortunate official.

I left about a minute to give the impression that I was busy with something other than a computer game, saved Football Manager in preparation for the next major confrontation, and strode across to the conference room.

The first thing that struck me on opening the door was the strong, feminine aroma. There was only one person in the world who gave off a pong like that, and I'd have known who it was even if I hadn't seen the top of his head, a balding pate with grey,

3

greasy hair scraped across it. He was sitting with his back to the door but turned round as I came in.

You know the way some people get a shudder down their necks when they see a spider? Rex Crawley has the same effect on me and, I imagine, most people. He is universally known as Creepy Crawley. His other, even less complimentary nickname is Tyrannosaurus Rex. You'd know why if you'd ever seen him savage a sirloin.

He must be knocking 70 now, but I shouldn't think he'll ever retire. He likes to call himself a publicist, but he seems to have spent most of his life doing the opposite: hushing things up that celebs don't want papers to hear about. Which is ironic, since he made his name flogging kiss and tell stories by people who think they can earn fame and fortune for having shagged someone famous. Say what you like about Creepy, he doesn't mind what people say about him. That's just as well, since he's universally despised.

"Allo, Charlie," he said, showing his surprisingly white teeth, which must have cost him at least twenty grand. "Long time no see."

"Why, Rex Crawley, as I live and breathe," I said. "To what do I owe this inestimable pleasure?"

"Inestimable pleasure!" he chuckled. "I like that. Knees all right?"

"Last time I looked down," I said. "Mustn't grumble."

"But no more sliding tackles," he said.

"Those days are gone," I said. "And what are you up to?"

"The usual," he said. "A bit of this, and a bit of that."

"And a bit of the other, no doubt. I keep seeing your name in the papers."

"Oh yeah?" he said, evasively.

I took a look at the woman by the window. She looked at least thirty years more mature than his usual client.

"And now, Rex," I said, "perhaps you would be good enough to make the introductions?"

"I'm sorry," said the little man. "This is one of my most valued friends, Katasha Molotovski."

His friend turned from the window. Valued or not, she looked as though she required high maintenance, and plenty of it. She was a big, buxom blonde who had seen better decades. It was hard to tell her age, which might have been anything from thirty to sixty. Maybe forty-five with a facelift, which might well have necessitated the assistance of a forklift truck. She extended her hand and moved towards me, like the irresistible force she must have been in her teens and twenties.

"Mr Crawley has told me everything about you," she breathed huskily, with a voice that suggested a lifetime of Russian cigarettes and fancy cocktails, the kind that cost a lot of money and don't require umbrellas. I couldn't help wondering if she had been a welterweight boxer. Although she was on her best behaviour, she looked as if she might have a useful left hook.

"Nothing incriminating, I hope," I said.

"Rather the reverse," she said. "He say you are honest as day is long."

"Thanks, Creepy," I said. "But coming from you, I'm not sure that's entirely a compliment."

"Now, now, Charlie," he said shiftily, "I know we've had the odd run-in, but..."

"So you do still remember selling that rubbish story about me to the News of the Screws?"

"That was many moons ago," he said. "And I wasn't to know the tart was telling porkies. Besides, you got compensation. Generous compensation, as I recall."

"Yeah, they settled out of court," I said. "But it didn't exactly do my marriage any favours. Or my reputation. What was it you said on the *News At Ten*, about 'There's no smoke without fire'? Thanks a lot, chum!"

"Now, now, Charlie, why not let bygones be bygones?" he wheedled. "We've all passed a lot of water since then."

Just then, the door burst open to save me having to put up with any more of his cheery cockney badinage, and my son came in. His name's Tom, and he's my none too highly paid assistant. Tom was bright enough to have gone to university but he dropped out of school – expelled, actually, after a series of misunderstandings over alcohol and cannabis. After that he started to drift, so I took him on, to give him a bit of steady money and get him out of his mum's hair.

He's twenty now and a reasonably solid citizen. Still likes a drink now and again, but he doesn't do drugs, tattoos or eye make-up, which is a relief. He's more James Hunt than Amy Winehouse. I could see both my potential clients eying him speculatively.

"Sorry I'm late," said Tom. "Trouble on the tube. Someone threw himself on the line at Warren Street. Probably couldn't stand the suspense of waiting for the train. Marti told me you had people with you. Do tell me if I can help."

The thing about Tom is that he went to a public school until they hurled him to the wolves, so he talks a bit posher than I do. That and his looks make him an asset in my line of business. I'd be the first to admit that I've a few rough edges, whereas Tom could charm the birds from the trees. And his appeal isn't limited to winged wildlife.

"Ah, Tom," I said. "Glad you could make it. This is Tom, my beloved son and heir to the Charlesworth millions."

"Katasha Molotovski," said the Russian, extending her hand to be shaken.

"Pleased to meet you, Mrs Molotovski," said Tom.

Tom turned to face the little man whom Marti had recognised from the telly. I wondered if Tom knew who he was.

"And you're Rex Crawley, aren't you?" said Tom.

"Yeah," said Creepy, shiftily. "Maybe."

"And you've come here to consult my father?" asked Tom. "Or is it to chew the fat about the last time you stitched him up?"

"No," said Creepy. "Me and Mrs Molotovski have... a

6

problem. That we'd like to discuss with your father. Alone if possible."

"That won't be possible," I said. "Tom's an integral part of the operation."

"Really?" said Creepy. "I thought he must be on work experience."

"No," I said. "He's here full-time."

"When I'm not late," said Tom, with his usual lack of remorse.

"Indeed," I agreed, looking at my watch, 11 a.m. wasn't bad for Tom. "He helps me a good deal, in fact."

"I'm sure he does," purred Mrs Molotovski, looking my son up and down.

"You do realise I'm not paying any extra for him," said Creepy, with a gracelessness he might have learned from watching Alan Sugar on *The Apprentice*, or more likely came to him naturally. "It's you I came to see."

"I have no objection to young man staying," said Mrs Molotovski, with a flutter of her heavy black eyelashes, which looked like a pair of demented crows had crash-landed on her face.

"Oh well, suit yourself," said Creepy. "Now, let's stop farting about and get down to business."

"By all means," I said. "Would we all like coffee?"

There was a multiple murmur of assent, and I poked my head out of the door. As usual, Marti had her head deep in a celebrity magazine.

"Marti," I said, "if I can tear you away from your studies, could you fix us four coffees?"

"What? Oh. Yeah. Righto, boss," said Marti.

She tottered round from behind her desk, all long black legs and ridiculously high heels.

"Mind if I get myself one at the same time?" she asked.

"Feel free," I said.

"I do," she said, with a wink. "How's it going in there, all right?"

"It's a little bit early to tell," I said.

"Now," I continued, returning to the conference room, "perhaps you could tell me what this is about."

"It about my little girl Olga," said Mrs Molotovski. "She is vanished."

"I'm sorry to hear it," I said. "But surely that's a police matter."

"The police have been informed, of course," said Creepy, "but my client does not consider they are taking the matter seriously enough."

"How old is little Olga?" I asked.

"Seventeen," said Creepy.

"Eighteen in few days time. I have pictures," said the Russian. "Here."

She pushed them across the table towards Tom. I could tell straight away from Tom's exaggeratedly cool reaction that Olga was not all that little, and a definite looker. I looked at the photos, which had obviously been done professionally. She would have looked at home on page three of the Sun, if she hadn't been demurely clothed. I could see that Tom was already taking a keen interest in the case.

"These photos look as if they were done professionally," I said, turning them over to look at the back. There was a logo on the back, saying FLASH PHOTOGRAPHY, followed by an address in Notting Hill.

"They were," said the proud mother. "Olga made with the modelling."

"What kind of modelling?" asked Tom.

"Swimsuits, underwear, that thing," said the Russian. "But she get bored with that, so she stop."

"How long ago did she disappear, Mrs Molotovski?"

"Nine days," said Mrs Molotovski. "Saturday night. Last Sunday we get up and she is gone."

"Had she been out on the Saturday night?"

"No," said the Russian. "Was up reading in her room. She is good student. Just taken A-levels. Five of them."

"A year early?" asked Tom.

"Yes," said the Russian. "Super-intelligent, like my husband. She speak four languages. English, Russian, French and Spanish."

"Maybe she couldn't take the pressure," said Tom.

"I not think so," said the proud mother. "She star pupil. Learning come easy to her. And exams were over."

"Where is she at school?" I asked.

"The North London Academy for Girls."

I nodded. This was one of the posher North London schools, with a matchless reputation for high fees and spectacular rates of *anorexia nervosa*.

"I take it the police have talked to her friends at school, and the teachers?"

"I believe so," said the Russian. "But they know nothing."

"I'm impressed that the news hasn't leaked to the papers."

"The school has been very good, like the police," said the Russian, "but not so good at finding my daughter."

"Was she in the habit of disappearing?" I asked. "Has she ever gone off for days at a time?"

"Never," said Mrs Molotovski. "My husband would not allow it."

"And your husband is…?"

"Igor Molotovski," she said.

Tom whistled.

"I see," he said.

"I don't," I said.

"Dad, you must know who Igor Molotovski is. I know he doesn't own a Premiership club, but even so…"

"Igor Molotovski," said Creepy Crawley, "is an international entrepreneur."

"And he specialises in…?" I asked.

"Computer games," said his wife, shrugging. "I am not proud of it, but there it is."

"Dad knows all about them," said Tom. "Is Football Manager one of his?"

"I don't think so," said Mrs Molotovski. "His games are more into fantasy and action."

"Oh, violence," said Tom. "World of Warcraft? Everquest?"

Mrs Molotovski shook her head.

"His best-selling game at moment is Seven Deadly Sins."

"I know it well," said Tom. "I have it on my phone as an app. It's seriously addictive."

He turned and gave me a penetrating look.

"A bit like Football Manager," he added.

I decided to ignore the cheap jibe.

"Tell me about your family," I said. "Have you been married for long?"

"Twenty years."

"And you have how many children?"

"Just the one," she said.

"Which would make Olga an heiress."

"Yes," she said, "and kidnap victim, possibly. Which is why my husband keep her under strictest control."

"Except now she's disappeared."

"Exactly."

"From your home in…?"

"Totteridge."

I knew the kind of house she must live in. Huge. Big garden, too. The sort a Renaissance Pope might have built in order to impress his mistresses.

"Don't you have security cameras?" I asked. "Big iron gates?"

"Gates, yes," she said. "Cameras, not working."

"Why not?"

"My husband having new system put in. Not yet up and running. But we have security men. They no good, so we fire them, get new ones."

"And they didn't see your daughter leave?"

"No."

"I see. Does your husband have any enemies?"

"Many, many enemies," she said. "Is why we come to live in UK. Safer here. Or so we thought."

"Could your daughter just have walked out the front door?"

"Is possible. She have key. Let herself in and out. But where to?"

"So you think she's been kidnapped?" I asked.

"That is everyone's first thought," said Mrs Molotovski. "But no, there is no kidnap demand."

"And what do the police think?" asked Tom.

"Mystery to me," said Mrs Molotovski. "Is as if they think she run away from home."

"Could she have?" I asked. "Have there been any arguments?"

The conversation paused as Marti brought in the coffees and handed them around.

"No, no arguments," said Mrs Molotovski. "My husband very strong man. He not allow arguments. Over nothing."

"And your daughter, she obeys him?" asked Tom.

"Of course," said Mrs Molotovski. "She good daughter. Except…"

Her voice trailed away.

"Except what?" asked Tom.

"It is nothing. A year ago. She seem to be going, how you say it, astray."

"In what way?"

"Oh, she stay out all night, that kind of thing."

"With a boy?"

"No," she said. "With a girl. She very bad influence. But she got expelled from school."

"What for?"

"Drink, drugs, usual things," said Mrs Molotovski.

"Yes," I said, looking hard at Tom. "I gather that sort of thing happens all the time."

11

"Thanks for that, Dad," said Tom. "This girl. Do you remember her name?"

"Fairycakes," said Mrs Molotovski.

"I beg your pardon?"

"Her full name, it is Fairycakes Bonanza Parks."

"I've heard of her," said Tom. "Wasn't her father Dreggsy Parks?"

"Yes, I think so," said Mrs Molotovski.

"Would someone translate for me?" I asked. "Who are these people?"

"Dreggsy Parks was a rock singer," said Tom. "Started out in the mid-seventies with a punk band. The Prats."

"Never heard of them."

"You must have heard of Dreggsy," said Tom. "He went solo after the band broke up, and became this big animal rights activist. Kept on being arrested. Then he got together with Chantelle Titmus."

"Who?"

"The Page 3 girl. They had a kid."

"And this would be Fairycakes?"

"Yes," said Tom. "There was quite a lot about her in the press, especially when she was born, because of her name."

"It's memorable," I said.

"I think she was named after her mum's favourite food, and her dad's favourite TV programme."

"Fairycakes Bonanza," I said. "It all comes back to me. Didn't Dreggsy top himself?"

"Yes," said Tom. "A couple of years ago. He died of auto-erotic asphyxiation. He was found hanging in a hotel room with an orange in his mouth."

"Must have come as a shock to his family."

"You could say that."

"What about the Page 3 girl?"

"Chantelle? Oh, that was all a bit tragic."

"She fell to pieces after his death?"

"I think the verdict was death by misadventure," said Tom.

"What happened?" I asked.

"I can tell you that," said Rex Crawley. "She was one of my clients. She was always into self-harming, and she went a bit bonkers after Dreggsy died. She got obsessed with animal rights."

"Oh, I remember," I said. "Didn't she break into Regent's Park after dark?"

"That's right. She died, trying to liberate the lions in London zoo."

"They didn't want to escape?" I asked.

"They were more interested in tearing her apart and eating her," said Rex.

"Blimey," I said. "Poor old Fairycakes. That's not what you'd call a settled home background."

"Totally out of control," said Mrs Molotovski. "My husband tell her not to come near our daughter."

"Or what?" I asked.

"Or Igor do something to make her regret it," said Mrs Molotovski. "I not ask."

"And this all happened when?" I asked.

"Over one year ago," said Mrs Molotovski. "It ancient history."

"Did you tell the police about this?" asked Tom.

"No need," said Mrs Molotovski. "My daughter and this girl not see each other since my husband put foot down."

I exchanged glances with Tom. I could tell he was thinking there was an avenue to explore here.

"I take it your husband knows you're here now?" I asked.

"Yes, but..." said Mrs Molotovski, with a sideways glance at Creepy Crawley.

"What's wrong?" I asked. "You fear he might not approve?"

"I know he not approve," said Mrs Molotovski. "But I tell him I am anxious. I not sleep at night. And we have air conditioning. Not like in here."

13

"I'm sorry," I said. "Would you like the window open?"

"Please, yes," said the Russian. "I very hot. And, how you say in English, bothered."

"Which is why Mrs Molotovski came to me," said Creepy.

"That's what's puzzling me," I said, as Tom opened the window and let traffic noise from Soho Square seep into the room. "Why does someone with your resources go to someone like Creepy?"

"I'm not sure I like your tone," said Creepy.

"Look, Creepy," I said, "we've known each other a long time and I know what you do. You're a P.R., a fixer. You introduce people. You manage their publicity. You pay people off for their silence. What you don't do is track down missing persons."

"I go to Mr Crawley because I trust him," said Mrs Molotovski. "He manage things before when... well, when family want certain matters handled with, what you say, delicacy."

"And those matters would be...?" I asked.

"Those matters," said Creepy, "would be none of your business."

"I assure you," said Mrs Molotovski, "that they have nothing to do with Olga."

"I'd still like to know," I said.

Mrs Molotovski looked across at Crawley, as if to ask his permission to speak.

"My husband and I required an injunction."

"Against anyone in particular?"

"Against a national newspaper that was planning to reveal certain things about my past. Things that need be of no concern to the public."

I had a shrewd suspicion what that secret might be.

"Would this have something to do with a former occupation of yours?"

"It would," she said. "But I would rather not discuss these things. They are of no importance."

"But this newspaper obviously thought they were."

"That is because the woman who wished to write these things about me is a jealous bitch."

"Ah," I said. "I take it you're talking about one of our respected lady columnists. Which one was it?"

"Let me guess," said Tom. "Amanda Platell? Jan Moir? Stephanie Sharp?"

"It was that Sharp woman," said Mrs Molotovski, spitting out her surname as though it were poisonous. "What do they call her? The Queen of Mean?"

"And her column's known as the Palace of Malice," said Tom. "Though *Private Eye* calls it Bitch From A Ditch."

"That Sharp woman is jealous of my wealth," said Mrs Molotovski. "She take every chance to criticise my figure, my hair, my dress sense. It is not my fault that rich men have always been attracted to me. They are like moths to my flame."

"I'm sure they are," I said. "So why do you think you need me?"

"Well, Charlie," said Creepy. "You're a proper person. Proper Charlie. That's what they call you."

"Thanks for that," I said. "And your point is?"

"The point is you don't muck about. You're calm, loyal, discreet."

"Kind of you to say so."

"The Molotovskis want to keep this out of the media."

"Might not the media be able to help find your daughter?"

"We value our privacy," said Mrs Molotovski. "I don't want that Sharp woman telling her readers that we made our little girl run away."

"And how do the police feel about that?"

"They're happy enough at present," said Creepy. "As long as they think there's no kidnapping."

"Does she have a boyfriend?" asked Tom.

"No," said Mrs Molotovski. "Not that we know of."

"Girlfriend?" asked Tom.

"What are you insinuating?" asked Creepy.

"I'm not insinuating anything," said Tom. "But she's a good looking girl. Clever. Rich. Happy, apparently. She must have had friends of some sex or other."

"Why you mention sex?" asked Mrs Molotovski. "My daughter not have sex. She too busy studying."

"I'm sure she was," I said. "But it's our job to ask questions. Investigate. Find out why your daughter's disappeared."

"You will take case?" asked the Russian.

"I didn't say that," I replied.

"I not understand," said Mrs Molotovski. "You not take case?"

"Look, Charlie," said Creepy. "It's obvious from the state of this place you could do with some dosh. Just find Olga. Get her home where she belongs. No questions asked. And Bob's your uncle."

"I am sorry," said Mrs Molotovski. "Who is this Uncle Bob?"

"It's an expression," said Creepy. "Look, Charlie, this is the last chance saloon. Are you in or out?"

"I'm not sure if I'm the right person," I said.

I tried not to catch Tom's eye as he stared across at me. I could sense he thought I was mad. But then he hadn't had dealings with Crawley. Tom probably thought he could be trusted, whereas I knew he would sell his own grandmother to turn a profit, not to mention the rest of his family, if he had one, which I very much doubted. The idea of Rex Crawley ever having attracted another human to his bed seemed far-fetched in the extreme – unless money had changed hands, of course.

"Dad, we've tracked down missing persons before," Tom said.

"Yes, Tom. And I'm sure we'll do it again," I replied. "Under the right circumstances."

"Look, Charlie," said Creepy, "I know you don't owe me any favours, but as soon as Katasha came to me, I thought Charlie Charlesworth's the man for the job. A nice, tidy private detective who won't try and take her to the cleaners just because she's worth a bob or two."

"But I pay him plenty," said Mrs Molotovski, prodding Creepy with her finger. "You tell him how much."

"How much?" asked Tom, before I could stop him.

"Ten grand up front plus expenses," said Creepy. "Right?"

"No, really, I'm not sure," I said.

"Twenty," said Mrs Molotovski.

I could see that she could see that I was relenting. To be fair, I wasn't in the best position, defensively. We didn't have any work, and she was offering four times my normal price. And maybe the job wouldn't bring me into too much contact with Crawley. Besides, a girl was missing. It could be that she needed my help.

"Okay," I said. "But on one condition."

"What is that?" she asked.

"I must see your daughter's bedroom and talk to your husband."

"Okay, but I tell you he not approve," she said. "He say he trust English police."

"And you don't?"

"They not know my daughter."

"But we don't know your daughter either," I said. "Does she have a phone, a diary, an address book, anything like that?"

"No," replied the Russian. "Police take everything. And her laptop."

"That's a shame," I said. "It would have been handy."

"I know," said Mrs Molotovski. "But I have copy of hard drive. Took copy only two weeks ago."

She took a purple memory stick out of her handbag and gave it to Tom.

"If you don't mind my asking, why did you make a copy?" asked Tom.

"You not ask. None of your business," she said. "I have my reasons."

"You must realise," said Creepy, "that everything you find out must be treated with the utmost discretion. Nothing is to reach the media."

"I understand," I said.

"Sure," said Tom. "No problem."

"I am trusting you with this," she said, earnestly. "Please find her for me."

"Don't worry, Mrs Molotovski," said Tom, before I could stop him. "I'm sure we'll find her."

"You want to meet my husband now?" Mrs Molotovski asked me.

"Would that be possible?" I asked.

"Sure. He at home. He not get out much no more."

"That would be good," I said. "Tom, can I leave you to look at this memory stick while I'm gone?"

"Sure thing, Dad."

"Well," said Creepy, "I'll leave you in Katasha's capable hands. It's been a pleasure seeing you again, Charlie."

"Oh no!" cried Mrs Molotovski, slapping one hand theatrically to her forehead. "We forget about the dwarf!"

"I beg your pardon?" I asked.

"The dwarf," she said. "With red beard."

"I'm sorry," I said. "I'm still not following you."

"He come to our house day before she disappeared and handed her letter."

"What kind of letter?"

"I not know. I not read it. But maid not around, so I answer door and there he is. A little red-bearded dwarf."

"Clutching an envelope."

"Exactly."

"And he gave it to you?" asked Tom.

"No," said Mrs Molotovski. "He ask to see Olga. He say he have to give it to her personally."

"And she took it from him?"

18

"That's right."

"And she read it?"

"She take it to her bedroom and read it there. And she very, very silent after that."

"Something in the letter upset her?"

"I think so. Yes. But she not say what it was. All I know is the letter made her nervous. My daughter has, how you say in English, a stutter. It very bad again, all of a sudden. She hardly get word out. And the next day she is gone."

"And no sign of the letter?"

"No."

"Or the dwarf?" asked Tom.

"No. One other thing."

"What's that?"

"I think the beard, it was false."

"So," I said, "the key to her disappearance may lie with a dwarf wearing a false red beard."

"I think so. This is what I tell police."

"I don't suppose you have a picture of this dwarf on CCTV?"

"No. Security cameras, they not working when he come."

"But it's a good, solid lead," said Rex Crawley.

"That's right, Dad," said Tom. "I mean, how hard can it be to track down a dwarf wearing a false red beard?"

We were about to find out.

2

RICH AND STRANGE

Mrs Molotovski was very insistent on giving me a lift in her limo.

"You. Me. Come now," she ordered.

So I did.

As the limo drew up at the gates of Chez Molotovski, a couple of security guards came out to identify us. They were the size of Sumo wrestlers and didn't look as if they smiled. They glared at me with barely concealed aggression, like Millwall fans waiting to give someone a good kicking.

Mrs Molotovski gave them a regal wave. One of the goons talked into a lapel microphone, and the electric gates started to open, I looked through at the house, or rather mansion. It was a sinister alien presence, a brutalist nightmare of Soviet architecture, given a curious overtone of femininity by being a gaudy shade of pink. It was a bizarre building to find in a domestic area of North London, even though it was separated from the surrounding buildings by a long, high wall, topped off with broken glass and barbed wire. It was only missing towers and gun turrets, or it could have been a Russian women's prison camp.

"What you think of it?" asked Mrs Molotovski, proudly.

"It's very, er," I tried to find the right word, "palatial."

"Fit for a queen, no?" she said. "All my own design."

"It certainly dominates the landscape."

"And what you think it made of?" she asked.

"Concrete? Glass?" I hazarded.

"Not only concrete and glass," said Katasha proudly. "Do you know what produces that colour?"

"You mean that kind of prawn cocktail pink? You like it?"

"It's incredibly striking."

"Blood."

"Blood?"

"Yes," she said. "My husband expert on many things, even concrete. He read that Romans use many things to make concrete."

"Isn't that cement, pebbles, sand and water?" I asked, remembering a short, back-breaking time working on a building site.

"Ah, but the Romans added other ingredients," said Mrs Molotovski. "Milk, animal fat, horse hair and blood."

"Hence the pinkish tinge?"

"It is at its reddest towards the evening," said Mrs Molotovski. "My husband say whole building represents old Soviet Empire."

"Is your husband political?"

"He used to be. Big friend of Vladimir Putin."

"I see."

"But not any longer. Vladimir's people try kill him. Twice."

"Which is why he's in England?"

"Yes," said Mrs Molotovski. "He not want to wake up one morning to find himself dying of polonium."

"But you say he's not very well?"

21

"He not very well at all," said Mrs Molotovski. "You see."

Before I was taken to meet the master of the house, I asked if I could visit Olga's bedroom. This was not like a normal English girl's bedroom. There was nothing pink or fluffy about it. There were no posters of boybands. It was more like a western bachelor pad, with black leather and chrome furniture, and a massive plasma screen at the end of the bed. There weren't even any clothes draped anywhere. It was infinitely tidier than my office. Or my house, come to think of it.

"Do you know what clothes she was wearing when she disappeared?" I asked.

"That is curious thing. None of clothes are missing. They all in wardrobe and drawers."

"What about the clothes she was wearing on the Saturday night?" I asked.

"Them lying around on floor, like she take them off to go to bed."

"They're not here now."

"I have maid tidy up."

"What would she have been wearing in bed?"

"She never wore nothing in bed."

"So your daughter vanished from her bedroom, and she wasn't wearing nothing, I mean anything," I asked.

I don't mean to be repetitive, but I often sum up things that have just been said, to show I'm on top of things and give myself a bit of time to think. A lot of people like it because it shows them I'm giving them my full attention. Mrs Molotovski just shrugged.

"I say that already," she said.

"Could someone have climbed in through this window?" I asked.

"It was warm night," she said. "Window was open."

"But there were no signs of anyone entering or leaving by it?"

22

"No."

"And she could hardly have jumped," I said, taking a peek out of the window.

"Not without she injure herself," agreed Mrs Molotovski. "Must be ten metres."

I indicated the big, plasma screen.

"She liked to watch television?" I inquired.

"No," said Mrs Molotovski. "She play video game on PC."

"Did you ever play with her?"

"No," she said. "She play on her own, or over internet."

I looked at her bookshelves and saw that they were packed not with books but with video games.

"Was this one of her favourites?" I asked. "Carmageddon II: Carpopolis Now?"

"It used to be," said Mrs Molotovski. "Recently she play more this one."

She picked up a box and opened it.

"Look. It empty. Maybe she take it with her."

I went over and studied the front and back cover.

"The Seven Deadly Sins?"

"One of my husband's."

"Yes, I remember," I said.

"She say it good," said Mrs Molotovski, with a shrug. "I not know. I not play."

I replaced it where she had found it, next to the bed.

"Come," said Mrs Molotovski. "Now I take you meet Igor."

She took me down the wide, marble staircase and through the main hall, to the back of the house.

"He through there," she said, indicating a pair of double glass doors.

"You're not coming in with me?" I asked, seeing her hang back.

"No way," she said. "Room give me creeps."

"Ah," I said. "Righto."

I pulled open the doors and was surprised to find a second pair of glass doors no more than a few feet from the first. These opened automatically, as I stepped beyond the first ones. The effect was slightly unnerving, as if the person inside knew that I was coming but couldn't be arsed to greet me in person.

The first thing that struck me was the temperature, which was extremely warm, almost tropical. It was a clammy heat, the kind that makes you check whether your armpits are niffy.

The second thing I noticed was the size of the room. It was at least sixty foot in length and twenty wide, but the aspect that made it seem cavernous was the height. It was two or three storeys tall. The roof and one side of the room were made of glass panels. Look up and you saw the sky. Look out and you saw a dense shrubbery.

The next thing I noticed was a bird. At first, I thought it was trapped inside the room, but then I noticed more of them. They were flying around. As I watched, one – I think it was a tit of some kind – landed on a plant. Almost immediately, the plant bent over and swallowed it, head first. It didn't even have time to squawk an objection.

The room was a mini-rainforest, filled with plants that looked exotic but menacing at the same time. A stone path led through it, three foot wide. I walked along it and came face to face with Igor Molotovski.

He was not at all as I had imagined him. I had thought he would be one of those stocky Russians with a square build and belligerent jaw. Instead, he was a thin, almost emaciated figure, in a motorised wheelchair with an oxygen tent over his head and shoulders.

"Welcome to my domain, Mr Charlesworth," he said, with the exaggerated politeness of a Bond villain. The kind that keeps sharks in his swimming pool.

"Hello," I said. "I'm sorry to tell you but I've just seen one of your birds eaten by a plant."

"Good," he said.

"I thought you might be concerned," I said.

"Not at all," he said. "The birds in here are merely victims. They exist purely to provide food for the flora and fauna within. I have created an environment where predators can thrive. I am, I fear, something of an obsessive."

"What kind of predators?" I asked, looking around me nervously.

"Plants, reptiles and spiders," He said. "In fact, if you look down, you have a tarantula crawling up your trouser leg."

"Eurgh!" I said, shaking it off.

I controlled my natural inclination, which was to stamp on it. I've always had a fear of spiders, and this was the largest I'd ever seen. Gold and black, Hairy. Repulsive, unless you like that kind of thing, which my host clearly did.

"It's a Chinese bird spider," he said.

"It eats birds?"

"And cockroaches, crickets and mice," said Molotovski. "It won't hesitate to bite humans if it is disturbed. And it is highly venomous."

"You mean it could kill me?"

"Doubtful," he said. "I doubt if its neurotoxins would be deadly as long as you are in a relatively sound state of health. Which you appear to be. Excuse me a moment."

He unzipped his oxygen tent and lit up a cigarette.

"Want one?" he asked, offering me the packet.

"No thanks," I said.

"They're good," he said. "Imported from Mother Russia."

"No," I said. "Really."

"My wife says they'll be the death of me," he said. "And, of course, she's right."

"Aren't you worried about being surrounded by all these predators?" I asked.

"Not at all," he said. "I feel at home here. Besides, I have been bitten so often by spiders that I have built up an immunity. I am dying anyway. Lung cancer."

"I'm sorry to hear that."

"It is an unfortunate byproduct of my addictive personality."

"And Russian cigarettes."

"Indeed. How old would you say I am?"

"I don't know," I said. "Late sixties?"

You wouldn't think it to look at me," he said. "but I am 58, exactly the same age as Vladimir Putin. We were both born on 7th October 1952."

"Your wife tells me you were old friends."

"Yes, but we went our separate ways," he said. "Vladimir was more interested in power, while I was drawn to money. We fell out. Over what is not important. But now he keeps on trying to kill me."

"Not in Britain, surely?"

"Nowhere is safe," he said.

"Might he try to get at you through your daughter?" I asked.

"It crossed my mind," he said. "But that is not Putin's style. He is more direct. It is the Russian way. We did not defeat the Germans by kidnapping their children."

"Your daughter ran away?"

He shrugged.

"I think so."

"Why do you think that?"

"My wife told you of a mystery letter delivered by a dwarf?"

"She did."

"That may have played some part," he shrugged again. "But who knows? That is for you to find out."

"She mentioned that you didn't approve of Olga's friends."

He shook his head.

"Untrue," he said. "There was only one friend I did not care for. A poor little rich girl. The decadent daughter of some degenerate rock star and his whore."

"Fairytale Bonanza Parks?"

"The name is ridiculous," he said. "Her behaviour was even more absurd. I could see immediately that she was on drugs. I have seen it too many times before. And her language and demeanour demonstrated a disrespect for her elders that was intolerable."

"And what do you put that down to?"

"The lack of a father, perhaps," he said. "It is not my concern."

"But you warned her off seeing your daughter," I said. "Could that have made Olga run away?"

"I do not think so," he said. "That was more than a year ago."

"Is there anything else you can think of?" I asked. "Any little argument?"

"I told her she was spending too much time on her computer," he said. "But that is normal these days."

"More normal for boys than girls, I'd say."

"Yes," he said. "But Olga is like a boy."

"In what way?"

"All her life, Katasha has tried to dress her in pink, little dresses with bows in her hair, but Olga always preferred a t-shirt and jeans."

"Anything else?"

"Many girls like dolls," said her father. "Olga always preferred computer games."

"What kind of games?"

"The more killing, the better," he said nonchalantly.

"Didn't that concern you?"

"Why should it?" he asked. "That would be pretty hypocritical of me, no?"

"I hear you're in the video games business," I said. "I play a game called Football Manager."

"Ah, football," he said. "That kind of game does not interest me. But I imagine the thrill comes from beating rivals, buying and selling players, achieving a measure of success that you have failed to attain in real life?"

"I suppose," I said.

"And I imagine you are addicted," he said.

"I'm not sure I would go that far."

"How many hours a day do you play?"

"Around two or three," I lied.

"Which means four or five. So you are addicted. It is nothing to be ashamed of."

"Perhaps your own daughter is an addict."

"Indeed she is," he said. "And, I am proud to say, to my own bestseller."

"The Seven Deadly Sins?"

"You see," he said proudly, "even you have heard of it."

"I saw the box for it up in her bedroom. It was empty. That means she may have taken the game with her."

"Which would seem to indicate she was not kidnapped," said Molotovski. "Good work. The police did not spot that."

"Can you tell me a little about this new game she liked so much?"

"It is my most successful yet," he said. "And it came about because of an idea of mine. Did you ever see a film called *Seven*?"

"Is that the one with Brad Pitt and Morgan Freeman as a pair of cops?"

"That shows the difference between you and me," he smiled. "When I saw it, I thought of it from the point of view of the Kevin Spacey character. I enjoyed it as a film about a man trying to clean up America."

"You sided with the serial killer?"

"Didn't he have the moral high ground?" he asked. "Was he not punishing people for the seven deadly sins. Pride, Lust, Envy, Sloth, Gluttony, Avarice and... what's the other one?"

"Anger?"

"Anger," he said. "Quite right."

"So I instructed my designers to devise a game in which the

player tries to track down the most sinful inhabitants of a city and kill them. The more sinful they are, the higher you score."

"And how do you find out how sinful they are?"

"You study them," he said. "You look at their clothing, their race, their attitudes and you form an opinion."

"And then you slaughter them?"

"Exactly."

"And what if you get it wrong, and murder an innocent bystander?"

"Then you score negative points, and the police are more likely to arrest you. That is where the skill comes in. You have to be selective. And you're looking for seven different deadly sins, so there is no point killing only the lustful or the lazy."

"And this game is popular?"

"Extremely. For two years running, it has been voted the world's most addictive video game. So it is not just my daughter's favourite."

"Do you ever get hooked?" I asked. "Addicted to your own game?"

"I am from an older generation," he said. "My addictions lie elsewhere. In cigarettes. And vodka. If you won't smoke with me, would you care for a drink?"

"No," I said. "I have to get back. I have your daughter to find."

"That's if you can tear yourself away from Football Manager," he said. "Goodbye, Mr Charlesworth. I hope you find her in one piece."

"I hope I do, too," I said.

"By the way," he said. "That tarantula I mentioned."

"What?"

"It appears to have climbed on to your right shoulder."

He was highly amused when I attempted to shake it off without having to touch it, but in the end had to use my left hand. In fact, he was still coughing and spluttering with laughter when I left the room. The sweat was pouring off me, and I was shaking. It could have been the heat or the spiders. Probably both. One thing's for certain. If I'd known everything that was about to happen, I'd have been sweating an awful lot more.

3

REAR WINDOW

Monday, 1st August

I grabbed a sandwich for a late lunch and got back to the office mid-afternoon. I poked my head around the door of Tom's office, towards the rear of our building. It has the worst view of all our rooms, which Tom says he likes because it doesn't distract him. The rear window looks out on to a blank wall, and next to it Tom has a white board on which he scribbles ideas. He calls it his clueboard. There were just three words on it: Agency, Flash and Slope. Tom didn't look up as I came in. He was too busy fiddling away on his computer, with the purple memory stick sticking out of one side.

"Agency, Flash and Slope," I said. "I take it that they're not a firm of solicitors?"

"Correct," he said.

"What have you got to tell me?"

"All in good time, Sherlock," he said. "How was your home visit to the lovely Mrs Molotovski?"

"Okay," I said. "Except I nearly got bitten."

"By Mrs Molotovski?"

"No. A venomous spider."

"How come?"

"Mr Molotovski keeps it as a pet. Along with many others. Not to mention snakes and carnivorous plants."

"Eccentric," he said.

"Very," I replied. "I return severely traumatised."

"Sorry to hear it," said Tom.

"You should see the Molotovski home," I said. "It certainly gave me an insight into why Olga might have wanted to run away. It's like a Russian prison camp dipped in icing sugar."

"Sizeable?" asked Tom.

"Huge," I said. "Are video games really that big a deal?"

"Absolutely," said Tom. "I've been doing a bit of research into Mr Molotovski."

"I hoped you would," I said. "Care to give me the bullet points?"

He looked down at a pad on which he'd scribbled some notes.

"He's been called the Bill Gates of video games."

"Is that good?"

"He's the leading figure in the industry, and you know how large that is."

"Not really," I said.

"In June this year, the global video game market was valued at 65 billion US dollars."

"And Mr M is a top dog?"

"Only the world's most successful publisher."

"Jealous rivals?"

"Too many to mention. His enemies say that basically he brought the methods he'd learned in his previous professions into the games arena."

"And his previous professions were?"

"Gambling, drugs and prostitution," said Tom. "They say he's taken the violent video game and raised it to a whole new level of depravity. His first hit was a driving game."

"Sounds harmless enough."

"Not really. It was called Death Car. It showed how to run people down in the most imaginatively brutal ways. Detaching limbs and reducing pedestrians to steaming piles of flesh earned bonus points."

"Nice," I said.

"He moved on to war games. His were the first to encourage players to brutalise enemies for enjoyment. One of them was supposed to have inspired American torturers at Abu Ghraib."

"What a charmer," I said.

"He has one other nickname," said Tom, "which is meant to sum up his character."

"Go on," I said.

"They call him The Predator."

"Lovely," I said. "And here we are, working for him."

"At least we know he's got the money to pay us," said Tom.

"Good point," I said.

"So what about little Olga?" asked Tom. "Got any leads?"

"Two, I think. One is that Mr Molotovski is convinced that Vladimir Putin is trying to kill him."

"Interesting suspect," said Tom, adding 'Putin' to his whiteboard. "So does Mr M think Putin may have kidnapped his daughter?"

"No," I said. "He says that wouldn't be Putin's style."

"It does seem a bit subtle," said Tom. "Still, let's keep it on the board as a possibility. Though I'm not convinced we're going to be able to haul him in for questioning. What's the other lead?"

"Olga took a video game with her when she vanished."

"Interesting," said Tom. "So she wasn't kidnapped."

"Precisely."

"It also suggests," said Tom, "that wherever she was going, she expected to be able to play her video game."

"Good point," I said. "Watson, you're more than a pretty face."

"Did you notice what format it was?"

"PC," I said.

"Right. So wherever she was going, she expected to find a PC."

"Right."

Tom scribbled PC on his clueboard, then looked up.

"So what game are we talking about?"

"One of her dad's. The Seven Deadly Sins. You used to play it, didn't you?"

He nodded, as he scrawled '7 Deadly Sins' on his clueboard.

"I got hooked on it for a while, about a year back. I've still got it on my phone, as an app. You kill lots of people you think are evil."

"Is it fun?"

"You do get to play God, which is cool. And you can choose your own avatar."

"One of those tall, blue things from a politically correct planet?"

"Not that kind," he said. "Avatar just means an alternative identity. You choose your own name, personality, special strengths and so on."

"I see."

"One of the cool aspects is that there's a translator thingy which allows you to see what your name might be if you were a different nationality."

"Why is that cool?"

"Well, if your name is Smith, for instance, you can find out what the equivalent of a 'smith' or 'blacksmith' is in another language. My avatar was an Indonesian called Detektif Putra."

"What does that mean?"

"Son of the detective."

"So what gives, Detectif Putra?" I asked, "Fill me in about Agency, Flash and Slope."

"They're the three clues I've come up with so far," he said. "I reckon the police will have been through Olga's emails, and there's nothing I can see that's out of the ordinary. Mainly conversations with classmates about work, that kind of thing. The police are bound to have checked out her primary contacts."

There was something in his voice, though, that suggested he had something more up his sleeve.

"But you found something else?"

"Could be," he shrugged. "It might be nothing. But it struck me that if she had anything to hide, she would have hidden them."

"What? You mean encoded them?"

"Could be, but there's no evidence of that. I mean deleted them."

"But if she'd deleted them, they're no longer on the hard disc."

"Not necessarily. Just because you press the delete key doesn't mean they've gone completely."

"You can de-delete them?"

"With the proper software. And that's thrown up a few interesting items. Most of the files she's deleted are just old copies of files she's updated. But there are some emails which... I don't know."

"What don't you know?"

"Well, they're not the kind of emails you'd expect the average 17-year-old girl to be getting."

"What do you mean?"

"Well, there's about ten from this modelling agency she used to work for."

"Ah," I said, waving towards the word Agency on his whiteboard. "What do they say?"

"They're pestering her to come back."

"When do these date from?"

"Earlier this year. But not only has she not replied to them, she's deleted them."

"Maybe she didn't want her parents to know she was still in contact," I suggested.

"Could be," said Tom. "Except her parents must have approved of the agency, or they would never have allowed her to model."

"That's right," I nodded. "Mrs M said it was Olga's idea to give up modelling, not theirs."

"Which is odd," said Tom. "Psychologically."

"How do you mean?"

"You've met her dad and I haven't, but I get the impression he is quite strict with her. Right?"

"Right," I agreed.

"And yet he allows her to flaunt herself in photographs, with not much on."

I nodded.

"I mean, come on, Dad, you saw those photographs of her," said Tom. "She's definitely a looker."

"Like her mum used to be," I said.

"Better, if you ask me," said Tom. "Olga's the looker. Her mum's more of a…"

"Hooker?" I suggested.

"You said it," replied Tom.

"Have you tried looking up Mrs M?" I asked.

"Of course," said Tom.

"No clues there?"

"Not really," said Tom. "It's mainly society gossip, with a lot of broad hints that she used to be a working girl."

"She certainly conveys that impression."

"But it does make me wonder," said Tom, "if there's something fishy about this modelling agency."

"You think it could be a front?"

"Who knows? But I think one of the first things we do should be to check it out. Especially as they're only round the corner."

"Whereabouts?"

"Greek Street. I'll print out the address."

"Good," I said.

"Hang on," he said. "Okay, it's printing out now."

"What else have you got?" I asked. "Why have you written Flash on your board? Is it something to do with the photographs?"

"Got it in one, Sherlock," said Tom. "I've looked up the bloke who took her glossies. There are no emails from him, but the name of his company's on the back of the photos. Flash Photography. They're in Notting Hill. They might be worth a visit."

"Why?"

"Isn't it a great British tradition that photographers tend to seduce models?"

"You mean like David Bailey?"

"And the rest," said Tom. "What's the betting little Olga is having a secret affair with the bloke who took those photos of her?"

"It's possible," I said. "Set something up."

"Such as?"

"A photo session," I said. "Have you ever considered modelling?"

"Not really," said Tom.

"I'm your new agent," I said. "Let's get you a portfolio."

"Sure?"

"Sure."

"Well," said Tom doubtfully, "you're the boss."

"You're starting to sound like Marti," I said.

"Ha," he said, the way he always does when you've said something he knows is supposed to be funny but he can't be bothered to laugh. "Oh, one more lead."

"Would that be something to do with a slope?" I asked, indicating the whiteboard.

"This one's really intriguing," he said. "Little Olga is on Facebook."

"It would be more surprising if she wasn't."

"True, but then I looked to see who her friends were."

"And?"

"Well, one stood out."

"Out with it."

"It may be nothing, but he struck me as odd. He's three times the age of anyone else. And he happens to be an old mate of yours. Not."

"What do you mean?"

"Does the name Bill Slope ring any bells?"

"Bill Slope! Stroll on! I didn't know he was still alive," I said. "I haven't seen his byline in years."

"Didn't he once try to stitch you up?" asked Tom.

"Yeah," I said. "Slippery Slope! Talk of the devil!"

"Doesn't he have some connection with Crawley?"

"I don't know if he does now, but he did. He was Creepy's contact on the *News of the World*."

"Was?"

"I don't think he's there now."

"Nobody's there now," Tom pointed out.

"What I mean is he got fired from the News of the Screws, as a result of trying to stitch me up. It cost them a few quid, that did. Paid for what passed for your education. God knows what he's doing now. He must be well over 60."

"Don't you think Bill Slope is an odd bloke to be a 17-year-old's Facebook friend?"

"Too right he is," I said. "It's fishier than Grimsby."

"I've googled Mr Slope," said Tom, "and he's still working. As a freelance. Calls himself an investigative journalist."

"That's not what I'd call him," I said feelingly. "He was one of the biggest bastards in the business. He'd go through your bins as soon as look at you. Eavesdrop on telephone calls."

"Hack a phone?"

"Without a backward glance."

"Worth a visit?" asked Tom.

"I dunno," I said. "I wouldn't trust him an inch, but kidnapping Russian heiresses? I can't believe he'd have it in him. Even in his prime, he wouldn't have been up for that."

"Interesting, though, isn't it?" said Tom. "That a beautiful Russian heiress would accept a lowlife like Bill Slope as a Facebook friend?"

"Yeah, you're right," I said. "He's got to be worth following up. Track him down for me, would you?"

"Sure thing, Dad," said Tom.

I had a troubled sleep that night. When I wasn't dreaming of huge, venomous spiders, I found myself thinking about carnivorous plants that could eat a small bird in one gulp. There was one dream where Igor Molotovski turned into a crocodile and chased me through a rain forest. In another, I found Bill Slope going through my bins. Then he produced a cardboard box, like the one Brad Pitt opened in *Seven*. Out of it, Bill Slope produced a head. It was Olga Molotovski's. Then the police came and took me away to prison, where I was forced to share a cell with Rex 'Creepy' Crawley, who kept asking me what deadly sin I was guilty of. It was all very upsetting. It was a relief to wake up the following morning, and not find myself behind bars.

I soothed my nerves with an hour or three of Football Manager, and was playing with it on the kitchen table when my son walked in.

"Bloody hell," he said. "You're not still playing that thing, are you?"

"I like it," I said.

"You're obsessed with it," he replied. "It's not healthy."

"You play computer games."

"Not all the time," he said. "You need help. Everyone says so."

"What do you mean, everyone?"

"Marti, for a start. She's worried about you."

"It helps me relax."

"No, it doesn't. It leaves you twitchy and completely lacking in concentration. Half the time, I think you're not really listening to me. Just waiting to spend more time on the computer."

"Really?"

"Yes, really. I'm seriously worried."

"It's nice to know someone cares."

"Oh Christ, spare me the self-pity," said Tom. "Look, if I arrange an appointment, will you see someone?"

"Who do you mean? A shrink?"

"It might help."

"And who's going to pay for that?" I asked.

"Look, Dad, if it's such a big deal, I'll pay for it," said Tom.

"You must be crazy," I said.

"You're in a classic state of denial," said Tom. "Just humour me, will you?"

4

THE SKIN GAME

Tuesday, 2nd August

One of the biggest problems with being a private detective is persuading people to talk. If you're *bona fide* police, people don't have a lot of choice. They've got to do it, with or without their lawyers.

Fictional detectives also have it easy. Time and again, I've read thrillers when witnesses spill vital information as if they can't wait to be rid of it. Real life isn't like that. If people don't have to talk to you, chances are they won't, least of all if they know you're a private detective. So I've learned to be vague about my intentions.

It helps that I've been a minor celeb, played footie for England. It makes people feel they know you, even if they don't. Once you get chatting, you're half way there. People lower their guard, tell you what you need to know. I won't say it happens every time, but being a Z-list celeb certainly gives you an in.

Talking to a modelling agency was a bit different. It struck me I wasn't going to get much out of them if I just barged in, demanding to know about some Russian heiress they were pestering. I mean, they don't owe me any favours, do they? So I came up with a plan.

I don't know if I mentioned it, but Marti our receptionist is quite striking. Tall, long legs, nice chocolate brown colour, good figure. Athletic, if you know what I'm saying. So as soon as Tom mentioned the agents in Greek Street, I asked Marti if she'd ever considered modelling, and she said she hadn't, she was more into singing, dancing and acting. So I told her she should, because I needed access to this modelling agency. And she said all right.

At first they said they weren't looking for new models but she could send in some photos, and if they liked them they would get back to her. So she dropped them round some snaps of herself that she keeps in her drawer, in case an audition crops up, and the same day they gave her a bell, and told her to come over tomorrow. As I say, she's a good looking girl.

So here we are, a day after my visit to the Molotovskis, strolling round the corner to this agency in Greek Street. Loco Parente is the name on the buzzer, and it's up some stairs over quite a well-known restaurant. The reception area's done out in white, with glossy photos all over the walls, presumably their models. Covers of *Vogue*, *Vanity Fair*, *Harpers*, that sort of thing. I can see Marti's impressed, and a bit nervous. It's almost like she's really after a job.

The receptionist is a snotty gay bloke – oriental, with bright green hair. I don't mind admitting that this takes me right out of my comfort zone. It's not that I'm homophobic, not at all, but it's not really my world.

After about ten minutes of keeping us hanging about with not even an offer of a cold drink, the bloke with green hair says "Mr Parente will see you now" and he takes us upstairs.

Mr Parente is sitting in his shirtsleeves, very cool and composed behind a large desk. He's a big, leathery man, very tanned, as though he's made of the same cowhide as his armchairs. Looks a bit like that bloke who runs Venezuela, crossed with an elephant. His desk is strewn with folders, photos of models, the usual. The wall behind him is covered with even more photos, but they're group shots, all of them including Mr Parente. I look at Marti, and I can see she's feeling a bit sick and not at all sure of herself. If the truth be told, I'm not feeling too confident either. One glance at the wall behind him, and you can see he's well connected.

Mr Parente stands up and comes out from behind his desk. The chap hugs Marti as if he's known her all his life.

"I am Ricardo Parente," he says, "but you must call me Loco."

"I'm Marti," she says.

"Of course you are!" he says, beaming fondly down at her. He presses against her breasts with every appearance of enthusiasm before letting go, somewhat reluctantly.

"And you," he says to me, pointing and grinning. "I know you. You are famous footballer. Proper Charlie, no?"

"That's right," I say. "Alan Charlesworth. But most people call me Charlie."

"Good to meet you, Charlie! I like all things football. After all, I am Brazilian! But what you doing here?" he asks. "Are you lucky enough to be her boyfriend?"

"No," I say.

And before I can say "I'm her boss," Marti chimes in with: "He's my dad."

There's an awkward pause. Mr Parente goes back behind his desk and says "But how can this be?"

"I mean stepdad," says Marti, improvising. "He's come along to give me moral support."

"I see," says Mr Parente uncertainly. "Well, we are all one big, happy family here. You know what in loco parentis mean?"

"Innit something to do with parents?" said Marti.

"That's aright!" beams Mr Parente, as though she has just won a star prize on a game show. "It means I am like a father to my girls and boys. This is the secret of my success."

"You've got some influential friends," I say, pointing to the wall behind him.

"That's aright," he beams.

Most of the group photos behind his desk are of Mr Parente shaking hands and beaming at various world figures: Obama, Clinton, Putin, Blair, Berlusconi, Blatter... I notice an unusual one.

"I see you know Colonel Gaddafi."

"That's aright," he says.

"What do you think of Sarkozy, Cameron and Obama trying to bring him down?"

"To me, it is a matter for Libya," he says. "Life must be very hard for Gaddafi and his family."

"And for the people he's killing in Libya."

"If you believe the press," says Parente, with a dismissive wave of his hand. "Gadaffi is a man I have always admired."

"Really?" I asked.

"I am telling the truth," he says. "I know him, and his family. They are my friends."

"I've never met them," I say.

"Nice guys," says Mr Parente.

"You don't find Gadaffi a little... unstable?"

"Gadaffi is his own man. But hey," he says, "what do I know? They call me Loco!"

"It's good of you to see me," says Marti.

"It is always my pleasure to meet beautiful girl," says Parente expansively. "But – I hope you don't mind me saying – you look older than these pictures. Were they taken some time ago?"

"A couple of years," says Marti. "Maybe three."

"That explains it," says Parente, with a sigh.

"You can't mean Marti's too old to be a model," I say. "Look at her! She's gorgeous."

"Thanks, er, Dad," says Marti, blushing.

"But what are you?" asks Parente. "24? 25?"

"23!" says Marti indignantly.

"You are already a little mature," says Parente, "certainly for the runway. Have you done any glamour modelling?"

"No!" said Marti.

"I fear that your stepdaughter has left it a little late to come to me," says Parente. "Once the first bloom is lost… It has something to do with the skin."

He lets his voice die away, and I look across at Marti. I can see she's furious, and I'm going to have to think quickly, or we'll be ushered to the door.

"I do have another girl," I say. "A lot younger."

"Does she look like her?" asks Parente.

"Oh no," I say. "She's white. Fair. A bit Russian-looking,"

"Perhaps if you send in some glossies," says Parente. "I make no promises, but…"

"I have some photos here," I say, producing them and tossing them across his desk.

Of course, they're the pictures of Olga Molotovski.

I don't know why I did it. It was more of an impulse than anything else. To see how he reacted. After all, Olga had been on his books, and he'd wanted her back enough to keep pestering her. I wondered why she didn't want to answer his emails and had deleted them all. I don't know what reaction I was expecting. Maybe a smile of recognition, or a look of surprise. I don't think I've ever seen a man with a tan turn quite as pale, quite as suddenly.

"You know her?" I say.

"No," he says. "I never see her before."

"Are you sure?" I say.

"Why do you come here?" he asks.

"Her name's Olga," I say.

"I'm sorry," he says, pushing the photos back towards me. "She is not suitable."

"Then why do you keep emailing her?" I ask.

He shrugs, as though he doesn't understand English. So I decide to make one last try.

"She tells me she's worked for you before."

At this, he rises from his chair like a harpooned whale.

"I don't know what you're talking about," he says, breathing heavily. "I would like you to leave. Now. I have no more to say to you."

The last thing I do as I walk out of the door is turn and look back at Loco. Pools of sweat are appearing under his arms. It may be hot, but I don't think it's the temperature that's done that to him. He's gone a funny colour too. A sort of elephant grey.

Outside in the street, I turned to Marti.

"I hope we haven't killed him," I said. "He turned a very funny colour."

"What?" she said. "Oh, yeah."

Marti was deep in thought, or so I imagined. Her expression wasn't one I'd ever seen before. Not on her, at any rate. It was like she was on *Mastermind*, being asked a question in a foreign language.

"Are you okay?" I asked.

"Yeah," she said, snapping out of her mood and returning to her normal, cheery self. "I don't think modelling's quite my thing anyway. Boring, innit? Just trying on other people's clothes and taking them off."

We started to walk back towards Soho Square.

"What did you make of Mr Loco?" I asked.

"Bit of a perv, if you ask me," said Marti. "Did you see what he was up to when he hugged me?"

"No," I said.

"Checking out whether my breasts were real, and copping a feel of my bum, wasn't he?" she said. "Charming! I nearly clocked him one."

46

"Anything else strike you?"

"He had a lot of photos, didn't he?" she said. "Were they all world leaders? I recognized Osama."

"I think you mean Obama."

"Yeah. And that Italian bloke who goes with young girls."

"Berlusconi?"

"Yeah, him, and Kim Jong-Il."

"Who?"

"Kim Jong-Il," she said. "He runs South Korea."

"North Korea," I corrected her. "He's one of the last Communist dictators."

"Whatever. Scary little bloke. He was in that film with puppets. Dead funny, that was."

"And he was on the wall? I didn't spot him," I said. "I saw Sepp Blatter, though."

"Who?"

"Sepp Blatter. Another scary little bloke. Mid-seventies. Runs FIFA."

"What's FIFA?"

"They control world football."

"You mean, like the world cup?"

"That, among other things."

"Is he German?"

"Swiss," I say.

"Since when have the Swiss been any good at football?" asked Marti.

"Good point," I said.

"Didn't he just get re-elected, unopposed?" asked Marti, frowning. "Like one of them middle-eastern dictators?"

"That's the one," I said.

"I read about him on *Mail Online*," said Marti. "He sounds a right wanker."

"I don't think he's very fond of the British press," I said. "But then who is at the moment?"

I don't know what made me do it, but at this point I looked over my shoulder. I caught a flash of green.

"Don't turn round," I said, "but I think we're being followed."

"Who by?" asked Marti.

"I think it must be that receptionist. The one with green hair."

"Maybe he fancies you," said Marti.

"Unlikely. I think he's trying to find out where we're going."

"Really? This is so exciting!" said Marti. "Like you're Jason Bourne or something. Shall we try and give him the slip?"

"Not much point. We're already back at the office."

"Oh well," said Marti, "that's our cover blown. Mind you, I'm not sure Mr Parente was totally convinced that you were my dad."

As we climbed the stairs to the suite, Marti continued to prattle.

"You know what's doing my head in, boss?" she said. "What's someone like this Blatter fella got to do with modelling?"

"Beats me," I said. "But you might say the same about Blair or Clinton. They were all up there on his wall."

"Parente's quite a hot shot, isn't he?" said Marti.

"Looks like it," I said.

"That's another thing I can't get my head around," she said, unlocking the door to the offices. "This Olga girl doesn't seem to want anything to do with him."

"What makes you say that?"

"Well, Tom says she's been not replying to his emails. She even deletes them."

"That's right."

"That's what I do when I'm trying to get losers out of my life," said Marti, sitting down in her receptionist's chair. "But you'd think a bloke like Parente could do a lot for her."

"Maybe she doesn't want to be a model," I said.

"So why doesn't she tell him?"

"Maybe she did."

"Tom says she didn't reply to any of his emails."

"Perhaps she talked to him in person."

"Maybe," said Marti. "But I can imagine he might be a bit scary. Specially with all those connections. You know, powerful friends."

"But when I showed him those photos," I said, "it was as if he was scared of her. And us."

"Yeah, right," Marti agreed. "It was like he didn't want anything to do with her, or anyone who might know her."

"He couldn't get us out of his office fast enough."

"So, boss, do you think Mr Parente's got anything to do with our disappearing heiress?"

"I haven't a clue," I said honestly. "But one thing's certain. Two things, really. One is: he's got something to hide. The other is: we haven't the foggiest idea what that is."

"Never mind, boss," said Marti. "At least you haven't been told you're past it at 23."

So that was what had been preying on her mind. Parente had exposed to her the fleeting nature of youth. Probably for the first time, whereas for me youth was long gone. I looked down and saw the first signs of middle age spread. I should be in the gym, really, not playing computer games.

Once we were up in the office, I couldn't resist the temptation to go into the conference room and look down into the square. As I expected, the gay oriental with green hair was disappearing round the corner. I remember not being all that bothered. Maybe I was a bit naïve, but at that point I didn't have a clue what I was getting involved in. Just another teenage runaway, I thought. Certainly not mayhem and multiple murder.

5

THE SECRET AGENT

Tuesday, 2nd August

The next stop was Flash Photography, in Notting Hill. I didn't hold out a lot of hope for this contact, but at this stage I was pretty much clutching at straws, throwing them in the air, and seeing where they landed. Maybe I could get an insight into why Mr Parente had been in such a state. There was clearly something about Olga Molotovski that he didn't care to talk about in public.

Maybe someone at Flash Photography would be more forthcoming. Tom and I went there by tube, along the central line. I wasn't sure, but I had the feeling we were being followed. Every so often, I saw a flash of green in my peripheral vision. But whenever I turned round, he was nowhere to be seen. Tom told me I was being paranoid.

When we reached Flash Photography, it turned out to be considerably more flash than I had imagined. I had anticipated it being just one bloke in a mews house. Instead, it was a vast house on five floors, the kind that would go for nine or ten million plus. When we rang the doorbell, it was obvious that whoever lived there was security-conscious. He checked us out through a spy-hole and drew several bolts before the front door opened.

Once we were in, though, he was hospitality personified. Tall, thin and with an all-over tan that suggested long hours on a sun bed, Jack O'Riordan was in his late thirties or early forties. He wore a silver satin shirt open to the waist, and this exposed an immodest amount of chest hair.

"Darlings, come on in!" he ordered, marching ahead of us into his ground floor studio.

"Bloody hell," muttered Tom. "He looks like Simon Cowell."

"I'm Jack," he said, showing two rows of teeth that were too perfectly white and regular to have been made in Britain. "Welcome to my humble abode."

O'Riordan said he was happy to oblige with building up a portfolio of photos of my male model son. He even seemed interested in him, ready to talk about the modelling game, all that sort of thing. Although he sounded like an ex-public school type, he was approachable, friendly, easy to get on with. He just kept snapping away. That's until he asked who had recommended him, and I said Olga Molotovski. That stopped him in mid-snap.

"Really?" he asked.

He stared at me. Something told me that our cover story was about to unravel even faster than it had done at Loco Parente's. Maybe it was time to think up a new one. Frankly, Tom was much less believable as a fashion model than Marti had been. It was obvious that Tom wasn't used to being photographed. He was self-conscious, awkward, not remotely at ease with his own body.

"Yeah," I said. "She's a friend of my son's."

"You don't say," he replied, turning to Tom. "And how exactly do you know her, darling?"

"Through the internet," Tom improvised. "We game."

"Oh yes? And what game is that?"

"The Seven Deadly Sins," said Tom.

"But this isn't some kind of virtual relationship," said O'Riordan. "You have met her in real life?"

"Yeah," said Tom. "Of course."

"When was the last time you saw her?"

I could see right away that O'Riordan was on his guard. Suspicious. Something wasn't right. I decided to stick my oar in.

"That's the thing," I said. "Tom's worried about her."

"Yes," said Tom. "I am. It's like she's disappeared off the map."

"Have you seen her at all?" I asked O'Riordan. "I mean recently."

"You're not the only people who have been pestering me about Olga," said O'Riordan. "I've even had the police round. It seems she's run away from home."

"You don't think she's been kidnapped?" I asked.

"Now look, guys," said O'Riordan, putting down his camera and staring me in the face. "I may have this all wrong, but I don't think Tom here is all that serious about modelling. And I'm pretty sure what you really want is to pump me about Olga. And that's okay. I'm happy to be pumped. You don't have to spin me a line."

"That's good," I said. "It's just that some people don't seem to want to talk about her openly."

"Such as?" asked the photographer. "Sorry, we didn't really introduce ourselves, did we? I'm Jack O'Riordan. Hence Flash Photography. You know, like Jumping Jack Flash?"

"The Stones song."

"That was my nickname at school, and it kind of stuck," he said. "And you are?"

"I'm Charlie," I said, "Charlie Charlesworth, and this is my son Tom. We're private detectives, working for Olga's mother."

"I'm not really hoping to become a model," said Tom.

"Thank God for that," said O'Riordan. "It's not that you're bad looking, darling, but you have about as much hope of becoming a top model as you would of playing Dorothy in *The Wizard of Oz*."

"What a shame," said Tom. "And just when I'd learned Somewhere Over The Rainbow."

"Let's face it, darling," he said. "You're hardly flamboyant, are you? You need to know how to pose, how to present yourself. Like him."

He indicated a huge glossy picture of a well-known film star.

"He looks vaguely familiar," I said. "Is that Johnny Depp?"

"Dad!" exclaimed Tom. "That's Jean-Paul De Mode."

"He looks as if he works out," I said.

"Darling, all the Hollywood stars do," said O'Riordan. "And the gay ones like him work doubly hard."

"Isn't De Mode married?" asked Tom.

"Darling, half the hunks in Hollywood are in lavender marriages. And half the actresses started out as call girls, or in the adult sex industry."

"How do you know that?" I asked.

"Because, darling, I know them all, and where the bodies are buried," he said. "A place like this doesn't come cheap, you know. But there, I've said too much already."

The photographer tossed his head and gave me a roguish grin.

"I'm letting my tongue run away with me but, hey, that's another chapter in my autobiography. Now, darlings, I am going to have to charge you for the photo session, because it's, like, my line of business, but if you want to stop now and schmooze about Olga, I'm happy to do so. I hope she's okay."

"So do we," said Tom. "You don't seem surprised she's run away from home."

"Hardly, darling," said Jack.

"Why not?" Tom and I asked in near-perfect unison.

"I got the impression her father's a bit of a disciplinarian. She used to complain a bit about her dad, but then don't they all!"

"Oh?" I said. "What did she say?"

"Just that he was very strict, autocratic, that kind of thing. He didn't let her go out in the evenings, made her study, didn't approve of her friends."

"Any particular friend?"

"Well, I think there was one in particular. Daughter of a rock star."

"Fairycakes Bonanza Parks?" said Tom.

"Yes," said O'Riordan. "Terrible mouthful, isn't it? I know she and Olga used to be, like, super-close."

"But not any longer?"

"Olga's dad saw to that," said O'Riordan. "But I think they still chatted over the net. Played games together. You know the sort of thing."

"What kind of games?" I asked.

"God knows, darling," said O'Riordan. "I don't play them. Ghastly, violent things, mostly. The kind in which you kill people. Not my scene at all."

"And you didn't have a relationship with Olga," I said.

"Not a sexual relationship, if that's what you're getting at," he said. "It's not exactly a state secret that I'm gay."

"I'm sorry," said Tom. "We don't mean to be rude."

"That's okay," said Jack. "It's only natural that you'd want to talk to me. I mean, I am her agent."

"You are?" asked Tom.

"More of a secret agent, really. Ha!" O'Riordan threw back his head and flared his nostrils, like a prancing horse.

"Don't take this the wrong way," I said, "but why would she come to you if she wouldn't sign up to a top agent like Loco Parente?"

"Oh, you know Loco, do you?" he asked, a superior smile playing on his lips.

"Not well, but I paid him a visit yesterday."

"Did you now?" said the photographer. "And Loco agreed to meet you? You were honoured!"

"I showed him these glossies, and he behaved very strangely."

"How do you mean?"

"Well, he denied he knew Olga and turned a very funny colour."

"Mind if I look?" asked Jack.

He frowned at the pictures of Olga.

"These are quite old," he said. "I took these when she was thirteen."

"They're the pictures her mother gave us," I said. "Does she look different now?"

"Well, of course nowadays she's quite a bit more butch."

Tom and I looked at each other. This was a new piece of information.

"I, er, didn't know," I said.

"You didn't know Olga's gay?" said Jack, incredulously.

"I hadn't a clue," I said.

"Nor me," said Tom.

"I thought you said you knew her," said Jack.

"I haven't actually met her," said Tom. "As such."

O'Riordan turned to me.

"And her parents didn't tell you?" he asked.

"You mean they knew?"

"Of course. There was a big row, about a year back."

"What caused the row?"

"Her mother found her in bed with Fairycakes and, put it this way, they weren't playing Scrabble," he said. "Her parents blamed the other woman, of course, saying she'd corrupted her. But my guess is that it was six of one, and half a dozen of the other."

"And after that, Olga came out?" Tom asked.

"Yes. In a way, being discovered cleared the air. Olga doesn't mind who knows."

"Why wouldn't they tell us?" I asked.

"Who knows how these crazy Russians think, darling?" Jack shrugged. "I'm just a humble photographer."

"Not that humble," said Tom. "This place must be worth millions."

"I've been very fortunate," said Jack, fluttering his eyelashes.

"Have you ever worked for Parente?" I asked.

"Hasn't everyone, darling?" said O'Riordan.

"When Parente looked at these photos, he claimed not to recognise her. But surely he knew her quite well?"

"She worked for him for years."

"Any idea how long?"

"From when she was a child, maybe five or six, right up to the end of last year."

"So from 2000 through to the end of 2010?"

"That's about right."

"Why did they fall out?" asked Tom.

"I know Olga called him a dirty old man. I think that's why she asked me to represent her. She knew I wouldn't try to touch her up."

"Maybe that's it," I said. "When I showed him those photos, Parente must have thought I was about to accuse him of having it off with an underage girl."

"And did he?" asked Tom.

"Did he what?" asked O'Riordan.

"Did he have it off with Olga?"

O'Riordan thought for a moment.

"I imagine so," he said. "Loco thinks he enjoys a *droit de seigneur* over most of his models, male and female, and let's just say age was the least of considerations. In fact, for Loco it's always been a case of the younger, the better."

"You say she came to you for work?"

"Yes. Mainly hand modelling, that sort of thing. I found her the odd job her parents didn't know about. You know, for pocket money."

"And when was the last time you saw her?"

"I realty couldn't say. Lately she hasn't needed an agent,

because she wasn't looking for work," said O'Riordan. "She's been doing her A-levels."

"Just one more thing," I said.

"Uh-oh," said O'Riordan, with a smile. "Isn't that what Columbo always says just before he nails a suspect and accuses him of murder?"

"Has Olga ever spoken to you about Vladimir Putin?" I asked.

"Funny you should say that," said O'Riordan. "She once told me that seeing Putin pose bare-chested with a gun was one of the first times she realised she was definitely gay."

"You think she meant that as a joke?" I asked.

"Not at all," said O'Riordan. "I'm sure she meant it. Look, I have to get on. Nice to meet you both, and I'll get your photos to you as soon as I have time to print them up. I presume you do actually want them."

"Why not?" said Tom.

"Thanks for your help," I said.

On the way out, Tom pointed to some photos pinned up on the wall. They were of clowns. Three of them. Two normal sized, and one midget.

"God, I hate clowns," said Tom. "They give me the creeps."

"Do you?" asked O'Riordan. "I did them yesterday. The funny thing is, they kept asking about Olga too. At least the midget did."

"Really?" I asked, trying not to sound excited. "What sort of things did he ask you?"

"Same sort of things you were. Whether I thought she'd run away or been kidnapped. Whether she'd been unhappy at home. That sort of thing."

"Did they tell you how they knew her?"

"The midget did most of the talking. He said they were friends of hers from way back."

"Anything else odd about them?"

"You mean apart from them being clowns and a midget?"

"Yes," I said. "Apart from that, obviously."

57

"Mm, let me see. They did all have different accents. I think the two big ones might have been French, and the midget sounded American."

"Do you know what circus they belong to?" I asked.

"They didn't say."

"I notice the midget has a Hitler moustache."

"I think he would deny that. He called it a Charlie Chaplin."

I tried to think of a way to make the next question sound like the most natural thing in the world to ask.

"He didn't by any chance," I suggested, "have a red beard?"

"What on earth makes you ask that?" said O'Riordan.

"I don't know. Just a hunch."

"You know," said O'Riordan, "you're not as stupid as you look."

"Thanks," I said, "I think."

"He did have a few red hairs around his ears, as though he'd been wearing a fake beard and hadn't washed off all the glue. I remember because I made him clear it off. Once you noticed it, it was the only thing you could look at."

Tom and I looked at each other.

"Mind if I take this photo?" asked Tom.

Jack O'Riordan shrugged.

"Sure, if you want. It will cost you ten quid."

"What did you make of him?" Tom asked, as we walked away from O'Riordan's house.

"Well, I think we can rule him out as Olga's secret lover."

"Yes," said Tom. "But didn't you think there was something not quite right about him?"

"Apart from him being a raving queen who looked like Simon Cowell?"

"Apart from that."

"I'm not sure what you're getting at."

"Well, what about the size and location of that house, for a start? He's not by any stretch of the imagination a world-famous photographer, and yet he lives in a property like that."

"Maybe he's got a private income."

"Or some other source of revenue," said Tom. "It seemed to me he was hinting about some connection with the adult sex industry."

"I must have missed that," I said. "Anyway, is that something you can make serious money in?"

"Dad, you've had such a sheltered upbringing," said Tom. "It's huge. Some say it's bigger than Hollywood."

"Do you think Olga might be mixed up in that?"

"Nothing would surprise me," said Tom. "This case is starting to get really bizarre."

He waved the photograph at me and grinned.

"A red-bearded American dwarf and a pair of French-speaking clowns," he said. "Are the Cirque du Soleil in town?

"I don't think so."

"At least we have a picture now," said Tom. "I suppose you want me to find out who they are?"

"It wouldn't hurt," I said. "After all, if we could find the dwarf, we might be able to ask him what was in his note."

"The one he delivered to Olga?"

"Yes," I said.

"He might not know," says Tom. "He might just have been the delivery boy."

"You think?" I asked. "Incidentally, do you see that person over there. Pretending not to be watching us?"

"You mean the Asian-looking guy with fluorescent green hair?"

"He works for Loco Parente," I said. "You see, I'm not imagining things. You can see him too."

"Well, he's not exactly inconspicuous," said Tom. "That attempt to hide behind a tree is pathetic."

"Shall we see if we can lose him?" I asked.

"Look, there's a yellow light," said Tom.

"Taxi!" I yelled.

"Where to, guv?" asked the cab driver, as Tom and I piled in.

"Soho Square," I said, "but could you start off by driving in the opposite direction?"

"It's your money, guv," said the cabbie. "You can go via the North Pole, for all I care."

I looked back, to see the green-haired oriental watching us leave. I think I even saw him stamp his foot.

"This is exciting," said Tom. "Like being in an old-fashioned thriller. You know, like one of those Hitchcock movies you love."

"You don't think it's like a modern thriller?" I asked.

"Nah," said Tom. "Not enough action and no one's been killed yet. Far too tame."

"This is all a bit weird, isn't it?" I said. "I mean, here we are, being followed by a bloke with green hair. On the trail of two clowns and a midget."

"Investigating a crime that probably isn't one," said Tom. "I mean, do *you* think Olga's been kidnapped?"

"It seems unlikely," I said. "Still why should we care, as long as we're being paid?"

"It seems to me she's run away from home," said Tom. "And probably to be with her lesbian lover."

"Fairycakes?" I said.

"Presumably," said Tom.

"I think it might be an idea if you redoubled your efforts to find an address for Ms Parks."

"It would be my pleasure," said Tom.

"Fairycakes Bonanza Parks, here we come," I said, looking over my shoulder. "At least we seem to have shaken off our friend with the green hair."

"He's not following us?" asked Tom, looking over his shoulder.

"Not as far as I can see," I said. "But chances are that by the time we get back to the office, he'll be outside waiting. I mean, it's not as if we have anywhere else to go, and he does know where we live."

When we got back to the office, the bloke with green hair wasn't there. Perhaps he was reporting back to Loco Parente that we'd been visiting a photographer with a suspiciously large house in Notting Hill. The first thing Tom asked Marti was if she had made an appointment for me.

"Yeah," she said. "Most of the therapists were booked up, but one had a cancellation for six o'clock tonight."

"You can not be serious," I said. "We've got a runaway heiress to track down."

"Leave that to me," said Tom. "I'm on to it. In the meantime, Dad, you need professional help."

"If it helps get you two off my back," I said. "Just give me the address."

Marti also mentioned there'd been a couple of calls for me.

"It was someone who called himself Die Fuhrer," she said. "He pretty much ordered you to have dinner with him."

"Any day in particular?"

"He suggested tonight."

I shrugged.

"I don't see why not."

"He says he has a reservation for eight o' clock at Killingfield's."

"Blimey," I said. "I hope he's taken out a second mortgage."

"Why's that?" asked Tom.

"It's the most expensive restaurant in town," I said. "Haven't you heard of Edward Killingfield?"

"Not really my scene," said Tom.

"He's the trendiest chef in London," I said. "Calls himself a culinary alchemist. His restaurant is booked up months in advance. It's supposed to be the ultimate experience in extreme gastronomy."

"I'm more of a steak and chips man myself," said Tom.

"Me too," I said. "Can't say I'm much of an enthusiast for tarantulas on toast."

"Yuk!" said Marti. "You're not serious!"

"I am," I said. "Another of his specialities is barbecued bat. And freeze-dried goose foetus."

"Rather you than me," said Tom. "I take it, incidentally, that you're not actually planning to dine with Adolf Hitler."

"Oddly enough, I am not," I said. "The Fuhrer is an old pal of mine, of a German persuasion, named Joseph Gildenstern."

Wasn't he a great player in his day?"

"What they call a midfield general," I said. "And a right devious bastard. He'd foul you when no one was looking and then look all innocent. You could always tell when he'd done something really evil. He'd stick out his lower lip and shrug, with both his hands in the air, as though he was playing a three foot harmonica."

"Sounds like a charmer."

"One of the biggest bastards who ever bestrode a football pitch."

"Does he often invite you out for dinner?"

"Only when he wants something," I said. "Invariably football-related."

"Blimey," said Tom. "Don't tell me it's another job."

"Who knows?" I said. "This could be our lucky day."

"Don't forget to ask the Fuhrer if he knows the whereabouts of any Russian heiresses," said Tom. "Or French clowns. Or an American midget."

"I'll see if the topic comes up," I promised.

6

CHAMPAGNE

Tuesday, 2nd August

Tuesday evening began with my trip to the shrink. The address was a basement in Tufnell Park, which made me suspect that this was not the most successful psychotherapist in London.

When I rang the doorbell, it was the therapist herself who answered. She didn't even have a receptionist.

"Lobelia Briggs," she said, shaking my hand.

"Charlie Charlesworth," I said.

"Oh," she said. "I thought I was meeting an Alan Charlesworth."

"That's my real name," I said. "But most people call me Charlie."

"So you have two names," she said, as though I had two heads. "Interesting."

She asked me to come through to her consulting room, and this turned out to be a small study, just about big enough to accommodate an armchair, a desk chair and a small table. She indicated that I should sit in the armchair, which turned out not to have any springs. The sensation was a bit like falling down the rabbit hole in *Alice in Wonderland*. She sat at the table and looked down at me.

She was an efficient-looking woman with straight black hair, a piercing stare and extremely thin lips. I distrusted her immediately.

"Why have you come to see me?" she asked.

I have absolutely no idea, I thought. I've been bullied into it. I don't want to be here. Of course, what I actually said was:

"My son thinks I need help."

"Do you think you need help?"

"I don't think I'm bonkers."

"You mean your son thinks you are?"

"I think he thinks I might be getting that way."

"And why do you think he thinks that?"

"He says I'm addicted."

"Oh?"

"He says hopelessly addicted."

"To what?"

"It's a bit embarrassing."

"I'm not easily embarrassed."

I flushed.

"No, but I am."

"There's no need to be," the shrink said. "I can't believe it won't be anything I haven't come across before."

"I wouldn't be too sure about that," I said.

"So I take it, it isn't drugs?" she inquired.

"No."

"Alcohol?"

"No."

"Cigarettes?"

"No."

"Internet pornography?"

"You're getting warmer."

"Other kinds of pornography?"

64

"Colder."

"Mr Charlesworth…"

"You can call me Charlie."

"Mr Charlesworth, it might be a more productive use of our time if you just came out and told me what you are addicted to."

"I didn't say I'm addicted to it."

"No, but I understand your son does."

"Exactly."

"So?"

I paused. It wasn't easy to say out loud.

"I think, or rather he thinks, I may have a… video game addiction."

"Ah."

"You don't seem surprised."

"I have come across it before, though never – if you don't mind my saying so – in someone of your age."

"That's what's embarrassing."

"And how does this addiction manifest itself?"

"Well, I play a lot. On my computer. Obviously."

"How much is a lot?"

"Well…" I considered. "What level would you say might constitute addictive behaviour?"

"The normal estimate is two hours a day."

"Ah," I said.

"You play longer?"

"Much longer. Maybe six. Up to twelve. Sometimes fifteen."

"How do you find time to do anything else?" she asked.

"Business has been slow recently."

"And your business is?"

"I'm a private investigator."

"But not a busy one."

"No."

"Is it any game in particular, to which you're addicted?"

"I didn't say I was addicted."

"Let me rephrase that. Which game do you play so much that your son is worried about you?"

"It's called, er, Football Manager."

"How long have you been playing it?"

"Years and years," I said. "It helped break up my marriage."

"Why was that?"

"My wife didn't like it when I nearly burnt the house down."

"And this was to do with Football Manager?"

"All I'd done was set a waste paper basket alight, to recreate the atmosphere of a Champions' League away game in Istanbul."

"You think that's normal?"

"I did at the time. I might have had a drink or two."

"Would you say that you have an addictive personality?"

"Not really. I've cut back on the booze, apart from the odd glass of wine. But I am still a bit obsessed, with…"

"With this Football Manager," she said, staring at me with a scary impassivity. "So you chose a computer game over your wife?"

"That could be what she thinks."

"Is it what you think?"

"I'm not sure what I think," I said. "I mean, I'm a bloke."

"Yes," she said, raising her eyebrows and lowering them. "You most certainly are."

She pulled out a piece of paper, on which she had made some notes.

"I looked you up on Wikipedia," she said. "I gather you played football for England."

"Only twice," I said. "Just before my left knee went. That was in a so-called friendly against Austria, and it really was a case of Goodnight, Vienna."

"And why the nickname?"

"Oh that," I said.

"Proper Charlie."

"Yeah," I said. "The Arsenal fans used to call me that."

"Why?"

"There are two schools of thought," I said. "One is that it referred to my tackling, which was – I like to think – strong but fair. I never got a red card."

"But isn't Proper Charlie an insult?" asked the shrink. "Aren't they implying that you're…?"

She waved her hands around, while searching for the right expression.

"A couple of sandwiches short of a picnic?" I suggested.

She shrugged.

"That's the alternative scenario," I said. "We were in the Cup Final with two minutes to go, and some people say I should have taken a dive."

"I thought we were talking about football."

"Pardon me?"

"Are you telling me they wished you were a swimmer?"

"Oh, I see. Diving. It's an expression. I was in the opposition penalty area, and someone pulled my shirt, another one kicked me and, well, I didn't go down. A lot of people said I should have."

"And earned a free kick?"

"It was inside the box so it would have been a penalty and almost certainly the winning goal," I said, "But it wouldn't have been right. You know, proper."

"And you ended up losing the game?"

"We did, yeah."

"So that's when you were called a Proper Charlie?"

"Among other things," I said.

"What kind of things?"

"Well, the opposing manager, Alex Ferguson—"

"Ah yes, Liverpool, no?"

"No. Man U."

She looked blank.

"Manchester United. Alex Ferguson, he told me that I had a good footballing brain but lacked the killer instinct, which I told him suited me, as I was planning to be a professional footballer, not a trained assassin. I don't think that went down too well, because he never spoke to me again. I got the impression he doesn't like players who answer back. The one top club I've never worked for, as a footballer or a detective, is Man U."

"So why did you become a private detective?"

"I couldn't do much else. I wouldn't pretend to be the brightest or the best. I left school at 16 in order to pursue a career in association football, so I'm not exactly brimming with academic qualifications. Harry Redknapp once said I had an educated left foot, but the rest of me must have played truant."

My attempt at a joke brought no smile from her. Instead, she frowned.

"Who is this Harry Redknapp? An educational psychologist?"

"Not as far as I know," I said.

"It seems a leap," she said, "from footballer to private detective."

"Especially with a bad knee," I joked.

Like my other attempts at levity, this went down like a cup of cold sick.

"I'm not the only one who's done it," I said. "Ever heard of a bloke called Glen Mulcaire?"

The shrink thought for a moment.

"The name sounds familiar," she said.

"He's another footballer turned private investigator. Glenn used to play for AFC Wimbledon. Decent striker. But now, sadly, better known for that *News of the World* business."

"Ah yes," she said. "Didn't he hack phones for a living?"

I nodded.

"Glenn knew what a lot of private investigators like me didn't, which is that the voicemail services on most mobile phones have the same default access code, a four-digit number that most users can't be bothered to change. All you needed to know was the right mobile number, and putting in that bog-standard access code meant you had access to lots of private phone messages. Glenn was quoted as saying he didn't realise doing that was illegal, but he learnt soon enough that it carried a six month prison sentence."

"And you were involved with him?" she asked.

"No, no, I set up on my own."

"To hack phones?"

"No. I was never high-profile enough to be approached by any of the tabloid press to do their dirty work, for which I am eternally grateful."

"Maybe this is why you have so little work," she said.

"Oh, I've had work. You might think that being a private investigator specialising in football would be a niche activity, but you'd be surprised. It's big business these days, and where there's money, there's crime. The time was when gangsters were attracted to boxing, but now the big money's in football, worldwide."

"Ah. So you went into it for the money," she said.

"Not really," I admitted. "My dad used to be a copper, God rest his soul, and even before I got injured he used to tell me I should do something useful with my life. Safeguard society, that sort of thing. I never knew whether to take him seriously. He was always having a laugh. That's until he fell over with a heart attack. Which was when the laughing stopped, obviously."

"And you have been a private detective for a number of years?"

"I have."

"And you've survived," she said. "Until now."

"I've got by," I said. "But then I'm Proper Charlie, aren't I? Maybe not Sherlock Holmes, but I'm no wide boy. I'm known for being honest, discreet and relatively cheap, which has helped me get through the recession, and keep an office in central London. It's far from sumptuous, but perfectly adequate until the lifts and air con stop working, which occurs every summer, which is how I can afford an office in Soho Square."

"I see," she said. "And what is it you require from me?"

"I don't know," I said. "Is there any way you can help me play less?"

"Ah yes. Football Manager. I take it you've tried to give up?"

"Yes, but I keep going back to it. There's always more players to buy and sell, more matches to play, more trophies to win."

"Would you say you are more effective at this game than you are at life?"

I decided not to take offence. After all, there was more than a trace of truth in her observation.

"At the moment I'm doing really well."

"And how does this manifest itself?"

"Well, I've won the Premiership four times in a row, the FA Cup twice, the League Cup three times, and been to the final of the European Champions League twice. And now I have other responsibilities."

"Inside or outside the game?"

"Inside."

"And what are they?"

"I did so well as manager of Arsenal, that now I'm managing England as well."

"In your spare time?"

"That's the idea."

"I imagine having two jobs on your computer doesn't leave many hours of the day free for private investigating."

"Really it's more the other way round," I said. "It's because there's so little work coming in that I play a lot on the computer."

"Shouldn't you be out, advertising for work?"

"It doesn't work like that," I said. "I pretty much rely on word of mouth."

"What if the word of mouth was that you're addicted to computer games?"

"I never thought of that," I said. "You think the news might have leaked out?"

"I'm not sure," said the shrink. "But when a wife leaves a husband, their friends tend to discuss why that might be, and if she says it was because he was more attached to a computer game than her, the news might get around."

"You think?"

"I do indeed think," she said, looking at her watch. "I'm afraid our time is up, Mr Charlesworth."

"Charlie. So you'll need to see me again?"

"If you don't mind," she said, "I think you might be better off seeing a colleague of mine, a Mr Zsigmond von Bienhoff."

"He sounds German."

"Austrian. He works out of Harley Street. He's far more up to date on computer game addiction than I am."

"So you think that's what I've got?"

"Mr Charlesworth," she said. "You're the most advanced case I've ever come across."

"Advanced?" I said. "Is that good or bad?"

"It isn't good," she said.

"Ah," I said. "That bad."

"Bad enough for you to need it put right," she said. "Would you prefer to pay by cheque or credit card?"

Killingfield's turned out to be a discreet, tall building in Mayfair. You could easily have assumed it was a private house, because there was no evidence on the outside of commercial habitation. You had to press a bell to get in, and the door was opened by an elegant black man, dressed entirely in black and carrying a black menu. The walls were painted black, as was the floor. It was like being welcomed into an extremely upmarket funeral parlour.

I was ushered upstairs to a private room, also black, where the Fuhrer was already waiting, impeccably dressed in the establishment's colour of choice. He was chatting to a muscular young man with a shaven head, dressed inevitably in black. I was wearing a light blue shirt and dark blue trousers, and felt garish.

I'd never known Joseph Gildenstern be late for anything, and he hadn't made an exception this time. He'd already ordered a bottle of Dom Perignon, and had poured out two glasses of bubbly, one of which was half-empty, if you're Arsene Wenger, or half-full, if you're Harry Redknapp.

I thought about telling Joseph I'd prefer a beer but decided against it. I'm not saying that all Germans have no sense of humour – that would be, if not a foul racial stereotype, a definite over-generalisation, like saying that all Englishmen are rubbish at sex – but the Fuhrer was not renowned for his levity. Intensity was more his line. That, and world domination.

Gildenstern was now in his early fifties and, as he rose to his feet and greeted me, I saw that he had developed a small but quite noticeable paunch. In his playing career, he'd had very good feet and an excellent tactical brain. Superb passer of the ball, like a Germanic Paul Scholes. Also like Scholesy, he had a mean streak, and a way of getting his own back. It's more difficult to get away with that kind of thing these days, with the number of cameras they have all round the pitch, not to mention slow-motion action replays. But the Fuhrer was a cagey character and he was very adept at coming up behind you and causing damage with his studs, off the ball, when the match officials and most of the crowd were looking the other way. He often went for your testicles, which made him widely feared.

Shortly after he retired from playing, he inherited the family armaments business, and he's been very much the businessman ever since, doing a bit of this and a bit of that, and for all I know a bit of the other. But he's always kept up his involvement with football. He's got connections with FIFA, sits on its ethics committee and still does consultancy work for different clubs. I guessed that this might be why he wanted to meet me, and I was soon proved right.

"I hope you do not object," he said, "but I have taken the liberty of ordering us the tasting menu. It is the ideal way to sample the latest delicacies that Edward has to offer."

"I'm just impressed that you were able to get a table," I said.

"I am one of Edward's principal investors," he said. "I can always get a table. He reserves this room for me whenever I am in London."

"Very nice, too," I said. "Especially if you're fond of black."

"I am," he said. "I have many black shirts. And black suits. And, of course, black socks."

"Must make it easy to dress in the morning," I said. "I've been known to end up wearing odd socks."

"That would never happen to me," he said.

"I'm sure it wouldn't," I said.

"Please sit down," he said, indicating the chair opposite him.

"Thanks," I said.

"While I was waiting for you," he said. "I have been talking to Dries here. Charlie Charlesworth, Dries Helling."

I gazed up at the muscular young man with the shaven head, who had withdrawn a respectful couple of paces from the table.

"Dries is one of your biggest fans," said Gildenstern.

"Really?" I asked. "I'm always surprised when people remember my playing days."

"I used to watch you at Highbury," he said. "It was a shame your career was cut short."

"Yeah," I agreed. "So, Dries, I take it you are the maitre d'?"

"Not exactly," Helling replied. "I am Mr Killingfield's quartermaster."

"His right-hand man. Dries finds Edward his exotic ingredients," said Gildenstern. "From all over the world."

"Mr Killingfield used to do his own foraging," said Helling. "But now he spends most of his time in the kitchen, I'm happy to do his legwork."

"Any ambitions to be a chef yourself?" I asked.

"Mr Killingfield and his backers have kindly set me up with my own place. I must invite you to the opening," he said. "There I hope I will be able to pursue my own food ideology."

"Ideology?" I queried.

"Essentially, it's all about foraging. Nothing shapes a chef like foraging," he enthused. "If you see how a plant grows and you taste it in situ you have a perfect example of how it should taste on the plate. But it's more than that. When you get close to the raw materials and taste them at the moment they let go of the soil, you learn to respect them."

"So how does this foraging work? Mr Killingfield gives you a shopping list, and you go out to get them?" I asked. "That must involve a lot of travelling."

"It does," said Gildenstern.

"I travel all over the world," said Helling.

"But when Dries is in London, he stays in my house," said Gildenstern. "He even has his own key."

"Mr Gildenstern is generous with his hospitality," said Helling. "It is much more pleasant than staying at a hotel."

"You speak English very well," I said. "But your name?"

"Dutch," he said. "But I have spent most of my life in England. And I attended college in America. But now I must leave you two gentlemen to your dinner. Bon appetit."

"That's modern London for you," I said, after he had left us. "It's so cosmopolitan, it's a wonder there are any English people left."

"Fascinating boy," breathed Gildenstern, gazing at Helling's rear view. "Did you see those muscles? Edward finds him indispensable. And, of course, very easy on the eye."

He winked at me, roguishly.

"To me, he looks like Ross Kemp," I said. "But then a lot of blokes do these days."

"I do not know this Ross Kemp," said Gildenstern. "To me he looks more like that English film star. The one in action movies."

"Jason Statham?"

"That's the one."

"I can see the similarity," I said. "But I'm pretty sure Statham's a lot taller."

"I defer," said Gildenstern, "to your superior knowledge."

I wondered when Joseph would get round to why he had invited me there. In the meantime, I tried a little more polite conversation.

"So, Joseph, you have a house in London?"

"Just round the corner. Here in Mayfair."

"And that's where you're living at the moment?"

"If you can call it living," he emitted the long-suffering sigh of the world traveller. "I divide my time between the UK, Germany, the States and South Korea."

"South Korea?"

"We live in a global economy, and we all have to make sacrifices."

Having exhausted the Fuhrer's limited supply of small talk, we passed on to the main topic of the evening.

"Charlie, although it is delightful as always to see you," he said, "I have called you here in a professional capacity. Which means I shall need your discretion."

"Oh yes?" I asked.

Ever since Marti had told me of the Fuhrer's phone call, I had been wondering why Joseph Gildenstern was so determined to treat me to an expensive dinner. I attempted to register an expression of polite interest, while attempting to suggest by my poise of dignified reserve that a man of my status and sophistication was well accustomed to being approached professionally by leaders of world football, especially over matters of extreme delicacy.

"Yes," he said.

At this point, there was a pause, as the first course was brought to the table, accompanied by a glass of white wine, the name of which was possibly German, and certainly too long and complicated to catch. The first course consisted of an egg each. It looked like a hen's egg, or maybe a duck egg. It had been shelled and, as far as I could tell, lightly boiled, and served in a sauce that gave off a smell of chilli and vinegar.

"What is this?" I asked, hoping that my expression of ignorance, laced perhaps a little too audibly with fear, would not dispel my image as a man of the world. My attempt to suggest sophistication may well have suffered by my dropping my napkin, stooping to retrieve it and banging my head on the underside of the table, which unfortunately cause me to drop it again.

"Let me pick that up for you, sir," said the waiter, retrieving the napkin from the floor.

Another waiter moved in smoothly with another napkin, unsullied by contact with the floor, or indeed myself.

"You are not permitted to know," said the Fuhrer. "Edward believes that knowledge is a dangerous thing, for it can prejudice you against culinary endeavour. Every course at Killingfield's is an exercise in trust and obedience to the chef."

So saying, he bit into his egg, which had something grey and pink inside it.

Somewhat against my better judgment, I bit into mine. The taste was eggy, mixed with some kind of liver. Goose liver? There was also something weird about the texture. It was crunchy.

"Voila!" said one of the waiters, who had been watching us. I surmised he was French.

"Now that we have finished," I said, "May we know what that was?"

"Indeed, monsieur. It is Philippine Duck Embryo a la Killingfield."

I hastily took a drink of water, and washed away the memory of the course with a swig of the white wine chosen to accompany the course. Gildenstern seemed unmoved by the naming of the dish, and continued as the plates were being cleared away.

"You may not be aware," he said, "but I have been operating

for some years as a consultant to Mr Bernhard Spritzer who, as you no doubt know, owns 98.5% of Southern Athletic."

I should explain at this point that at various points in this narrative I have been obliged to change a few names of persons and football clubs in order to protect the innocent, the guilty and indeed myself from being bundled into the boot of a car and taken to a permanent abode not of my choosing.

"I wasn't aware of the exact percentage," I said.

"Well, now you know," he said.

"I do," I said. "Who owns the other 1.5%?"

"That is unimportant," he said. "Kindly concern yourself with essentials of the case and listen to what I have to say."

"Righto," I said. "This is very nice champagne, by the way."

"It is," he said.

The waiter was hovering with the next course, which appeared to be in liquid form. It was served in a cocktail glass.

"This, messieurs, is an appetiser," said the waiter.

"Thank you," replied the Fuhrer.

"It is best if you down it in one," said the waiter.

"Very well," nodded Gildenstern.

He swigged it back, with every appearance of enjoyment, so I did too. There was an explosion of fishy flavour on the palate, mixed with what seemed to be cream sauce.

"Was it to your liking?" asked the waiter.

"Very nice," I said.

"Cod shirako," he said.

"Shirako?" I inquired.

"Semen, or sperm," he said.

"So that was cod sperm."

"It was indeed, sir."

I did my best to look grateful. I turned back to my host.

"So you work to Mr Spritzer rather than to the manager?" I said.

"Exactly," said the Fuhrer. "I am the troubleshooter."

"So what is this trouble you are currently shooting?"

The former footballer nodded, as though appreciative that I was coming straight to the point.

"Mr Spritzer is troubled with the form of his strikers," he said. "One striker, in particular."

"And I think I can guess who that is," I said.

"That would not surprise me," said the Fuhrer.

"Lorenzo Fettucini?" I hazarded.

"The same," he said, sipping his wine.

"Lorenzo's a nice boy," I said. "Thick as vegetable soup, but he can't help that."

"You knew him when he was playing in the north, didn't you?"

"I did, yes," I replied cagily.

"I understood this to be the case," he said.

"Lorenzo hasn't scored yet for Athletic, has he?" I asked, knowing the reply.

"He has not," said Joseph. "And Mr Spritzer is not well pleased at the return on his investment."

"What was it? Twenty million?"

"Considerably more," he said, "if you include dispensations and what have you. Nearer thirty."

"Ouch," I said.

"Naturally, his arrival unsettled the other strikers at the club, who have been less than delighted at the number of games Fettucini has been given to find his form, while they…"

"Have been left festering on the bench," I said.

"Or loaned out to other clubs," said Joseph, "where they have scored ten goals between them, while Mr Fettucini has scored precisely none."

The next course arrived. It appeared to be broad, thin slices of meat, covered in batter, and served with sautéed, sliced mushrooms.

"What do you think this is?" I asked.

There was a pause while the Fuhrer tasted the dish.

"It is difficult to say," replied Gildenstern. "The meat appears to have been marinated in oil, lemon juice, chopped parsley, with I think salt and pepper, then fried in batter, sliced and cooked in a butter and cream sauce. Am I correct?"

"You have a fine palate, sir," said the waiter.

"It's a bit chewy," I said.

"That is all part of the experience, sir," said the waiter. "And, gentlemen, it is said to be good for the sexual prowess."

"I have it," said Gildenstern, triumphantly. "It is testicles of bull."

"It is indeed, sir."

To calm myself, I took another swig of champagne.

"Where were we?" asked Gildenstern. "Ah, yes. Fettucini's inability to score."

"Plenty of strikers take a while to settle into a new club," I said.

"Fettucini has not scored in twenty games," said Joseph. "A statistic that Mr Spritzer finds unacceptable. As do I."

"Perhaps he isn't fully fit," I suggested.

"Needless to say," said Joseph, "Mr Spritzer has had every aspect of his game measured and evaluated, on match days and in training."

"And the result?"

"There has been no discernible diminution in his speed or impairment of his passing accuracy. And he scores freely enough in training."

"I see." I thought for a moment. "Couldn't Mr Spritzer sell him?"

"No."

"Why not?"

"Because his market value is now half what Mr Spritzer paid for him. Perhaps even less."

"Has he tried sending Lorenzo to a shrink?"

"We have employed the services of three sports psychiatrists," he said, "but all they have come up with is that Fettucini seems distracted. It is as if his mind is not upon the game. It is almost as if he is frightened of scoring."

"Never a good thing in a striker," I said.

"Precisely," he said. "Which is where you come in."

"Joseph, old buddy, I'd love to help," I said, "but psychoanalysing soccer superstars isn't really my area of expertise."

"On the contrary," he said. "You are the only one who can help him."

"I am?"

"You are a good listener," he said. "I am not. My patience is not inexhaustible. Neither is Mr Spritzer's. It is evident to us both that Fettucini has some... secret that is bothering him, but which he is unwilling to tell us."

"Have you tried torturing him?" I suggested, with a grin.

"We never employ torture at Southern Athletic," said the Fuhrer, sitting bolt upright. "Who has been telling you that we do?"

"No, no, I was joking."

"Torture is something that you British joke about?" he asked. "I am not sure if I understand you. Or perhaps my English is not so good."

"No, your English is excellent. Better than any British Premiership footballer, I'd say."

"You flatter me," he said.

"No, I don't," I said. "Sadly."

"Sirs, I bring you your dessert," said the waiter.

"Oh my god," I said, looking at what had been brought before us. "These are moths."

"Yes, sir," admitted the waiter. "And what could be sweeter than a fat moth delicately baked? They are beautiful on the outside and sweet within, for they are nourished on nectar, the fabled food of the gods."

I braced myself, took a forkful, and was astonished to find that they did, indeed, burst open with a distinct taste of honey. Hairy honey, but honey nonetheless.

A few furry mouthfuls later, and I sensed thankfully that the meal was drawing to a close. But then the waiter reappeared with a couple of steaming dishes.

"Your savoury course, gentlemen," said the waiter.

"I'm not sure I can manage anything else," I said.

"But you must!" said a new voice.

The newcomer was a strikingly ugly woman, with an off-puttingly baritone voice. She must have been six foot six, and at least 25 stone. She was wearing chef's overalls and carrying a riding crop. The other noticeable thing about her was that she had black nail polish on her fingers. It was reminiscent of Liza Minnelli in *Cabaret*. What was it she said in the film? "Divine decadence, darling." On this woman, the effect of black nail polish was decadent but not divine.

"How are you, darling?" she asked, swiping at Joseph playfully with her crop.

He did not seem to mind her beating him around the shoulders.

"Edward," said Gildenstern, "I would like you to meet Alan Charlesworth. He is a former professional footballer, now a private detective."

"How thrilling!" boomed Edward Killingfield, for it was he – or she. "But I mustn't detain you, darlings, or your final course will be getting cold."

"The meal has been excellent, as always," said Joseph. "You are indeed the Queen of Extreme Cuisine."

"I do my best," said Edward Killingfield. "The challenge lies in finding the right ingredients. Of course, Dries is a godsend."

"I gather you're setting him up with his own restaurant," I said.

"I am!" he beamed. "You must come to the opening!"

"Is he, er, serving the same sort of food you do?"

"I'm sure he'll give it his own spin," said Killingfield. "But heaven knows how he'll find time to forage when he has his own kitchen."

"Maybe he'll delegate," I said. "After all, you did. Maybe he'll hire an assistant."

"A *sous chef?*" cried Killingfield, as though I have said something extremely indelicate. "I can't be having anyone else in my kitchen. I am an *auteur!*"

"You mean, like Hitchcock?" I said.

"No meal leaves my kitchen that has not been cooked with these fingers, conceived by this brain! Really!"

As he tossed his head and flounced off, I felt I should apologise to Gildenstern.

"Sorry," I said. "I seem to have said something wrong."

"That's just Edward," said Gildenstern. "He is so touchy about letting anyone into his kitchen, let alone another chef. He's always convinced they'll steal his ideas."

"What about Dries?" I asked.

"Oh, that's different," said Gildenstern. "He regards Dries as his protégé. And, of course, he's desperate to go to bed with him."

"But there's nothing between them?"

"It isn't for want of trying on Edward's part," said Gildenstern. "But I fear that when it comes to matters sexual, Dries is horribly straight."

As I pondered what was so horrible about preferring sex with a woman, I dug a fork into the food before me. It resembled a cheesecake, though I was willing to guess that it did not contain cheese.

"Ah, my favourite!" enthused the Fuhrer. "Alligator cheesecake!"

I forced myself to take a mouthful. This was certainly cheesecake with a bite. It was spicy, sweet and savoury, all at the same time, with curious lumps and textures that hit you as you bit into it.

"Do you like the little lumps of alligator sausage?" asked Gildenstern, happily. "Is it not perfectly teamed with the snappy shrimp?"

"Mm," I said, chewing furiously. "And there's something else."

"That will be the brain," said Gildenstern. "It has the consistency of tofu but the creaminess of a rich paté, or foie gras. There are those who believe this will increase your brain power."

"It's a little bit, er, rich for me," I said.

"May I have yours?" asked Gildenstern.

I tried to stop my gorge from rising as he piled my alligator cheesecake upon the remains of his. I asked the waiter where the gentlemen's was, and he directed me to the half-landing upstairs. I went into the one and only stall, and downloaded the contents of my stomach. I definitely wasn't cut out for fine dining.

After I had removed all traces of my lack of good taste, I returned to the table, where I was glad to see to see the Fuhrer had devoured the last of the alligator cheesecake.

"We are, of course, willing to pay you for your time," said Gildenstern, throwing his napkin on the table.

"That's good of you," I said.

"With ten thousand pounds up front," he said.

"That's even better of you," I said. "But I don't understand why you think Fettucini might confide in me."

"Is it not obvious? Because you have done things for him in the past."

"Well, yes, I was able to help him out over a little something."

"Involving a prostitute and a Sunday newspaper."

"You heard about that," I said.

"I have my spies," he said. "I notice that you do not deny it."

"He was guilty of a youthful indiscretion, which I was able to help him with, yes."

"I take it you paid off the prostitute," he said.

"It seemed the best solution all round. That way, Lorenzo's wife in Italy didn't need to know anything."

"In my opinion, Lorenzo may have need of your services now."

"That's as may be," I said. "But if he does, surely he would have hired me himself."

"I do not think Fettucini fully realises the precariousness of his situation," said Joseph.

"How do you mean?"

"As I mentioned, Mr Spritzer's patience is not inexhaustible, and neither is mine."

"And you don't think Lorenzo fully appreciates that?"

"I think that Lorenzo is, as you say, as thick as vegetable soup. If not thicker."

I stared at him. This was as near to humour as I'd ever experienced from the Fuhrer.

"And you wouldn't want anything to happen to him," I said.

"It would be a tragedy if his career – or life – were to end prematurely," said Joseph, impassively. "But that might be the only way Mr Spritzer might be able to recoup on his investment."

"I imagine the club has Lorenzo insured," I said.

"Exactly," said Joseph, "and at present he is worth a good deal more to the club dead than alive."

"And you would like me to put this to Lorenzo?"

"With the utmost discretion, of course," said Joseph, with the regret of a professional mourner. "It would be dreadful, quite dreadful, if anything were to happen to him."

"And if I were to say no?"

"I think you know better than to say no to me," said Joseph, with a roguish wink, "if you value your testicles."

"Don't get me wrong, Joseph," I said hastily. "I do. I really do."

Around this point, the coffee arrived.

"Shall I be mother?" asked Gildenstern.

"Please," I said.

To my surprise, the coffee – though served in a cup not much larger than a thimble – looked more or less like coffee. It tasted like it, too, though it seemed richer and sweeter than usual, and without the kick of caffeine. It was tasty but restful.

"That wasn't bad," I said.

"Excellent, sir," said the waiter, before turning to Gildenstern. "Was it to your liking, as well, sir?"

"It was," pronounced the Fuhrer. "But it is always one of my favourites. Kopi Luwak, was it not?"

"Yes, monsieur," said the waiter.

"And that is…?" I hazarded, not sure if I really wanted to know the answer.

"Dung, sir," said the water. "Coffee derived from beans consumed, digested and excreted by the common palm civet, a cat-sized mammal that has the facial markings of a raccoon."

"A close relative of the mongoose," said Joseph.

"How nice," I said. "I wonder if they spend Christmases together."

"Farmers pluck the beans from the faecal matter," continued the waiter. "After a thorough scrubbing, the beans are roasted, ground and brewed."

"I am glad to hear abut the scrubbing," I said. "Well, Joseph, this has all been extremely educational."

"Why end it here?" he asked. "You must come back to my place. Did I mention that it is only round the corner?"

"You did," I said.

"I may also have mentioned that I have houses everywhere," he boasted. "New York, Geneva, Berlin, Seoul. But I am especially fond of this one."

"Why's that?"

He leant forward, conspiratorially.

"It has an excellent dungeon," he whispered. "I have a sling."

"Oh, yes?" I asked weakly. I wasn't sure what you'd want a dungeon for, let alone a sling, but I was pretty sure it wouldn't be my cup of tea, or civet dung.

"You know, Charlie," he said, sliding his foot up my leg. "I have always admired your calves."

"That's... very kind of you," I said. "But I think I must be going."

"Do you not feel the effects of the meal?" he asked. "The aphrodisiac effects?"

I thought it politest not to say that only a few minutes previously I'd thrown most of the meal up.

"Don't get me wrong," I said. "The food was ace. Not what I'm used to, but very stimulating."

"So why do you not come home with me?"

"Joseph, maybe you should know that I'm straight. Horribly straight."

"Straight? Crooked? What's the difference?" he said. "A civilised man should be prepared to taste any dish once."

"But I'm not civilised," I said hastily. "I come from the East End. At least my dad did. And one of the things he told me was to try anything once, except anal sex and morris dancing."

"Oh? That is a new one on me," said Gildenstern. "Perhaps I should take up morris dancing."

"It's been a terrific evening," I said, "and thanks for the job. But I have to be up bright and early in the morning."

"A pity," said the former German midfielder. "Perhaps another time, ya?"

"Yeah, maybe," I said, starting to get up.

As it was the end of the meal, I thought I'd try out a long shot. You know, one of those speculative punts from the halfway line. Not something you'd try normally, but in extra time it might take a goalie unawares.

"Joseph," I said, sitting down again. "One last thing. Do you happen to know a bloke called Igor Molotovski?"

"You mean the Russian businessman?" he said. "I've heard of him, of course."

"I don't suppose," I said, "you've ever met his daughter?"

And here I produced a photo of her. Joseph scrutinised it for a moment, before rising to go.

"No," he said, with his face as taut as a death mask. "I have never met her before in my life. No, no, absolutely never."

As he did this, he stuck out his lower lip and shrugged with both hands in the air, as though he was playing a three foot long harmonica. The last time I'd seen that body language, he was telling a referee it was nothing to do with him that Gary Lineker was rolling around in agony, clutching his bollocks. Interesting.

7

THE RING

The next day, Wednesday, was hot and sticky. It was as though a storm was about to break. All three of us in the office were irritable, including me. Tom had been out all night, and I didn't like to ask him where. When he marched into my office, his first words were to ask me about my encounter with the shrink.

"So how did you get on with her?" he asked.

"Not too bad."

"What did she say?"

"She said I might have a problem."

"I could have told you that," said my son. "Did she do anything? Prescribe anything?"

"Not really. She said I should see another shrink."

"Anyone in particular?"

"An Austrian," I said. "I've got his name written down. He operates out of Harley Street."

"Sounds expensive," said my son. "But it's worth it, if it gets you off that Football Manager game. I don't suppose you could just give it up? Go cold turkey?"

"I tried that," I said. "But this morning I got up early to play it. I couldn't sleep."

"You don't seem to have any trouble falling asleep in the evenings."

"How do you know? You're hardly ever in."

"Well, when I do get in, you're usually slumped in front of the television, fast asleep. You usually blame whatever's on telly."

"Look," I said, "aren't we getting the father-son bit reversed here? I mean, I'm meant to be worried about you, not vice versa."

"I'm not doing anything you should be worried about," said Tom.

"Are you sure?" I asked. "I mean, where were you last night?"

"That's none of your business," Tom said. "But take it from me, I wasn't playing computer games."

"Fine," I said venomously.

"So," said Tom, "have you booked an appointment with this Austrian shrink?"

"Not yet."

"Do you want me to do it?"

"I can do it myself."

"Why don't you do it then?"

"All right. I will," I snapped, pulling down the screen on my laptop so that he couldn't see what I had been doing.

"Oh bloody hell," he said. "You're playing it, aren't you?"

"It's a very delicate stage of the season. The January transfer window."

"Dad," he said, "for God's sake get help. Somewhere they must have pills for this kind of thing."

It was then that Marti dropped the bombshell that changed the whole complexion of our case. She came into my office, and I was initially relieved that she had some news. Anything to get my son off my back about my so-called addiction.

"I think you two should sit down," she said.

"I am sitting down," I pointed out.

"You too," she said to Tom.

"Why? What's happened?" asked Tom, sitting.

"That bloke you went out to see yesterday," she said. "The one in Notting Hill. Wasn't he called Jack O'Riordan?"

"Yeah," said Tom. "What of it?"

"And he was a photographer, right?" she asked.

"Why are you talking about him in the past tense?"

"Because he's snuffed it," she said.

"Blimey," I said. "He looked in good health to me. Fit, tanned. What was it, a heart attack?"

"The police say he was murdered. Foully and brutally murdered, it says on the internet."

"Does it say what time?"

"They say it was late yesterday evening. Around 11 p.m."

"That puts us in the clear," I said.

"We were with him in the afternoon," said Tom.

"But that means you might have been the last people to see him alive," said Marti. "Apart from the murderer, that is."

"Do you think we should go to the police?" I asked.

"And do what?" asked Tom. "I can't see we have anything to tell them."

"It might speed up their inquiries," I said. "I mean they might waste hours of police time, trying to work out who we are."

"I see your point," said Tom. "I'll ring up Scotland Yard and give them our contact details. You don't think we'll be on their list of suspects?"

"They'll have a job coming up with a motive," I said. "It's not as if we'd even met the guy before."

"Yeah, but do you have an alibi?" asked Tom. "Where were you at eleven o'clock last night?"

"I was in bed, having only narrowly survived a meal at Killingfield's."

"You were on your own in bed?" asked Tom.

"Of course I was," I said. "Where were you?"

This time, Tom looked sheepish.

"Actually," said Marti, "he was round at my place. And I can vouch for him being there all night. We didn't get much sleep."

She gave Tom an affectionate squeeze.

"So now you know, Dad," said Tom, blushing.

"Great," I said. "But please, no snogging in the office. I'm an old man, remember?"

Half an hour later, I asked Tom if he'd heard back from the police.

"Nothing," he said.

"How about Fairycakes?" I asked. "Have you managed to track her down?"

"Not yet. I'm waiting for a call back."

An hour later, I asked Tom if he'd had any luck finding Slippery Slope, and he said he was on to that as well. He told me he was awaiting information, and he'd let me know if he had any luck, and could I just leave him alone please.

An hour or so after that, he came into my office and told me he'd managed to find out something disturbing about Bill Slope.

"How disturbing?" I asked.

He paused to ponder.

"Potentially quite disturbing," he said.

"So what is it?"

"He's a paedophile."

"Is that something to do with feet?"

"No, Dad, that's a podiatrist. Paedophiles fancy children."

"Dirty old bugger. So they caught him at it?"

"Apparently. He's a convicted paedophile."

"So he's in prison."

"Has been. Got out a year ago. Only served eight months. His original sentence was two years, reduced to sixteen months on appeal. He was found guilty of downloading child pornography."

"Not great for his career, or presumably his personal life. So where's he living now?"

"Not sure. He moved house, and I gather he's living on his own, under a false name."

"What name?"

"I have no idea," said Tom. "But I have a phone number for him. And I've left him a message asking him to call me back."

"But you haven't heard from him?"

"Not yet."

"So what's he up to being a Facebook friend to Olga Molotovski?" I asked.

"That is the question," said Tom.

"Mind you," I said, "if he's a paedophile, isn't she a bit old for him?"

"That thought did cross my mind," said Tom. "But as he's a convicted sex criminal, it might be an idea if we could get to him before…"

"He can get to her?"

"I mean, she may be 17 years old," said Tom, "but if she looks younger…"

"All right, all right, I follow your line of reasoning," I said. "Get on to this as quickly as you can."

"I'm doing my best, Dad," said Tom. "There's no need for you to snap at me."

"I'm not snapping at you."

"Yes, you are."

"Maybe that's because you've got me worried."

"I'm worried too," said Tom. "Do you think we should tell her parents?"

"Not yet," I said. "There's no point in making them even more anxious."

"Should we tell the police?"

"I'm not sure," I said. "There might be an innocent explanation. Let's see if Slope gets back to us before the end of the day."

An hour after that, I asked Tom if he'd heard anything about Fairycakes or Bill Slope, and he said that if he had I would be the first to know. So I asked him if he knew why Joseph Gildenstern might be based in South Korea, and Tom asked me irritably what that had to do with anything, and I said I didn't know what it had to do with anything, it had been preying on my mind. And he said that if it had been preying on my mind, why didn't I go and look it up on the internet myself, so I did.

I found what I needed and returned to Tom's office, a few minutes later. He was drumming his fingers on his desk. I could tell Slope had not called him back, and things were not going well. As a father, one notices these things.

"Now what is it, Dad?"

"I found out why Joseph Gildenstern has to keep visiting South Korea."

"And that is interesting because…?"

"I'm not sure," I admitted. "I thought it might be relevant."

"Relevant to what?"

"To why he wanted to see me."

"And was it?"

"I'm not sure," I confessed. "Mind if I run the information past you?"

"Why not?" Tom said. "All I'm doing is wait here for people to call me back. And sweating a lot. Neither of which I'm enjoying. So fire away."

"Fire away," I said. "I like that."

"I'm not sure I follow you, Dad," said Tom. "Is this heat making you delirious? Or is it too much Football Manager?"

"Sorry," I said. "I'm not making myself clear."

"Too right you're not."

"It turns out that Joseph Gildenstern's main income is from his family business."

"And that is what?" Tom asked. "Something to do with football?"

"No," I said. "He's in armaments."

"Right," said Tom.

"And not just any old armaments," I said. "Land mines."

"Nice," said Tom, meaning the opposite. "Aren't land mines illegal?"

"Well, they are and they aren't," I said. "Since 1999, the manufacture of land mines has been outlawed in most countries, including Britain and Germany."

"But not South Korea?" said Tom.

"Exactly. South Korea was one of only a few countries not to ratify the treaty."

"So Gildenstern moved that side of the family firm to South Korea?"

"Yes."

"That's fascinating, Dad, of course, but if you don't mind my asking, what has any of this got to do with disappearing Russian heiresses, or highly paid footballers who can't score in front of an open goal?"

I considered for a moment.

"That's an extremely good point, Tom. I haven't the foggiest idea."

"Dad," he said, "has it ever occurred to you that your problem is having too much time on your hands?"

I paused to consider.

"Tom, you may be right," I said. "What do you think I should be doing?"

"Well, while I'm waiting for developments on our vanishing and possibly imperilled Russian heiress, why don't you see if you can make contact with your perversely non-scoring footballer?"

"Good idea," I said. "I should have done that hours ago. It must be the heat. I'm not thinking straight."

I called Lorenzo Fettucini on his mobile, and he sounded surprisingly happy to hear from me.

"Hiya, Charlie," he said. "It'sa been a long time."

"Hello, Lorenzo," I said. "Hot day, isn't it? I was wondering if you fancied a drink."

"That would be nice," he said. "But tomorrow I go back to Italia to see my momma and poppa."

"What are you doing tonight?" I asked.

"Packing," he said.

"Before you do that," I said, "let's grab a quick one. There's a sports bar round the corner from me, in Soho. Gordano's."

"Oh yes, I know it," he said.

"See you there, then," I said. "6.30 all right?"

No sooner had I finished the call than Tom came in, with a smile on his face.

"Bingo!" he said.

"Success?"

"Yeah, Slope finally called me back."

"Does he admit to knowing Olga Molotovski?"

"He does."

"That makes a change," I said. "Every other person I meet seems to know her face but not want to talk about it. Anyone would think the kid was Myra Hindley. Or Rosa Klebb."

"Who's Rosa Klebb?"

"I thought everyone knew that. She was the female Russian agent in *From Russia With Love*. The one who had knives in her boots. Played by Lotte Lenya."

"Bit before my time, Dad."

"Blimey," I said. "Don't they teach you anything in school?"

"Not unless it's connected with the Holocaust or slavery," said Tom.

"I dunno what the world's coming to," I said. "Remind me to show you all the Bond films some day."

"Sure, Dad. But it's good Slope called me back, isn't it?"

"Even better that Slippery is happy to own up he knows the girl."

"Well," said Tom, "Him being her Facebook friend is a bit of a giveaway."

"Good of the dirty old sod to talk to us," I said. "Did he remember me?"

"Yes. I think that may be why he's willing to meet us."

"What do you mean?"

"He told me to pass on that he was sorry."

"Sorry about what?"

"He just said sorry."

"He's got a lot to be sorry about," I said.

"His accent sounds a bit odd," said Tom. "Is he South African?"

"An Aussie."

"But he must have been living over here for years."

"Decades," I said. "Like a perverted Rolf Harris."

"Nice," said Tom.

"Doesn't bear thinking about," I said, deciding a joke about Two Little Boys might not be in the best of taste. "Still, you've got a result."

"Let's hope so."

"You think he's willing to chat about Olga?"

"Apparently so," said Tom. "But he sounds weird. Very, very paranoid. Refused to talk about her on the phone. He invited you and me to see him."

"When?"

"Tomorrow."

"Where?"

"At his place."

"Where does he live?"

"Sounds like the back of beyond. Up in north-west Norfolk. East Creake? Ever heard of it?"

I shook my head.

"What time is he expecting us?"

"We're booked in for eleven o'clock. It'll mean we have to

leave home about 8.10. Marti says she'll hold the fort for us down here."

I wrote in my diary.

"Back of beyond. 11 a.m. Right. Whoo!"

"It's not that exciting, Dad."

"No, but this is. We've just put seven past Tottenham!"

Tom left the room, shaking his head. About a minute later, he returned. He looked excited.

"Another mini-breakthrough," he said. "I've found an address for Fairycakes."

"Watson," I said, "you're a genius."

I was in a good mood already, having just been voted Manager of the Month and hailed as a tactical genius by legions of adoring fans.

"She lives in Hackney," he said. "13, Downhill Road."

"That's round the corner from my sister," I said. "Got the phone number?"

"No," he said. "I think she's ex-directory."

"What about her mobile?"

Tom shook his head.

"Well," I said, "if we can track down Fairycakes, Olga may not be far away."

"That's what I reckon," said Tom. "What do you say to paying her a surprise visit?"

8

NUMBER 13

Wednesday, 3rd August

Number 13, Downhill Road was a tall Georgian house, next to a row of shops in Hackney, not far from my sister's place in London Fields. The shops here reflected a multiplicity of ethnic backgrounds: Turkish, Polish, Indian. Number 13 was residential accommodation on five storeys. It had once been smart but now looked dilapidated. I estimated it hadn't been repainted in the last twenty years.

"Number thirteen," I said. "Unlucky for some."

"Mostly the people who live in it," said Tom. "Do you think it's a squat?"

Beside the door were two buzzers. The top button had a handwritten name 'Parks'. I pressed it, but there was no reply.

"Try the other one," said Tom.

I pressed the lower button, labelled 'Castle'. After a moment, the door opened, and a man looked out at us warily.

"What can I do for you?" he said.

He had a surprisingly educated voice for a run-down house

in Hackney. Posh, even. He was a grey-faced man with his long hair pulled back into a ponytail. He looked about sixty, and wore the wire spectacles that John Lennon rejected. He was unshaven, and sniffing, as if he had a bad cold. He wore a t-shirt, a little too tight for him, bearing the legend 'This t-shirt hates fascists.'

"Hello," I said. "I understand that Miss Parks lives here."

"Not here," he said. "Gone away."

"But she does live here normally."

"Yeah," he said. "Insofar as she can be said to do anything normally. She's not what you'd call a conventional young woman."

"She lives here with you?" asked Tom.

"She has a room at the top of the house," said the man. "I rent it out to students."

"Could we ask you a few questions?" I asked.

"What kind of questions?" he asked.

"May we come in?"

"Why?" he asked, after another sniff, a more suspicious one. "Are you the police? Do you have a warrant? I have rights, you know."

"No," I said. "We're private investigators. We're trying to find a missing girl."

"Fairycakes isn't missing," he said. "Is she?"

"Maybe not, but a girlfriend of hers is."

"Oh?"

He still seemed disinclined to let us in. Tom attempted to find the magic word that would get the man on our side.

"The girl we're trying to trace is an immigrant," said Tom. "We're trying to help her."

"Oh," he said. "I see. Right. Come in."

He took us into the room next to the front door. It resembled a student's room, with posters of revolutionary leaders and rock bands. I recognised Che Guevara, Lenin and John Lennon, but most of the music posters were for black groups I'd never come across.

"You can sit on the sofa," he said. "Just dump those papers on the floor."

The place looked as if it needed a good clean. It reminded me of that sitcom starring Rik Mayall and Ade Edmondson. *The Young Ones*. But he was definitely an Old One.

"Are you a student?" I asked, looking around me.

"No," he said. "I'm a professor."

"A professor?"

"I am Oliver Avery-Castle," he said. "Professor of Modern Cultural Studies at the University of South-East London."

"Isn't that the old Deptford Poly?" I asked.

"Yes," he said stiffly. "But we've been a university for over two decades."

"Is Fairycakes one of your students?" I asked.

"Yes," he said, "and one of my better ones. I have high hopes that she will be part of that select minority that finishes my course and graduates with a degree."

"What's she studying?" asked Tom.

"Our basic course on the foundations of western culture," he said. "It covers the political thought of Jean Luc Godard, the genius of Peter Greenaway and the contribution of rap music to modern culture."

"So no Shakespeare," I said.

The professor didn't deign to reply.

"And you teach all those things?" I asked.

"Goodness no," he said. "My specialism is rap, and that happens to be the area of study Ms Parks is really into. I often hear her playing it at all hours of the night."

"Isn't that a nuisance?"

"Not really," he said. "After my many years on the cultural front line, I'm quite deaf. I find the rhythms often help me get back to sleep."

"Have you heard of a girl called Olga Molotovski?" I asked.

"Of course," he said. "At one point she and Ms Parks were very close."

"Have you seen her recently?"

"Not for months," he said. "She used to come here all the time. She even used to stay overnight."

"Would you say that she and Fairycakes were lovers?" asked Tom.

"What are you?" he asked. "The gutter press?"

"I'm sorry," I said. "We haven't introduced ourselves. I'm Charlie Charlesworth, and this is my son Tom."

"Hi," said Tom.

"Sorry to intrude on your space, professor, but we are private investigators. Trying to find out more about a missing person. In order to help her."

"You mean Olga?" he asked.

"Yes."

"Do you know anything that might explain why Olga would run away from home?" asked Tom.

"She's very keen on rap," he said, "and hip-hop. That can cause friction with insensitive parents."

"Why?" I asked.

"It's the lyrics," he said. "The poetry of the streets. The heartfelt cry of the dispossessed."

"She was into gangsta rap?" asked Tom.

The professor nodded.

"Isn't that a strange thing for a white girl to be into?" I asked.

"No, no, no," the Professor said pityingly, as though I was being exceptionally slow-witted. "Gangsta rap is an exciting and progressive area, dealing as it does with issues of physical violence, drive-by shootings and murder."

"That's exciting and progressive?" I asked, feeling that I was missing something.

"Why would two white girls be attracted to music that condones violence?" asked Tom. "Especially violence against women?"

"Gangsta rap has been accused of many things, including – it

101

is true – the objectification of women. I imagine you're referring to tracks such as Slick Rick's 'Treat Her Like A Prostitute', or Notorious B.I.G.'s 'Me and My Bitch'."

"And Olga and Fairycakes actually bought into what they're selling?" asked Tom.

"I'm not sure I would accept your mercenary metaphor," said the professor, sniffing.

The professor's habit of sniffing was so pronounced that I wondered if it might be associated with the ingestion of cocaine. I also noticed some white powder just inside his nostrils. That might account for why he was being so talkative. I decided to keep pumping him for information.

"Were they – I mean, are they – into drugs?" I asked.

"Who can say?" he said.

"I read on the net that Fairycakes was once arrested for dealing marijuana," said Tom.

"That's hardly surprising in a country like ours," he said, "where the young are deliberately marginalized and unable to find jobs. I—"

Before he could embark on a monologue, I decided to abandon that line of inquiry.

"So you don't have any idea where Fairycakes is now?"

"Of course I do," said the professor. She's in The Thirty-Nine Steps."

"You mean in the West End?" I asked. "I had no idea she was an actress."

The professor gave a long-suffering sigh, followed by another sniff.

"Not the West End."

"Are they remaking the Hitchcock film again?" I asked.

"I have absolutely no idea," said the professor.

"I think, Dad, that The Thirty-Nine Steps the professor is referring to is a rehab centre."

"Like the Priory?"

"But more exclusive," said the professor. "It's where the rich go to dry out, and recover from their addictions."

"Maybe that's what you need, Dad," said Tom.

I decided to ignore the jibe and turned back to Avery-Castle.

"So you're telling me that Fairycakes is an addict?"

"I am not the kind of person to pin judgmental labels on people," he replied. "But she does have certain problems."

"Such as?"

"The usual kind of things," he said. "Chronic fatigue syndrome, obsessive-compulsive disorder, anger management, substance abuse, eating disorders. Normal stuff."

"Normal?" said Tom.

"So The Thirty-Nine Steps," I said, "provides them with a 12-step programme?"

"No," said the professor. "Thirty-nine. Much longer, more thorough and intense."

"Sounds expensive," I said.

"I'm sure she's having the best treatment money can buy."

"And who's paying for it?" I asked.

"Why, she is, of course," said the professor. "She's quite a wealthy young woman."

"Inherited from mum and dad, presumably," I said.

"If she's so well off, why does she need to push drugs?" Tom asked.

"Until recently, all her money was held in a trust fund."

"Which is why she lived here," I said.

"She turned twenty-one about a month ago, and that's when her trust fund released all her funds," said the professor. She's planning to move into her own house shortly. I believe it's quite a large one in Pimlico."

He rose and obviously expected us to do likewise.

"Thanks for sparing us some of your valuable time," I said. "Oh, just one more thing."

"Make it quick," he said.

"How long has Fairycakes been in rehab?" I asked

"About three weeks," said the professor. "Or possibly longer. Yes it must be a month, because she owes me a month's rent. Look, I can't stand around here all day."

"Thanks, professor, you've been very educational," I said.

Outside, I turned to Tom.

"What an inspiration to the young," I said to Tom.

"You know something, Dad?" asked Tom. "I wasn't cut out for tertiary education. If I'd had him as a tutor, I'd have decked him."

"Or dropped out," I said.

"You can see why he loses so many of his students," said Tom.

"And he obviously thinks Fairycakes is one of the better ones," I replied.

"So what did we learn from that?" Tom asked.

"You mean, apart from their taste in music?"

"Apart from that."

I considered.

"Olga and Fairycakes are still close. But the timing's all wrong. Fairycakes went into rehab around a month ago – that's about three weeks before Olga ran away."

"Looks like we've hit a brick wall," Tom said. "I was sure Olga had moved in with her old pal."

"Me too," I said. "But there's still a chance that Fairycakes could lead us to Olga."

"She's the only lead we've got," said Tom. "At least until we see Bill Slope tomorrow."

"Fancy trying to climb The Thirty-Nine Steps?" I asked.

9

THE THIRTY-NINE STEPS

"Have you made an appointment?" The woman at the front desk was icily suspicious.

The Thirty-Nine Steps proved to be a rambling Regency mansion in Hertfordshire, with a faintly antiseptic smell. It was impressive but cheerless, not unlike the woman at the severely functional front desk.

"We're here to visit a Ms. Parks," I said. "F.B. Parks."

She stared at me disparagingly.

"We don't encourage visitors," she said.

"You do have Ms Parks staying with you?" I asked.

"I am not at liberty to divulge such information," she said. "Are you reporters?"

"No," I said. "We're—"

At this point, my son broke in.

"I'm afraid my father's a bit confused. And in an advanced state of denial. He's here as a potential patient."

"Oh?" The woman seemed sceptical. "Has he a referral letter?"

"A referral letter?" asked Tom.

"From his GP."

"No. But his family are worried about him. And we are extremely wealthy."

The mention of extreme wealth seemed to mellow the woman considerably.

"Here's a form for you to fill in," she said. "Hand it back to me, and I'll see what I can do."

A little old man was staggering across the hall, resting his shrivelled carcass on a zimmer frame.

"Allo, darlin'," he said to the woman at the front desk. "Fancy a spot of rough and tumble?"

The woman at the front desk looked at him as if he was a more than usually unpleasant example of pond life. Then she looked down, as if trying to pretend he didn't exist.

"What are you getting me into?" I muttered.

"This place, hopefully," said Tom. "And maybe we'll get a free consultation about your problem."

"I don't have a problem," I said.

"That's how I know you have a problem," he said. "You don't think you have one."

"Do I have to use my real name?" I asked.

"Aren't you Charlie Charlesworth?" said the little old man, passing by and resting on his zimmer frame. "I used to watch you down the Arsenal."

"Yes," I said, dismally. "That's me."

"Didn't you have trouble with your knees?" he asked.

"I did," I said.

"That's my trouble too," said the old man. "Both of them have gone. Good to see you, Charlie."

"So much for anonymity," said Tom.

"On the bottle, are you? Don't worry. They're very discreet here," said the old man, with a wink. "Your secret's safe with me."

"Thanks," I said.

"What do you think of her?" asked the old man. "Bit stand-offish, but I know she fancies me."

Something about his face seemed familiar.

"Don't I know you?" I asked.

"You've probably seen me on the telly. Ted Chester. Stand-up comic," he said, before tapping his zimmer frame. "Only now I can't stand up."

He wheezed with laughter at his own joke.

"What are you in for?" I asked.

The old man looked around him, theatrically, as if he didn't want anyone to hear.

"Sex addiction," he whispered. "My wife insisted I came in."

"To give her a rest?"

"Nah. It was my own fault," said the old man. "I warned her about my little problem when we got married. I told her that I kept a box in my study that helped me control my addiction. and she was never to look inside."

"And did she?"

"Not for years," he said. "Besides, I always kept it padlocked."

"So what happened?"

"Mavis and me, we were happily married for forty years. But one night, I got careless and left the box unlocked. The next morning, she woke me up and told me she'd looked in the box."

"What had she found?"

"Three empty beer cans and twenty grand in cash."

"So what did she say?"

"She said she was pleased about the money, but wanted to know me why I kept the empty cans, so I told her. I reckoned that after all our years together, she was entitled to the truth."

"What did you say?" I asked.

"I told her that whenever I was unfaithful to her, I put an empty beer can in the box to remind myself not to do it again."

"How did she take it?"

"Okay at first. She told me she felt sad and disappointed, but maybe three times in forty years was not that big a deal."

"That was good of her," I said.

"So we hugged, and then she asked me why I kept all that money in the box."

"So I told her the truth. That, whenever the box filled up with empty cans, I took them to the recycling center and redeemed them for cash. And that's why she put me in here."

He zimmered off down the corridor, wheezing gently as he went.

"Funny guy," said Tom.

"Not that funny if it's true," I said.

We were interrupted by the woman at the front desk. She had been listening to someone on the phone, and put it down.

"Mr Boomla will see you now," she said. "Down that corridor. Room 11. Straight ahead and turn left. Take your form with you."

Mr Boomla turned out to be an elderly man of Indian origin. He sat behind a large mahogany desk, with a large window behind him. He was dressed in a white coat, with the logo '39' emblazoned on one of its pockets. His desk was neat, and he seemed to be a man who liked orderly lists. They were everywhere. He looked up with a practised, friendly smile.

"Come in! Come in!" he enthused. "Now what seems to be the problem?"

I handed him the form. He glanced down at it, then up at me.

"Oh, I see. You're the prospective patient."

"And I'm his son," said Tom. "I'm very worried about him."

"My son thinks I need help," I said.

"It says here that you're addicted to computer games."

"Not computer games in general," I said. "One in particular."

"And that is?"

"Football Manager," I said.

He looked at me blankly.

"It's about football management," I added.

"I haven't come across that one," he said. "Why do you think this particular game attracts you?"

"Well, I used to be a footballer."

"So that made you wish to manage a club?"

"Not really," I said. "I thought I could be more useful in some other walk of life."

"So what did you become?"

"A private investigator."

"I see."

Tom decided to butt in.

"Look, Mr—"

"Boomla," he said.

"Are there any tests you can run on my father? Find out whether he's all right in the head?"

"I'm sure there are things we could do," he said. "But curing someone of an addiction, any addiction, can be a long and arduous process."

"And, I imagine, an expensive one," I said.

"We try to keep our fees down to a minimum," said Mr Boomla, "but they do mount up over time."

"Perhaps you could let us look around?" asked Tom.

"I'm afraid that would not be possible," said Mr Boomla. "We prize our patient's privacy above all else."

"Good grief!" said Tom suddenly, looking out of the window.

'What?" asked Mr Boomla, startled.

"There's a naked old man out there, chasing after a girl!"

"What? Where?" asked Boomla, getting up and crossing to the window.

"Keep him occupied," muttered Tom.

I joined Boomla at the window.

"I saw him too," I said. "I think I recognised him from the telly. Ted Chester, I think his name was."

"Are you sure?" asked Mr Boomla. "He's pretty much lost the use of his legs."

"I think they've had a new lease of life," I said. "Is that him behind those bushes?"

"Where?"

"I think I just caught a flash of elderly male buttock."

"Oh my God," said Mr Boomla.

"What step of your programme is he on?" I asked.

"Thirty-three," he said.

"I fear he may be back to square one," I said.

"Perhaps you should call the police," came a voice behind us. It was Tom, sounding ineffably smug.

"I'm sure that won't be necessary," said Mr Boomla. "A mild sedative should suffice."

"Look," said Tom, "perhaps we can come back another time, when you're not so busy."

"Perhaps so," said Mr Boomla. "Besides, we are full at the moment. Perhaps you would drop this form back to the lady at reception, and she could fix a date when we might be able to admit you. Would you like me to show you out?"

"No need to bother," said Tom. "We can find our own way."

But instead of turning right outside the door and making for the front desk, Tom steered me to the left and up a flight of stairs.

"Where are we going?"

"To visit Fairycakes," said Tom. "Room 26."

"How do you know that?"

"Didn't you see that piece of paper he had on his desk? It had all the patient's room numbers. All I needed was a chance to look at it. Nice diversionary tactics, by the way."

"Thanks."

"Look, there's a sign. Her room's down here," said Tom. "Let's hope she's in."

The name on Room 26 said 'F.B. Parks', but when the door

opened, it revealed a young, white man of considerable girth. He wore a Mohican haircut and a scowl. Apart from that, nothing.

"What you looking at, man?" he asked.

"Nothing" said Tom. "At least, I'm trying not to."

"Who's you, dude?" he asked.

"I'm Tom Charlesworth," said Tom, with a pleasant smile. "And this is my father, Charlie."

"Ain't you footballer, man?" asked the man. "Didn't you play for England, blood?"

"I did indeed have that honour," I said.

"You were shit, man," he said.

"You are not alone in that opinion," I said. "Sir Alex Ferguson himself expressed a similar sentiment, though not in precisely those words."

"Why you talk in long sentences, man?" he asked. "You some kind of snob or somet'ing?"

"We seem to have come to the wrong place," said Tom. "We're looking for Fairycakes Bonanza Parks."

"This her crib, man," said the man. "Me and her were shagging."

"I'm so sorry," said Tom. "We didn't mean to interrupt."

"Not just now," he said. "She nipped down the corridor for a pee."

"Oh," said Tom. "You don't have en-suite facilities."

"Yeah, we do, man, but right now it's all blocked up and shit."

"I'm sorry to hear that," said Tom.

"We'll wait outside," I said, "until she comes back."

"No, man, that's all right," said the man. "Come on in. We finished fucking. It be nice to have some masculine company, know what I mean?"

We followed him into the room and sat in chairs on either side of the bed. It was a small double, and looked a little insubstantial to take a man of his considerable weight.

"I pee blood," he said.

"I'm sorry," I said. "Shouldn't you see a doctor about that?"

"No," he said. "That my name, innit. I.P. Blood. At least that's my rappin' name. My real name is Sidney."

"Which would you rather we used?"

"Call me I.P.," he said. "All my fans do."

"So you're a rapper," I said.

"Ain't that the troot," said I.P., scratching his genitals, which fortunately were covered by an enormous flap of fat.

"And why are you in here?"

"Bitch-slappin'," he said. "Bitch-slappin's taken over my life."

"So you're trying to practise abstinence?" asked Tom.

"Fuck that," he said. "I'm still on step 3."

"Step 3?"

"I've cut down to slappin' one bitch a day."

"Good for you," I said, in the most encouraging way I could.

"I think I've heard one of your songs," said Tom.

"Yea? Which one is that?"

"I think it's about killing people."

"Ah!" he said, smiling. "You mean 'Kill All The Motherfuckas'."

He got up and started doing some moves, which were impressively close to dancing for a man of his size.

"Kill all the white people,

They're the worst,

Kill all the white folk

But buy my record first."

"That actually rhymes," said Tom.

"You think that because I talk like this, I didn't go to school?" demanded Blood.

"I'm sure you did," said Tom.

"Tom was expelled from his," I said.

"You were, man?" beamed I.P. "So was I!"

"Small world," said Tom. "Thanks for that, Dad."

"What you expelled for, bro?" asked I.P.

"They found some pot on me," said Tom. "How about you?"

"I didn't take no shit," said Blood. "I beat up a teacher."

"Any reason for that?" I asked.

"She wouldn't show me no respect," said I.P. "She was my English teacher, and she kept correcting my English. Said I was dyspeptic."

"Dyslexic?" I suggested.

"Don't you start, man. No one disrespect me."

"How badly did you beat her up?" asked Tom.

"Not that bad, man," said IP. "She out of hospital after a week. But I got her fired, bro."

"Why was that?"

"She racist, man. All the brothers and sisters, we got together and said she don't teach us no English no more."

"Wasn't that tough on her?" I asked, mildly.

"Whose side you on, man?" demanded I.P, staring into my eyes. "You thinking just because I's white, I can't show solidarity with the streets?"

After an awkward hiatus, the door opened, and Fairycakes Bonanza Parks walked in. She was a pretty girl, or would have been if her face hadn't been covered with studs, spikes and a black eye, ill-concealed beneath make-up. She was wearing a t-shirt bearing the legend 'I survived the 39 steps'.

"Who the fuck are you?" she asked. "What are you doing in my room?"

"I let them in," said I.P.

"Why the fuck did you do that, I.P?" she asked.

"I don't know, bitch. But don't you diss me or I might have to hit you."

"You're so cute," she said, sitting down on the bed beside him and kissing his bare shoulder.

"I know," he said.

"So," she said. "Who are you two losers?"

"I'm Charlie Charlesworth," I said, "and this is my son

Tom. We're private investigators, and we're looking for Olga Molotovski."

"Olga?" she said. "Is she missing?"

"So you haven't heard," I said.

"They don't allow much contact with the outside world in here," she said. "Has she been in the papers?"

"No, her family are keeping it to themselves."

"Call that a family?" she said. "Per-lease."

"You know her parents?"

"Never met them," she said.

"We met her mother, and she didn't seem to approve of you."

"Why should I care what that old slapper thinks?" she said. "Can't even speak English proper. As for her father, all he thinks about is power and money."

"You don't think they care about her?"

"If they did," she said, "they wouldn't have treated her the way they did."

"And what way was that?"

"She wouldn't talk about it. But every time she mentioned them, she used to start stuttering," said Fairycakes. "That's not normal, is it?"

"She never told you what the matter was between her and her parents?" I asked.

"Fuck all that. You're the investigators. Why don't you fuck off and investigate?"

"That's why we're here."

"Yeah, well," she said, "Even if I did know, I don't tell tales on my friends."

"That's right," said I.P. "Respect."

"What do you know about respect?" she said to I.P. "You're a fucking moron."

"No, I'm not," he said.

"Course you are," she said.

"Then why are you letting me fuck you?"

114

"Cos you're the only person in here under thirty," she said, "and I have extremely low self-esteem."

"Who told you that?"

"Everyone," she said. "You'd know it too, if you weren't such a fucking moron."

"Sorry," said Tom. "I don't mean to interrupt your discussion, but we're anxious to know if Olga was having any kind of – I'm not sure how to put this – any kind of a relationship with you."

"Olga and me?" she said. "We haven't been together in months."

"What?" demanded I.P. "You telling me you're some kind of dike?"

"Fuck off, would you?" she said.

"Don't I have a right to know?"

"You don't own me," she said. "Tomorrow I'll be out of here. I might never see you again."

"Don't say that, Fairycakes," he wheedled. "Or…"

"Or what?" she demanded. "Or you'll hit me again?"

I decided to interrupt.

"Sorry, but do you happen to know if she's been seeing anyone else?"

"Well, yeah," said Fairycakes, after a pause. "I happen to know she is, yeah."

"Who is it?" asked Tom.

"He's someone pretty famous, actually," said Fairycakes, with a superior smile.

"Not more famous than me?" asked I.P.

"Yeah," said Fairycakes. "A lot more famous than you. Thinner, too. Not that that's difficult. You're such a fucking disgrace. Why don't you work out? You disgust me."

"Can you tell us who it is?" asked Tom.

"I could, but I'm not going to," said Fairycakes. "Now get the fuck out of here."

"Right," I said. "Thanks for your time."

We started to leave, but Tom turned back at the door.

"So are you sure you don't have any idea of where Olga might be now?" Tom asked.

"Look," said Fairycakes, "I've told you to fuck off twice. Don't make me tell you three times. A right pair of divvy shits, you are."

Outside, in the corridor, I found myself pondering the scene we had just witnessed.

"Did we learn anything there?" I asked.

"Olga Molotovski has rubbish taste in girlfriends," replied Tom.

"Apart from that."

"We know Olga was having some kind of a relationship with a celebrity."

"But she wouldn't say who it was." I pointed out.

"True," said Tom. "But she did let drop it was a 'he'."

"Good point," I said.

"And we know he's thinner than I.P. Blood," said Tom, "though that doesn't exactly narrow it down."

"It rules out John Prescott," I said.

"So what we do next, Dad?" asked Tom. "I take it you don't fancy checking in here to cure your addiction."

"Why don't you try and find Olga's celebrity squeeze?" I said.

"That could be easier said than done," said Tom.

"And while you're doing that," I said, looking at my watch. "I have to go and have a drink with a footballer who's forgotten how to score."

10

SABOTAGE

Wednesday, 3rd August

Lorenzo Fettucini wasn't hard to spot as he drew up outside in his yellow Ferrari, parked on a double yellow and strode into the sports bar. He greeted me like a long-lost friend, and planted kisses on both my cheeks.

"Charlie!" he exclaimed. "Long time no see!"

"So you braved the congestion charge," I said.

"What congestion charge?" he asked.

It's true what they say: the rich are different from us. Mind you, even for a multi-millionaire footballer, Lorenzo had acquired a reputation for eccentricity. He was rumoured to have a lifesize statue of himself in his front garden, and he famously announced on arrival at his latest club that he was bigger than Lionel Messi. This was met at the press conference with hoots of derision, after which his manager explained that what Lorenzo had meant to say was that he was taller than Lionel Messi, and therefore more of an aerial threat in set pieces. Then Lorenzo went and spoiled it all by saying that of course he was bigger than Messi. It was just that the world did not fully appreciate his genius yet. This, he went on to explain, was because the sporting press was full of idiots.

As bad luck would have it, they had the telly on in the bar, showing comic highlights of the previous football season. I imagine they had it on pretty much all the time, with it being a sports bar. It didn't do much for Lorenzo's spirits that one clip showed him having trouble pulling on his training bib during a pre-match warm-up, struggling for five or six minutes, before losing his temper and ordering his manager to do it for him.

It was followed by match footage taken from towards the end of the season. It depicted the Southern Athletic striker blazing a shot more than a yard wide of the goal, only for a defender to stick out a foot and stick it into his own net. The comedy lay not only in the defender's expression, but also the way the Italian kept shaking his head when his team-mates surrounded him and pointing at the defender on the ground, who was beating his fists on the grass with frustration. It was as if Lorenzo didn't want to claim credit for the goal.

"Look!" said Lorenzo gloomily, surveying the punters looking up at him on the big screen and jeering. "They all try and make fun of me."

"Cheer up, Lorenzo," I said, pouring him the Italian beer he had requested. "At least you're more telegenic than Wayne Rooney."

"Rooney look like Shrek, but even he is able to score," he said miserably.

"Only if he's playing away," I said. "Boom boom!"

Lorenzo looked at me. Clearly, 'playing away' didn't have the same connotations in Italy that it did in the UK.

"I saw him score at Old Trafford only other week," he said.

"Really? I must have got that wrong," I said, on the principle that if you've got to explain a joke, it probably wasn't much of a joke in the first place.

"And cheer up," I added. "Look at that motor you drove up in. It's a Ferrari, isn't it?"

"What of it?" he said. "Do you think I should get a Lamborghini?"

"Didn't you know Alex Ferguson threw a party for his players? Rio came in his Bentley. Giggs came in his Range Rover. But all Rooney wanted to come in was a battered old escort."

"Is this a joke?" asked Lorenzo.

"Not much of one," I said. "If you don't mind my saying so, Lorenzo, you don't seem yourself. A trifle under the weather."

"I can not wait to get out of England," he said.

"Is the weather getting you down?" I asked.

"It is not the weather," he said. "The weather, she is ok."

"Is it your team-mates?" I asked.

"No," he said. "Most of them are very supporting. Though not all of them."

"Oh?"

"One came up to me and asked me if I knew the difference between a motorbike and Southern Athletic Football Club."

"And?"

"And he said the difference was that a motorbike can only carry one passenger."

At this point, I'm ashamed to say I did the nose trick. I covered it up as best I could, turning it into a cough and wiping away the beer on my shirt with a paper napkin.

"Maybe he wasn't getting at you," I said. "You know what footballers are like. Always making jokes. You mustn't take it too personally. I heard one the other day about my own team."

"The Arsenal?"

"Yeah. Why do women love the Arsenal football team?"

"I don't know," he said, after a pause. "I don't know that they do."

"No, that's not what you're meant to say," I explained. "You're meant to say 'I don't know – why do women love the Arsenal football team?'"

"Oh," he replied.

"Well, go on then."

"Right. Why do the women love the Arsenal football team?"

"Because they stay on top for ages and always end up coming second!"

"But they don't," he said. "Often they come third. Or even fourth. Like last season. Which is why they still have to qualify for the Champions' League."

I looked at him. Could he be taking the piss? I decided to give him one more try.

"What about this one, Lorenzo. What do you say to a footballer with a good-looking bird on his arm?"

"I don't know," he said.

"Nice tattoo," I said.

He looked down at his own arm. Until now, I hadn't noticed that it had a seagull tattooed on it.

"Thank you," he said.

I decided to try another tack.

"What's the problem? It's not woman trouble, is it?" I asked.

He shook his head, miserably.

"No. My wife, she is here with me in London. And the bambino. He look a little like Wayne Rooney, but I think he is mine."

"In that case, why aren't you happy? These should be the happiest days of your life. You're playing for a big club, earning millions, and you have a beautiful wife and child, even if he does look like Rooney."

"That is not problem," he said.

"Then what is?"

"Charlie, I should never have made transfer to another English club."

"Why not?" I asked. "They paid a lot of money for you. They're a decent outfit. Play European football. You must be on way more than a hundred grand a week. What more do you want?"

"I want to score goals," he said, "but I can not."

"You're bound to start scoring again," I said. "You know what they say: form comes and goes, but class is permanent."

"You don't understand. I can not score goal."

"You have some kind of mental block?"

"Look, Charlie," he said, looking around him to make sure we were not overheard, "if I tell you this, you are not to mention it to anyone else. You swear?"

"Sure," I said. "You know me. My lips are sealed."

"I am getting death threats," he said.

"You don't want to pay any attention to those," I said. "A lot of people get them in football. Like that Celtic bloke. Neil Lennon."

"No, but these are real."

"Those were real," I said. "Didn't you read about them in the papers? Three people got parcel bombs. Or would have done, if they hadn't been intercepted."

"They are threatening to cut off my legs if I score goal," said Lorenzo.

"Who are?"

"Supporters at my old club," he said.

I nodded. Suddenly, this was starting to make sense. This kind of thing had happened before, like when England star Eddie Parrott (not his real name) was about to agree terms with Southern Athletic in 2006, and supporters of his old club, let's call it Northern City, had threatened to massacre his entire family if he moved. Including his pets. Which, I gather, upset him a good deal. Apparently he was very attached to his goldfish.

"You mean, like Eddie P?"

"Just like Parrott," he said, nodding vigorously. "They threaten my baby and my wife, too."

"Why don't you go to the police?" I asked.

"They tell me that if I go to police, they will shoot me in the brain."

"If they can find it," I thought.

"I see," I said.

"This is why I want to return to Italy," he said.

"I can see that," I said. "It's not as if they have any organised crime in Italy."

"You make joke?" he asked. "You should not make joke about things like this!"

"No, don't get angry, mate," I said. "I do take what you say seriously."

He took another swig of overpriced beer, which seemed to calm him down a bit.

"I try security," he said. "But it is like I am living in a prison, and my wife she say she want to go home. In Italy, I would have my own protection."

"Then that's what you need over here," I said. "Protection. Do you know who these bastards are?"

"You mean, the people threatening me?"

"Yeah," I said.

"Of course I know," he said. "You think I am stupid?"

I decided to let that question pass unanswered.

"Are you going to tell me their names?" I asked.

"I only know one name," he said, "but people say he is the boss. *Molto pericoloso.*"

"And I bet I know who that is," I said. "He's been going round the last five years, boasting he's the man who kept Eddie Parrott at Northern City."

"Then you know who he is," he said.

"You're not going to tell me his name, are you?" I said.

"I can not," he said, tapping his head meaningfully, "or he will shoot me in the knees."

"But if I was to say the name Desmond Mad Monkey Mullarky," I said, "you wouldn't have to tell me if I was right or wrong, just whether I was maybe moving in the right direction."

He stopped to consider. I could almost hear the whirring of cogs in what passed for his brain. After a time, he spoke.

"But you can do nothing to stop him," he said. "Can you?"

"No," I said. "Of course *I* can't. I'm just a humble private detective. But if other people more influential than myself – and perhaps less instinctively law-abiding – were to lean on him, maybe make him reflect upon the error of his ways, it might be that they could get The Monkey off your back. Persuade him that it doesn't pay to be a nuisance."

"You could do that?" he asked.

"I'm not saying I could," I said. "But I might be able to put out a few feelers, spy out the lay of the land, know what I mean?"

"I pay you," he said, softly.

"No, Lorenzo," I said. "That's not necessary. But I hate to see a good striker losing his form, for no good reason."

"You're a good man, Charlie."

"I hope so, Lorenzo," I said. "I hope so."

"I must go now," he said, smiling, "or it will be my wife that shoots me in the knees."

"That's the spirit, Lorenzo," I said. "You go on holiday, visit your aged parents. Commune with your ancestors. Mark my words, everything's going to work out. Come the start of next season, I have a feeling you'll be scoring goals again."

I was a tad embarrassed when Lorenzo kissed me on both cheeks. You know these Mediterranean types. Over-emotional.

Outside, a black woman traffic warden was attaching a parking ticket to his car. Lorenzo tore it off the windscreen, extracted a wad of fifty pound notes out of his back pocket and thrust them into her hand. It must have been five hundred quid or more.

"You can't do that!" she remonstrated.

"Yes, I can," said Lorenzo, just before he drove off. "I am Fettucini. I am legend."

11

THE MAN WHO KNEW TOO MUCH

Thursday, 4th August

The journey to north-west Norfolk took us two and a half hours, via the superb vernacular architecture of Brandon and the trend-setting wind-energy capital they call Swaffham. Eventually the satellite navigation gave up the ghost as we were travelling along a country road.

"Look," said Tom, "we're literally off the map."

I glanced down. Sure enough, according to the sat nav, the countryside around us didn't exist. Nor did the road we were on.

"Are you sure the postcode he gave us is correct?" I asked.

"He didn't give me a postcode," he said. "He told me we should go to South Creake, and then he gave me directions."

"So where does he live?"

"There should be a ruined tower on our right. Standing in the middle of a field."

"An old church?"

"I suppose so. He didn't say. But we're supposed to turn right when we see it, drive along a lane, and he's on the left."

A few miles later, we turned a bend. There, indeed, was a ruined tower with a cart-track running along one side. I turned down it, bumped along for a few hundred yards. Ahead of us was a cottage, made of brick and flint. It looked a bit dilapidated. The only sign of human habitation was a Sky dish on the roof.

"This must be it," Tom said.

I looked around. Without the directions we'd been given, you'd never have known there was a cottage beyond the ruined tower. The cottage was all alone, except for some wooden outbuildings in a state of collapse. It was the ideal hideaway for a hermit, a social leper or a murderer wanting to play with a victim before taking a chainsaw to him. Even though it was a sunny morning, I felt a chill down my spine. The guy was a convicted paedophile. I had a sudden mental image of him bringing children back to this place. Or young women. This couldn't be where Olga Molotovski had disappeared to, could it?

"You okay, Dad?" asked Tom.

"Yeah," I said.

"This place gives me the creeps," said Tom.

"Me too," I said. "Let's see what the dirty old devil has to tell us."

Tom rang the doorbell, but it didn't seem to work, so we knocked on the door. After a while, there was a shuffling inside, and the door opened an inch, to check who it was. Then it opened wide, and we saw the occupant.

He was a tubby, unshaven man of well over sixty. Although it was mid-morning, he already stank of booze. From the bottles by the door, his favourite tipples were brandy, whisky and red wine. He was wearing khaki shorts that were baggy around his knees, and an old check shirt he hadn't bothered to button up properly. It revealed grey chest hair and a rather nasty skin infection.

"G'day," he said.

"Charlie Charlesworth," I said.

"I know who you are," he said. "How are the knees?"

"Mustn't grumble," I said.

"Well," he said without enthusiasm, "since you're here, you might as well come in."

The bottom floor of the house made my office look as minimalist as something from *The World of Interiors*. Books were stacked two deep on sagging shelves. A computer sat on a battered desk, surrounded by old coffee mugs and scrunched up balls of paper.

The other concession to modernity, a widescreen television with a Sky box perched precariously on top, sat in the corner. Under it was a DVD player, with a few DVDs scattered around it. Mainly action stuff, as far as I could see. I recognised a few faces on the covers: Stallone, Jason Statham (twice), Liam Neeson with a gun in his hand. Evidently, Bill Slope's taste in movies did not extend to the art house. Facing the screen was a solitary armchair. The lack of a sofa indicated that he rarely entertained guests. Except possibly on his lap.

Tom was checking out some photographs which also adorned the bookcases. They were virtually all of little boys.

"Who are the kids?" asked Tom.

"What kids?" asked Slope. "Oh them. They're all my kid, at different ages. My son, Ben."

"How old is he?" asked Tom.

"Oh, those pictures were taken years ago," said Slope. "He grew up. Went into the army. Iraq. Afghanistan. Got himself blown up."

He shook his head, and suddenly looked very old and tired.

"I'm sorry," I said.

"It still makes me angry," said Slope, "I blame all those video games he used to play. Kids play them and they think you don't get killed or mutilated. All you have to do is press reload and you've got yourself another life."

Tom paused by another photo of Slope's son, aged about

three, holding the hand of an elegant, if hard-faced, woman with very red hair.

"Isn't that Stephanie Sharp?" Tom asked.

"Too right it is," said Slope. "My ex-wife. The bitch. I only keep it because it's a nice picture of Ben."

"Do you still see her?" I asked.

"Nah," he shook his head. "The less I see of her, the better. She's turned into a monster. What do they call her, the Queen of Mean? That's a flaming understatement. She took me for every penny I had, and a few I hadn't. Now look at me!"

He was certainly a pathetic sight. For a moment, I recalled the man Stephanie Sharp must have married. Slope had once been a go-getting investigative reporter with a reputation for fearlessness. Now he looked like a worn-out old man, presumably still mourning the death of his son. I noticed for the first time that he was wearing odd socks. I suspected they had holes in them.

Out the back was an old-fashioned kitchen, where I was confident last night's dishes would still be sitting in the sink. Personal and domestic hygiene did not seem to loom large in his priorities.

"Sorry about the mess," he said. "I'm working on something. Something important."

"What's that?" I asked.

"Ssh," he said, ostentatiously putting one finger to his lips. "Walls have ears. I haven't swept this place in a month."

"Looks more like a year," muttered Tom.

"You certainly have a lot of books," I said.

"Research material," said Slope. "The ones over there are all mine."

He indicated one shelf, upon which a number of tomes could be discerned that did, indeed, seem to have been written by Bill Slope. They tended to have lurid covers and titles containing the words SCANDAL, FIX or CRIME.

I strolled over to the bookshelf, where one other item caught my eye.

"Aren't you a bit old for video games?" I asked, lifting up a copy of The Seven Deadly Sins.

"It's research," he said.

"I presume you know this has made millions for Olga's dad."

Bill Slope then did an extraordinary thing. He looked around nervously, as though masked gunmen were about to break in through the walls. Then he stared at me and Tom, as though we were John Travolta and Samuel L. Jackson in Pulp Fiction.

"Did he send you here?" he gasped, backing away. "Who are you people?"

"I thought Tom told you," I said. "We're here, looking for a missing person. Olga Molotovski."

"I talked to you about it on the phone," said Tom. "Don't you remember?"

I could see Tom was worried the old codger was turning senile.

"He's sent you to kill me, hasn't he?" said Slope, backing away.

"Who has?" I asked.

"Igor Molotovski," he said.

His face had turned a nasty shade of grey. Reminiscent of the way Loco Parente had looked when I showed him the pictures of Olga. I was worried Slope might be about to have a heart attack.

"Of course not," I said. "Bill, we're just looking for his daughter. He doesn't even know we're here."

At this, Slope visibly relaxed.

"Woo... hoo," he said, like a winded owl. "I thought... It doesn't matter. Sorry. I've got to sit down."

"You, er, do remember me, don't you?" I asked.

"Course I do," he said, sitting down, hanging his head and breathing deeply.

"It was a long time ago," I said, "but even so..."

"Yeah," he said. "Of course I remember you. You were one of my biggest cock-ups."

128

"I beg your pardon?"

"It was my own fault," he said.

He looked up at me. He no longer seemed terrified. Colour had returned to his face, now that he was talking about the safely distant past.

"I should have double-checked my sources," he said. "I wasn't to know that tart was lying about you. And I made the mistake of believing Rex Crawley. Got me into a lot of trouble, that did. Lost me my job on the News of the Screws."

"It nearly lost me my reputation," I said.

"Yeah, well, as I told your son," he said. "I'm sorry about that. Still, you're all right now, aren't you?"

"Yeah," I said. "Mustn't grumble. Now, Tom here says you may have something to tell us."

"Yeah," said Slope, "but not in here."

"Why not?" I asked. "It seems as good a place as any."

"I told you already," he said, struggling to his feet. "Are you half-witted or something? Walls have ears."

"Look, Bill," I said, trying to appear a good deal friendlier than I felt, "don't you think you're being a trifle paranoid?"

"I'm not paranoid," he said. "A paranoiac thinks he's being persecuted. I know I'm being persecuted. And I've had the jail sentence to prove it. I only got out a year ago."

"I heard," I said. "Are you telling me you weren't guilty?"

"Of course not," he said. "Do I look like a paedophile?"

Tom and I glanced at each other and collectively decided not to answer.

"So," I said, deciding to humour him, "why didn't you plead not guilty when they accused you under the Sexual Offences Act?"

A crafty look crossed the old man's face.

"Ah, but that's what they were expecting me to do," he said. "And then the judge would have thrown the book at me. I knew that if I pretended I was guilty but very, very contrite, and told them a lot of bollocks about being abused as a child, I'd get away with a light sentence. And I did. It also helped on appeal that I happened to know the judge was a raving paedo."

"So who was trying to frame you?" asked Tom, who was looking through Bill's collection of DVDs.

Slope shrugged.

"It was my own fault, in a way," he said. "I was living in London then, with my wife. I didn't notice that one day, while I was out, someone had broken in, used my credit card to download a whole lot of kiddie porn on to my computer."

"How had they got hold of your credit card?" asked Tom.

"I'd left it beside the computer," he said. "In those days, I was using it a lot to buy books from Amazon."

"And DVDs?" asked Tom. "I see you're a Jason Statham fan."

Slope made a non-committal grunt. Or it might have been a Jason Statham impersonation. Hard to say.

"And you didn't know that you had this porn on your computer?" I asked.

"Not until the police burst in," said Slope. "Someone tipped them off. Presumably the same people who set me up."

"How much stuff was on your computer?"

"Only about ten photos," he said. "But that was enough to get me sent away."

"And what did they show?"

"Buggered if I know," he said. "But I imagine it wasn't snow scenes in Narnia."

"And that ended your marriage," I said.

"Oh, that? That was pretty much over anyway," he said. "The court case supplied the finishing touches."

"And who are these people out to get you?" I asked, hoping my incredulity wasn't too obvious.

"A man like me," he said, with more than a trace of self-importance, "has many enemies."

"Is that why you live here?" I asked. "It's very secluded."

"Nobody knows me here," he said, "and that's the way I like it. People round here know me as Harry."

"Why Harry? Isn't your name Bill?"

"After all the nasty publicity," he said, "I thought I'd call myself Harry Evans."

"Wasn't there an editor called Harold Evans?"

"That's right," he said. "My old editor, when I was on *The Sunday Times* Insight team."

"You worked for *The Sunday Times*?"

"That's right. Back in '63, on thalidomide and some other stories. Then I moved on to expose the International Olympics Committee, the FIFA cash for votes scandal and most recently curious accountancy practices in the European Union. And do you notice something missing in this room?"

I looked around. It seemed full of every kind of stuff. It was hard to know what else he could have crammed in.

"I'm not sure what you mean."

"Awards for investigative journalism," he said. "Even in this country, you don't get too many brownie points for exposing the truth, if it happens to be unpopular."

"You've never won an award?"

"Not unless you count the jail sentence they imposed on me in Switzerland for alleging that members of the International Olympics Committee took bribes."

"And did they?"

"Course they did. But if I ever wanted to go skiing, I'd still have to give Switzerland a wide berth."

"So, Bill – do you mind if I call you Bill?"

"I don't mind what you call me in here. Outside, I'd prefer it if you used the name Harry."

"So, er, what Tom and I were wondering was, how do you know Olga Molotovski?"

"Ssh! Not here," he said, shiftily. "Let's go for a walk on the beach."

"What beach?"

"We'll go to Wells beach," he said, loudly. "I'll take you in my car. I've a parking permit."

It wasn't too long in his car, a beaten up Honda CR-V, before we passed a sign to Wells, which he ignored. He then drove past a sign saying 'to the beach'.

"I thought we were going to the beach," I said.

"We are," he replied. "But we'll go on to Holkham."

"Why Holkham?" asked Tom.

"Because they'll be expecting us to go to Wells," he said. "You can't be too careful."

Tom and I exchanged glances. The old man seemed to be well off his trolley. I wondered if we would get anything useful out of him, except maybe a wild conspiracy theory. I was sure he'd have plenty of those.

We got out and walked east along a path that Slope assured us ran parallel with the sea. It was a pleasant enough walk. Occasionally we passed people, usually with small children or dogs. Almost everyone said 'Hello', which surprised me.

"Do you know all these people?" I asked Slope. "They all seem to know you."

"No," he said. "That's what they're like up here. Everyone acts as if they know each other. It's the exact opposite of London, where everyone avoids eye contact. And prison, where the other inmates try and beat you up if they think you're a nonce."

We walked on through pine woods, very nice and fragrant, until we reached a beach, which seemed virtually deserted.

"Where are the tourists? I asked.

"That's the beauty of around here," he said. "Huge beaches with nobody on them. Reminds me of beaches back in Oz. No sharks, either. Just the occasional seal."

"It's a long way from Fleet Street," I said.

"Fleet Street doesn't exist any more," he said. "Everything's fucked. Including me. So what is it you wanted to ask?"

"Tom explained we've been asked to find a missing person," I said.

"Yeah," he said. "Olga Molotovski. Tell me what you know about her."

"All I know is that she's a good student. Son of rich Russian parents. Lives in Totteridge. Now she's disappeared without leaving a note, and there's been no kidnap ransom. Her parents are worried, but the police are treating her as just another runaway."

"And where do you think she's gone?"

"I think she's run away to be with someone. At first we thought it might be a girlfriend, but now we think it might be a male celebrity. Any ideas who that might be?"

Slope grunted, non-committally, then looked at me with a suspicious expression.

"And you're working for her father?" he asked.

"Mother, mainly," I said. "She's got some sort of connection with Rex Crawley."

"That scumbag," said Slope.

"And Crawley suggested she came to me. To see if I could find Olga."

"But no luck so far?" asked Slope.

"Not much," I said. "But Tom here noticed you were one of her Facebook friends. Which seemed a bit odd, considering the age difference. And your, ah, reputation."

"Did you approach her to be your friend, or was it the other way around?" asked Tom.

"She invited me," said Slope.

"And how did you two know each other?"

"She, er, helped me out with some of my inquiries," said Slope. "You really don't know much about her, do you?"

"We know she did modelling" said Tom.

"That's one way of putting it," said Slope. "Does Loco Parente mean anything to you?"

"Yes," I said. "He runs a modelling agency. We found emails from him, urging Olga to come and work there, but she'd deleted them."

"And you know why?" asked Slope.

"Not really," I said.

"She used to work for them when she was a kid," he said. "She joined them when she was maybe five or six. And they... well, let's just say they worked her pretty hard."

"And that's why she fell out of love with modelling?" asked Tom. "She found it hard work?"

"The kind of modelling she was doing wasn't only hard work," said Slope. "It involved more than that."

"You mean travel?"

" I don't suppose you've seen Olga's passport," said Slope.

"No," I said.

"She showed it to me," said Slope. "It was quite an eye-opener. And when she told me what she did on her travels, that was even more of an eye-opener."

"I take it it wasn't just modelling," I said.

"No," said Slope, after a long pause. "It wasn't."

Just then, Tom's mobile rang.

"Oh, hi, I can't talk right now," he said. "What?"

He stood, listening for a few moments.

"Yeah, I'll pass that on to dad. Tell the police we'll be back in London tonight. We could see them in the morning."

He put the phone back in his pocket.

"That was Marti," he said.

"It sounded important," I said.

"Yeah," he said. "It is."

"Is it about O'Riordan?" I asked.

"O'Riordan?" said Slope. "You mean Jack O'Riordan?"

"You know him?" asked Tom.

"Of course," said Slope. "He's one of the lowest forms of life."

"Like an amoeba?" I asked.

"More like amoebic dysentery," said Slope.

"Well, not any more," I said.

"What do you mean?" asked Slope.

"Someone's killed him."

"Not before time," said Slope. "I expect one of his boyfriends did him in."

"Isn't that a bit homophobic?" inquired Tom.

"Look do you want my help or don't you?" asked Slope.

"What did Marti tell you?" I asked Tom.

"It's none too pretty," said Tom. "The gory details are all over the internet. Bits are missing from his body. Eyes and fingers. The police think he may have been tortured, then dismembered."

"Bloody hell," said Slope. "Pooftas…"

I thought I would intervene before he treated us to a dissertation on outlandish homosexual practices.

"So the police want to interview us?" I asked Tom.

"Marti said he did seem very keen. Insisted we talk to him when we're back in London."

"Who was it?" I asked.

"Someone called Frank Drake," said Tom. "Came round to our office today. Miffed when we weren't there, apparently."

"I know that name," said Slope.

"Me, too," I said. "Specialises in murders. Tends to get the big ones. A lot of people reckon he's the best at Scotland Yard. Very thorough."

"Can't do any harm to talk to him, can it, Dad?"

"Tom, if Frank Drake wants to speak to us, we're involved in something very serious indeed. He's not the kind of person you want to piss off."

12

YOUNG AND INNOCENT

Thursday, 4th August

Bill Slope seemed strangely silent as we walked back through the trees.

"So," I asked him, "do you think Olga's been kidnapped, or did she run away?"

"It seems to me," he said, "there are one or two things you need to know about Igor Molotovski."

"What kind of things?" I said. "I noticed you reacted quite strongly when I mentioned his name."

"He's a very dangerous man," he said. "In fact, I've been writing a book about him for some time. It's called The Evil Umpire."

"Catchy title," I said.

"But surely a bit melodramatic," said Tom.

"Oh, you think that, do you?" asked Slope, aggressively.

"Well, I don't know," said Tom. "I realise it's a play on words. Umpire and empire. But he's hardly on a par with Stalin, is he? Or Hitler? Or even Pol Pot?"

"How do you know?" asked Slope. "Have you been doing research on him for ten years?"

"No," said Tom. "Of course not. I just thought."

"No," said Slope. "You didn't think. You just talked, without thinking. Like the rest of your generation."

"Oh," said Tom. "Sorry I spoke."

"Tom didn't mean to insult you," I said.

"Look," said Slope. "Molotovski's been mixed up in some pretty sleazy businesses. Pornography, prostitution, sport."

"What's sleazy about sport?" I protested.

"You don't get out much, do you?" said Bill. "I first came across him when I was investigating the world figure-skating championships. The Russian pair fell over in the final but still managed to win."

"And you're saying?"

"Some of the judges had been got at. Enough to swing the result. The crowd booed, but no one was able to prove anything."

"And you reckon Molotovski was behind it?"

"Too right he was."

"Maybe he was being patriotic," said Tom.

"Maybe. But he had money riding on the result," said Slope.

"How do you know?"

"Contacts," said Slope. "But I was never able to stand it up well enough to publish anything. And my only informant died in a car crash, a month after he talked to me."

"It could have been an accident."

"You reckon?" said Slope.

"What's that got to do with Olga's disappearance?" I asked.

"You don't get it, do you?" said Slope. "Olga's father doesn't just use bribery to get his own way. He uses blackmail."

"What kind of blackmail?"

"Well, say he wants to fix the result of a football match, he might decide to get at the referee. Set him up with a prostitute, then take photos of him and threaten to send them to his wife. Or, if it's an underage prostitute, to the police."

I considered for a moment. Was he saying what I though he was saying?

"Are you telling me that Igor Molotovski was willing to prostitute his own daughter?"

"Yeah. At least that's what Olga said he did."

"She told you that?"

"Not in so many words," said Slope. "But I'm not stupid. I could get the gist of what she was trying to tell me."

"Yuk," said Tom.

"Well, that's enough to make anyone run away from home," I said.

"You might think so," said Slope. "But my impression is that she put up with it for years, since she was a nipper."

"God, that is so disgusting," said Tom.

"Surely her mother would object?" I said.

"I don't know about that," said Slope. "You've met Katasha Molotovski. She used to be a high-class hooker. God knows what age she started, so maybe the old trout thought it was okay that her daughter was following in her footsteps."

"But why would Olga run away now?" I asked.

"Maybe she'd finally found somewhere to run to," said Slope. "Or it could be there was something particularly bad she was being asked to do, and she didn't want to do it."

"Any idea what that might be?"

"Not a clue," said Slope.

"Wow!" I said. "What have we got ourselves into?"

"That's why I thought I should have a word with you and your boy," said Slope. "After all, I owe you one."

"Thanks," I said.

"If you want my advice, you might do well to back out of this business now. Both of you," Slope said. "Suppose she did run away from her father and mother. That might be the most sensible thing the kid could do. And the worst possible thing you could do might be to find her."

On our way back to his cottage, Bill Slope stopped off at a garage, just outside Burnham Market.

"Sorry, guys," he said, "I need to fill up with petrol. It's nearly on empty. I won't be a minute."

"Do they sell newspapers?" asked Tom. "There might be something about Jack O'Riordan's death."

"Yeah, they've got papers," said Bill Slope. "Just inside, on the left hand side. They'll probably have a copy of the *EDP*."

"What's that?" I asked.

"The *Eastern Daily Press*," said Slope. "It's the nearest thing they have up here to the *Standard*. I'll fill the car up and see you both inside."

We checked out the *EDP*, but nothing about O'Riordan's death had yet reached the East Anglian press. There was, however, a story on the front page which had more than a little relevance to our visit.

There was a picture of Bill Slope and over it a headline reading, SICK PAEDO LIVES IN NORFOLK.

Slope came into the shop and brought out a handful of ten pound notes from his pocket.

"You all right, Doris?" he asked the woman at the till.

"Oh, I'm alright," she said meaningfully. "But are you?"

"Yeah, I'm alright," said Slope, happily impervious of her wintry demeanour.

He turned towards us.

"You found a copy of the *EDP* then?" he asked. "Is there anything about O'Riordan?"

"I haven't looked inside yet," said Tom, "but you might want to have a look at the front page."

"Yeah?" asked Slope, taking it from Tom.

"Is one of you paying for that paper?" asked Doris, staring

beadily at us, for all the world as though we were a gang planning to rob her shop, or worse.

"Oh, stone me," said Bill Slope, seeing his own picture on the front page.

"I'll pay," said Tom.

"Are you with him?" asked Doris, accusingly.

"We're up here on a visit," said Tom. "From London."

"Well, we don't want people like you up here," said Doris. "Go back to where you belong. And that goes for you too, Harry – or should I call you Bill?"

Bill Slope couldn't get out of the garage quickly enough. He didn't even bother to count his change.

"I was only here yesterday, filling up, and she was all over me," said Slope. "You see? That's what you're up against, once you're branded a paedophile."

Having briefly experienced what it might feel like to be branded a dangerous pervert, I started to feel a grudging sympathy for the old man. Most of all, I suppose, I felt grateful that nothing like that could ever happen to me.

13

SUSPICION

Friday, 5th August

The first hint that we might be suspected of first degree murder came the very next day, when Frank Drake and his immaculate sidekick turned up at our office and asked to interview first Tom, and then me.

"What do you think, dad?" asked Tom, before he went in to see them in the conference room.

"I think they're checking to see if our stories match," I said.

"Does that mean we're under suspicion?" Tom asked.

"I imagine it does," I said.

About half an hour later, Tom came out of the room. He raised his eyebrows and puffed out his cheeks, as though he'd been through an ordeal. Bad sign. Before Tom could say anything to me, Drake's sidekick emerged and ushered me into the conference room.

Frank Drake looked up from a file he was studying. He was a man in his late fifties or early sixties, grey-haired, lined and serious-looking, with heavy black glasses. He could easily have been an academic. He looked old to be an active copper, and I wondered why he hadn't retired. Maybe he needed the money, or enjoyed chasing villains. He reminded me of that bloodhound who used to be in the commercials with Clement Freud.

"Are you Alan John Daniel Charlesworth?" he asked.

"I've been called worse," I replied.

"I am Detective Chief Inspector Drake," he said, holding out his hand.

"I've heard of you," I said, shaking his hand, "but I don't think your friend and I have been properly introduced."

"I am detective sergeant Anwar Patel," said his sidekick.

"Sit down, Mr Charlesworth," said Drake. "Make yourself at home."

"I am at home."

"In a manner of speaking," said Drake. "No need to be nervous, Mr Charlesworth."

He was looking at my hands, which I couldn't help noticing were trembling.

"We are conducting a murder inquiry," said Drake. "Possibly a double murder inquiry."

I couldn't believe my ears.

"Double murder?"

"Yes. And you seem to have been with both victims shortly before they died."

"I'm not sure I understand," I said. "I thought this was about Jack O'Riordan."

"Indeed it is," said Drake. "But it's no longer just about him."

"We've found a second body," said Patel. "Who died on the same evening."

"But, for reasons we needn't go into, he was only discovered last night."

"And who is this?" I asked.

"You mean you can't tell us?" asked Drake, with a quizzical expression.

"I haven't a clue what you're talking about."

"Does the name Loco Parente mean anything to you?"

"Yes," I said. "My assistant Marti and I went to see him earlier in the week."

"And when might that be?"

"Tuesday morning."

"Would it surprise you if I told you he was dead?"

"I'd be very surprised. Mind you, he did look a funny colour when I left."

"Oh?"

"As if he might be about to have a heart attack."

"I see," said Drake. "And do you normally have that effect on people?"

"Of course not," I said.

"It's just that on Tuesday you seem to have been a bit like Typhoid Mary," said Drake. "You visit someone, and a few hours later they're dead."

"Maybe it's a coincidence."

"I don't believe in coincidences," said Drake. "Perhaps if you started off by explaining how you knew the two victims."

I won't bore you with the details, but I came clean about the missing heiress, and why I'd thought Parente and O'Riordan might be able to help me trace her. I mentioned that I thought Parente had had me followed to O'Riordan's house by his green-haired receptionist.

"Interesting," said Drake. "And have you any idea who might want to kill these men?"

"Not really," I said. "I imagine Parente must have a lot of enemies, if he was involved in the seedier side of modelling."

"That's a curious way to describe underage prostitution," said Drake.

"So that is what he was into," I said.

"I'm not saying he was, and I'm not saying he wasn't," said Drake impassively. "What about O'Riordan?"

"I imagine he must have enemies too," I said. "I got the impression that he might have been involved in the sleazy side of photography."

"By which I take it you're referring to porn," said Drake.

"Maybe," I said.

"Would it surprise you to learn that he was one of the world's leading directors of pornography, under the name Dirk Masterson?"

"Well, it would explain the size of his house," I said.

"It appears that he also had a profitable sideline in blackmail."

"Sorry?"

"You heard. Blackmail," said Drake. "He wasn't, by any chance, blackmailing you?"

"Me?" I said. "Do I look like someone with a guilty secret?"

"You are an ex-footballer," said Drake.

"And you know what I was called? Proper Charlie!"

"Yes, I've always wondered," said Drake. "Was calling you that meant to be insulting, or affectionate?"

"Probably both," I admitted. "The point is, I've got values."

"I'm glad to hear it," said Drake. "But maybe you went round to see O'Riordan because he didn't share those values. Or he had something on you that would have destroyed your reputation. Such as it is."

I could see he was deliberately needling me.

"If he had, I'd hardly go round there with my son to sort him out, would I?"

"Maybe he was blackmailing both of you," said Patel.

I could tell they were clutching at straws.

"Well, if you believe that, you'll believe anything."

"Or perhaps you were investigating on behalf of someone he was blackmailing?" Drake suggested, looking me straight in the eyes.

"I'm afraid you're barking up the wrong tree," I said. "All I know is what he told me, that he'd got to know a lot of secrets about famous people. He told me that most of the leading men in Hollywood were gay, and the leading ladies had been either tarts or porn actresses."

"He did, did he?" asked Drake. "Did he name names?"

"Only one. This bloke who looks like a young Johnny Depp. He had a big picture of him up in his studio."

"You mean Jean-Paul De Mode?" asked Patel, leaning forward excitedly.

"I think that was his name, yes."

"So what you're telling me," said Drake, "Is that O'Riordan wasn't blackmailing you, your son or any of your clients."

"That's right."

Drake looked down at his notes, then up again.

"Perhaps you won't mind telling us what you were doing last Tuesday evening?"

"You mean, apart from killing the people I'd been meeting during the day?" I asked.

"I take it, that isn't a genuine confession," said Drake.

"It certainly bloody isn't," I said.

"No reason to raise your voice," said Drake. "We're just trying to get at the truth."

"What times do you want to know about?"

"Perhaps if you start around 6 p.m.," said Drake.

"Er, well at that time I was visiting a, er, thingumybob. You know."

"No, I don't," said Drake.

"A therapist."

"What kind of therapist?"

"A psychotherapist."

"How interesting," said Drake, as if it was the next-best thing to a full confession. "And how long have you been seeing him?"

"It's a her. Lobelia Briggs, Operates out of a basement flat in Tufnell Park. It was my first and probably only visit. My son can give you the address. He arranged it."

"And why did he do that?"

"He was worried about me."

"Anything in particular?"

"It's got nothing to do with the case."

"Perhaps you'll let me be the judge of that," said Drake.

"It's about, um, something I do in my spare time. And it isn't murdering people."

"So what is it?"

"It's this computer game," I said. "Called Football Manager."

"I know that one," said Drake. "My daughter plays it. A big Arsenal fan, poor girl."

"Yeah, well my son thinks I'm a bit, I don't know, obsessed by it."

"Hence the psychotherapist?"

"Yes. I went there to humour him."

"And how long were you there?"

"About half an hour. Then I went home, changed into something smarter and went off to Killingfields."

"Expensive," said Drake.

"I wasn't paying," I said.

"Who was?"

"Joseph Gildenstern," I said. "He's an old contact from my football days."

"When did you get there?"

"Around eight. Exactly eight, in fact. I was there on time, but my host was early."

"And where can we find him, to corroborate your alibi?" asked Patel.

"God knows," I said "He has a house in London but he jet-sets all over the world. For all I know, he's in South Korea."

"Is there anyone else who can place you there, at around eight o'clock?"

"We ate in a private room," I said. "But, come to think of it, I did meet Edward Killingfield himself."

"What time would that be?"

"That would be later. Maybe nine-thirty, ten."

"Was there anyone who could testify to seeing you around eight?"

"The waiters, obviously. Oh, and some Dutchman who works for Killingfield. Collects exotic ingredients for him. Looks like Jason Statham. I can't remember his name."

"Very good," said Drake, scribbling. "Patel, check him out, would you? And when did the meal end?"

"About ten," I said.

"You don't seem very sure."

"Look, I was having an evening meal, not clock-watching."

"So where did you go then?"

"I went home."

"Any witnesses?"

"No," I said. "Not unless someone saw me on the tube."

"Your son says he lives with you," said Patel.

"Yes, but he wasn't there. As I daresay he's already told you."

"Indeed," said Drake. "And, unlike you, he has witnesses to corroborate his story."

"I expect he has," I said. "But then I wasn't to know I would need witnesses. As far as I was concerned, it was just a normal Wednesday night. I didn't know I had to fit myself up with an alibi, did I?"

"It's a shame you were on your own," said Drake. "Parente died at about eight. Maybe nine. And O'Riordan was murdered around eleven."

"And they were both murdered?"

"We can't be sure," said Drake, "until forensics have done their bit, and maybe not even then. Parente swallowed a lot of pills."

"What kind?"

"Prescription pills. He had a history of heart trouble."

"So isn't that more likely to be suicide?"

"Possibly, but he didn't leave a note."

"He lived on his own?"

"He had a flat in the Albany. One bedroom. That was where he was found. By his maid."

"And what makes you think he might be linked to O'Riordan?"

"You visited them both, on the same day they died. And O'Riordan had worked for Parente."

"Yes, he said as much," I said. "Look, perhaps the two of them fell out. Parente went round to his house, murdered him and then, in a fit of remorse, committed suicide."

"That would work if the deaths had been the other way round," Drake pointed out. "But one thing we can be certain of is that O'Riordan died after Parente."

"Yes," said Patel. "What have you to say about that?"

"I don't have anything to say about it," I snapped.

"Why are you being so belligerent?" asked Drake.

"I didn't know I was," I said. "But it's not every day the police come to your office, acting as if you might be guilty of a double murder."

"Don't lose your temper, Mr Charlesworth," said Drake.

"I'm not losing my temper," I said.

"Then perhaps you won't mind lowering your voice."

"I'll speak at whatever volume I care to, thank you very much!"

"Clearly," said Drake.

"Will that be all?" I asked

"That's all for now," said Drake.

"So am I a suspect?" I asked.

"It's too early to say," said Drake. "Not unless you'd care to make a full confession."

"I barely knew these people. Why would I want to kill them?"

"You tell me, " said Drake. "We'll check out your alibi for the early part of the evening with this Dutch fellow."

"There is one other thing," I said. "It's probably nothing but…"

"Go on," said Drake.

"O'Riordan did mention to us that he was gay."

Drake pushed his glasses up his nose and looked into my eyes.

"That would seem to square with what we know of his history, yes."

"Has it occurred to you that that might be relevant to his demise?"

"It has crossed our mind, yes," said Drake. "You mean, it could be some sexual pick-up or rent boy coming back to his place, indulging in some hanky-panky that goes wrong, turns nasty, and leads to the other bloke going bonkers and tearing his head off?"

"That kind of thing, yes," I said. "You mean O'Riordan had his head torn off?"

"That's not to go beyond these four walls," said Drake. "I shouldn't have said that."

"Mr Charlesworth," said Patel, "are you a homophobe?"

"I don't think so."

"Do you fear or loathe homosexuals?"

"No," I said. "Though I can't say I'm attracted to them."

"Are you aware," said Patel accusingly, "that you have just made, or at the very least implied, a shockingly homophobic accusation against the entire gay community?"

"No," I said. "I just thought..."

"You can leave the thinking to myself and Mr Drake," said Patel, huffily tossing his head.

"Oh God," I told Tom, after they had taken down the address of Lobelia Briggs and left, "I think I've just got up the nose of the only gay Asian policeman in London."

"Oh shit," he said. "I forgot to tell them about the clowns and the midget."

"Who cares?" I said. "Sod them."

Marti looked up.

"Boss, this arrived by messenger," she said. "Very posh."

I opened the black envelope and read the card inside it, embossed in gold.

"Is it an invitation?" asked Marti.

"It is," I said. "It must be from my new best friend, Joseph Gildenstern. But I don't think I'll be going."

"Why not?"

"Killingfield's are opening a new restaurant, run by this Dutch guy," I said. "And if it's anything like the old one, the food will be a bit rich for me."

"Tom and me could go in your place. Is the invitation for two?"

"Alan Charlesworth and guest," I said. "But it says 'Strictly Non-Transferable'. You'd better ring them up and tell them I can't go."

"Shame," said Tom. "I quite fancied hob-nobbing with the rich and famous."

His words seemed to remind Marti of something.

"Oh, I almost forgot, two things cropped up while you were in there with the pigs."

"Yeah?"

"One is I've managed to book you on the early morning train to Bruges, like you asked me to."

"What's that for?" asked Tom. "You think Olga's run away to Belgium?"

"No, that's our other case," I said. "Nothing for you to worry about. But I promised Lorenzo Fettucini I'd try to sort out his little problem in front of goal."

"How come that involves travelling all the way to Bruges?" asked Tom.

"Because Desmond Mad Monkey Mullarky lives there, and I'm going over there in an attempt to reason with him."

"Why is he called Mad Monkey?" asked Tom. "Doesn't that kind of imply that he might not be all that easy to reason with?"

"He does have a somewhat unhinged reputation," I said. "But don't worry, I'll handle him."

"Now why," said Tom, "do your words not instil in me a boundless amount of confidence?"

"Go to your room," I said. "And get looking for Olga."

"So we are still looking for her, are we?" asked Tom. "I wondered if we were planning to abandon that case. Bill Slope seemed to think we should."

"Son, I'll be the first to let you know when Bill Slope takes over the running of this detective agency," I said. "In the meantime, we're still employed by Mrs Molotovski to find her little girl, even if she is a rampant lesbian prostituted by her parents from an early age."

"Ahem," said Marti.

"What is it?" I asked.

"I did say there's one other thing," she said. "Or maybe I should have said one other person. In your office."

"Not another job!" I said. "I've got more than enough on my plate."

"Believe me," said Marti, with a smirk, "this is one job you'll be more than happy to take on."

14

SPELLBOUND

Friday, 5th August

When I went into my office, I saw what Marti meant. There before me was a vision of beauty, elegance and what I can only describe as glamour.

You may have noticed from the chapter headings that I'm a fan of Alfred Hitchcock. Like the Master of Suspense, I've always been drawn to the mysterious, Grace Kelly type. This most definitely fitted the template: cool, calm and collectable.

Seeing this exotic creature in the unkempt surroundings of my office, which even at its tidiest would most politely be described as functional, reminded me of a nature documentary I once saw about a flock of macaws living on the roofs of slums in Rio de Janeiro, like a living explosion of colour and energy, set against a background of grim grey and dingy brown.

Everything about her was way out of my league, and I immediately knew who she was. Marion Brooke was a young, blonde British actress who had featured in gossip columns long before she had made any films. I was dimly aware that her husband was some Hollywood heart-throb.

Even now, I'd be hard put to name any pictures she'd been in, but papers would use any excuse to put her on their front page, as half of what the gossip columns would call 'the hottest couple in Hollywood'.

She turned to me and flashed a smile that revealed white teeth of crystalline perfection.

"Oh, hi!" she exclaimed, rising and extending a hand. "I'm Marion Brooke."

"I'm Charlie. Charlie Charlesworth," I murmured.

"I hope you don't mind me just dropping in on you like this," she said. "But I wondered if I could make an appointment to see you."

"Now is as good a time as any," I said.

"That's so kind!" she said, flashing another smile of the sort that would make most heterosexual men go weak at the knees, and might have caused even Jack O'Riordan to check his preferences.

"What can I do for you?" I asked, sinking into my chair with, I hoped, an appearance of calm professionalism, spoiled by a farting sound which came from the chair.

"Sorry," I said. "That's my chair, not me. I should really get it fixed."

"Don't worry," she said, transfixing me once more with that smile.

"What can I do for you?" I asked.

"I have this little problem. And it's really embarrassing," she said, leaning forward conspiratorially. "I wouldn't like what I'm telling you to go beyond this office."

"Anything you tell me," I said, "is in strictest confidence."

"I knew I could rely on you," she said.

"I presume it isn't football-related," I said.

"God, no!" she said. "It's more of a marriage thing."

"Is it something to do with your husband?"

"Yeah. It is," she said. "I'm really, really worried about him."

"And your husband is a film star, isn't he?"

"Well, yes. I expect you know his work. Jean-Paul De Mode?"

Oh, Christ, I thought. That bloke on O'Riordan's wall. Didn't O'Riordan say De Mode was gay? But how could he be gay if he was married to a woman like this? I decided to play the innocent, a role that comes pretty easily to me.

"Sorry, I don't go to the movies much. He's American, isn't he?"

"Canadian, originally, but we have homes here and in Beverly Hills."

"And you're in London at the moment," I said, unnecessarily.

"I am, obviously. But Jean-Paul's been away on location doing his latest movie, *Frat Party*, and then took a little vacation on his own, so I've been getting our house in Primrose Hill redecorated."

"That sounds nice. Whereabouts in Primrose Hill?"

"Chalcot Grove. Fortunately, I'm between jobs, so I've been able to supervise. Jean-Paul is due back today. Round about now, in fact. He's due at Heathrow."

"So why aren't you meeting him?"

"He wouldn't like that. He'd say I was checking up on him."

"He sounds a bit crazy."

"What? Well, you probably know what they call him – Jean-Paul The Mood."

"I had no idea."

"He's quite, I don't know, mercurial. Little things make him angry," said Marion, "so I know which buttons not to push."

"And why have you come to me?"

"Well, the thing is… I've become aware of certain things on the internet."

"Such as?"

"You know about Twitter and tweets?"

I nodded.

"Well, I'm sure it's very shallow and egocentric of me, but on my computer I have this system of google alerts that make me aware of everything that's being said or written about me on the net, and recently there's been a whole lot of stuff that hasn't been… Well, it hasn't been very nice."

"About you or your husband?"

"Both of us. There's a lot of people claiming he's taken out some kind of legal injunction. Like a gagging order?"

"You mean, there's something or things he doesn't want known about his private life?"

"That's what they say. Obviously, I don't know if it's true. And now there's this really bitchy piece about me in the paper."

"Who by?"

"This total cow called Stephanie Sharp. Do you know her at all?"

"I've heard of her," I said. "I don't know her personally."

"Lucky you. She's a grade A bitch. In this morning's paper, she's hinting that all is not well in our marriage. She always calls Jean-Paul 'The Mood' and makes out I married him only in order to advance my career. This morning, she says that Jean-Paul and I didn't sign a pre-nuptial agreement, it was more like a mutual suicide pact."

"Nice."

"Oh, it gets much worse. She as good as says Jean-Paul is sleeping around, though of course she turns it into a joke. She says he's so thick he thinks monogamy is something you make dining tables out of."

"I hope you won't mind me saying this," I said, "but someone once told me he was gay."

"Oh, I've heard all the rumours," she said. "A lot of people are jealous about his looks, and that's the way they get back at him. Look at Tom Cruise. Married three times and with kids, and they still won't leave him alone."

"But you think there might be something in all this?"

"I wish I knew," she said. "That's why I need someone like you to find out. Discreetly, of course."

"Wouldn't it be cheaper if you asked him yourself?"

"I don't think that would be a good idea," she said. "You see, if he has taken out an injunction, it will be because he doesn't want me to know something."

"So if you ask him about it, that will make him angry?"

"Also, I think it would hurt him a good deal, and I wouldn't want to cause him pain," she said, with a hint of melodrama.

"That's very thoughtful of you," I said.

"Just because I'm an actress," she said tragically, "that doesn't mean I think only about myself."

"I'm, er, glad to hear it," I said. "But I'm not yet clear what exactly it is you want me to do."

"It's quite simple. I'd like you to find out if there really is an injunction," she said. "And if so, why Jean-Paul has taken it out."

I thought for a moment.

"You do realise," I said, "that if he's trying to shield you from the truth, there might be a good reason for that."

"Yes."

"But you'd rather know the truth than not?" I said.

"Exactly," she said.

"Have you any reason to think that your husband may have been unfaithful to you?"

"Well," she said. "He's an attractive man. I'm not his first wife, and he's been in and out of rehab a few times."

"What for? Drink? Drugs?"

"Mainly heroin. And cocaine. And alcohol. And steroids," she said. "Three times. Or maybe four. I mean, who's counting, right?"

"Oh," I said.

"I know it sounds awful," she said, "but I'm not telling you anything you want be able to find out for yourself on the internet."

"But as far as you know, he's been faithful to you."

"Yeah," she said. "I think so. Since we married, at any rate. It's just that, lately, I've noticed one or two things."

"Such as?"

"He's been in contact with this awful... man."

"And you think they might be having an affair?"

"What? Oh no!" she said, turning her smile on again, full beam. "Nothing like that!"

"So who is this awful man?"

"His name's Crawley. Rex Crawley."

"I see."

"You know him?"

"Yes. I know him. But how does your husband know him?"

"Jean-Paul's used him in the past to hush up things that he didn't want to reach the media."

"Such as?"

"Drug busts. Fights with paparazzi. That sort of thing."

"You make it sound normal."

"Well, let's face it. It's not abnormal. I mean, we are talking big movie stars. Most of the rich and famous have someone like Crawley to go to, when they think they might be getting into trouble."

"And you think Crawley might have arranged this injunction for your husband?"

"It has crossed my mind."

"So why not talk to Crawley about it?"

"He makes my flesh creep. Besides, I don't think that would be a good idea," she said. "He'd only tell Jean-Paul."

"Forgive my saying this," I said, "but you sound a bit frightened of your husband."

"Do I?" she asked, with a suddenly stricken look in her eyes. "I don't mean to."

"How long have you and Jean-Paul been married?"

"A couple of years. It's our anniversary next month."

"But no children."

"No," she said. "Not that that's likely."

"Why not?"

"Well, I have my career, and Jean-Paul is always off, making some film or other."

"Isn't he in that action series?" I said. "*The Terminator*?"

"No, you're thinking of Arnold Schwarzenegger. Jean-Paul is in *The Exterminator*. One, Two and Three. They're about to make number four."

"So they're successful."

"With audiences," she said. "Not with critics, obviously."

"And what do you think of them?"

"I hate the bloody things," she said. "They're total crap, and Jean-Paul is always at his worst when he's making them."

"In what way?"

"Well, he takes lots of stuff to beef himself up, pump up his physique. Pills, etcetera."

"You mean steroids?"

"I've no idea what they are," she said. "But they make him pretty aggressive."

"Is he aggressive towards you?"

"Oh, don't worry about me!" she said, brightly. "I can look after myself."

Looking at her, so feminine and slender, I rather doubted that. She looked to me as if she needed protection. And perhaps I was the one to do it. Not that I was bodyguard material. But then you could say that about Kevin Costner in *The Bodyguard*. I pondered the pros and cons of working for her, and came to the obvious conclusion.

"When do you want me to start?" I asked.

"Well," she said, "I know it's short notice, and you might be doing something, but... Jean-Paul has a premiere tonight. I've got spare tickets."

"Is this one of those *Exterminator* films?" I asked. "They don't sound like my scene."

"Oh no," she laughed. "This is one of Jean-Paul's spasmodic bids for intellectual respectability. It's called *The Grapes of Peace.*"

"I can't say I've heard of it."

"It's a period piece, set in the Napa Valley. Directed by Alfredo Di Cojones."

She paused and looked in my eyes, as though she expected me to be impressed.

"I don't think I've heard of him," I said.

"He's terribly famous," she said, "though I suppose he is something of an art-house director. He's only made five films over thirty years."

"Are they any good?"

"They're very big with critics."

"But not audiences?"

"That's why he finds it so difficult to get funding. The only reason he gets such brilliant actors is they all do his films for practically nothing. Just so they can say they've hung out with Cojones."

"So that's why Jean-Paul did the movie?"

"Well, it certainly wasn't for the money. It would be great if you could go tonight and keep an eye on him. It's not so much the film itself, but the party afterwards."

"Can't you keep an eye on him yourself?"

"Oh, I'm not going," she said. "I attended the cast and crew screening. The movie lasts 186 minutes. Sitting through it once was enough. Besides, I hate premieres."

"Aren't they glamorous?"

"Not particularly. And I hate the expense. The new clothes, the hair, the make-up. And then you get photographed, and if there's a hair out of place, or anything remotely see-through, people slag you off in the papers and online. You know?"

I shook my head.

"Not really."

"The *Mail Online* is the worst. People pour out their envy and hatred, and then thousands of other people click on a green arrow to show they agree. I once had over three thousand people telling me I looked fat."

"I find that hard to believe."

"You'd be surprised. Besides, it's no fun going as Jean-Paul's wife. His fans hate me, you know. They all want to marry him, or at any rate sleep with him."

"Couldn't you just attend the party afterwards?"

"Not really," she said. "I've already had to text Jean-Paul and say I'm not going to the film because I don't feel well. It wouldn't look good if I recovered in time for the party."

She pulled some tickets out of her handbag.

"Look, I have four spare tickets," she said. "Maybe your son would like to go too? Take his girlfriend. I have two for you, so you could take your wife."

"Unlikely," I said. "She lives in Spain. We broke up a few years back."

"Your girlfriend, then," she said.

"I don't have one."

"Boyfriend?"

"I'm not that way inclined."

"Well, I'll give you a couple of tickets anyway," she said. "Maybe you'll think of someone."

"Aren't these tickets in demand?"

"Only among people who haven't seen the movie," she said.

"You mean it isn't great?"

"Oh, it *looks* great," she said. "Cojones' films always do. He'll only shoot during the magic hour, you know?"

"Sorry?"

"The magic hour is the hour before sunset, when everything gets a sort of hazy, nostalgic feel. Cojones' films are like that. Kind of beautiful and moody."

"I suppose he doesn't do bright and cheerful."

"Not his style," she said.

"Well, I'm not doing anything else tonight," I said. "So sure, I'll keep an eye on your husband for you."

"I'd be eternally grateful," she said, flashing another radiant smile that would have made buckle at the knees if I hadn't been sitting down.

"Are you really sure you want to do this?" I asked. "You could be opening a right old can of worms."

"I wouldn't be here if I didn't, would I?" she said.

I told her my fee, which didn't seem to concern her at all – so much so that I wondered for the first time if I wasn't undercharging. As she stood up to leave, I thought of one last thing.

"If you don't mind my asking," I said, "who suggested you come to me?"

"What? Oh," she said.

For the first time since I met her, she seemed flustered.

"I must have heard someone talking about you," she said.

"Do you remember who it was?"

"I can't say I do," she said. "Anyway, then I looked you up in Yellow Pages, and here I am!"

She smiled brightly.

"Fame at last," I said.

"Word of mouth," she said. "It's the best publicity there is."

"I'm glad you came," I said, standing up and going to her side of the desk. I hoped that I wasn't looking as hot and bothered as I felt in her presence.

"Me too," she said, kissing me on both cheeks. "You're really not bad looking, you know, Charlie. Especially not for an ex-footballer."

"Thanks," I said.

"You should try wearing make-up," she said. "A lot of men do."

"Not really my scene," I said.

"I knew you'd say that," she said. "You're a man's man, aren't you?"

"I haven't had that much luck with women."

"Really?" she giggled. "You surprise me!"

She saw me blush, beamed that smile at me, turned on her high heels and left.

"Wow!" I said, going out to the reception desk as soon as I had regained my composure. Tom was out there, chatting with Marti.

"She's quite something, isn't she, boss?" said Marti.

"She is," I said, feelingly.

"But definitely a man's woman," said Marti. "She barely noticed me."

"She seemed to notice me," said Tom.

"Don't even think about it," said Marti. "She'd have you for breakfast."

"Well, that's our third case on the go," I said.

"Dad! We can't take on another one!" said Tom.

"We can't afford to pass up work," I said. "Jobs are like busses. You're waiting ages for one, and then three turn up at the same time."

"How did she come to choose us?"

"She says she found us in Yellow Pages," I said.

"That's odd," sad Marti. "We're not in there."

"True," I said. "Maybe it was word of mouth. Anyway, what does it matter?"

"Well, I've got my hands full with our Russian heiress," said Tom. "Which, in case you haven't noticed, has got us tangled up in a murder. What are your plans?"

"Tomorrow I'm off to Belgium about this Fettucini thing."

"I know that," said Tom, "but what does Marion Brooke want us to do?"

"Check up on her husband."

"Jean-Paul De Mode?" said Tom.

"Me, me, me!" cried Marti, hearing his name.

"Don't get ideas above your station," I said. "We need you to run the office."

"So how are we going to cope with three jobs at once?" demanded Tom.

"I've been thinking about that," I said. "I'm going to have to bring in Tracey."

"Your sister?" asked Marti.

"I'll give her a bell," I said, "and see if she's available."

Tom and Marti exchanged glances.

"I know, I know," I said. "She's a bit dizzy. But she's got the right instincts. She used to be a cop."

"Come off it, Dad! That was years ago. Before she got married and did the full-time wife and mother thing," said Tom.

"Look, I need someone glamorous, a bit of a party girl, to check out Jean-Paul De Mode."

"Me, me, me!" exclaimed Marti again.

"Oh God, you don't fancy Jean-Paul De Mode, do you?" asked Tom.

"Course I do," said Marti. "He's smokin'."

"He's so up himself," said Tom.

"So?" asked Marti. "If I looked like him, I'd be up myself. A lot. He's well fit."

"And he's meant to be gay," said Tom.

"As if," said Marti. "He's married to Marion Brooke. That doesn't look very gay to me."

"Lots of gay Hollywood actors marry," said Tom, "to put the media off their scent."

"Surely," I said, "you don't think Marion Brooke would have married him if he was gay."

"I dunno," said Tom. "Maybe she's gay as well."

"I don't think so," I said. "She seems extremely heterosexual to me."

"My God," said Tom, staring at me. "You really fancy her, don't you?"

I decided to ignore him.

"Look, Marti," I said, "if Tracey won't do this, I'll get back to you. But I need someone older than you. Experienced. Someone who can look after herself."

"I can look after myself!" protested Marti.

"What about that time at Boujis?" said Tom.

"I was pissed!"

"Exactly!" said Tom.

"I may have got over-excited about meeting Prince Harry."

"You took your top off."

"I was hot."

"And you got thrown out."

"Could have happened to anyone."

"It happened to you," said Tom. "And I had to take you home."

"Did you?" said Marti. "Oh, yeah. You were quite the gentleman. You didn't even try to take advantage of me."

"You wouldn't have remembered if I did."

"You didn't, did you?"

"No," said Tom, "But on reflection, dad has a point. Auntie Trace may look like an airhead, but she knows how to look after herself."

"Thank you, son," I said. "I am still here, you know."

"I thought you were going to ring Aunt Trace up."

"I intend to," I said. "Just as soon as you two lovebirds have stopped quarrelling."

I meant that to be my exit line, then remembered I had something else to tell them.

"By the way, I have a couple of presents for you," I said. "Spare tickets for a film premiere tonight, and the party afterwards. A Jean-Paul De Mode premiere."

"You're joking!" said Marti. "Look Tom, we're going to be hob-nobbing with the rich and famous after all!"

"Oh no," said Tom, looking at the tickets. "*The Grapes of Peace*."

"What's wrong?" I asked.

"Look what it says. 'An Alfredo Di Cojones Film'," he said.

"I know," I said. "I'm told he's very good."

"His pictures are unbelievably boring," said Tom. "And pretentious."

"You shouldn't prejudge," I told him. "Our new client told me it looked wonderful."

"So she's going, is she?"

"No," I said. "She's seen it once and didn't fancy sitting through it a second time."

"Well, there you are, then," said Tom. "It's obviously crap."

"You young people," I said. "So judgmental."

"You're not going to come as well, Dad?" asked Tom.

"Sure," I said. "I've got to keep an eye on Jean-Paul. Marion asked me to."

"Oo la la!" said Marti. "It's Marion, now, is it?"

"Dad, you do realise," said Tom with withering sarcasm, "that there aren't going to be any goals in it?"

I rang my sister, and as usual it sounded as if World War II was happening in the background. The first person I got was Gareth, her stunningly dull husband.

"Hi, Gareth, how are you?" I asked.

"How long have you got?" he said. "The odd ache and pain, but not too bad, thanks."

Any normal person would then have asked me how I was, but Gareth didn't do normal conversation. He either gabbled on for ages about nothing in particular, or stopped talking suddenly, as he did now.

"Is Tracey there?" I asked.

"She's around," he said.

"Do you think you could get her for me?" I asked.

"I could try," he said.

"What's that going on in the background?" I asked. "It sounds like World War II."

"That would be the kids' new video game," he said.

"Do you think you could fetch Trace?" I asked. "Or would that be pushing your luck?"

The minute I said this, I knew it was a mistake. Any cliché is liable to get Gareth's stream of consciousness going, and I had an ominous feeling that might be one of them. I wasn't wrong.

"You say I might be pushing my luck," he said. "But what am I supposed to do? Wait until luck pushes me? Luck has to push pretty hard before the likes of me get moving, and luck is at a disadvantage because it has roller skates on. It can't get the traction. Whereas, when you push your luck, those wheels work in your favour. The slightest touch gets luck rolling. Of course, there is a risk that, if you push too far, it will roll right away. But if you ask me, a nudge will do just fine."

"That's really interesting, Gareth," I said, "but I'm in a bit of a hurry. Is Tracey there?"

"As it happens, here she comes now," he said. "Nice talking to you, Alan. You must come over soon, and we'll continue our chat."

"That sounds great, Gareth," I said with all the insincerity I could muster.

"Here's Tracey," he said abruptly. "Bye bye."

I heard him tell Tracey, "it's your brother."

"Hi, bruv," she said.

"Hi, sis," I said.

"Can you speak up a bit?" she asked. "Damian and Johnny are playing this horrible killing game, and I can hardly hear myself think."

"Couldn't you ask them to turn down the volume?" I asked.

"Not really," she said. "They say it's essential for the atmosphere."

"What's the game?"

"Something about the Seven Deadly Sins," she said. "You heard of it? It seems to involve an awful lot of bloodshed.

Damian's just shot an old age pensioner. One of his arms just fell off."

She was delighted to hear about the premiere, and even more happy that I wanted her to do a surveillance job on Jean-Paul De Mode. I told her this would involve her going with me to the premiere this evening, and then keeping his house under observation for the next few days.

"No probs!" she said. "He's so hot! Hubba hubba!"

"You're the first person I've ever heard actually say that," I told her.

"Say what?"

"Hubba hubba."

"We say things like that all the time in Hackney. You should visit us more often."

I ignored the veiled accusation.

"Is babysitting a problem?" I asked.

"No," she said. "In fact, it's brilliant timing. I've got Gareth's mum staying, and she loves looking after the kids. I think it helps that she's deaf as a post."

"And how is Gareth?" I asked politely.

"Those astrology hotlines of his are going from strength to strength," she said. "Do you know he gets more from them than he does from writing in the paper?"

"Good heavens," I said.

"I know you think astrology's just for the thick and gullible," said Tracey, "but you won't catch me complaining."

"I forgot to give Gareth my regards," I said.

"I expect you couldn't get a word in edgeways," she said. "You know Gareth. Wind him up and away he goes!"

I made a non-committal grunt.

"So what time do you want me?" she asked.

"Why don't you come over here for about seven, and we'll walk down to Leicester Square."

"Magic!" she said. "Look forward to it, bruv."

I'd hardly put the phone down, when Marti popped her head round the door.

"Boss, do you mind if I nip off a bit early, find myself something to wear?"

"Sure, I said. "No problem."

Tom came in, a few moments later, carrying about thirty pages of print-outs.

"I've done a bit of research into Jean-Paul De Mode for you."

"Oh God," I said. "I can't read all that now. Just give me the edited highlights."

"A few surprises, actually. Not the usual rags to riches story. He was born into a privileged background. De Mode cosmetics."

"His father made the millions?'

"Grandfather. French-Canadian. Hence the French name. The family weren't too pleased when Jean-Paul decided to go into acting."

"But they didn't cut him off without a penny?"

"Not exactly. He's inherited a big share of the company. He doesn't need to work."

"Nice for him."

"Must come in useful when he takes time off to be in art movies."

"He does that a lot?"

"Occasionally. *The Grapes of Peace* is the most prestigious yet. It turns out he knows the director from way back. He studied under him at college."

"The director also teaches?"

"Alfredo Di Cojones is one of these guys, like Terrence Malick, who doesn't make a lot of films. Either he's lazy, or he can't get the funding. Like Malick, he teaches film. I bet he's a boring lecturer."

"And De Mode was one of his prize students?"

"Not exactly. Dropped out after a year."

"Couldn't stand the excitement?"

"No, there was some kind of scandal."

"Sex scandal?"

"No. Details are vague, but he seems to have assaulted a fellow student. With a knife."

"Male or female?"

"Don't know. Nothing went to trial. It must all have been settled out of court. Presumably the De Mode family paid off the victim."

"But the anger management issues persist?"

"You could say that," replied Tom. "I found Jean-Paul on a list of The 50 Angriest People In Hollywood."

"Where was he in the pecking order?"

"Number three. Just below Christian Bale and Sean Penn. Above Lindsay Lohan, Kiefer Sutherland and Tom Sizemore."

"Is that bad?" I asked.

"It means he's pretty angry."

"It doesn't sound to me as if he has much to be angry about."

"Quite. He still has a long record of attacking paparazzi, former girlfriends, traffic wardens…"

"Is there anything on the net about him marrying Marion Brooke?"

"Plenty. His fans didn't like it, calling her a stuck-up English bitch and worse."

"How did his family take it?"

"They were okay about it. In fact, as soon as they got engaged, the company made her The Face of De Mode. She appears on most of their adverts."

"Anything about these super-injunction rumours?"

"They're all over the net," said Tom. "It looks as though he's had a super-injunction to protect his privacy, but unlike some it's been pretty effective."

"Any rumours?"

"Plenty. Some of it about female co-stars, probably put out by the publicists."

"What about male co-stars?"

"All through his career there have been rumours that he's gay. But that's nothing new. Virtually every good looking Hollywood leading man attracts them."

"You mean, like Tom Cruise, John Travolta, Richard Gere..."

"Yeah. George Clooney, Jake Gyllenhaal, Leonardo DiCaprio, Tobey Maguire, Elijah Wood, Vin Diesel..."

"You think Vin Diesel is good looking?"

"Some people like tattoos," said Tom.

"One thing I can't work out," I said, "is why there's still this stigma to being gay. I can understand it in the old days, but now virtually everyone in Hollywood claims to be cool about homosexuality, and they wear these red ribbons to show how concerned they are about Aids."

"And yet hardly any gay actors admit they're gay?"

"That's right."

"As far as I can see," said Tom, "the problem is that if you're straight and playing a gay role – like, say, Colin Firth, Tom Hanks or Sean Penn – you know?"

I didn't know, but I nodded.

"You're half-way to an Oscar. But if you're openly gay and you want to play a straight role, no one will cast you – and if a gay man wants to play a gay role, he won't get cast either."

"Why not?"

"I guess they think the public won't accept it."

"That must be why *The Lord of the Rings* bombed at the box office," I suggested. "It had a gay bloke playing Gandalf."

"And, if the internet rumours are to be believed, a gay Frodo."

"At least they didn't have any love scenes together."

"Maybe they did in the director's cut," said Tom.

"Who do you think they'll get to play us in the film of our lives?"

"I dunno," said Tom. "As long as it's not Daniel Radcliffe."

"No," I said. "Too butch."

"Too short," said Tom.

"What about me?" I queried. "A young Clint Eastwood?"

"Nah," he said. "Someone like Paul Bettany. Big, blokey but not quite A-list."

"You know how to hurt," I said.

"Mind if I go home early," he asked, "and slip into something smarter?"

"You do that," I said. "I don't need to. My one good suit's hanging on the door."

"Want me to bring you a clean shirt?" he asked.

"Nah," I said. "This one will do."

Before he could go, Marti's head popped back round the door.

"What do you reckon?" Tom asked me. "Beyonce?"

"Nah" I said. "Will Smith in a wig."

"What are you two on about?" she asked. "No, don't bother. I'm off. But there's a bit of good news for you. Earlier, I nipped out for some milk, and the lift is back in working order."

"At last," I said.

"How long has it been?" asked Tom.

"It's got to be two weeks," I said.

"They must have rented out one of those offices on the third floor," she said. "There was this other bloke in the lift with me. He was quite sweet. He had to get me to press the right button for him."

"Why was that?" I asked.

"He was a dwarf, wasn't he?" said Marti. "Couldn't have been over four foot."

"He wasn't by any chance wearing a red beard?" asked Tom.

"No," she said. "I'd have definitely noticed."

"Or a Hitler moustache?" I asked.

"No," she said. "What are you two on about? He looked pretty normal. I mean, normal for a dwarf."

"Tom," I said. "Before you nip off home, I think you and I should pay a visit to our upstairs neighbour."

There were two offices on the floor above us, and both had been vacant for some time. We knocked on the doors, but there was no reply.

"No sign of dwarven habitation," said Tom.

"What are you expecting?" I asked. "A discarded fishing rod? Snow White's hairband?"

"Touchy," he said.

"I don't like it," I said.

"What do you mean?" asked Tom.

"In our own building," I said. "It feels like we're under surveillance."

"It might be a coincidence," said Tom. "I mean, it might not be the same dwarf."

"Have you any idea how lame that sounds?" I asked.

"Sorry," he said. "But it's a possibility. A remote one, admittedly."

"You know what this means," I said.

"What?"

"It means that we're not only looking for him. He's looking for us."

"Why?"

"I don't know. But something tells me we should be careful."

"You think we should step up security?"

"Yes. And warn Marti. We'd better lock all the windows and double-lock the doors."

"We can't do anything about him this evening," said Tom. "We've got a premiere."

I stared at the door of the two offices. I wondered for a moment if it was worth breaking in, and decided against it. What if the dwarf was someone unconnected with the case?

And who was to say which of the two office suites he was inhabiting?

"Okay," I said. "Let's take a rain check on this for now. We'll address the dwarf infestation when I get back from Belgium."

15

FRENZY

Friday, 5th August

You could hear the frenzy from several streets away. The unmistakable sound of teenage girls screaming. The nearer you got, the more distinct the cries became. A few girls were screaming 'Jean-Paul!' Many more were yelling the names of Sting and Bono.

"I had no idea Sting and Bono were still that popular," said Tracey. "Are they in the movie?"

"I don't think so," said Marti, who was attracting a few wolf-whistles herself and a few hopeful cries of 'Look over here, Beyonce!' "I read about this in a mag. The premiere's in aid of the Amazonian rain forest, or ozone emissions or something. So a lot of celebs have flown in to be associated with the event."

"And to hell with the carbon emissions," said Tom.

"Oh Tom," said Marti, "you're such a cynic."

It was the first movie premiere I'd attended, so I wasn't prepared for the number of fans jammed against the barriers in Leicester Square. Many stared with undisguised hatred as those of us with tickets proceeded towards the Odeon, on the eastern side of the square. As we passed one group of schoolgirls, I distinctly heard one ask "Who the fuck are they?"

"I feel like we're here under false pretences," I said.

"Lighten up, bruv," said Tracey. "Pretend you're a celeb for the evening."

"You look more like a celebrity than I do," I told her.

And she did. Tracey was wearing an all-white outfit to show off her tan, no doubt expensively acquired at some trendy beauty salon. She looked every inch a footballer's wife – ironic, as she was only a footballer's sister, and happily married to one of the most boring men in England, the aforementioned Gareth. Gareth's full name was Gareth Edwards – not the former rugby player, but the welsh astrologer known to his followers as the Mystic of the Marches.

I'd always thought Tracey would marry someone interesting and attractive – and then along came Gareth. He hadn't been an astrologer when she met him; he'd been a weather forecaster. But then he'd been fired from his job on BBC Wales – they told him that he had a face like a wet weekend in Welshpool – and embarked on a career in astrology. His ability to forecast the future was no better than his talent for predicting the weather, but somehow or other he'd managed to wangle a spot on a national newspaper. From then on, as they say, he'd never looked back. Only forward, and even then with nothing comprehensible to say about anything.

"Look!" she said. "Isn't that the girl who was on the *X Factor* until they found out she worked as a prostitute?"

"I wouldn't know," I said.

"I'm sure it is," said Tracey. "And from the look of her, she's taken Simon Cowell's advice."

"What was that?"

"Not to give up her day job."

I gazed at those ahead of us on the long, red carpet. Just

outside the cinema, under huge arclights were people I didn't recognize, preening and posing for the cameras.

"Who are these people?" I asked.

"Celebrities!" cried Marti.

"Poor old Charlie," said Tracey. "None of this means anything to you, does it, bruv?"

I shook my head.

"Don't mind Charlie. He's just being boring," said Tracey. "Look over there!"

"Oh my God!" screamed Marti.

"Who am I supposed to be looking at?" I asked. "Not those two funny-looking boys with sticky-up hair, who look like Tintin?"

"That's Jedward!" said Tracey.

"Who?"

"John and Edward," said Tracey.

"Why are they leaping about like that?" I asked.

"They want to be noticed," said Tom.

"They look as if they need a good smack," I said.

"Don't say that!" said Tracey.

"What are they famous for?" I asked.

"You must have seen them on *The X Factor*," said Tracey. "Aren't they cute?"

"So they can sing?" I asked.

"Not really," said Tracey.

"Only out of tune," said Tom.

"They can't keep in rhythm either," said Marti. "Have you seen them try to dance? It's like their limbs are all uncoordinated. Like collapsing puppets."

"So why are those girls screaming at them as if they're a cross between Nureyev and the Beatles?"

"You just don't get it, Dad," said Tom. "People admire people for having no talent but being famous anyway. It's the same thing with Jordan."

"Who's Jordan?" I asked.

"Jade Goody?" said Tom, as if I was impossibly ignorant. "Abi Titmuss? Rebecca Loos?"

"Oh I know her," I said. "Didn't she have an affair with David Beckham?"

"Gawd, give me strength," said Tracey.

"It always comes back to football," said Marti.

"Let's go inside and sit down," suggested Tracey.

"Right," said Marti. "Come on, Tom. And you, boss."

The four of us moved into the cinema and found our seats. Up on the big screen was a highly excitable young woman interviewing celebrity guests, none of whom I recognised.

"Who is she?" I asked.

"She's only Daniela Diaz!" said Tracey.

"She's famous," said Marti. "She's a veejay on MTV!"

"And here is the man we've all been waiting for," said the hyperactive young woman. "Director extraordinaire, Alfredo Di Cojones!"

"Ola. I speak only little English," said the great director, who was so vast that he was almost popping out of his flamboyant, lavender-coloured suit. "You must forgive me."

"Alfredo," said Daniela, "you are world-famous."

"I am," he said simply. "My films are seen everywhere. By the workers, the oppressed, the poor and dispossessed."

"And that's what this film is about?" asked Daniela.

"My film is about the exploitation of Mexican immigrant labourers in the Napa Valley. My very good friend Sean Penn plays a whip-wielding patriarch."

"Married to a much younger wife, played by Cameron Diaz," said Daniela.

"And she has the, how you say, hots for immigrant Mexican labourer Juan."

"Played by Jean-Paul De Mode."

"Exactly," said the director.

"And, of course, the whipping scene has been compared to the climax of Mel Gibson's film about Christ."

"No, no, it is totally different," said the director.

"But it shows De Mode's brown, glistening, naked body being lacerated by the white patriarch's whip. And it lasts a very long time. Not that us girls are complaining!" giggled Daniela.

"It lasts twenty-three minutes," said Di Cojones. "I do not consider that long."

"Are we ever going to see this movie?" I asked. "Wasn't it meant to have started ten minutes ago?"

"Ssh," said Tracey.

"Another highlight of the movie," said Daniela, "is a half-hour section when you travel back to the dawn of time itself."

"Yes," said the director. "This is to show a clan of black cavemen with rocks being routed by white cavemen with superior weaponry."

"Is he going to go on forever?" I asked.

"Ssh!" said Tracey and Marti.

On the big screen, the great director continued to expound the philosophy behind his film.

"My aim is to demonstrate the brutalising face of technology, as the white Neanderthals brutally rape and murder the black and Hispanic Neanderthals. The message is that this is how it has always been."

"Well," said Daniela, with a nervous giggle. "Plenty of food for thought there!"

"Is there food?" asked the great director. "I look for it inside."

He pushed Daniela aside.

"Alfredo Di Cojones there!" she gurgled. "Over there I can see the hottest rising star in Hollywood, Jean-Paul De Mode. Come over here, Jean-Paul!"

"Oh my God," I said. "Are we never to see this film?"

"Ssh!" Tracey, Marti and Tom.

"Hi," mumbled the actor, over the screaming of his fans.

Daniela decided to begin her interview with a tough question.

"How does it feel to be mobbed by so many fans?"

"It feels great, man."

"I see you're wearing an Aids awareness ribbon."

"Am I?" he murmured. "Yeah, I guess I am, like, kinda…"

He tailed off into a series of grunts and unfathomable mumblings.

"Am I going deaf," I asked, "or is his diction really bad?"

"Ssh!" said Tracey. "I can't hear him."

"You and me both," I said.

Nothing on the presenter's face suggested that she had the slightest idea what he was saying either. She just looked down at the questions she had prepared, and prattled on.

"What's like it to be one half of the hottest celebrity couple in the world right now?"

"It's like, really great," he said.

"Where is Marion tonight?"

"She couldn't be here," he said. "She'll be really bummed out to miss it."

"Why do some people call you The Mood?"

"I guess it's because I've hit a few cameramen."

"You mean paparazzi?"

"Yeah, them too. But I don't like cameramen either. I can't stand people shining lights in my face."

"Doesn't that make acting difficult?"

"Acting is easy, man. It's the cameramen who are difficult. All those lights."

"So, Jean-Paul, I gather you've jetted in to be here?"

"Yeah, I've been on holiday, man."

"Where to?"

"I've been to Cuba, man.

"And did you meet Fidel Castro?"

"As a matter of fact, I did," he said. "Meeting him was, like, very spiritual. It was an experience of a lifetime to sit only a few feet away from this guy who's done so much for his country, and I guess the world."

"And what did you think of Cuba?"

"It proves that socialism works, man. And their healthcare is second to none."

"So you went to Cuba because you'd just been playing a Hispanic?"

"No, man, I saw this Michael Moore picture. About how great it was there."

"So it didn't bother you," said Daniela, looking up from her notes, "that Cuban jails are full of political prisoners, most of who have done nothing more than speak out against the Castro regime or try to leave the country?"

"What are you talking about, man?" he asked. "Have you ever been to Cuba?"

"No," said Daniela, "and there's a reason for that."

"This is starting to get interesting," I said. "I don't think she likes him."

"Ssh," said Tracey.

"My father, God rest his soul," she continued, "was one of the thousands of Cubans who fled that country, along with his brothers. And you know why they fled?"

"How should I know?" mumbled Jean-Paul.

He started looking around him for help. The interview clearly wasn't taking the line that he had expected.

"Because two of them tested positive for HIV," said Daniela. "And you know what happens in Cuba if that happens?"

"Free healthcare?" guessed Jean-Paul.

"You get thrown in jail," said Daniela. "No contest. No due process of law."

"That's heavy, man," said Jean-Paul.

At this point, Jean-Paul was rescued from the interview by a familiar figure. Rex Crawley evidently felt the interview had gone on long enough.

"We have to be going inside, Jean-Paul," said Crawley. "Say goodbye to the nice lady."

"Yeah. Bye," said Jean-Paul.

As he was led away, the actor could be heard mumbling "I think that went well." I couldn't help wondering what he'd been smoking. I doubted if they were Cuban cigars.

I wish I could tell you something about the film, but I fell asleep after ten minutes, and woke only as the credits were rolling, to a smattering of dispirited applause.

"You were snoring," said Tracey.

"Sorry," I said. "How was it?"

"Long," she said. "Very, very long."

"And unbelievably boring," said Tom.

"What did you think, Marti?" I asked.

"Don't ask me," she said. "I flaked out too. I woke up towards the end, when Jean-Paul was being whipped to death, but I can't stand the sight of blood so I closed my eyes and drifted off again."

"Did you miss the cavemen?" asked Tom.

"What cavemen?" she asked.

"Which one was Danny Glover?" asked Tracey. "His name was on the credits."

"I think he might have been the old Neanderthal at the back of the cave," said Tom. "But it was too dark to see. It might have been a rock. The fight between the two tribes was the best bit. Of course I am speaking relatively. My God, I need a drink."

The party took place at the VIP Club, which was in Soho, and about equidistant from the Odeon Leicester Square and our offices. I was by the bar, waiting for Tracey to emerge from the Ladies, when I saw Rex Crawley. He was still chaperoning De Mode and looked like a thundercloud.

"Hi, Rex," I said. "You enjoying yourself?"

"No, I am not!" he fumed. "Did you see Daniela Diaz? Trying to bring politics into her interview with Jean-Paul?"

"I'm not sure that's the way I saw it," I said.

"That wasn't the time or place," he said. "I'll make sure that bitch never works again. Need another drink, Jean-Paul?"

"Yeah, man," said De Mode, before turning to me. "Do I know you?"

"No reason why you should," I said. "I'm a nobody."

"Rex seems to know who you are."

"Rex and I go way back," I said. "Unfortunately."

"But you know who I am, right?" he asked. "How did you love my movie?"

"It's very... artistic," I said.

"It is," he said. "Did you know Di Cojones and I go way back?"

"To your college days," I said.

"That's right," he said. "I was on the director's course, but I guess I was too good-looking ever to become a director."

"I heard you were thrown out," I said.

"Yeah, well," mumbled De Mode. "There was a misunderstanding."

"Didn't you stab someone?" I asked.

"Not really," he said. "This guy kinda walked into a knife I was holding. We were making this film, and he kept shining lights in my face."

"Hello, Mr de Mode," said a familiar voice.

I guessed Marti had come up to him for an autograph, but I was mistaken.

"I hope you won't mind me asking," she said. "But you claim to be a progressive."

"Well, yeah," said De Mode. "Doesn't everyone?"

"Doesn't it bother you that in this movie you played a part that might have been filled by a Mexican or Hispanic actor?"

De Mode looked at her with barely suppressed hatred.

"Who the hell do you think you are to talk to me like that?"

"Who the hell do I have to be?" she asked.

To her credit, Marti didn't flinch as he stepped forward and thrust his face into hers. This involved him stepping on tiptoe, as he was several inches smaller than he looked on screen.

"Why are you such a bitch?"

"I'm only asking you a question."

"What gives you the right to ask me a fucking question?"

"Why shouldn't she ask you a question?" asked Tom.

"Nobody asked you for an opinion," snarled Jean-Paul. "Why don't the two of you get out of my face, or..."

"Or what?" asked Tom, who looked quietly confident that he could hold his own against a vertically challenged actor from Hollywood.

"Or I'll put you and your girlfriend here in a fucking rose garden, you cunt! You understand that?"

"I see you've attended the Mel Gibson charm school," said Tom.

At this point, Rex Crawley returned with two drinks, one for himself and one for De Mode

"Rex," I said, " could you take control of this little chap? He seems to be either very drunk or very stoned. And profoundly unpleasant."

"You know these people?" De Mode asked me. "I bet you're a Jew. You've got one hell of a big nose."

I'm not Jewish, but I was interested to see how this conversation would go.

"What if I were Jewish?" I asked.

"The Jews are responsible for all the wars in the world."

"They're not half as much trouble," I said, "as obnoxious little creeps who can't hold their liquor."

"Fuck off, you filthy yid!" cried Jean-Paul, raising his fist to strike me.

At which point the star fell to the floor. He never knew what hit him. This was just as well, as it was his elderly publicist, who had administered a smart rabbit punch to the back of his neck.

"I wasn't expecting that," I said.

"I used to be in the army," said Crawley. "Worst time of my life. Don't tell him I did that. I'll blame the paparazzi. You're not Jewish, are you?"

"Not as far as I know," I said.

"I am," said Crawley. "And if there's one thing I can't stand it's anti-semitism. Help me take him outside, will you? I'll get a cab and take the angry little bastard home."

Tom and I hitched one of De Mode's arms around each of our shoulders and dragged him through the party. Rex Crawley walked a little ahead of us, so it was he who nearly collided with Stephanie Sharp, as she emerged from powdering her nose.

"Rex Crawley," she drawled. "Don't tell me Jean-Paul is drunk and disorderly again."

"Why, if it isn't the SS," said Crawley. It was immediately obvious that his enmity towards Stephanie Sharp went back over many years. "Mr De Mode is a little indisposed."

"He looks as indisposed as a newt," remarked the Queen of Mean, tossing her mane of very red hair and thrusting out her boobs.

"That," said Crawley, "is the ugliest top I've seen in years. It complements your personality perfectly."

"Dear Rex, you've never really forgiven me for refusing to sleep with you, have you?"

"If I throw a stick," said Crawley, "will you leave?

"Oh I see what you're trying to achieve," she said, with a careless laugh and another toss of her head. "It's like humour, but without the comedy."

"Stop harassing me and my client," said Crawley.

"Who's harassing who?" she asked. "It's you who took out an injunction against me."

"I have nothing more to say," muttered Crawley.

"How much did you have to pay the judge?" asked Stephanie Sharp.

"Stephanie Sharp," said Rex Crawley, "you are the most vile human being on the face of the earth. And remember, I've met Michael Winner."

He went off to find a cab. Tom looked at me, and I looked at Tom. Jean-Paul De Mode hung between us, his feet not quite touching the floor.

"You know something?" said Tom "I'm starting to warm to Rex Crawley."

"No one can be all bad," I said.

"I don't know," said Tom. "I can see that this little fella might come close."

"Look, Rex is waving at us. He's found a cab. Let's get this idiot over there," I said. "I don't fancy being around when he wakes up."

"I thought movie premieres were supposed to be glamorous," said Tom, as we carried De Mode towards the taxi. "This one's been more like flypaper for freaks."

"Uh-oh," I said. "Talking of which…"

"What do you mean?" asked Tom. "Oh."

That last exclamation came about as he too registered the arrival at the party of Fairycakes Bonanza Parks. She definitely looked more cheerful that when we had seen her last. Without her piercings and with some make-up, she looked almost attractive. She stopped to watch us loading De Mode into the back of Rex Crawley's cab.

"Maybe you two aren't such losers after all," she said.

"What do you mean?" I said.

"I'm impressed," she said. "You managed to find Olga's secret lover. And I didn't have to help you at all."

"Well, we are investigators," said Tom, playing for time. "It's what we do."

"So how did you find out?" she asked.

Perhaps the alcohol was slowing me down, but I wasn't quite following.

"Find out about what?" I asked.

"About Olga and Jean-Paul?"

"I'm afraid we can't reveal our sources," said Tom. " How did you?"

"Well, I knew she was seeing someone, and I suppose I was a bit jealous," said Fairycakes. "So one day I followed her. All the way to Primrose Hill."

"Ah yes," I said. "Chalcot Grove."

"Right," she said. "And he opened the door, stripped to the waist, and he kissed her, and it was, like, so totally obvious."

"Right," I said.

"I mean, it does make sense. He is gorgeous," said Fairycakes. "Tiny, but perfectly formed."

"So did you ask her about him?"

"I didn't need to," said Fairycakes. "It was obvious that she was in love. I mean, why not?"

"Well, he is married," I said. "To Marion Brooke."

"So?" she said. "I'd fuck him. "

"Really?" I asked.

"Sure," she said. "He's Jean-Paul De Mode."

She turned on her heels and left.

"Does any of that make sense to you?" I asked Tom.

"Well," said Tom, "now we know why De Mode got Crawley to take out an injunction."

"To stop Sharp telling the world about him and Olga?" I asked Tom.

Tom nodded. I shook my head.

"It doesn't feel right to me at all," I said. "I mean, what man in his right senses would choose a callow 17-year-old over Marion Brooke?"

"My God!" said Tom. "You're totally infatuated with her, aren't you?"

"What if I am?" I said. "You've got to admit she's lovely."

"Who's lovely?" asked Marti, coming up to us with Tracey, who had finally emerged from the Ladies.

"You talking about me again, bruv?" asked Tracey.

"I was just telling Trace about our little altercation with Jean-Paul," said Marti.

"What a creep," said Tracey. "How disappointing is that?"

"We think De Mode may be having an affair with Olga," I said.

"Which is why he took out an injunction," said Tom.

"Blimey," said Tracey. "You'd think Marion Brooke would be enough for any bloke."

"My sentiments entirely," I said.

"But, as we just witnessed for ourselves, Jean-Paul De Mode's not just any bloke," said Tom.

"Yeah," said Marti. "Maybe he's the kind of guy who can't resist new conquests."

"Or he gets off on Russian heiresses worth billions of pounds," said Tracey.

"But why the need for secrecy?" I said.

"Dumping Marion Brooke wouldn't come cheap," said Tracey.

"It might not do his reputation much good either," said Marti.

"Or maybe he wants to keep two women going at the same time," said Tracey.

"Some men are like that," agreed Marti.

"Not my Gareth," said Tracey. "He's barely got enough energy for one woman."

I wasn't at all sure if I wanted to hear about Gareth and Tracey's sex life, or lack of it.

"Oh, look at the time," I said. "I've got to be up early in the morning. Shall we go?"

"Yeah, I'd better be off," said Tracey.

"Gareth will be wondering where you are," I said.

"Doubt it," she said. "By this time he'll be in the land of nod."

"Mind if Marti and I stay on for a while?" asked Tom.

"Yeah, you two enjoy yourselves."

"Oh, while I remember," said Tracey. "You want me to keep De Mode under surveillance, but you never told me where he lives."

"Chalcot Grove," I said. "I don't know the number."

"Leave that to me," said Tom.

"Text me the number, Tommy, right?" said Tracey.

"I wish I didn't have to go to Belgium tomorrow," I said.

"Look, you sort out the Fettucini case," said Tom. "Leave finding Olga to us."

16

NOTORIOUS

Saturday, 6th August

When a bloke's one of the most violent criminals these islands have ever produced, and his nickname is Mad Monkey, it's a major surprise to find he isn't covered with tattoos and piercings, and his knuckles don't graze the pavement when he walks.

When Desmond Mad Monkey Mullarky strolled into one of the classiest restaurants in Bruges, he treated the greeter like an old friend. He was togged up in a smart suit that couldn't have cost less than two grand. He looked like a respectable businessman, or maybe a wealthy tourist enjoying early retirement. Certainly not a bloke who'd been barred from more football grounds than anyone dead or alive.

Our paths had never crossed, but he recognised me at once, came over and shook me by the hand.

"Des Mullarky," he said.

"Charlie Charlesworth," I said.

"Don't worry, I know who you are," he said. He had a curious mixture of accents, in which I detected Irish, Scouse and all-purpose north-western, the kind of voice that southern actors put on when they're in Coronation Street, plus something different and sing-song. It sounded a bit like the Dutch accent that Steve McClaren was ridiculed for adopting when he started coaching in the Netherlands. I guessed that, though Mullarky obviously came from somewhere up north, he didn't go back there often.

"I've ordered some sparkling water," I said apologetically. "I wasn't sure what you'd want."

"That will do me," he said. "I'm trying to cut down on the booze at lunchtimes. I need to watch my figure."

He tapped his stomach, which was indeed perilously close to obese.

"Too much fine dining," he said.

"A few nights ago, I had a meal in Killingfield's," I said.

"Never been there," said Mullarky. "Any good?"

"A bit rich for my taste," I said.

"Oh yeah?" he said. "Aren't they opening a second restaurant at the top of that new skyscraper, The Pyramid? I'm not sure why, but I got an invitation for the opening next Friday."

"I met the chef," I said. "Seemed like a nice bloke."

"Not another genderbender, is he?" asked Mullarky. "I'm not sure if that bloke Killingfield is a man or a woman."

"The new bloke seemed pretty straight to me," I said.

"Maybe I should go," said Mullarky. "My wife's already nagging me that I don't take her to London."

"I got an invite too," I said. "But I don't think I can go."

"Pity," he said. "Too much work on?"

"Yeah," I said. "And I'm not good at big social events. I never know anyone, unless they happen to have something to do with football."

"I know what you mean," said Mullarky. "Half of them are poofs, if you ask me. Which reminds me, what's the difference between Michael Jackson and a plastic bag?"

"I, er, don't know," I said.

"One is white, plastic and dangerous to young children," said Mullarky. "The other is a plastic bag."

I contorted my face, to look as though I was laughing, but no sound would come out.

"Here's another," he said. "How does Michael Jackson know its time for bed? When the big hand is on the little hand."

He roared with laughter. Again, I tried to look as though I was enjoying his wit.

"Anyway, enough of these pleasantries," he said. "You know, Charlie, I've always been a fan of yours. We could have done with a central defender like you at our club. It's never been the same since we got in these foreign managers. Always employing nancy boys to do a real man's work."

It hadn't really occurred to me that the recent troubles of his favoured club – let's call it Northern City – had been caused by a surfeit of airy-fairy homosexuals at the heart of the back four. Still, I thought it best not to argue with him. After all, he was the most vicious football hooligan of the past thirty years. And I was buying him lunch and about to try and convince him not to do something he was undoubtedly very good at: threatening people.

"Ah," I said, non-committally.

"Or, let's be fair," he said, "poofs and wogs."

"So you think there are too many foreign players in the Premiership?" I hazarded.

"Far too many," he said. "Look at Arsenal. Ever since they lost their back four – Adams, Keown, Dixon, Winterburn – they've been struggling to win anything."

"But surely Ashley Cole…"

"Don't talk to me about Ashley Cole," he said, darkly. "Poof!"

"He's hardly a poof," I said. "Doesn't he send pictures of his todger to random women?"

"Looks like a poof to me," said Mullarky. "Like that Tony Blair. Wears make-up. Dyes his hair. And Mandelson. You can't tell me something gay wasn't going on there."

"You can't seriously be suggesting…"

"All I'm saying is that Mandelson knew where the bodies were buried. Why else would he keep on being re-employed, know what I mean?"

I wasn't at all sure what he meant, so I decided to study the menu.

"And look at that pinko Cameron. They're all in the pay of Murdoch, if you ask me," he said. "And Israel. Bring back Tebbit is what I say. Best Prime Minister the country never had."

"Nice food here," I said, studiously avoiding the subject of politics. "I thought from the name of the place that they might only serve fish."

"Nah," he said. "Den Gouden Harynck is one of the best restaurants in Bruges. I come here all the time."

"So what drew you to Bruges?"

"It's quiet here," he said, "Fewer poofs. And hardly any crime or violence."

The irony of a former hooligan requiring peace and quiet had evidently never occurred to him, so I let it pass.

"Do you still get to watch football?" I asked.

"Only on the box," he said.

"So your hooligan days are behind you," I said.

"Long gone," he replied. "Great days, but it was never the same after Hillsborough and the Heysel. I couldn't summon up the same enthusiasm. The all-seater grounds didn't help."

"You miss those days?"

"I try not to live in the past," he said. "But yeah, to be honest, I enjoyed a good riot. If things had been different, I might have gone into the army. I'd have been a general by now."

"Why didn't you?"

"Dunno, mate. I didn't come from an army background," he said. "If you ask me, the kids of today don't have what it takes to be proper hooligans."

"How do you mean?"

192

"Well, it may not have looked like it, but there was a good deal of planning and preparation went into a good rumpus," he said. "I mean, I spent days, weeks even. And there was a lot of discipline involved."

"How do you mean?"

"Well, the footsoldiers looked up to me," he said. "The kids of today, they don't respect no one."

"What about these gangs?" I asked. "They must have leaders."

"Yeah," he said, "but they're usually recruited along racial lines. My followers were from all races, all walks of life. We were multicultural before they'd even thought up the word."

"So you do miss it?"

"I miss the adrenalin rush, yeah, and the sense of belonging," he said. "But I'm too old for it now. Too old, too slow and too rich."

"Yes," I said. "I heard you were a successful entrepreneur."

"That's one way of putting it," he said. "It's too bad you didn't contact me earlier in the week. I was in London on Wednesday. I had some business to attend to."

"I didn't know then that I needed to meet you."

"Never mind," he said. "Bruges is well worth a visit. It's too bad you can't stay longer. Or can you?"

"I have to go back later this afternoon."

"Make sure you catch a few of the sights before you go," he said.

"I'll try."

"Were the sights the reason you came here?" I asked.

He shook his head.

"I married a Belgian girl, Berthe. She wanted to be near her family. Anything to keep the little lady happy."

"You moved here from Britain?"

"Nah," he said. "The Costa. It got a bit hot for me there. Too many spics, dagoes and Russkis trying to muscle in on my territory. So I moved my operation to here."

"And what kind of operation is that?"

"Oh you know, wheeling and dealing," he said, vaguely. "This and that. I made a shedload of money in krugerrands."

"How did you do that?"

"Me and some business associates bought a whole lot of them – they didn't carry VAT, see? – and melted them down into gold ingots, which did. Then we sold them back to the bullion house, and collected a nice little wedge of VAT in the process."

"And that made you a living?"

"Yeah. Eight million quid in a single year. Brilliant scam, that was."

As the waiter hovered, Mullarky pointed to the menu.

"As my friend here's paying, Gaston, I think I'll be having a soupcon of your lovely lobbo."

"For you, the lobster starter, sir?" said the waiter, with professional deference. "And for you, sir?"

"What's the soup of the day?" I asked.

"That would be pea soup."

"That will do nicely," I said.

After the culinary experiments of Edward Killingfield's establishment, I felt like dining conservatively. Or at least like not eating anything that would make me throw up.

"Just make sure you don't pee in it!" said Mullarky.

"No, sir," said the waiter, with barely a wince.

"Not much sense of humour, Belgians, but lovely people," said Mullarky. "Wouldn't hurt a fly. So now you're one of these private detectives?"

"That's right."

"What do you detect?"

"I get a lot of cases to do with football. Some of it is about celebrities, matrimonial matters, things like that."

"Sounds interesting," he said. "You must know a lot of guilty secrets. I expect you know about these super-injunctions."

"I don't think there are that many super-injunctions."

"Didn't John Terry have one? And Fred the Shred? Andrew Marr?"

"You're well informed."

"We get the *Daily Mail* over here, only a few hours later than in the UK. And I go on the internet. And, as I say, I get over to London now and then, on business."

There followed a brief conversation about the identity of various footballers and other celebrities currently involved in injunctions and gagging orders, which of course it would be illegal of me to reproduce here.

We were well into the main course – on his recommendation, I'd chosen the turbot – before Mullarky got round to raising the matter of why I had wanted to meet him.

"It's a ticklish subject," I said, "but you're well known as a supporter of Northern City."

"Guilty as charged," he said.

"And you weren't keen when Eddie Parrott tried to move to Southland Athletic."

"Too right I wasn't. He was the life and soul of the club. Northern City, through and through."

"In fact, if he went through with the transfer, you threatened to break his legs and murder his wife and children. And, I believe, his goldfish."

"Did I?" he paused with turbot in mid-air. "I can not, for the moment, recall."

"Well, that is the perception," I said.

"If that's the perception," he said. "I don't have much control over it, do I? It's not as if I'm in a position to go to a judge and get a gagging order. Specially not this long after the event, if it occurred, which I'm not for a moment saying it did. I'd look a right ponce."

I paused for a moment, then decided to take the plunge.

"What do think of Lorenzo Fettucini?"

"Apart from the fact he's a fuckwit?"

"Apart from that."

"In my opinion, Northern did well to get rid of him."

"Really?"

"Yeah. What did they get for him from Southern Athletic?"

"Round about thirty million," I said.

"What a waste of money," he said. "How many goals has he scored for them?"

"None yet."

"Well, there you are."

"It's the fact he hasn't scored that concerns a lot of people," I said. "Are you sure that has nothing to do with you?"

"Why would it?" he asked. "I don't follow."

I looked at him, hard. As far as I could see, he was genuinely perplexed.

"I just wondered," I said, "or rather others were wondering if you had been... putting pressure on him."

"Never met the bloke," said Mullarky. "Don't want to, neither."

"Then why do you think he hasn't scored for Southern?"

"Maybe he panics in front of goal," shrugged Mullarky. "Or owes someone a favour."

"What do you mean by that?"

"I don't know how much you know about these things," said Mullarky. "After all, you date from a bygone era."

"I wasn't playing that long ago."

"You know what I mean," he said. "Nowadays these geezers are on over a hundred grand a week. You were never on anything like that."

"That," I said, "is only too true."

"The players today are mostly uneducated fuckwits, over-rewarded for their dubious talents with way too much money," said Mullarky. "So what do you think they do with it?"

"Spend it on cars," I said. "Big houses, expensive wives."

"Nah, you're forgetting the major thing," he said.

"What's that?"

"I don't know why you're in Belgium, talking to me," he said. "You should be in England, talking to Bill Slope. Ever heard of him?"

"Yes," I said. "Oddly enough, I have."

"I used to go to football matches with his son," said Mullarky. "Ben. Nice guy. Took to soldiering, didn't he?"

"I gather he got blown up in Afghanistan," I said.

"Did he? I'm sorry to hear that," said Mullarky.

"But it's his father I should be talking to?" I asked.

"Absolutely. Very well informed," he said, tapping one side of his nose.

"So I've heard."

"He knows more about this kind of thing than I do," he said. But it seems to me the key to a lot of what's going wrong with football at the moment is gambling. Lots of the players gamble."

"Well, I've heard about Rooney," I said. "I gather he ran up debts of 700 grand with one betting company."

"Yeah," said Mullarky. "Not one of mine, unfortunately."

"You own a betting company?"

"I'm a businessman," said Mullarky. "And I like to diversify. So it's only natural that I have interests in gambling."

I tried to think back to the players who were around in my own day.

"I do remember Paul Merson and Tony Adams," I said. "They lost millions gambling."

"Yeah, Merson lost seven million, at least," said Mullarky. "And don't forget Eidur Gudjohnsen."

"Icelandic, wasn't he?"

"Yes, an Icelandic banker, as you might say in Cockney rhyming slang. Got himself six million quid in debt. A berk of Mersonian proportions. But they're just the tip of the iceberg. There's lots more that make sure they never make it into the papers."

"You mean, by taking out injunctions?" I asked

"Yeah, or they use PR people for damage limitation."

"Like Rex Crawley," I said.

"He's one of the biggest," said Mullarky.

"And you're saying that Fettucini gambles?"

"Of course he does. I heard he was going to finance a film about himself. 'Lorenzo Fettucini Superstar'. That kind of thing. Got it all set up with a director and everything, then went out gambling and lost all the money."

"So no film?"

"Well, every cloud has its silver lining," he said. "At least there's one fewer crap film in the world."

"It does sound in character," I admitted. "I gather he has a life-size effigy of himself in his front garden."

"I heard it was slightly larger than life-size in certain of its measurements," said Mullarky. "If you catch my drift. He fits the classic profile. You know, before he made the move to Southern, Fettucini lost form and spent weeks on the bench?"

"So?"

"That's when a lot of players get depressed and miss the adrenaline rush of playing. The nearest these footballers get to that buzz is by gambling. And for some of these guys, it turns into an addiction."

"You seem to know a lot about it," I said.

"I've made a few grand out of them," he admitted. "Just because they're mugs doesn't mean I have to be."

"But it isn't you who have been pressurising Fettucini?"

"I've better things to do with my time."

"Such as?"

"Well, football obviously. My bovver boy days are over, but I still follow City during the season. Especially when they play in Europe. And my wife's an artist. We enjoy art galleries. No, don't laugh. We've several in Bruges. You should let me take you to one."

Something in the tone of his voice told me he was telling me the truth. It was glaringly obvious that he didn't care enough about what I thought to lie to me. He was a man perfectly at ease in his own skin, and own extremely expensive wardrobe, which was a lot better than anything I could conceivably afford.

"I take it you don't gamble yourself?"

"Come off it, Charlie!" said Desmond Mad Monkey Mullarky, rolling his eyes in mock-horror. "Do you think I'm mad?"

It was when I was trying to settle up at the restaurant that I discovered one of my credit cards was missing. I said as much to Mullarky.

"You're not trying to sting me for the bill, are you, Charlie?" asked Mullarky.

"Not to worry," I said. "I have another card."

"That's all right, then. So when's your train back to London?" asked Mullarky.

"Not for a couple of hours," I said.

"You should let me take you to the hospital."

"There's nothing wrong with me," I said.

"I mean the old Saint John's Hospital. It's within walking distance, the Memling museum."

"The what?"

"Memling. The 15th century painter, Hans Memling?"

I shook my head.

"Never heard of him," I confessed.

"Top man," said Mullarky. "He painted four pictures for the sisters of the hospital, and they're a must-see. I'll treat you to a visit."

Outside in the street, I took out my mobile phone.

"I'd better call my office," I said. "Do you mind?"

"Don't mind me," he said. "I'm a slave to my iPad."

I got through to Tom, almost immediately.

"Any news about Olga?" I asked.

"Not yet. I've managed to track down De Mode's address. Number 17, Chalcot Grove. I'll alert Tracey to stake it out, see if there's anything suspicious, such as a runaway Russian heiress on the premises."

"Good. But in the meantime, Tom, can you check if I left my Visa card by my computer?"

"Sure," said Tom, returning after a few moments. "No sign of it, Dad. But Marti says you gave it to her to book you on to the Eurostar."

"That's right, I did," I said. "Does she have it?"

"No. That's the odd thing," said Tom. "I'll put Marti on."

"I can't find it, boss. I had it on my desk yesterday," she said. "But it had gone by this morning, so I assumed you took it back."

"Do you remember when it disappeared?" I asked. "Was it during the morning or afternoon?"

"I'm not sure," she said. "Sorry."

"Was it there when you left work?"

"I'm not sure about that either," she said.

"Oh damn," I said, "I'd better cancel it. Can you look up the number I have to call in order to cancel the card?"

"Sorry about this," I said to Mullarky.

"No sweat," he said. "You can't be too careful these days. There's too much crime about."

When I called up Visa to cancel the card, I heard something even more alarming. The card had been used to pay £150 for some transaction with an internet company I knew nothing about. Luckily, the bloke at Visa seemed to accept my word that I hadn't authorized it, and promised to cancel it.

But something wasn't right, and it reminded me of something Bill Slope had told me only a couple of days before. So I dialed the office.

"Tom," I said. "Me again. It may be nothing, but someone used my card for some internet transaction I know nothing about."

"That's weird," he said.

"Does it remind you of anything?"

"It sounds like what Bill Slope was telling us about."

"Exactly," I said. "My computer is on my desk in my office. Could you get on it and check if there have been any downloads?"

"You mean, last night?"

"Any time over the last day or two. But most likely overnight, yes. I left my computer in the office."

"There's been no sign of a break-in."

"I know. It may be nothing," I said. "I expect I'm just being paranoid."

"You probably are, Dad," said Tom. "But don't worry, I'll look into it."

"This is my favourite piece," said Mullarky, inside the Memling museum.

"It's three pictures in one," I said.

"Yeah. A triptych. One of Memling's biggest," said Mullarky, "and in my opinion, his best."

"The colours are very vibrant."

"Indeed they are," said Mullarky.

"What was it for?"

"It was an altar-piece, painted in the late 1470s," said Mullarky. "In the middle there's the holy virgin with the baby Jesus on her lap."

"Why is he putting a ring on the finger of the woman on the left?" I said.

"Because she's Saint Catherine of Siena," said Mullarky. "Don't ask me why. He likes her, I suppose. The woman on the right is another Saint Catherine – Catherine of Alexandria. Don't know anything about her, either."

"What's happing on the right of the triptych?" I asked. "It's like a man with a think-bubble coming out of his head."

"You're not so far wrong. It's a vision of the Apocalypse, as seen by St John the Evangelist."

I studied it closely.

"Are those the four horsemen of the apocalypse?"

"Yeah," said Mullarky. "You can see hail and fire upon the land, and a mountain hurling itself into the sea.'

"Smashing up all the ships."

"That's right. And there are soldiers on animals with fire-breathing lions' heads and a red, seven-headed dragon."

"You wouldn't want to run into one of them on a dark night."

"Specially not on the Day of Judgment," said Mullarky.

"Do you believe in all that?" I asked.

"Course I do," said Mullarky. "I was brought up a Catholic. Original sin and all that."

Finally, I went to the left side of the triptych, and immediately it reminded me of why the police had been keen to interview me a couple of days before.

"This one's grisly," I said.

"John the Baptist," said Mullarky. "Decapitated by Salome. That's his head on the plate. You know the story?"

"Refresh my memory," I said.

"Salome is one of the Bible's most notorious femmes fatales, though to me she sounds more like a spoiled brat," said Mullarky. "She was the step-daughter of King Herod, and her mum had a grudge against John the Baptist for saying her marriage to Herod was unlawful."

"Didn't Salome do some kind of sexy dance in front of Herod?"

"Yes, on his birthday, which makes him sound like a dirty old man, if you ask me. Then, as a reward, he told her she could have anything she wanted. Presumably, he thought she'd go for jewels, or the biblical equivalent of an iPod."

"But instead she asked for John the Baptist's head?"

"Apparently, she went to her mother, and mum suggested she ask for it."

"I take it Herod wasn't keen?"

"I imagine he thought it might stir up trouble with John the

Baptist's fans, whoever they were. But Herod gave Salome what she wanted, and there is the end result. Head on plate."

"Hmm," I said. "You know what? It reminds me of a murder in London this week. That guy had his head cut off too. And his name was Jack, which means he was probably christened John."

"So maybe the police should be looking for his personal Salome."

"Yes," I said. "I hope you don't mind my asking, Des, but does the name Olga Molotovski mean anything to you?"

"Nah," he said. "Can't say that it does."

"The daughter of Igor Molotovski?"

"Sorry, mate," he said. "Not my world."

My mind was racing. We knew from Fairycakes that Olga wasn't exclusively lesbian. O'Riordan was a good-looking guy. Could he have rejected Olga's advances, with fatal consequences? But would any modern girl seriously respond to a gay man saying he wouldn't go to bed with her, by cutting his head off?

"What was the dead bloke's name?" asked Mullarky.

"Jack O'Riordan," I said. "He was a photographer."

"Oh yeah, it was all over the papers," said Mullarky. "A pillow-biter, wasn't he? It was probably one of his boyfriends done him in."

"Could be," I said. "Or maybe a woman whose advances he'd rejected."

"Or someone trying to rid the world of poofs," said Mullarky. "When I read about it, it reminded me of that movie."

"What movie?"

"The one about the serial killer."

"*Silence of the Lambs*?"

"Nah, not that one. What was it called?" mused Mullarky. "It starred that wog actor."

"Will Smith? Denzel Washington?"

"No. Older. Uglier. Morgan Freeman. And Brad Pitt. And that stupid veggie actress married to that singer who does all that moaning in the world's most boring band. Ends up with her head in a box."

"Gwyneth Paltrow?"

"Yeah," he said. "*Seven*, that was the title. About this serial killer who kept bumping people off. Like he wanted to rid the world of corruption."

"I think he wanted to punish the seven deadly sins," I said. "It's funny you should say that, because it's just inspired a very successful computer game."

"Not my area," said Mullarky. "I can't be doing with them things. Far too much gratuitous violence. Mind you, there are plenty of sinners who would be well worth taking out, if you felt so inclined. Personally, I'd start with Gordon Brown, for screwing up the British economy. Bloody poof."

I made a few calls on my way back to London, starting with Lorenzo Fettucini.

"Lorenzo," I said.

"Who is this?" asked Fettucini. "How you get my number?"

"It's Charlie Charlesworth," I said. "I'm on the train back to London from Bruges."

"Who is this Bruges?"

"Bruges is a city in Belgium."

"What you doing there?"

"I feel as if I've been living out a chapter in *The Da Vinci Code*."

"What?"

"Never mind," I said. "I've been chatting to Mad Monkey Mullarky."

"Who?" he replied.

"The man you told me was threatening you."

"No, I no say that."

"And he says he hasn't threatened you."

"I never say he did."

"You certainly implied that he did, which is why I went to see him. All the way to Belgium."

"Where are you now?"

"On a train back to St Pancras."

"That was wasted journey," said Fettucini. " I know nothing about this."

"Lorenzo," I said, "Is there something you're not telling me?"

"I don't know what you're talking about," he said. "You don't bother me no more, okay?"

"Lorenzo," I said, "I'm not sure you realise what kind of trouble you're in."

"Sorry," he said. "I no understand English so good. Bye bye."

Shortly afterwards, as I was still pondering what precisely Lorenzo was up to, my phone rang.

"Hold on to your hat," said Tom.

"I'm not wearing a hat," I said.

"Hair, then. Someone did get into your computer. There's stuff on it which… well, you don't want to see. And you definitely don't want anyone else to see."

"Oh," I said. "I see."

"So what do you want to do?" asked Tom.

"Can you delete it?" I asked.

"I can, but I don't think that's going to do the trick," he said. "The police might be able to undelete it, like I was able to undelete Olga's files."

"So what should we do?"

"I have a feeling we may have to move fast. If you're being set up, like Slope said he was, the safest thing would be to trash the whole computer and report it as having been nicked, at the same time as your credit card was stolen."

I thought for a few moments.

"Can you trash it for me?" I asked. "But keep a copy of all our business files. That's everything in Word and Excel."

"Consider it done."

"Oh – and my Football Manager files."

"I was afraid you'd say that."

"And can you give me Slope's number?"

"What for?"

"We never did find out who he thought framed him."

"I'm not sure he knows. Anyway, you know how paranoid he is. He's never going to tell you over the phone."

"Maybe we can meet up. We need to talk to him."

"I'll text you his number," said Tom. "But he doesn't always answer his mobile. You'll have to leave a message, and see if he calls you back."

"That's okay," I said.

But when I did call Slope, he answered immediately. He sounded breathless, and there was a lot of noise in the background.

"Hello? Is that Bill Slope?"

"Who's that?"

"Charlie. Charlie Charlesworth."

"It's not a good time, mate."

"Where are you? I can't hear very well. Are you in East Creake?"

"More like Shit Creek, mate," said Slope.

"What's the matter?"

"My house is burning down."

"Are the fire brigade there?"

"Yeah, but they're too late. The fire's taken hold. The only thing I've managed to save is my car and my laptop. Everything else is gone."

"Was it arson?"

"Looks like it."

"Do you think it's connected with the piece in the *EDP*?"

"Looks like it."

"What do you mean?"

"Over the last twenty-four hours, I've had hate mail, bricks through the window. This looks like the ultimate measure to run me out of town. Or rather village."

"I'm sorry to hear that," I said. "I just wanted to let you know that I've been set up in the same way as you were. You know, over, how can I describe them, illegal downloads."

There was a lengthy pause.

"Look," said Slope, "we can't talk about this over the phone. Have you got a place I could crash for a few days?"

"Not at home," I said. "Our spare room is full of junk."

"How about your office?"

"I suppose there's the conference room."

"Perfect," said Slope.

"There's no bed."

"I can sleep on the floor," said Slope. "I used to be in the army. I'll get a sleeping bag. No worries."

I gave him the address of the office, and asked what time he would be getting down to London.

"I've got a few things to sort out overnight, so I'll stay in a motel. I could get down to London by midday tomorrow. It's Sunday, so with any luck there won't be too many people around. I need somewhere I won't be found by… you know, my enemies."

Only a few days ago, I'd have thought Slope was being needlessly paranoid. Now, I wasn't so sure.

"Okay. Noon. I'll meet you at the office and let you in."

"Right. And we'll have a chat," said Slope. "I'm still not sure you fully realise what you've got yourself into."

"I'm not sure I do either."

"You sound a bit funny," said Slope. "Are you on a train?"

"Yes. I've been to Bruges for the day."

"Work, or pleasure?"

"Work. I've been talking to someone who seems to know you. Or know of you. Desmond Mullarky."

There was another long silence.

"Look, I've got to go," said Slope. "The roof just fell in. Literally. See you tomorrow. And don't be surprised if you get an early-morning visit from the police."

17

UNDER CAPRICORN

Saturday, 6th August

They were waiting for me as I got off the train. I didn't know who
they were, but I knew at once the sort of person they were. Both
appeared to be Asian in origin. One was the Muscle, around six
foot five with no neck, the kind of person who gets employed for
protection by rock stars. He had the kind of nose which suggested
that football was probably not his sport. Boxing, more likely, or
Rugby.

The other was the Brains. That's not to say he was Albert
Einstein or even Stephen Fry, but unlike his mate he did not
appear to be educationally sub-normal. He was small and wiry, a
weasel of a man. Shifty eyes and sticky-up hair. Looked as if he
carried a knife. And knew how to use it.

It was Brains who did the speaking.

"You're Charlie Charlesworth," he said, unimaginatively.

"Indeed I am," I replied.

"We'd like you to come with us," he said.

"And if I said I didn't want to?"

"I wouldn't advise that."

"And where do you want to take me?"

"It's not far," said Brains.

"Does your friend speak?" I asked.

"Not much," said Brains.

"But he still has vocal chords," I said.

"I've never checked," said Brains.

"He must be a boring companion," I said.

"I make my own amusement," said Brains.

"How do you do that?" I asked.

"I persuade people," he replied, "to do as I say."

He attempted a smile, which came across as more of a sneer.

"You have a car?" I asked.

"Sure."

Another Asian gentleman, in a chauffeur's outfit complete with cap, was waiting outside the station on a double yellow line. The car was a black Mercedes. There was no sign of a traffic warden. Presumably if there had been one, he or she had either decided to move on or was in the boot, dying of stab wounds.

The Muscle opened the door for me.

"How kind," I said.

Brains shoved me from behind.

"In," he said.

The journey did not last long. I was vaguely relieved that no one put a bag over my head, though my attempts to make conversation resulted in stony silence. We ended up on the north side of Hampstead Heath, in Bishop's Avenue. Electric gates whirred open. We alighted from the car, in front of several million pounds worth of prime real estate.

"Nice place you have here," I said to the Muscle.

"Wait," said the Brains.

The front door opened, and a prosperous gentleman came out, beaming. He, too, was Asian.

"I am so glad you could join me," he smiled.

"Lovely house," I said.

"Yes," he said. "I am most fortunate. Lady Luck has smiled upon me. Please."

He ushered me into a luxurious living room. His taste in interior design is probably best described as colour-blind Saddam Hussein. A spectacularly horrible picture of my host was over the mantelpiece, smiling down benevolently in a three-piece suit.

"Very baronial," I said.

"You will sit down," he said. "Please."

I sat and looked around me. There were numerous statues of goats. Some were gold. Others were silver. Others reflected my host's dominant predilection for marble and onyx.

"You seem fond of goats," I said.

"I am," he said. "That is because I was born under Capricorn. It is the most aspirational sign in the Zodiac. I deplore hardship and failure. What sign are you?"

"Aries," I said.

"Ah yes," he said. "Impulsive and risk-taking. I do not care to take risks. I prefer to, as it were, load the dice of destiny so they fall in my favour."

He turned to Muscle.

"Cigar me," he said.

Muscle hurried to a cigar boss, cut the end off a cigar and handed it to his boss.

"Light!"

Muscle fumbled inside his trouser pocket and took out a very small gun. For a moment, I thought he was about to shoot his employer. But when he pulled the trigger, there was the familiar clicking of a cigarette lighter refusing to work. Muscle carried on clicking, while Brains brought over a box of matches from the fireplace and lit his boss's cigar.

"Thank you," said his boss, before cuffing Muscle round the head.

The bigger of the two goons seemed to accept his punishment and backed away, bowing. I decided to make polite conversation.

"I see you like people to do as you say."

"You are correct," he said. "Some might see that as a weakness, but I regard it as a necessary strength, especially in my line of work."

"And that is?"

"I am so sorry. Most rude of me. Allow me to introduce myself," he said, puffing on his cigar. "I am Chin Sun Fong. You have already met my assistants. Their names are unimportant."

"Have you brought me here to threaten me?" I asked.

"Why would I do that?" asked Mr Fong. "I am a respected businessman."

"In what field is that?"

"In the area of leisure," he said. "I come originally from South Korea."

"Oh yes?" I asked.

"Yes," he said. "I am a footballer's agent."

"And will I have heard of the footballers you represent?"

"Undoubtedly you will have heard of some of them," he said, "but not all."

"Do any of them play in the Premiership?"

"Indeed they do," he said. "But I am concerned with more than the Premiership. My clients play in many countries. Turkey, South Korea of course."

"Isn't there a scandal about South Korean football at present?"

"Yes," he said. "It is most regrettable. Prosecutors have accused a handful of players of taking bribes."

"Aren't there around 50 of them?" I asked.

"I would not know the exact figures," he said. "Perhaps 46."

"46 is one hell of a handful."

"I do not think anything has yet been proved," he said.

212

He made a dismissive gesture, as though he wished the conversation to move on.

"As for Turkish football," I said, "haven't scores of people just been arrested there for corruption? And didn't the authorities there postpone the Turkish Super Cup final between Fenerbahce and Besiktas because both teams were implicated in match-fixing?"

"You seem extraordinarily well informed," he said.

"I read the sports pages."

"You should not believe everything you read in the British press. I also have footballing interests in Thailand and Malaysia"

"I read something about that, too," I said. "Didn't the captain of the Zimbabwe national team and four of his team mates admit taking bribes to lose matches on a tour to Thailand and Malaysia in 2009?"

"Did they?" he asked. "I really don't recall."

"Yes," he said. "The players were paid quite a lot of money to lose 3-0 to Thailand and 6-0 to... Syria, I think it was."

"How extraordinary," said Mr Fong. "But I daresay FIFA are looking into it, under my old friend Sepp Blatter. I myself have advised the FIFA Ethics Committee, on a formal and informal basis."

"You like Sepp Blatter?" I asked.

"I do," replied Mr Fong. "He is much misrepresented in the infamous British newspapers."

"Really?"

"Very much so."

"So there's no truth in the allegations that he's guilty of corruption, theft and fiddling his expenses to keep his mistresses in the lap of luxury?"

"There is not a shred of evidence that has ever found any backing on the FIFA Ethics Committee."

"No," I said. "Funny that."

"A man in his position is entitled to expect a luxurious lifestyle."

"Well, you're obviously doing well too," I said. "Houses like this can't come cheap."

"This is merely one of several houses that I own," said Mr Fong, "but it pleases me that you admire it."

"So what precisely do you want of me?" I asked. "I'm afraid you're out of luck if you need my professional services. I'm a bit over-committed right now."

"No, no," he said. "I do not require your services. All that I require of you is that you do not bother my clients."

"Such as?"

"I think you know the one I mean."

"Would one of your clients, by any chance, be Lorenzo Fettucini?"

"I do have the good fortune to represent him, yes."

"And he asked you to meet me off the train and threaten me?"

"I never threaten people," said Mr Fong. "But I find that people aware of their best interests tend to accept my guidance as to their future behaviour."

"I expect they do," I said. "But I'm not sure why Lorenzo called you in. All I'm trying to do is help him."

"Perhaps he feels that he has no need of your assistance."

"And perhaps he's wrong."

"Why do you say that?"

I pondered a moment. I considered whether to tell Mr Fong that if Lorenzo didn't start scoring goals for his new club, he ran a considerable danger of being murdered for his own insurance value. But I decided that telling the truth might just land me in more trouble.

"I don't know," I said. "My only concern was to help him start scoring goals again."

"I am sure he is touched by your concern," said Mr Fong. "I take it you are a fan of Southern Athletic."

"Not really," I said. "I'm more of an Arsenal supporter."

"Ah," sighed Mr Fong. "You have my sympathy."

"Thanks. But I think I understand what you're telling me."

He glared at me, before remembering to give me the benefit of a mirthless smile.

"Excellent," he said. "I very much hope that you do."

"So am I free to go?"

"Of course you are," said Mr Fong. "It has been a pleasure to meet you. There is just one condition."

"And what's that?"

"You must agree never to make contact with my client again."

"You're talking about Fettucini?"

"That is the client I mean."

"And if I refuse?"

"That would be most unfortunate," said Mr Fong, "and I feel instinctively that you are a sensible man, despite your enthusiasm for the Arsenal. I hope you will allow my chauffeur to drive you home."

"That's most kind of you," I said.

"It is," said Mr Fong, beaming. "And there is no need for you to tell him your address."

He beamed that mirthless beam at me again, before adding:

"We know exactly where you live."

It didn't improve my humour to get home and discover that someone had spray-painted "MERDURER" across my front door. It was either in blood, or very red paint.

When I unlocked the door, Tom was waiting for me. He had a paint pot in his hand.

"Why didn't you warn me?' I asked.

"I've only just got home myself," said Tom.

"Any idea who might have done it?"

"It would appear to have been written by a dyslexic," he said.

"Who do you think we're meant to have murdered?"

"Not sure. I imagine it's either O'Riordan or Parente."

"What's that you've got?" I asked him.

"Grey paint," he said. "As soon as I've located a paintbrush, I'm going to paint over it. I don't want to alarm the neighbours. They might think there's something in it."

"Good idea," I said. "It'll dry overnight. Tomorrow, that door will be as good as new."

18

THE WRONG MAN

Sunday, 7th August

The next morning, the roof fell in. Or, should I say, the door.

It's not every day you're raided by the boys in blue and accused of being a paedophile. On the whole, I wouldn't recommend it. Even if you're innocent, it's not relaxing, and the plod, even when they're being polite, tend to leave a mess. It's just as well I saw them coming, or I could have been in a nasty predicament. Not to mention prison. And being a convicted child sex offender in chokey is no picnic, or so I understand.

It was about 5 a.m. on a fine Sunday morn when the police broke down my front door in Islington. For security reasons, I don't plan on being too specific about where I live. Suffice it to say that when the wind's in the right direction, you can hear the groans of the Arsenal supporters as they watch the Gunners throw away a two-goal lead against Tottenham.

I was on my way downstairs to see what all the banging was about, when the door came off its hinges and half a dozen of

London's finest poured in. They looked young and incredibly nervous, as if I might be Mr Big about to mow them down with a tommy gun. In an American cop series, they'd have been carrying shooters but, this being England, they had their truncheons out, which struck me as comical.

The only one not brandishing a copper's knob was a woman. She was tall, tidy and not in uniform, which I presumed meant she was the bloke in charge. So it was her that I addressed.

"Good morning," I said. "I was just on my way down to let you in."

The woman spoke.

"Are you Alan John Daniel Charlesworth?" she asked.

"I am," I said. "And who, might I ask, are you?"

"I am Detective Inspector Carol Smith," she said, flashing her badge.

"And I," said the man beside her, "am Sergeant Karp."

"Like the fish?" I asked.

"With a K," he said.

"Unusual," I said.

"Not in my family," he said.

I couldn't help flinching as the remains of my front door collapsed. The dust made my eyes itch. I felt a teeny bit tetchy, so I decided to give them both barrels of my lethal sarcasm.

"I take it this is not a social call," I said.

"No, Mr Charlesworth," said the detective inspector. "We are here on behalf of Child Abuse Investigation Command."

"Ah," I said, trying to look as if I knew what that was. "In that case, you've got the wrong man. I haven't abused a child for ages – unless you count calling my son a lazy sod, and he's 20 and I doubt very much if he's lodged a formal complaint, because he *is* a lazy sod at times."

DI Smith appeared not to have much of a sense of humour. She didn't crack a smile. Sergeant Karp looked as if he was sucking a prune.

"We have a warrant to search these premises," she said, producing a piece of paper, which certainly looked official.

"I should hope you have," I said. "An Englishman's home is his castle, or so they keep assuring us in Her Majesty's press, and I wouldn't like to think you do this kind of thing without a warrant."

"Other members of our department are simultaneously searching your offices in Soho Square."

"Feel free," I said. "I've nothing to hide. I'm on your side of the law. A private investigator."

I got the impression she knew this already. She didn't seem impressed.

"May we see your personal computer?" she asked.

"No, I'm afraid you can't," I said.

"We are authorised to take it away," she said coldly.

"I have no doubt you are," I said, "but you'll have to find it first. And if you can do that, you're a better man than I am."

"What do you mean?" she asked.

"I mean it's been pinched," I said. "It's a laptop. Apple. Less than a year old. Still under guarantee. Disappeared yesterday. A significant nuisance. It's just as well I have a backup of my important records."

"In that case, I would like to see that backup. Where do you have it? Here or at the office?"

"Here," I said. "But if you're going to take it away with you, may I take a back-up of my backup?"

The Detective Inspector looked across at Sergeant Karp, who I imagine was her technical advisor on all things computerised, and he nodded.

"If you have an empty disc drive," she said, "we would find that acceptable. But we'll have to examine it first, to make sure you're not trying to erase anything."

"No skin off my nose," I said. "It's not as if I'm an executive at News International. My emails are an open book."

"We also need to see your credit cards," she said. "And credit card statements."

"No problem. Anything else?"

"We are authorised to make a thorough search of your premises," she said.

"Looking for anything in particular?" I said. "I might be able to point you in the right direction."

"I don't suppose you have any pornography?" she said, with – I thought – a trace of unwarranted sarcasm.

I considered.

"I might have a very old copy of *The Joy of Sex*, but I'm not sure where it's got to. I think my ex-wife may have it."

Just then, my son came down the stairs, yawning and scratching his head, as though hoping this might reactivate his brain.

"What's all the noise about?" he asked.

"It's the constabulary," I said, somewhat unnecessarily as the hall was full of them. "They've decided to pay us a visit."

"Oh, hello, officers," he said. "Blimey, look at that door. What have you done now, Dad?"

"I'm not entirely sure, son," I said, "but they seem to think it involves child pornography. You haven't been downloading any, have you?"

"Oh, um, let me think," he said. "Can't say that I have."

"A simple yes or no would suffice," said DI Smith.

"In that case, no," said Tom, yawning. "Of course not."

"It is a pity about that door," I said, observing its shattered remains. "I was getting quite fond of it."

"Never mind, Dad," said Tom. "It could have been a whole lot worse."

"How's that?"

"If this had happened a week or two ago," he said, "I expect one or more of these guys would have tipped off a tabloid, in return for a little something."

"Surely not?" I said. "Wouldn't that be against the law? I take your point, though. Ex-England footballer accused of paedophilia. I can see the headlines now."

"But now," said Tom, "with the untimely demise of the *News of the World*, there must be a better than even-money chance of keeping this out of the papers."

"Not to mention the Prime Minister ordering an inquiry into illegal transactions between police and press," I said. "I do hope you're right."

I couldn't help noticing that two of the policeman were smirking and glancing sideways at Sergeant Karp. Following their eye line, I saw him pulling down one of his cuffs.

"That's a very enviable watch you have there, sergeant," I said. "I only wish I could afford one like that."

"You're right, Dad," said Tom. "That's a gold Oyster Rolex."

"Blimey," I said. "Police pay must be on the up. How much does one of those go for?"

"I saw one on the net for over twenty grand," said Tom.

"It's a copy," mumbled Karp, pushing past.

He looked flushed and embarrassed, so I decided not to pursue the point. I noticed one of the junior coppers stifling a laugh, but neither Karp nor his boss seemed in the mood for banter, which was fair enough. After all, as far as they were concerned, I was a sex criminal. I made a snap decision that now might not be the best moment to ask how to get compensation for a new front door.

Over the next hour or so, they turned the whole place over with a significant lack of finesse, and went away with boxes of stuff, none of it even slightly relevant to what they were looking for. Tom had to hand over his laptop, and me my backup disc drive. But he and I knew what the police were really looking for, and they were never going to find that.

The reason was simple. Tom had destroyed it all the day before.

19

TO CATCH A THIEF

Sunday, 7th August

At noon on Sunday, not so long after our close encounter with the paedo-hunting rozzers, Tom and I met up with Bill Slope outside our offices in Soho Square. He took his belongings up to the conference room, and Tom showed him the bathroom and tiny kitchen facilities. The police hadn't left much trace of their intrusion. A few folders needed putting back into filing cabinets. Nothing that couldn't wait until Monday morning. I took Bill Slope into the conference room and was about to tell him he could sleep on the couch, when he put one hand to his lips. Then he spoke.

"Nice of you to show me round," he said. "It's a shame I won't be staying."

"Sorry?" I said.

He took a grey metal cube out of his holdall, and plugged some headphones into it. He turned it on, and it emitted a red glow.

"What's that?" asked Tom, entering the conference room.

Again, Bill Slope raised a finger to his lips.

He began moving slowly round the room, aiming his device at every corner. Evidently he heard something significant over his headphones, because he made for the centre of the room and looked up. Then he climbed onto the conference table, reached up to the light fitting and disengaged something. At first it looked like a dead spider, but when he put it in my hand I saw it was a small camera with an even tinier microphone.

Slope signalled that he wanted to go next door into my office and I nodded.

Slope repeated the process in every room, and we accumulated three bugging devices, from the conference room, my study and Tom's little room at the back. Only when Slope had swept the offices again did he condescend to speak.

"And the moral of that is," he said, "don't let the buggers grind you down."

"How did they get there?" asked Tom.

"We haven't had any break-ins," I said.

"No break-ins that you know of," Slope corrected me. "Whoever installed these was a pro. I'll check out your phones later. It wouldn't surprise me if they've been bugged as well."

"What is that thing?" I asked, pointing to his metal cube.

"That?" he said. "It's a dual mode wideband RF and GSM/3G detector. It takes handheld counter-measures to a whole new level."

"I thought everything you had got lost in the fire."

"Not this little beauty," he said. "I keep it in the boot of my car. You never know when you're going to need it."

"Bill," I said. "What the hell have we got ourselves into?"

"Yeah, I've been wondering that," he said. "I suggest we continue this conversation outside. Is there anywhere it's good to eat round here? I didn't have any breakfast."

"Not that I know of," said Tom. "It's a bit early, and there's not many places open on a Sunday."

"Okay, I'll cook something up for us," said Bill.

"I don't think we've anything to cook on," I said.

"That's okay," said Bill. "I've got a portable hob in the car. And we can get our ingredients in the square."

"Soho Square?" asked Tom. "It's not exactly chock-a-block with goodies."

"You'd be surprised," said Bill. "When you've been broke and out of work as many times as I have, you get a nose for foraging."

"This isn't Norfolk," I pointed out.

"I know," said Bill. "But it's warmer here in London, so plants develop earlier. All we're gonna need are scissors and a plastic bag."

"I think we've got those," said Tom.

He rummaged around in Marti's reception desk and brought out a pair of nail scissors.

"They're a bit smaller than I had in mind," said Bill. "But I guess they'll do. I've got a penknife if we need something more substantial."

"And here are some plastic bags," I said. "There were a couple of bags in my desk, originally from Foyles, the bookshop round the corner."

Bill Slope looked these over with satisfaction.

"They'll do fine," he said. "Follow me outside, and I'll give you an education. Suppose you bring me up to speed on what's been happening at this end."

So Tom and I told him about the police raid, the graffiti on the front door and my being menaced by a South Korean football agent.

"No worries," said Slope. "In fact, this is all starting to get a bit tasty. Taste that."

He passed me a blackberry. I bit into it. Even though it was early for blackberries, this one had ripened during the warm summer, and it was delicious, hitting my tongue with a tangy freshness.

"Did you know there are 375 kinds of blackberry?" asked Bill.

"No idea," I said.

"Is it all right to pick them?" asked Tom.

"Sure," said Bill. "Anyway, who's here to stop us?"

He had a point. Soho Square, normally full of cars and people, was weirdly deserted on a Sunday. In fact, we had the middle of the square to ourselves, something I had never experienced before.

"At least we can't be overheard out here," I said.

"Don't you believe it," said Bill. "There's such a thing as lipreading, and there are around five million surveillance cameras in Britain. There are 16,000 spy cameras on the underground alone."

"Well, at least that will give terrorists something to think about," said Tom.

"I'll give you something to think about," said Bill. "That there are people in positions of responsibility who think *1984* was an instruction manual."

I looked around the square. Even at a cursory glance, there were half a dozen cameras that might conceivably be trained on us.

"A good job we don't live in a police state," I said.

"You don't think so?" asked Bill. "It might still be a good idea if we keep our heads down when we talk. As you may have noticed, most of the cameras are up high so they won't be noticed."

"Yes, I've seen six," I said.

"I've seen twelve," said Bill. "But then I've been at this longer than you have."

Weirdly, I started to feel I could put my trust in this ramshackle old man. Nothing seemed to upset him – not even the burning down of his home. And here I was, jittery over just about everything. Bugging devices, surveillance cameras, being framed for paedophilia.

"Look, Bill," I said. "I'm sorry we don't run to a bed in the office, but there's always the couch."

"No problem," said Slope. "That'll do nicely. I've a new sleeping bag in the car. It's good of you to put me up."

"Any idea how long you'll be staying?" asked Tom.

"Just until I'm back on my feet," said Slope. "In the meantime, I'm ready to cook us lunch, and sing for my supper. I think I might be able to help you."

Tom glanced across at me. I could tell from his expression that he still regarded Bill Slope with a good deal of distrust. But I could see the old guy needed a lifeline, and Tom and I could do with all the help we could get.

"Look over here," said Bill. "See what I see?"

"I see nettles," said Tom. "It's just a bit of waste ground."

"Precisely," said Bill. "Nettles are the staple diet of any forager. You see them the whole year round."

"I know you can make nettle soup," I said dubiously. "I've never had it, though."

"They can be used to make soup, tea, beer and even haggis. Do you know, they contain more vitamin C than oranges?"

"Don't they sting your mouth?" asked Tom.

"Not when you've boiled them," said Tom. "The main thing to remember is: only harvest the youngest leaves. The old ones could give you kidney failure."

"This is proving quite educational," I said.

"Yeah," said Bill. "I used to take my son out foraging when he was young. Happy days."

"What about these?" I asked, pointing to a small tree with white flowers.

"Are they edible?"

"Sure," said Bill. "They're elderflowers. You can eat them raw, cooked, dried or powdered. You can even turn them into elderflower champagne. Don't eat the leaves or the stems, though. They're poisonous."

"Why's the square so deserted?" asked Tom. "Is it always like this on a Sunday? I haven't even heard a police siren."

"That's because no one is rioting here," said Bill. "I take it you've heard what happened in Tottenham last night?"

"No," I said. "What with being raided by the police, I didn't get a chance to read the papers."

"You should," said Slope. "Tottenham's practically next door to Islington. There's been a riot."

"They've decided to sell Luka Modric, then?" I said flippantly.

"No, mate," he said. "It's more serious than that. It started off as a protest about some bloke being shot dead by the police. Then it escalated into full-scale mayhem. Not sure why. Doesn't sound as though the fuzz did a lot to stop it."

"Maybe they were too busy planning how to knock down my front door," I said.

"Is that what happened to you, Mr Slope?" asked Tom.

"Call me Bill," said Slope. "No, they didn't need to break down my front door. My wife let them in."

"I imagine she got quite a shock," I said.

"She wasn't impressed," he said.

"Apart from that, though," said Tom. "Do you think the same people could be trying to disgrace dad as went for you?"

"It looks like it," he said. "It's déjà vu all over again."

"Do you think the police are watching us now?" I asked.

"I imagine they've got other things on their mind," he said. "And you're sure you didn't leave anything incriminating on your hard drives?"

Tom nodded.

"Sure," he said.

"Come over here," said Bill. "Look at these little beauties."

"Aren't they dandelions?"

"The most edible flower in any garden," said Bill, "and available throughout the year."

"They don't look very appetising," I said.

"Appearances can be deceptive," said Bill. "You can eat the whole plant. The leaves can be eaten in sandwiches, salads and even pies. You can put the flowers to use in an omelette or risotto."

"Can't you make dandelion tea?" asked Tom. "Or is that only in Japan?"

"No, mate, you're thinking of chrysanthemum tea. But you can make dandelion coffee. It's totally caffeine free and tastes a bit like chocolate."

He pulled up a dandelion and inspected it.

"Even the roots come in handy. They can be chucked into stir-fries or added to vegetable dishes."

"What about these?" I said, pointing to some mushrooms. "Are they mushrooms or toadstools? I never like to pick them in case they're poisonous."

"I'm amazed they're still here," said Bill. "There are so many restaurants here in Soho, you'd think they'd have been snapped up the moment they appeared."

"So they're harmless?" asked Tom.

"Delicious," said Bill. "They're chanterelles. You mostly find them in woodland, but they can be found under trees anywhere. Try one."

I took one out of his hand. It had a peppery taste and smelt mildly of fruit.

"Can you smell the apricots?" he asked.

I nodded.

"Amazing," I said. "How do you cook them?

"You just cook 'em in a bit of oil or butter and add to pasta. Or you soak them in vodka. They make for a very tasty liqueur."

We had a delicious lunch.

"That meal was a real eye-opener," I said.

"Glad to be of service," said Bill. "Now let's crack the case."

"Is it safe to talk in here?" I asked.

Bill looked around the conference room, then at the broken bugging devices on the table.

"It is now," he said.

"By the way, on the housekeeping front," I said, "we'll warn Marti you're staying overnight, so you don't surprise her in the morning."

"Marti's what? Your cleaner?" asked Slope.

"Our receptionist," I said.

"And Marti's a Sheila?"

"Yes," said Tom. "She spells it with an I."

"Course she does," said Slope. "You bloody Londoners. What time in the morning do you two get in?"

"It varies," I said. "We try to be in by nine, unless we've been up late on a case. Marti's always in around then, in case anyone wants to contact us."

"Sounds good to me," said Slope. "I'll make sure I have my strides on by the time she gets here. Wouldn't want to give Marti a nasty shock."

"Okay," said Tom. "It's been very interesting, all this foraging, but it doesn't have anything to do with our problems."

"You really think that?" asked Bill. "The thing about foraging is that it makes you look at things – even quite familiar things – in a completely different way. Which is precisely what you need to do as an investigative reporter or, indeed, a private investigator."

"You think we've been looking at things the wrong way?"

"I dunno, mate," said Bill. "You tell me."

"To be honest, I'm confused," I said. "We've got all these things happening to us, and we're completely clueless."

"Yeah," said Bill, "I can see why you might find that upsetting."

"None of it makes any sense," said Tom.

"It's starting to make sense to me," said Bill.

"How do you mean?" I asked.

"I don't know about these two murders," said Bill. "If they are murders. The good news is that the police don't seem to think Charlie's in the frame for either of them. Is that right?"

"Frank Drake didn't seem to think I had the killer instinct," I agreed.

"So let's leave the murders on one side for a minute," Bill said. "The police are investigating, and they've presumably got access to stuff that we haven't. Right?"

"Right," said Tom.

"So it seems to me," continued Slope, "that you've got three other mysteries here, and we're pretty sure they must be inter-related, except we don't know how."

"Agreed," I said.

"And one mystery is the graffiti on your front door," said Bill.

"It's hardly the most important," said Tom. "It's not like dad being accused of being a paedophile."

"In a way it's worse," said Bill. "Someone thinks one of you two is a killer."

"But that's crazy," I said.

"Maybe," said Bill. "But try and look at it from their point of view. Who is it they think you've killed?"

"Jack O'Riordan?" suggested Tom.

"Or Loco Parente," I said.

"Right," said Bill. "Let's hold those two possibilities. What else do we know about this graffiti artist?"

"He or she can't spell," said Tom. "Which means they're thick," said Bill.

"Or foreign," I chipped in.

"Or dyslexic," said Tom. "I'm no good at spelling."

"Okay," said Bill. "So does anyone else spring to mind?"

Tom and I shook our heads. Then I remembered something. "I.P. Blood."

"I'm sorry to hear that," said Bill. "You should see a doctor."

"No, I'm not peeing blood," I explained. "I.P. Blood is a rapper. A friend of Fairycakes Parks. And he told us he's dyslexic."

"Actually, he said he was dyspeptic," Tom pointed out.

"Yes, but he meant dyslexic," I said.

"This is good," said Bill. "So what is Mr Blood's connection with the murders? Anything to do with O'Riordan or Parente?"

"Not directly," I said.

Tom shook his head too.

"Not that we know of," he confirmed. "He's just a friend of a friend of Olga."

"Okay," said Bill. "Let's leave Blood on the back-burner."

"Don't forget the main mystery for us," said Tom, "which is what we're being paid to follow up. It's where's Olga?"

"You know my views on that," said Bill. "If I had her parents, I'd run away too. But I hear what you're saying. After all, that is how you were dragged into this whole dodgy scenario."

"The trouble is we don't have any leads," I said.

"That's not altogether true, Dad," said Tom.

"What do you mean?" I asked.

"Remember what Fairycakes told us about Olga having an affair with De Mode?"

"You really think someone called Fairycakes is a reliable witness?" asked Bill.

Tom and I both shook our heads.

"But she's all we've got," said Tom.

"Yeah, worse luck," said Bill. "Okay, so let's assume the improbable, which is that she's telling the truth. In which case, you've got to keep watching De Mode."

"But it's hardly likely he's keeping our runaway heiress on the premises," said Tom.

"Exactly," I said. "His wife's living there, for heaven's sake."

"You're sure?" asked Bill.

"Yes," I said, "and Marion told me they've just redecorated."

"That can be a sign of a failing relationship," said Bill. "I speak from personal experience."

"One thing bugging me is why did Marion come to see me?"

I asked. "She said she saw me in the Yellow Pages. We're not in the Yellow Pages."

"A lot of people don't remember where they first heard things," said Bill. "Why do you think she came to see you?"

"She seemed anxious to save her marriage."

"Don't forget the woman's an actress," Bill said darkly. "Don't underestimate these Hollywood types."

"I can't believe it of her," I said. "She's so, I dunno, fragrant."

"I think my father's in love," said Tom.

"Rule number one in any investigation," said Bill. "Never get involved emotionally with clients."

"I hardly think someone like her is going to get emotionally involved with me," I said.

"I don't know," said Bill. "You're not bad looking, with the light behind you. And this De Mode sounds a nasty little shit."

"He is," said Tom.

"Okay," said Bill. "So the sensible thing is to keep De Mode under surveillance. If this Fairycakes is right and he's Olga's squeeze, there's got to be a chance he might lead us to her. Has young Tom here got time on his hands?"

"It would be difficult for him not to be noticed," I said. "De Mode's already threatened him with violence at a party."

"I hope you thumped him," said Bill Slope to Tom.

"Not really," said Tom. "But if he ever saw me again, I'm sure he'd recognise me."

"There's no problem, Bill," I said. "We've put my sister on to him."

"Is she reliable?" asked Bill.

"She's an ex-cop," I said.

"So?" said Bill. "Is she reliable?"

"She's okay," said Tom. "She's cool."

"I wish I was," said Bill. "This bloody weather. Now, let's turn to the third mystery, which is the one that's probably worrying Charlie here the most right now."

"The paedophile accusation," I said.

"Right," said Bill. "Have you any idea who might be trying to get you in trouble with the police?"

"Not really," I said.

"Hey," said Tom, "let's talk about the elephant in the room."

"What elephant?" I asked, looking around. "There's hardly room in here to swing a medium-sized cat."

"It's not literally an elephant, Dad. It's something big that's staring us in the face, and we haven't yet addressed," Tom turned to face Bill Slope. "Do you have any idea who set you up, Mr Slope? Whoever it is seems to have used exactly the same methods on dad here. It's hardly likely to be a coincidence."

"You're right," said Bill. "I was thinking about that on my way down in the car. The trouble is, I have too many enemies. Dozens. Scores. Even hundreds. Any one of them could have been out to get me."

"But I don't have many enemies," I said. "At least I don't think so."

"The question is, Mr Slope," said Tom, "are any of your enemies the same people who might be out to get dad?"

"Yeah, that's my thought too. There must be an overlap," said Bill. "Here we are in Soho Square. Maybe there's a FIFA connection."

"Bill," I said, "I haven't done anything to offend FIFA."

"Don't be too sure," he said. "From what you've been telling me, you might have made yourself some influential enemies."

"Who in particular?"

"One of the guys I was doing research into at the time of my untimely arrest was called Joseph Gildenstern. Have you ever come across him?"

"Recently," I said. "I had dinner with him only the other evening."

"Now that is interesting," said Bill. "Did you invite him, or did he invite you?"

233

"He invited me."

"With what end in view?"

"Well," I said. "It was with regard to Fettucini."

"The food or the footballer?"

"The footballer. He's not scoring for his club, and Gildenstern seemed to think that was suspicious."

"Really?" asked Bill. "Lots of strikers go through a goal drought."

"Not for this long," I said. "He told me Fettucini was trying not to score. And that's not normal. He asked me to look into it."

"What interest did Gildenstern have in this?" asked Bill.

"He told me he was asking me on behalf of Southern Athletic Football Club, and in particular its chairman, Bernhard Spritzer."

"Bernie Spritzer," Bill mused. "Hmm. So what, if anything, have you discovered?"

"I had an off-the-record conversation with Fettucini, and I got the impression he was being threatened."

"Who by?" asked Bill.

"Desmond "Mad Monkey" Mullarky," I said.

Bill nodded. He obviously knew the name.

"So I went to see Mullarky."

"Brave of you," said Bill. "I wouldn't want to get on the wrong side of Mad Monkey."

"He's retired from hooliganism, and living in Bruges."

"So you travelled all the way to Belgium?"

"I did. I wanted to see if Fettucini's theory stood up."

"And did it?"

"No," I said. "Mullarky seemed to have no interest in Fettucini. And then there was this curious chain of events."

"Oh?"

"On my way back to Britain, first Fettucini tried to get me off his case. Then I was threatened by his agent. This South Korean guy."

"Does Gildenstern know about this?" asked Bill.

"I haven't talked to him about it yet," I said.

"Still," said Bill. "Gildenstern approached you, and he's always up to something. Ruthless, too. He could be our guy."

"How did you come up against him, Mr Slope?" asked Tom.

"His name kept cropping up with regard to corruption."

"Do you mean match-fixing?" I asked. "I wouldn't have thought that was his scene."

"No, Gildenstern operates on a much grander scale. He doesn't fix games. He fixes tournaments. A lot of people said he was responsible for getting the 2006 World Cup played in Germany."

"I don't remember much about that," I said. "But weren't we one of the unsuccessful bidders?"

"Yeah. England came in third, behind Germany and South Africa. South Africa were the favourites, but Germany beat them by one vote after a very controversial abstention."

"I remember now," I said. "Wasn't that some bloke from New Zealand?"

"Yeah," said Bill. "His home football organisation instructed him to vote for South Africa, but on the day he was meant to vote he went AWOL."

"And if he had done as he'd been told, and voted for South Africa?"

"They would have won, and not Germany. The score would have been 12 all, giving the casting vote to the FIFA chairman."

"Blatter?" asked Tom.

"Yes," said Slope, "and Blatter had already voted for South Africa."

"So you think Gildenstern may have outwitted Blatter," I said.

"Or outbribed him," said Bill. "Of course, Blatter was furious, but what could he do? Admit the whole system was corrupt?"

"And did anyone solve the mystery of the vanishing kiwi?"

"Not really," replied Slope. "He's always refused to talk to me.

All he told the press was that the pressure had got to him. He said there'd been an attempt to bribe him, which he'd resisted. But he never would say who or what made him abstain."

"But," said Tom, "you think the guy behind it was Gildenstern."

"That's my educated guess. He's one of the biggest scoundrels on the FIFA Ethics Committee. And believe me, that's saying something."

"And you were exploring his activities when the police paid you a visit?" asked Tom.

"I was," said Bill.

"Well, that's progress," said Tom. "Let's put Gildenstern at the top of our list of suspects."

"I still don't get it," I said. "What can I have done to Gildenstern, to make him bug my premises?"

"Hang on a moment," said Bill. "When you had this dinner with him, you didn't by any chance tell him about your Russian runaway?"

I racked my brains.

"As it happens, I did. I showed him a picture of her."

"How did he react?"

"He pretended not to know her," I said. "But there was something about his body language that told me he did."

"And you confronted him about that?"

"No," I said. "But I might have given the impression that I didn't believe him. Without meaning to, obviously. But drink had been taken, and maybe my face gave something away."

"Stroll on, mate!" said Slope. "Well, there you are!"

He clapped his hands, as though applauding me.

"I'm not sure what you mean," I said. "Am I missing something?"

"Look, mate," Bill said, softly as though I was a very small boy who needed to be told the facts of life, "bribery takes many forms. Usually money, but not always. Sometimes, it takes the form of women, or boys, or girls. Underage girls."

"You think Gildenstern might have used Olga?"

"It wouldn't surprise me one little bit," said Bill. "I reckon Olga was brought up to work as a prostitute from a very early age. The vote for the 2006 World Cup took place in Zurich in July, 2000. Olga would have been six."

"The same year she joined Parente's modelling agency," said Tom.

"Which Bill thinks was a front for prostitution," I said.

Bill nodded.

"Especially child prostitution. If Gildenstern thinks you're on to him," said Slope, "there's no telling what he might do to you."

"Oh," I said.

"And it may be," said Bill, "that it's not only him who thinks you're on to them."

"You mean Loco Parente?" asked Tom.

"Among others," said Bill.

"Dad did make a visit to Loco Parente's modelling agency recently."

"Yes," I said. "I was trying to track down Olga. I showed him pictures of Olga, and he claimed he'd never met her before in his life. But he obviously had."

"Like Gildenstern?" asked Bill. "Did his body language give him away?"

"Yes," I said. "And I think he knew he'd given the game away."

"That must really have put the wind up him," said Bill.

"Why?" I asked.

"Look, he's a football fan. He must know you used to represent England, one of the unsuccessful countries that competed to host the 2006 World Cup."

"You mean he might reckon I'm working for the FA?"

"Or, worse, the British press," said Bill. "Thanks to these phone tapping scandals, everyone knows they use private investigators."

"Come to think of it, Parente did have me followed," I said.

"A guy from his office with green hair followed me back to where we are now."

"Exactly. Soho Square," said Bill. "And it's not only you who are based here, is it?"

"You're right," I said. "That's the FA headquarters, over in the south-eastern corner."

"But we don't work for the FA," objected Tom. "Never have done. It's just a coincidence we're in the same square."

"It's not me you have to convince," said Bill. "I'm not a crazy Brazilian kiddie-fiddler."

"And you know what?" said Tom. "That receptionist of his followed us to O'Riordan's house."

"Now we're cooking," Bill said, "Parente must have thought you were in league with Jack O'Riordan."

"Is that worse than working for the FA or a newspaper?" I asked.

"Sorry," said Bill. "I keep forgetting you're new to all this shit. How do you think O'Riordan made his money?"

"I dunno. The porn industry?" I suggested.

"Yeah, but not only that," said Bill. "The guy used to run a protection racket."

"How do you know that?" asked Tom.

"Never you mind," said Bill. "But my information is that Parente had to pay O'Riordan a retainer, to keep his mouth shut."

"So if he thought we were working for O'Riordan…" I said.

"That might have made him decide to silence O'Riordan, once and for all."

"And then Parente might have killed himself out of remorse?" I asked.

"Could be," said Bill.

"No, it couldn't," said Tom. "The police told us Parente died at eight or nine, while O'Riordan was murdered two or three hours later. The timing's back to front."

"Don't jump to conclusions," said Bill. "Parente might have

commissioned someone to kill O'Riordan, then had second thoughts. Maybe he thought Charlie was closing on him, or that the police were bound to find out, then decided to take the easy way out."

"It's possible," I said. "And maybe he took steps to disgrace me by having someone break into my office and download stuff on to my computer."

"Could be," said Bill.

"So maybe Jack O'Riordan's murderer is already dead," said Tom.

"It's possible," said Bill. "And so is the guy who tried to frame your father as a paedophile."

"Was Parente in your sights too?" I asked Bill. "You know, when the police raided you?"

"Too right he was," said Bill. "Olga had just told me what a sleazebag the guy was."

"So Parente might have seen you as a threat, and set you up as a paedophile?"

"It could have been him. Or it could have been Gildenstern. Both had an interest in silencing me."

"Okay," I said.

Tom had been quiet for a few moments, but now chimed in.

"Sorry, but I don't buy it. Don't forget Parente died only a few hours after dad went to visit him. Would he have had time to disgrace dad as a paedophile?"

"Good point," said Bill. "It could be that someone else killed Parente, but then thought he'd better silence Charlie here. Not by killing him, but by putting him away for a few years, or simply disgracing him."

"Such as who?" asked Tom. "Gildenstern?"

"He's the person who springs readily to my mind," said Bill. "But what about someone you haven't even mentioned yet. Igor Molotovski?"

"But he's employing us," I said.

"No he isn't, Dad," Tom reminded me. "It was his wife who employed us. Maybe he really didn't want us involved."

"He could have done more to dissuade us," I said.

"Maybe this paedophile rap is his way of dissuading you," said Bill. "It could have been his way of dissuading me."

"You think he might have behind that?" asked Tom.

"Maybe he knew that I had been talking to Olga," said Bill. "He certainly knew I was trying to dig up dirt about him."

"You mean, about allowing his own daughter to be used as a prostitute?" I said.

"Oh no, it's worse than that," said Bill. "You know who co-owns Parente's agency?"

I shook my head.

"Igor Molotovski," said Bill.

I shook my head. I was having trouble getting my head round this.

"You look confused," said Bill.

"My head's spinning," I said. "Where's Hercule Poirot when you need him?"

"Now you've lost me," said Bill.

"He's a Belgian detective," I said.

"Did you meet this guy in Bruges?" asked Bill.

"No, he's fictitious," I said. "Sorry, I digress. Okay, let's add Igor Molotovski to our list. Any more bright ideas on who might be out to get me?"

"Yeah, mate. I have," said Bill, "It could be that this has nothing to do with your missing heiress, or bribery over the World Cup. It might have something to do with match-fixing."

"I don't get it," I said. "I have no inside knowledge about match-fixing."

"No. But other people might *think* you have."

"You mean Fettucini?" asked Tom.

"Lorenzo's no match-fixer," I said.

"There's a lot you don't know about Fettucini," said Bill.

"Please don't try to convince me he's some kind of criminal mastermind," I said. "I simply won't believe it."

"No," said Bill. "But you mentioned you'd been talking to Des Mullarky. Did he tell you anything you didn't know?"

"He told me how many footballers get involved in gambling."

"I thought he might," said Bill. "That could be his special subject on Mastermind. Along with poofs, of course."

"I had no idea so many footballers gamble," I said. "But what's that got to do with me?"

"Let me explain," said Bill. "The thing is, gambling leaves a footballer open to corruption."

"How does that work?" asked Tom.

"Well, some footballers find it hard to pay up on their debts. It can be easier just to throw a match."

"But football's a team game," I said. "It can't be easy to lose a game on purpose."

"You'd be surprised," said Bill, "especially if more than one player's involved – or a goalie."

"Isn't Fettucini a striker?" said Tom.

"Yeah," said Bill. "But a lot of gambling these days isn't only on results. It's on the number of goals, the gap between the two sides. You must have seen the ads."

"I know the sort of thing," I said. "Ray Winstone coming on and shouting the odds on who's going to score next, how many corners, that kind of thing?"

"Exactly," said Bill. "And you can gamble across a number of games, not just one, and accumulate a very nice profit indeed."

"So where does Fettucini come in?" I asked.

"Think about it," said Bill. "One of the things you can bet on is how many games a striker can play for a team without scoring. In fact, I happen to know that someone did just that. They placed a lot of money, at extremely long odds."

"How do you know that?"

"I have contacts in the gambling world," said Bill.

"Like Mullarky?" I asked.

"I never reveal my sources," said Bill. "But they contact me when there's been a suspiciously large bet on some really unlikely event, which then just happens to occur."

"Does that happen a lot?" I asked.

"No," said Bill. "Not in this country. But in the far east and some countries in Europe…"

"Turkey?" I asked.

"That's one of them," he said. "And Italy."

"You think there's something fishy about Fettucini?" asked Tom.

"There were rumours about him when he was playing in Italy, and I'm told he's run up a lot of gambling debts while he's been in England."

"What do you mean?" asked Tom. "Surely Fettucini wouldn't risk his career to do that?"

"Your son's half right," Bill told me. "Not even Fettucini is dumb enough to lay a bet on himself not scoring for thirty matches, even if the odds were fifty to one. Which they were."

"But someone else might have done?" I asked.

"Exactly."

"Someone not a million miles from his own agent?" I hazarded. "I forget his name…"

"Chin Sun Fong," said Bill. "You're beginning to grasp the principle."

"And don't tell me you were on to Mr Fong as well," I said.

"I have been for years. He's behind more footballing scams than anyone, right across the world. He makes Sepp Blatter and the FIFA Executive Committee look like choirboys. But he's incredibly difficult to nail."

Tom chimed in again at this point.

"Mr Fong doesn't sound like the kind of person you want to make an enemy of."

"That, young fella," said Bill, "is an understatement. But one of Mr Fong's hallmarks is that he only gambles on certainties."

"So betting on Fettucini not scoring and then making sure he didn't dare to score would be right up his alley?"

"Classic Fong," said Bill.

"I don't know," I said, shaking my head. "Fong doesn't strike me as the kind of guy who'd go round bugging offices or framing me as a paedophile. Brute violence would be more his style."

"You have a point," said Bill.

"So have you got any more contenders?" asked Tom.

"How long have you got?" said Bill. "But from what you've been telling me, those have got to be the front-runners. I'm not convinced by this I.P. Blood character. And if it's Parente, our problems may already be over. The guy's dead, and the cops are on his case. For my money, it's more likely to be one out of Gildenstern, Molotovski or Fong."

"Okay," I said, "so how do we find out which of them it is?"

"Right now, my money's on Fong," said Bill. "But there's an old Aussie saying that if you're going to catch a croc, first you have to tempt it out of the water."

"And that means?" asked Tom.

"What do you think I was doing earlier?"

"De-bugging our offices," I said.

"Yeah, but not only that. I was laying bait."

"Sorry, I'm confused," I said.

"It's a safe assumption that it was one of these scumbags who bugged your office," said Bill. "And it's human nature that any bugger is going to be curious about why his devices aren't working any more."

"You think they'll break in again?" I asked.

"I wouldn't be surprised," said Bill. "But this time I'll be here, waiting for them."

"I can't let you do that," I said. "They might beat you up, or worse."

"Don't you worry about me," said Bill. "I can look after myself."

Once again, he put a finger to his lips. With his left hand, he took something out of his pocket.

"Shit," said Tom.

"Is that thing loaded?" I asked.

Bill Slope nodded and bared his teeth in a dangerous smile.

"It's my old service revolver," he said, "and I know how to use it."

20

THE TROUBLE WITH HARRY

Monday, 8th August

The next morning, Tom and I booked a minicab to the office, and got there just after nine thirty. We would have got there earlier, but we had to wait in for a carpenter, who told us our front door could be patched up for now, but needed to be replaced.

"Can you do it right now?" I asked.

"You mean patch it up?" he said.

"Or replace it."

"I've got a lot of work on," he said. "Didn't you hear? There was more of them riots last night. Enfield and Brixton."

"Better patch up the front door then," I said. "At this rate, it won't be long before Islington goes up in flames."

When we did get in, Marti was already at the office, and she had a weird expression on her face: flushed and excited.

"What's up with you?" I asked. "Has someone rung you up and asked you to be on *The X Factor*?"

"Ha ha," she said, mirthlessly. "You've got a visitor."

"Already?" I asked.

"He paid us a visit during the night," she said, mysteriously. "Mr Slope's been looking after him."

"Where?"

"In your office," said Marti.

And, sure enough, there in my office, bound to the guest chair with a length of thick rope, was an exceptionally bad-tempered visitor, with a black eye. I suppose you could describe him as a dwarf, but he wasn't the kind of merry soul you'd find in *Snow White*. Sitting in my chair, with his feet up on my desk, was Bill Slope. He had a smug expression.

"Morning, Bill," I said. "Who's our little friend?"

"One thing's for sure," said Tom. "He isn't Happy."

"Grumpy, more like," I agreed.

"Bollocks," said the dwarf.

"I've been through his pockets," said Bill, "and his name appears to be Harry Crouch."

"But, by the look of him, no relation of Peter Crouch," I said.

"Not the heading ability," agreed Tom, "and a much lower centre of gravity."

"Are you two some kind of failed comedy double act?" said the dwarf.

"He sounds American," said Bill.

"Canadian," said the dwarf.

"And chippy," I said.

"Charming," said the dwarf.

"I think it's the Prince who's called Charming," I said.

"Bollocks," said the dwarf.

"How did you find this jolly little chap?" Tom asked.

"In the middle of the night, I heard a noise from your office," said Bill, "and found Harry here, dangling by a rope, face down."

I looked up to the ceiling. A couple of the damaged tiles had been removed, just enough for a small person to be lowered through from the floor above.

"Kind of you to drop in," I said.

"I was lowered in," said the dwarf.

"Like Midget Impossible," said Tom.

"I am not a midget," said the dwarf. "And that is an offensive term."

"Sorry," said Tom. "What do you like being called?"

"He seems to like the name Bollocks," said Bill.

"I prefer to be called by my name," said the midget. "Your tame psycho is right. The name is Crouch, Harry Crouch."

"So what were you doing being lowered through our ceiling, Mr Crouch?" I asked.

"I was doing my job," he said.

"And what's that?" asked Tom. "A spot of burglary?"

"How could you stoop so low?" I asked. I know, I know, but I couldn't resist it.

"I," said Crouch with a baleful stare, "am a private investigator."

"That's a coincidence," I said. "So are we."

"Good heavens. Really?" said Crouch, as though he were addressing a moron. "I am aware of that. It's why I came through your ceiling."

"Who are you working for, Harry?" asked Bill Slope.

"I told you," said Crouch. "I am not at liberty to say."

"Presumably, it isn't Santa," said Tom.

The dwarf rolled his eyes.

"Look, I've heard every dwarf and elf gag going," he said. "A hundred times or more. Please don't feel you have to keep me entertained."

"We would like to know who you're working for," I said. "And I daresay you'll have to tell the police. That's if we turn you over to them."

Harry shrugged, but I could see a tiny glimmer of hope in his eyes. The idea that we might not turn him over to the police clearly appealed.

"Harry says he was being lowered," said Tom, turning to Bill. "Does that mean he had an accomplice?"

"At least one," said Bill, "and possibly two. But I couldn't go after them. I had my hands full with this one."

"Put up a fight, did he?" asked Tom.

"He knocked the gun out of my hand," said Bill. "But I did a spell in the army. I'm good at finding pressure points."

"What a load of baloney! He punched me in the eye and knocked me out," said Crouch. "That's what he did."

"Well, if you're going to break into people's property," said Tom, "you can't be surprised if they defend themselves."

"Call that self-defence?" said Crouch. "Your friend's a raving psycho!"

"I don't care for guys who break into other people's premises," said Bill. "I like them even less if they set people up for crimes they haven't committed."

"I don't know what you're talking about," said Crouch.

"Are you denying that you tried to set me up as a paedophile?" I asked.

"Sure I'm denying it," said Crouch.

"Was that what you did to me?" asked Bill. "Was it you who had me sent to prison?"

"I don't know anything about that," said Crouch, "In any case, whatever I do, it ain't personal. It's business."

"So who employs you?" asked Tom.

"I'm not telling you that," said the little man. "It's a matter of professional etiquette."

"In that case, answer me this," I said. "Are you in possession of a false red beard?"

Crouch shifted uneasily in his seat.

"What if I am?"

"And did you wear it while delivering a letter to a young Russian heiress named Olga Molotovski?"

A long pause.

"I might have done."

"Why?"

He thought for a moment, then clearly decided there was no reason to lie to me.

"There were security cameras. I didn't want to be recognised."

"Who gave you that letter to deliver?"

"No comment."

"And what was in it?"

"I never looked. And before you ask, I wasn't told."

"You were just doing your job," said Bill. "So you didn't ask awkward questions."

"You got it," said Crouch.

"And why did you go to visit Jack O'Riordan a few days before his death, this time wearing a Hitler moustache?"

"It was a Charlie Chaplin moustache."

"So it was you."

Crouch thought for a moment, and clearly decided he could tell me a few other things without contravening his code of professional etiquette.

"I was looking for someone."

"Olga Molotovski?"

"Could be," he conceded.

"So you went to him with a couple of assistants, posing as clowns?"

"Sure," he nodded. "We told him we needed publicity photos."

"And did you find her?"

"O'Riordan pretended he didn't know where she was," said Crouch. "But I could hear someone walking around in the room above us. He said it was his dog."

"And you don't think it was?"

"Not unless his dog had two legs."

"So did you confront him?"

"No," said Crouch. "I kept him under surveillance. Which is how I came to know that if he had a dog, he never used to take it out for a walk. It's also how I came to see you two deadbeats."

I imagine he meant Tom and myself.

"I saw you lose the guy with the green hair, and I had one of my assistants tail you back here, which is how I got to know you are private detectives. So I put two and two together, and worked out you were also trying to trace Olga Molotovski."

"Which made you curious about how far along we were with our inquiries."

"Yeah, and I knew my boss would be even more curious," he said. "The office above you was up for rent, so I put in an offer they couldn't refuse. And the rest, as they say, is history."

"You say you kept O'Riordan under surveillance," said Bill. "Does that mean you were watching him the night he was murdered?"

"From a distance, yeah," said Crouch. "I told you, I was working under cover. I'm a master of disguise."

"We never saw you," I said.

"If you'd looked a bit harder at the house opposite," said the dwarf, "I was in the third dustbin on the left."

"So what did you see?" asked Tom. "After we'd gone?"

"I'm pretty sure I saw Olga Molotovski leave his place," said Crouch. "With a woman."

"What kind of woman?"

"It was between 10.30 and 11, so it was dark. But I could see she was blonde. And she seemed like a youngish woman, though it was hard to tell – she was wearing dark glasses."

"At night?"

"Yeah. She arrived in a taxi, got out like she was a young woman, not stiff or anything. She knocked on the door, and Olga let her in."

"So the taxi drove off?"

"That was the odd thing. It didn't. It just stayed there, with lights on and the engine running. And after a while two people came out of the house."

"How much later?" I asked.

"I don't know. Three minutes. Maybe four. And the taxi drove off with these two people in it, and some hand luggage. One was the woman who'd just arrived. And the other was Olga. At least I think so. The same build and everything."

"Did you follow the cab?"

"I tried to," said Crouch. "But my colleague had taken our car to follow you two. I was on foot, and I couldn't get a cab right away. Because of the way I was dressed, I guess."

"Why was that a problem?"

"I was wearing a burka," said Crouch. "I wanted to look inconspicuous. There's a lot of Arabs in Notting Hill."

"And no cabs?"

"There were cabs, but a couple of them ignored me. By the time I found one, Olga and her friend had disappeared."

"In which direction?"

"Towards the West End. But it could have been going anywhere. Up towards Mayfair, or down towards Chelsea."

"So can you tell us why you were trying to find Olga?"

"Not in any detail," said Crouch. "Let's just say that my client had feelings towards her, and didn't want to see her getting into trouble."

"And who is your client?" I asked. "Igor Molotovski? Joseph Gildenstern? Loco Parente?"

The dwarf just looked back at me, and shook his head.

"You won't get anything out of me," he said.

Tom took another line of inquiry.

"Why do you say Jack O'Riordan was trouble?" he asked.

"I don't like to speak ill of the dead," said Crouch. "But the word on the street is that the guy was a nasty, blackmailing piece of shit, and it was no loss to humanity when whoever it was cut his head off."

"You mean Olga and this woman?"

"How do I know?" said Crouch. "But no, I don't think so. If they'd killed him, they'd have been covered in blood. My guess is someone murdered him after I left."

"You're sure it wasn't you?" asked Tom.

"Why would I do a thing like that?" asked Crouch. "Be serious."

"And you didn't see who did?" asked Bill.

"From what I've heard, the cops think he died around 11, so if you want my opinion it was someone who arrived after I left."

"Following the two women," I said.

"Yeah," said Crouch. "Except that didn't work out. I lost them. So I went back to my hotel and tracked down who you were."

"And then you decided to see if we'd had any more luck than you," said Tom. "Hence your nocturnal visit, and your bugging devices."

"That's about the size of it," said the diminutive private detective.

"Shouldn't you have told your story to the police?" I asked.

"That's not my job," said Crouch. "Besides, my client is anxious to keep his interest in the case out of the newspapers. He had nothing to do with Jack O'Riordan. He just had the best interests of the girl at heart."

"That's all very touching," I said.

"Yes," said Bill. "I'm feeling very moved."

"Do you think we should let him go?" I asked.

"He's guilty of breaking and entering," said Tom.

"But he's given us a new lead on little Olga," said Bill. "I don't think we should bear him too many grudges."

"It's not much of a lead," said Tom. "A mystery blonde, who lives somewhere east of Notting Hill. Or north-east. Or south-east."

"I don't know why I bothered to break in here," said Crouch. "You guys don't have a clue, do you?"

"As to where she is?" I asked. "Not much, no."

"I bet you don't even know why she's in danger," said Crouch.

"Is she?" asked Tom. "Who from?"

"Oh my God," said Crouch. "You're jokes, you are. From her own parents, of course."

"What do you mean?" I asked.

"Look," said Crouch, "I've said enough. In fact, I've told you too much. Now let me go."

"You know, Charlie," said Bill, "I think we should. It's going to get very complicated if we call the police. And this little guy is only trying to do his job."

I stared at Bill.

"Are you sure?"

"Let's cut the guy some slack," he said.

So we did, and Harry Crouch didn't waste too much time in taking his leave of us, after a long, hard glare at Bill.

"It's too bad we don't know who employed him," I said to Bill afterwards.

"Oh, don't worry about that," he said. "I have a shrewd idea."

"Why do you say that?" asked Tom.

"While the little chap was out for the count," said Bill, "I took the opportunity to hack into his phone."

"That's not very ethical," I said.

"I know," said Bill. "But under the circumstances, it seemed the sensible thing to do. And it became pretty obvious who his employer was. In fact, I recognised the private phone number, even before I heard his voice."

"So put us out of our misery, Bill," I said. "Who is it?"

"Igor Molotovski?" Tom asked.

"No way," said Bill.

"Loco Parente?" asked Tom.

Bill Slope shook his head.

"Joseph Gildenstern?" I suggested.

"You're getting closer, but no."

"Lorenzo Fettucini? His agent?"

"You're getting colder again."

"I give up," I said.

"You were on the right track with Gildenstern, but you need to set your sights a bit higher."

"You don't mean Sepp Blatter?"

"That kind of level."

"I don't know," said Tom.

"Neither do I," I said. "I give up."

"Bernhard Spritzer," said Bill Slope.

"The owner of Southern Athletic?" I asked.

"The same," said Bill.

"What's he got to do with all this?" Tom inquired.

"You heard," said Bill. "He takes a strong personal interest in little Olga."

"He's not another paedophile, is he?"

"Interesting idea," said Bill. "Come to think of it, his girl-friends are getting younger and younger."

"Where can we find him?" asked Tom.

"Isn't he a foreign national?" I said.

"Bernie's mainly resident here but he's American," said Bill. "Though I suspect that may not be where he pays his taxes. If he pays any taxes."

"This is way too complicated for me," I said. "Why is Spritzer so interested in finding Olga?"

"An intriguing question," said Bill. "To which only he knows the answer. I think it's time that we paid the big fella a visit."

"What makes you think he'll see us?" asked Tom.

"Oh, he'll see us all right," said Bill. "Bernie Spritzer and I go way back. Are you doing anything this afternoon?"

21

THE BIRDS

Monday, 8th August

Bill Slope made a couple of phone calls, and proved as good as his word. Within an hour, we were off to see Bernhard Spritzer. Tom seemed miffed not to be going with us.

"It's a personal invitation," said Bill. "Your dad is going as my hot date."

"Where does Spritzer live?" asked Tom.

"He has this massive spread in Essex. Sixty acres, big house, deer park, heli-pad, the works. It turns out he's having a weekend house party."

"But it's Monday," Tom objected.

"For people like Bernie," said Bill, "the weekend begins and ends when he says it does."

"Any idea what he's celebrating?" asked Tom.

"I'm not sure," said Bill. "He's got some sort of unveiling, followed by a drinks do. The moment he heard I was back in town, he extended an invitation."

"What should I wear?" I asked. "Is it black tie?"

"No worries," said Bill. "Bernie's not that sort of guy. We can go as we are. Smart casual."

I noticed Tom suppressing a smile. Bill Slope's idea of 'smart casual' was not the same as most people's. Bill had changed into a powder-blue safari suit that might have been fashionable in the 1970s, but certainly hadn't enjoyed a revival in forty years. I was at least wearing a white shirt and black trousers. With the addition of my best jacket, hanging on the back of the office door, I would look halfway respectable.

"How are we going to get there?" I asked. "Are we taking your car?"

"I re-parked that yesterday," said Bill. "Well out of the congestion zone and the reach of traffic wardens. Bernie's sending us his chauffeur," said Bill.

A big black man in full livery turned up half an hour later, driving a silver Rolls Royce Phantom. By this time, Bill had given Tom and myself a crash-course in the world of Bernhard Spritzer.

"Why do you call him the big fella?" Tom asked.

"Because he's short," replied Bill. "Five foot three. In heels, maybe five foot five. But business-wise, he punches well above his weight."

"And what is his business?" asked Tom.

"Over the years, he's diversified," said Bill. "Property, publishing, shops, lingerie, racehorses. But essentially he's a pornographer, and proud of it."

"Like Molotovski used to be?" I asked.

"They're old business rivals."

"So how do you know Spritzer?" asked Tom.

"He's been a good friend to me over the years, and a very useful contact." said Bill. "He's pathologically indiscreet."

"Can't keep a secret?"

"Especially when he's high."

"What on?"

"Cocaine, mostly. And amphetamines. Other than that, he's a pretty straight sort of guy."

"You mean, like Tony Blair?" asked Tom.

"Yeah, well, maybe I should choose my words better," admitted Bill.

"I've looked him up on the internet," said Tom. "His nickname is the Sultan of Sleaze."

"One man's sleaze is another man's erotica," said Bill. "What I've always liked about Bernie is that he's always marched to his own drummer. He's true to his own beliefs."

"And those are?" I asked.

"Mainly, he believes in extracting as much money as possible out of mug punters," said Bill, "But at least he's honest about it. There's nothing hypocritical about Bernie."

"He sounds delightful," I said.

"He's fine as long as you don't cross him."

"I don't intend to," I said. "I take it he responds to flattery?"

"He loves it. Most billionaires do."

"I don't know any billionaires," I said.

"You know Molotovski."

"I'm beginning to wish I didn't." I said. "Anything else I need to know about Spritzer?"

"Apart from his temper, his one major problem," said Bill, "is his penis."

"What's wrong with it?"

"He can't keep it in his trousers. He's never married, but I've lost count of his fiancées. That's how he strings them along until he dumps them, or they discover one of his infidelities and dump him. And they're getting younger. The chances are that on his deathbed he'll end up marrying an embryo."

"Or Olga Molotovski?"

"I think Igor would have something to say about that," said Bill.

Bernhard Spritzer's country pile was in the neo-Georgian style, with post-modern extensions to each side that appeared to have been inspired by *Star Trek*.

But I'm getting ahead of myself. Before you could see that, you first had to negotiate armed guards, stationed at exceptionally high gates. A new-looking brick wall led away in both directions, with barbed wire entanglements along the top. There were CCTV cameras at regular intervals, and next to the gate a huge sign reading 'PRIVATE PROPERTY. KEEP OUT. Firearms are in continuous use on these premises. Enter at your own risk'.

"This is all new," said Bill to one of the security men.

"Six months old," said the guard. "The guvnor's turned a whole suite into panic rooms, with heavy, triple-bolted steel doors. Inside, he's got a direct line to the police and can watch the whole estate via the CCTV cameras. He's got guards patrolling the grounds, 24-seven.

"Security conscious," I said.

"So would you be," said the guard, "if you were as rich as him. ID, please."

"Will a driving licence do?" I asked.

"A passport would be better."

"I'm afraid I don't have that with me."

"Oh," said the guard. "Still, you're Charlie Charlesworth, aren't you?"

"Guilty as charged," I said.

"You were a good player," he said. "Hard luck about your knees."

He looked down at a handheld computer, and a message flashed up.

"All right," he said, "you're cleared to go in."

The host and hostess had clearly been alerted by the front gate as to our arrival, for they came out to greet us.

"Bill! Charlie!" said Bernhard Spritzer, for all the world as though we had been friends since childhood.

"Bernhard!" said Bill.

"Mr Spritzer," I said.

"Call me, Bernie," said Spritzer.

"Thanks, Bernie," I said.

"You're welcome. And this is my new fiancée, Tamara Slingsby-Smythe," said Spritzer, pointing to the beauty next to him.

She was blonde, about six foot tall, with astonishing breasts like protruding zeppelins. She did not appear to be wearing a bra, and looked about twenty-three. Her breasts looked, if anything, younger.

"Congratulations!" said Bill. It was with a shock that I realised Bill was addressing the word to her.

"I know," she simpered. "I'm so very, very lucky. Bernhard has told me so much about you, William. And you must be...?"

She held out her right hand to me, so I shook it.

"Charlie Charlesworth."

"Oh hi," said Tamara, exposing two rows of perfect teeth. I was instantly reminded that Bernhard Springer enjoyed the company of racehorses. "Glad you could drop by. Make yourself at home. We've put you in the blue suite. Are you two sharing a bed?"

"No," I said hurriedly. "We're just friends."

"Great," she said. "But we're completely non-judgmental here. If you want to make love to each other or anyone else, feel free. All sex aids in the bedrooms are available for your enjoyment."

She turned on her high heels and swayed away, revealing extremely long legs and a neat little bottom.

"Isn't she wonderful?" breathed Bernhard. "Do you know she's three hundred and sixty-fourth in line for the British throne?"

"Amazing," I agreed.

For a moment, I had a nightmarish flash of how, possibly in the wake of a nuclear holocaust, Britain might look if Tamara Slingsby-Smythe were on the throne, with Bernie Spritzer as her adoring consort. I shook my head. It didn't bear thinking about.

"You're in time for the unveiling," said Bernie.

"Unveiling of what?" I asked.

"Him," he said.

259

He pointed to a huge grey bag in front of the mansion.

"Who is that?"

"You'll see," he said. "You'll find champagne over there. In the meantime, I'll ask the butler to summon the guests."

He whispered a few words to an elderly butler who looked like Ian McKellen's supercilious elder brother. The butler nodded to another servant, who walked inside the front door. Moments later, a gong sounded, and guests converged from all directions.

Many of the female guests had obviously been selected for their physical beauty. Some of them, I recognised from the newspapers or television. A few of the less glamorous guests, I knew personally. Because of his business relationship to Spritzer, I wasn't altogether surprised to see Joseph Gildenstern.

"Ah, Charlie!" he nodded. "Bernhard mentioned you were coming. You must fill me in later on about how you're getting on with you know who."

At this, he inclined his head a little to his right. I followed his eye line, and was surprised to see Lorenzo Fettucini.

"I thought he was in Italy," I said.

"He was," said Gildenstern, "but Bernhard had him flown in this morning in his private jet. He wanted him to attend the party, to show there were no hard feelings about last season."

"I don't think Lorenzo will be very happy to see me," I said. "He had his agent warn me, in no uncertain terms, to keep my distance."

"How intriguing!" said the Fuhrer. "You must tell me more. In the meantime, I believe you have met my friend, Edward Killingfield."

"We met briefly at your restaurant," I said, shaking Killingfield's limp right hand.

The award-winning chef and restaurateur was flamboyantly decked out in an outfit that resembled a Ruritanian prince's idea of military dress.

"Why, yes," he said. "I remember hoping we three would have

mad, passionate sex together afterwards, but Joseph tells me you declined the offer."

"Well, I had a lot of things on," I said.

"Spoilsport!" he said, with a toss of his head. "Well, perhaps a few glasses of champagne will make you less, shall we say, tight-arsed. Bernhard's very free and easy, you know, and I... Well, I may not be free, but I am incredibly easy."

"If you'll excuse me," I said, "I think someone's trying to attract my attention."

I moved across to where Bill Slope was standing.

"What kind of apparition is that?" he asked.

"Edward Killingfield," I said. "You know, the celebrity chef? I think he and Joseph Gildenstern are some kind of item."

"I thought Gildenstern was married."

"I believe he is," I said. "And to a former Miss World."

"Christ," said Bill. "There really is no accounting for taste."

"You've seen Fettucini is here?" I asked.

"Yeah," said Bill. "But one look at you and he went haring off in another direction. Look, he's over there, hiding."

I followed his gaze, and recognised another familiar face.

"Oh God," I said. "That's his agent. The Asian-looking gentleman."

"Ah yes," said Bill, "Chin Sun Fong. I wouldn't have recognised him. All those Koreans look the same to me. But maybe all Australians look the same to him."

"He doesn't look too pleased to see me," I said.

"I'm not sure I rank high in his popularity charts either," said Bill. "The last time we met, he offered to break both my legs."

"Why was that?"

"I think he thought I was trying to expose him for racketeering, match-fixing, that sort of thing."

"And were you?"

"As a matter of fact, I was," he said.

"And did he break both your legs?"

"As it turned out, he didn't have to," he said. "Both the guys who promised me they'd testify against him in court were found dead."

"Lucky for him."

"Not so lucky for them."

"He doesn't sound like the kind of guy you want as your enemy," I said.

"You're fond of understatement, aren't you?" said Bill. "You're very British. You've seen who else is here?"

"Do you mean Prince Andrew?"

"Is he here?"

"I'm pretty sure he's standing over there, next to Peter Mandelson."

"No, I meant the film star," he said. "The bloke from the Exterminator movies."

"Jean-Paul De Mode?"

"That's him," said Bill. "I can see why they call him 'The Mood'. He looks a surly bastard."

The actor was more sober than when I had seen him last, but no happier. He was slouching and scowling, as though this was the last place he wanted to be. To his right was a face I instantly recognised. Marion Brooke. I caught her eye. She gave a nervous smile and turned away. Evidently, she didn't wish to acknowledge that she knew me – at least, not in front of her husband. Fine by me. At least I would know how to play things, were we to meet later on.

"Isn't your sister meant to be trailing De Mode?" asked Bill.

"Yes," I said. "I wonder if she's nearby."

As if on cue, my mobile phone started vibrating.

"Hello?" I said.

"Was that you and Bill I just saw arriving?" asked a familiar voice.

"That was us," I said. "Where are you, Trace?"

"Outside," she said. "I followed our target with his wife, and

I'm wondering what to do next. You're inside. Maybe you should keep tabs on him."

"I've a few other things on my mind," I said. "Look, just hang around outside. I don't know how long they're going to be here."

"Okay, bruv. Will do."

"Was that your sister?" asked Bill. "She outside?"

I nodded.

"You could have saved some money and sent her home," said Bill. "De Mode's hardly likely to stray with his wife slap bang next to him."

"True," I said.

"Good looking, ain't she? And I have it on very good authority that Marion Brooke's quite a goer."

"What?" I asked.

"That's according to Bernie Spritzer," he said. "And he tends to know about these things."

"What do you mean, a goer?" I asked.

"You know," he said. "A raving nympho."

"I can't believe it," I said. "I expect it's just one of these malicious rumours."

"I dunno, mate," said Bill, eying me doubtfully. "Are you sure you're cut out for this investigating lark? You seem a shade too trusting."

Bernhard Spritzer cleared his throat, and the assembled multitude fell silent. He spoke without notes, and evidently from the heart. His use of short sentences, often without a verb, reminded me of Tony Blair. Maybe they used the same speechwriter.

"We're all here today," he said, "to witness the unveiling. Of this statue. To a remarkable man. All the more remarkable, since... Most people have never even heard of him. But he changed many lives. I met him many times. Like a father to me. The father I never had. He took me. Under his wing. And taught me. All he knew. About business. The industry. The calling that I have pursued ever since. He taught me. Everything I know. Some of you know him. As Reuben Sturman. To me. He was. Quite simply. The Pornfather."

Spritzer indicated to his fiancée that she pull on a string. She did so, and revealed a golden stature of a small, paunchy man with a sinister leer. The audience applauded politely. Spritzer took a sip of champagne.

"Never heard of him," I whispered to Bill.

"Me neither," he whispered back.

"Born in 1924," said Spritzer, "Reuben Sturman began his business life. Selling comic books. From the boot of his car. But when he started selling magazines. With a sexual content. He found he could make big profits. His first major success came in 1964. With a magazine entitled *Sex Life of a Cop*. Nothing to do with you, was it, Frank?"

He waved his champagne glass jovially in the direction of a man I instantly recognised: Frank Drake, the inspector who had interrogated me the previous Friday. Next to him was a young woman, dark-haired and attractive. She struck me as vaguely familiar. But for the moment I couldn't place her.

"Over the next 25 years," Spritzer continued, "thanks to sheer hard work. Charisma. And drive. He managed to gain control. Of all the pornography circulating. In America. By the mid-80s. He owned 200 adult bookstores. He also pioneered. The sex-aid industry. Personally inventing. The Pocket Rocket. Joy Jelly. And Motion Lotion. What Carnegie was to the steel industry. And Ford was to cars. Reuben Sturman was to sex toys. Peep shows. And pornography. He managed to avoid prosecution. By using more than 20 different aliases. And arranging protection with the highly respected. Gambino family. From whom we have several. Representatives here today."

A group of large, Italian men raised their glasses in acknowledgement. A murmur of appreciation could be heard from the partygoers. Or it might have been fear.

"By the end of the 80s," continued Spritzer. "He had a virtual monopoly. On the porn industry in America and Europe. And was pulling in hundreds of millions. Of dollars each year."

This news was greeted with even more appreciation.

"Today he is widely applauded. As a protector of free speech. And a sexual revolutionary. Sad to say, envious business rivals had him arrested. For tax evasion. He died in prison on October 2nd, 1997."

There were a few cries of "Shame."

"But this statue will endure. And ensure. That he will not be forgotten. I give you. Reuben Sturman. The Walt Disney of porn."

After the applause, it was time for canapés, served on silver salvers, and more champagne. I couldn't resist sidling up to Frank Drake.

"I'm surprised to find you here," I said. "Being matey with a self-confessed pornographer."

"Oh, nowadays Bernie's considered quite respectable," he said. "He doesn't go in for the really raunchy stuff. No kiddie porn, or anything like that."

I couldn't work out whether Drake was deliberately needling me. I decided to change the subject.

"Haven't we met somewhere before?" I asked the young woman beside Frank Drake.

"Oh, how rude of me," said Drake. "I should have introduced you. My daughter, Carol."

I flushed. Now I knew why I recognised her. She was the woman who had broken through my front door the previous Sunday morning. Detective Inspector Carol Smith.

"We've met," she said. "But I don't think it would be appropriate to describe the circumstances."

She turned on her heel and walked off. Frank Drake raised his eyebrows.

"Oops!" he said. "You two have a history?"

"Not in that way," I said. "She raided my home on Sunday.

Her unit had evidently had a tip-off that I was downloading child pornography. I wasn't, needless to say."

"Glad to hear it," said Drake. "The prisons are overcrowded as it is."

"Good champagne, this," I said.

"It always is at Bernie's," said Drake.

"Incidentally," I said, "I have a lead for you. There was a dwarf who visited Jack O'Riordan shortly before his death."

"Oh?

"Called Harry Crouch. He's a Canadian private investigator, currently working in London."

"You don't say," said Drake, taking out a pen and writing the name in a small pocket book. "How did you find him?"

"It would be more accurate to say that he found me," I said. "I don't know if he'll be much help to you, but…"

I shrugged.

"Thanks for the lead," said Drake. "And now if you'll excuse me, I must circulate. Isn't that the Home Secretary over there?"

Bill Slope joined me.

"I had no idea you were matey with the cops," he said.

"Frank Drake?" I said. "He's in charge of the O'Riordan case. I was just tipping him off about Harry Crouch."

"Harry won't thank you for that."

"Well, if Harry must break and enter, he has to learn to live with the consequences."

"True."

"What have you been doing?"

"A spot of mingling. Jean-Paul De Mode just threw a punch at me."

"What did you say to him?'

"Nothing. I thought it would be interesting to see how short his fuse was. So I nudged him and made him spill his drink."

"And he hit you?"

"No, he missed."

"Did you hit him back?"

"Not worth it, mate. I said I was sorry, and moved on. That was when he tried to hit me again."

"Any more success, the second time?"

"He hit me a glancing blow on the shoulder."

"And what did you do then?"

"I told him that if he did that again, I'd have to kill him."

"And that quietened him down?"

"I think he thought I might be some kind of gangster, and that did take the wind out of his sails, yeah."

"He really is an angry young man, isn't he?"

"Yeah," said Bill. "In a world full of wankers, he's one of the biggest. God knows what he's got to be angry about. He must be one of the luckiest bastards on the planet."

"You think so?"

"Well, he must have made millions out of the *Exterminator* movies. And he inherited money. And he's married to the woman you fancy most in the whole wide world. No, don't deny it. I've seen the way you look at her."

"It is really that obvious?"

"Yeah, mate. Don't look at her like that in front of De Mode, or he'll hit you. Harder than he hit me."

I felt myself reddening, and thought it might be a good idea to change the subject.

"Met anyone else interesting?"

"Only Prince Andrew," said Bill.

"I had no idea pornographers were so respectable."

"Look around you, mate," said Bill. "They're taking over the world."

"Hello hello hello," said someone behind me. "Look what the cat's dragged in."

I didn't need to turn round in order to know the owner of that voice.

"Rex Crawley," I said. "I should have known you'd be here."

"I'm usually to be found where the bubbly's flowing," he said. "Here's a good one. Why is Bernie Spritzer's house like a public urinal?"

"I don't know, Rex. Why is it?"

"Because it's where the big knobs hang out!"

He cackled appreciatively at his own joke.

"Funny," I said.

"It's been too long," said Crawley.

"Excuse me?"

"I've been waiting for you to give me a progress report on Olga," he said.

"We've made a lot of inquiries but we're not much further forward," I admitted. "Except she was probably with Jack O'Riordan on the night of his murder."

"Bloody hell!" said Crawley. "Keep your voice down. You don't think she murdered him?"

"I don't think so," I said. "But it looks like she lodged with him a few days after she left home then left just before his death, with a mystery woman."

"What kind of woman?" asked Crawley.

"That's the mystery," I said. "She was youngish, blonde and wearing dark glasses."

"At night?" said Crawley. "She sounds like a celebrity. You know, wanting not to be recognised. Blonde hair, you say?"

"The blonde hair could be a wig," said Bill Slope.

"Bloody hell," said Rex Crawley. "Bill Slope? What are you doing here?"

"I'm an old friend of Bernie's," said Bill. "And I'm giving Charlie here a bit of help."

"Finding Olga?" asked Crawley, before turning to me. "I'm not paying anything extra. If you want him on board, he'll have to come out of your budget."

"So why are you working for Katasha Molotovski?" Bill asked Crawley.

"Sssh!" said Crawley. "Don't mention her around here. Didn't you know, she and Bernie used to be an item?"

"That must have been some time ago," I said.

"It's got to be nearly twenty years," said Crawley. "Ugly business. She ditched Bernie, then married his biggest business rival. Bernie was very cut up about it at the time."

"Any idea why she ditched him?" I asked him.

"The usual," said Crawley. "Bernie's always had a problem controlling his one-eyed trouser snake. The story is that she found him in bed auditioning a couple of future fiancées. I believe they were identical twins."

"What brings you here?" asked Bill.

"They want me to do a bit of PR for one of Bernie's restaurants. You've probably heard of it. Killingfield's."

"I've been there," I said.

"Really?" asked Crawley. "I wouldn't have thought it was your kind of place at all. Too classy."

"Thanks," I said. "It was. Much too classy."

"Fancy a refill?" asked Bill.

"Thanks," I said, giving him my empty glass.

No sooner had Bill left me than Joseph Gildenstern was at my elbow.

"And now," he said, "you must tell me all about Lorenzo Fettucini. But not here. Come with me to the gazebo."

The gazebo turned out to be an elaborate neo-classical construction, several hundred yards from the house.

"Here, we can be alone without distractions," said Gildenstern, patting my knee affectionately before laying one hand upon my thigh.

I removed it.

"Charlie, Charlie, Charlie," he sighed. "You always play so hard to get."

"Let's keep things on a professional basis," I said.

"Okay," he said. "Shoot!"

"I spoke to Lorenzo, and he told me he was being threatened by fans of his old club."

"They told him that if he scored for Southern Athletic, they would kill him?"

"Something of the sort."

"Did he name names?"

"He implied that it was Desmond Mullarky."

"That would make sense," nodded Gildenstern. "He did the same thing to Eddie Parrott."

"That's what I thought," I said. "But I've talked to Mullarky, and he denies all knowledge."

"So?" asked Gildenstern. "Why should he tell you the truth?"

"I know he's a thug and all that, but I'm sure he was telling me the truth," I said. "The fact is, he never rated Fettucini much as a player, so he wasn't that bothered when he moved to Southern Athletic.

"I see," said Gildenstern. "Or rather I don't."

"There's more," I said. "When I confronted Lorenzo with this over the phone, he got very evasive and started denying that he'd ever said anything about being threatened. And then he had me picked up and menaced by his agent. Who's here, by the way. That Korean bloke."

"Chin Sun Fong?"

"That's the one."

"So you are no closer to knowing why Fettucini can not score goals?"

"Actually, I think I have a pretty good idea," I said. "An associate of mine has been talking to his gambling contacts, and just after Fettucini signed for Southern Athletic, someone bet a shedload that he wouldn't score in his first thirty games for his new club."

"Surely Fettucini would not be so stupid as to lay such a bet himself," said Gildenstern. "It would be professional suicide."

"No, but his agent might."

"And then pressurise Fettucini to deliver?"

"According to my associate, Fettucini has a history of gambling. And, despite his earnings, he's heavily in debt."

"And Fong?"

"He's behind a lot of footballing scams, and my associate claims that a large bet was laid on Fettucini not scoring in his first thirty games for Athletic, at odds of 50 to one."

"So let me get this right," said Gildenstern. "You think Fettucini and his agent are in league over this?"

"That's my hunch," I said.

"Mr Spritzer will not be pleased," said Gildenstern.

"Don't tell him yet," I said. "I'm pretty sure I'm on the right track, but I've nothing that would stand up in a court of law."

"Doesn't matter. You've convinced me," said Gildenstern. "Keep up the good work."

"I'll try to," I said.

"We appear to have a visitor," said Gildenstern.

He stood up and clicked his heels.

"I was wondering who those two men were, sitting together so romantically," said Marion Brooke, smiling her heart-stopping smile. "I'm not interrupting, am I?"

"Of course not, dear lady," said Gildenstern. "Charlie and I were merely discussing football."

"But it's not the start of the season yet," said Marion. "Shouldn't you be discussing cricket?"

"I have never understood the English passion for cricket," said Gildenstern. "Perhaps if you were to concentrate on football, you would be better at it."

"Would you mind if I borrowed Mr Charlesworth for a moment?" asked Marion.

"Not at all," said Gildenstern. "Where is your delightful husband?"

"I think Jean-Paul is somewhere over there," said Marion, vaguely. "Glowering. I don't think he likes it here."

"Perhaps I can brighten his day," said Gildenstern.

The footballer clicked his heels again and strode off.

"I don't think I've ever seen anyone actually click their heels before," said Marion. "He really is frightfully Germanic."

"And you sound frightfully English," I said.

"Do I?" she asked. "I suppose I do. Maybe I've been playing the English rose too long."

"But you do it so well," I said.

"Thank you, kind sir," she said. "Incidentally, I'm impressed."

"By what?"

"That you knew we were going to be here. But I don't think Jean-Paul is likely to do anything terribly incriminating with me beside him. He's far more likely to get up to no good when I'm not around. I gather he did misbehave at the premiere party."

"A bit," I said. "He got very drunk and argumentative. Threatened me, my son and my receptionist, as a matter of fact."

"Rex Crawley brought him home," she said. "Said he fell over after he was knocked on the head by a paparazzo."

"I didn't see that," I said truthfully. "But so far I have no evidence that he's been unfaithful."

"Don't you footballers call it playing away?" she asked. "Is that why your marriage broke up?"

"Have you been checking up on me?"

"I googled you and found out all kinds of things," she said.

I flushed. It was almost as if she was being flirtatious.

"I'm sorry I haven't got back to you about Jean-Paul," I said.

"So you still don't know whether this super-injunction rumour is true?"

I hesitated. Should I tell her about Olga Molotovski? I decided that Fairycakes Bonanza Parks was not the most reliable of witnesses. Besides, I didn't want to cause Marion unnecessary heartbreak.

"Not yet," I said. "But I'm working on it."

"Let me know if you find out anything," she said. "Don't spare my feelings."

"I – I wouldn't do that."

"I can see that you might," she said. "You have kind eyes."

"Thanks," I said. "You have beautiful eyes."

They sparkled merrily.

"You and your compliments," she said. "Still, I'd better be off, I wouldn't want to monopolise you."

"That's okay," I said. "It's lovely to see you."

"Yes," she said. "It's good to see you too. You scrub up rather well, don't you?"

"Do I?" I asked.

"Yes," she said, turning to deliver another of her killer smiles. "But you really must learn to control your blushing."

22

I CONFESS

Monday, 8th August

Returning to the party, I nearly walked into Lorenzo's agent. I had a strong feeling that now was not a great time to confront the South Korean with any accusations about gambling or his goalmouth-challenged client. I couldn't see either of Mr Fong's henchmen, but instinct told me that they would not be far away.

Walking round the corner of the house to avoid him, I found myself behind Lorenzo Fettucini himself. He was surrounded by adoring females. Though he had his back to me, I could hear him holding forth on a variety of topics.

These included love ("Love is a game, but football is serious."), the superiority of football over any other game ("If you don't like getting dirty, go play tennis."), and the importance of looking successful ("I'm rich. What am I supposed to do. Hide it?").

The girls seemed to find his Italian accent charming, and his occasional verbal gaffes cute. ("It no matter if I hit ball with my left foot or right foot. I am amphibious.")

He expressed confidence in the coming football season. ("I will be at my best. There is no I in team, maybe, but there is a Me in Phenomenal.") And predicted that the goals would soon start coming again. ("I can see the carrot at the end of the tunnel.")

He expressed his loyalty to Southern Athletic and Bernhard Spritzer, ("I am the most loyal player money can buy.") and blamed his current unpopularity with the fans on the press ("Sometimes they write what I say, not what I mean.")

His speech was slurred, and his manner belligerent. It was evident that sun and champagne had made him garrulous.

So perhaps it wasn't surprising that when he caught sight of me, he raised his finger, pointed and said "You! I have something to say to you!"

"Are you sure of that, Lorenzo?" I asked. "The last time I saw your agent, he was very insistent that you had nothing whatever to say to me."

"That's right. I want to say that I don't have nothing whatever to say to you!"

"Okay, Lorenzo," I said, and turned away.

But he came after me.

"No! You let me say something, Charlie," he said.

"You could try saying sorry," I said.

"Why should I be saying sorry?"

"For lying to me," I said.

"About what?" he asked, a picture of aggrieved innocence.

"About Mad Monkey Mullarky, for a start," I said. "No one was threatening you if you scored goals for Southern Athletic."

"I no understand."

"You understand perfectly well, when it suits you."

"Maybe," he said, "but not all the time."

"Look, we're on our own now," I said, "with no witnesses, so let's just talk like grown men. I know about your gambling debts."

"What?" he said. "How you know that?"

"I just do," I replied. "And I know about your deal with your agent."

"What deal?"

"The one about his bet that you won't score for your first thirty matches with Athletic."

"How you know?"

"I'm a private investigator, remember? I investigate things."

"You no tell anyone this," he said.

"Probably not," I said.

"It no do my reputation any good. Besides, thirty matches will soon be up, and then I start scoring again."

"Why are you doing this?"

"I've been unlucky," he said, "but I'm gonna turn my life round 360 degrees."

"If you do that, you'll end up exactly where you were before."

"What? Okay. 180 degrees. Whatever."

I saw his agent moving purposefully towards me.

"I appreciate the off-the-record confession. But I suggest you get your agent to take you home," I said.

"You won't say nothing to Mr Spritzer, will you?"

"I don't know," I said. "It depends if the topic of you comes up. As Gazza once said, I don't make predictions, and I never will."

I turned on my heel, and went off to find Bill Slope. As it turned out, he was trying to find me. Bernhard Spritzer had made it known he wished to speak to us.

"Remember what I told you in the car?" said Bill. "Use plenty of flattery. And wait until Bernie's high. Then pump him for information."

23

FAMILY PLOT

Monday, 8th August

We found the multi-billionaire enjoying some recreational drugs. His latest fiancée was sprawled naked on the billiards table, and Spritzer was snorting cocaine from between her breasts, which pointed straight upwards like twin Matterhorns.

"Would you like to join me?" he asked. "I can heartily recommend this. I had it brought in specially for the occasion. I know Frank Drake might not approve, but hey, we don't have to tell him, do we?"

"Not for me, thanks," I said.

"Drugs don't agree with me, mate," said Bill. "Tried them in prison and they kept me awake at nights."

"Fair enough," said Spritzer.

He sniffed another line of cocaine and indicated to his fiancée that she should make herself scarce. Pausing only to bend down and French kiss her husband-to-be, she left the room. She didn't bother to put on any clothes.

"I'll wait for you upstairs," she told him.

"Sure, honey," he said. "Why don't you start without me?"

"Don't be long," she said. "Missing you already!"

Spritzer was in expansive mood.

"I gather from Gildenstern that you've cracked the Fettucini issue."

"I think so," I said. "Really, I should share my fee with Bill here. Lorenzo's pretty much admitted his failure to score is part of a gambling scam, organised by his agent."

"Never trust a Korean," said Spritzer. "It doesn't matter if they're from the south or the north. As for Fettucini, he's played his last game for Southern Athletic. You can take my word on that. I can't thank you guys enough."

"Glad to be of service," I said. "Especially on this special day."

"You think my speech went down well?" asked Spritzer.

"It couldn't have gone better," Bill assured him. "Everyone was deeply moved."

"I was moved myself," said Spritzer happily.

Wow, I thought, he really does respond to flattery.

"I must be one of the luckiest guys on the planet," he continued. "I feel so alive. I know they say this is an age of austerity, but for me things have never been better."

"I guess you're giving people what they want," said Bill.

"That's right," replied Spritzer. "You know there have been three great inventions in human history. Fire. The wheel. And pornography."

"You're helping people live the dream," said Bill.

"I am," replied Spritzer. "I am the American dream. I am the constitution. I am the pursuit of happiness. I represent the pioneering spirit that made America great. That's why I wanted to build a statue to Reuben Sturman. He taught me everything I know."

"Excellent celebrity turnout," said Bill. "It was quite a coup, getting that Hollywood actor."

"Jean-Paul De Mode?" asked Spritzer. "He comes to all my parties when he's in the country."

"He didn't look as if he was enjoying himself," I said.

"He never does," said Spritzer. "But you know what?"

"No," I said.

"He owes me his movie career."

"He does?"

"Yeah," said Spritzer. "Like a lot of Hollywood actors, he started out in porn. Not under his own name, naturally. He used to be known as Dick Du Jour. But he was in a lot of hardcore. Mainly the gay stuff."

"You're telling me he's gay?"

"He certainly was," said Spritzer. "Spent the best part of three years being smacked around the face with a penis."

"I don't need to know the grisly details," I said.

"You should see them. Maybe you have. *Raiders of the Lost Arse? Shaving Ryan's Privates? E.T. – The Extra Testicle?*"

"I seem to have missed those," I said.

"Any time Jean-Paul gets above himself," said Spritzer, "I tell him 'No matter how rich or successful you may become, to me you'll always be the second stud from the left in *White Men Can't Hump*.'"

"You said you wanted to see us," said Bill.

"I did," replied Spritzer. "I gather you've met an employee of mine, a pint-sized individual named Harry Crouch."

"That's right," said Bill.

"And you're curious about what he's been up to on my behalf."

"You could say that," I said.

"Okay," he said. "I can understand why you're curious. But I don't want what I am about to tell you to get out from within these four walls. Or I might have to kill you."

"Really?" I asked.

"Nah," he said. "Only joking. But I wouldn't want it to reach the press. Can I trust you?"

"You can trust me," said Bill.

"Me too," I said.

"Okay," said Spritzer. "The truth is I'm not getting any younger. None of us is. Right?"

"Right," said Bill.

"Sure," I said.

"And, having never married," said Spritzer, "I have no legitimate heirs."

"But presumably you'll start a family," I said, "with your new fiancée."

"No chance," said Spritzer. "I've been firing blanks for years. A legacy of certain, let's just call them, complaints. So a legitimate son and heir ain't on the cards. No way."

"Are you saying that you may have an illegitimate son and heir?" asked Bill.

"Not to my knowledge," said Spritzer. "But I do have a daughter."

"How long have you known this?"

"That's the thing," said Spritzer. "I didn't know a thing until a few weeks back."

An idea was starting to form in my mind.

"And did she know about you?" I asked.

"No, she didn't."

"Until you told her, via a message carried by Harry Crouch," I said.

"Exactly."

"And then she disappeared."

"Yeah. And to this day it bugs me that I don't know why."

"So you sent Harry Crouch to find her, and he tracked her down to Jack O'Riordan's house. But then he lost her."

"That's about the size of it."

"But surely Olga is Igor Molotovski's daughter," I said.

"That's what I thought," said Spritzer. "And it's certainly what he thinks. But then I did the math, and figured out I could just as easily have been the father."

"Because you were having an affair with his wife," I suggested.

"I'd been screwing Katasha on and off for years," said Spritzer. "She used to be a beautiful woman, you know? Did a few porn films for me, as a matter of fact. Specialised, exotic stuff. Did you ever see *Lawrence of Her Labia? In Diana Jones And The Temple of Poon? Spankenstein?*"

"But she threw you over for Igor."

"Yeah," he said. "She saw that he was more entrepreneurial than I was, a little bit richer, and a lot more ready to commit, so she and Igor got hitched. But hey, I kept on banging her for old time's sake. Never let it be said that I harbour a grudge."

"So nine months later Olga came along."

"And I thought nothing of it," he said. "I was banging a few other broads at the time, and who's counting? But then recently I saw pictures of Olga, and she looked nothing like Igor, and a lot more like me. So I bribed one of her teachers to get me some of her DNA."

"Clever," I said.

"I know," he said.

"And when you got the results back from the lab?" asked Bill.

"There was no doubt about it," said Spritzer. "The kid was mine. One thousand per cent. So I wrote her."

"What did you say?"

"That she was my flesh and blood. She has my DNA. And I wanted her to come and live with me."

"You didn't think it might be an idea to talk to Katasha first?"

"I figured the kid's about to turn eighteen. It's time for her to find out who her real father is."

"And did she reply to your letter?"

"No," said Spritzer. "And that's what gets me worried. At first I figure she wants nothing to do with me. But then I hear she's run away from home. And I wonder why she hasn't run away to me."

"It's possible," I said, "that she may want nothing to do with you."

"But why would that be?" Spritzer asked. "Look at me. Look

at this place. I have everything money can buy. And I'm offering it all to her. What's not to like?"

"Maybe she didn't want to be pressured," I suggested. "Your letter may have left her confused, uncertain where to turn."

"Yeah, but where does she go?" demanded Spritzer. "First, to a gay guy who used to take kiddie porn photos of her. Then she's off with some mystery woman. When she could come to her old dad and inherit my billions. Where's the sense in that?"

At this point, the butler came in and whispered something in the billionaire's ear.

"Oh no, I'd completely forgotten," said Spritzer. "I told this reporter I'd give her an interview. Look, tell her to stay for dinner, and I'll talk to her later."

He turned to Bill and myself.

"You guys will stay for dinner and overnight, right? Most of the guests are going back to London, but a few are staying over."

"We'd be honoured, mate," said Bill.

Bill waited until we were out of the room and grinned.

"That guy knows where so many bodies are buried. Wait until he's got a few more drinks inside him. Then he'll be really indiscreet."

Sadly, dinner did not turn out the way Bill had planned. Nor did breakfast, the following day. But that's a whole new chapter.

24

MURDER!

Monday, 8th and Tuesday, 9th August

I was pleased to see Marion Brooke at drinks before dinner. She looked ravishing in a dark green evening dress. It showed off her complexion, long neck and breasts to perfection. I was even more pleased that Jean-Paul De Mode was nowhere to be seen.

"Jean-Paul had to go back to London," said Marion, anticipating my question. "That German footballer gave him a lift."

"Joseph Gildenstern?" I asked.

"I think that's what he was called. Isn't he a little old and portly to be a footballer?"

"He's retired now. Devotes himself to international arms dealing and high living."

"Yes," she said. "It looks like it."

"But you've stayed for dinner."

"Oh, I've nothing better to do," she said. "Besides, Bernhard told me you were staying the night, and I thought it would give us the chance to get to know each other a little better."

I hoped I wasn't blushing again. She looked at me with an amused expression.

"You're not exactly at ease when you're around women, are you?"

"Er, well, um, not when I'm around you, no," I admitted.

"Oh my God," she said, looking over my shoulder. "Tell me it's not her."

I turned round. Stephanie Sharp was coming through the door. She was looking more than usually bad-tempered, like a red-headed Morticia Addams with a migraine. I followed her eyeline and saw that she was staring at Bill Slope. He hadn't seen her yet, and was talking to Bernhard Spritzer.

"Spritzer said he was being interviewed by a reporter," I said. "But he didn't say it was her. Do you think he knows she used to be married to Bill Slope?"

"Is that his name? The way she's looking at him now," said Marion, with an amused glint in her eye, "I'd say there's no love lost between them."

Stephanie took a glass of champagne from a waiter's tray, and came across to join us.

"Why, Marion," she trilled. "Is Jean-Paul not with you? That must be why you're looking so happy and relaxed."

"He was here," said Marion, "but he's gone back to London."

"You're so trusting," said Stephanie. "Some wives wouldn't let a husband who looks like that out of their sight. Why only the other night, I saw him being carried out of a party, drunk."

"That was by me, actually," I said.

"I beg your pardon" said Stephanie Sharp. "Have we met?"

"We haven't been formally introduced," I said.

"Allow me," said Marion. "Stephanie, I'd like to introduce Charlie Charlesworth. He used to play football for Arsenal and England, but now he's a private investigator."

"Really?" said Stephanie, grins at me with her usual insolent expression. "When I saw you the other night, I assumed you were a bouncer."

"Funny you should say that," I said. "I have occasionally worked as a bodyguard."

"No doubt that's why you're standing so close to Miss Brooke." I took a step away.

"Dear Marion," said Stephanie, "I'm so glad you've agreed to come on my new chat show. You weren't my first choice, but Cameron Diaz had to go back to America, and my producer insisted."

"Then your producer has good taste," said Marion. "Who else is on the show?"

"That awful, fat Mexican director," said Stephanie. "The one who's so lazy, he hardly ever directs."

"Oh, Alfredo Di Cojones," said Marion. "Did you know he taught Jean-Paul film studies at college?"

"I had no idea Jean-Paul went to college," said Stephanie.

"He dropped out after a year," said Marion.

"I expect it was too much of an intellectual challenge," said Stephanie.

"Do you know the thing I like about you, Stephanie?" asked Marion.

"No, darling. What's that?"

"You're living proof that a sharp tongue does not mean you have a keen mind."

"Thank you so much, Marion. I'm always so refreshed and challenged by your unique point of view."

"Well, of course I'd love to see things the way you do," said Marion, "but I'm not sure I can stick my head quite that far up my arse."

Stephanie gave a little tinkling laugh of false merriment.

"I'm sorry, I just can't find anything mean to say to you," she replied. "It must be 'Be kind to dumb animals' week."

Marion stamped her foot.

"Don't stomp your little last season Jimmy Choo shoes at me, darling," said Stephanie. "It's so cute that you think I might actually care what you think about me."

"Oh, Christ," said Bill.

He'd obviously come over to talk to me and failed to notice his ex-wife with her back to him.

"William!" said Stephanie. "You're looking perfectly dreadful. Who's cutting your hair these days? The county council?"

"What are you doing here?" he asked.

"I've come to interview Bernie Spritzer," she said, "and meet his new fiancée. She looks even younger and less intelligent than the last one."

"I thought for a moment you'd come here to torment me," said Bill.

"Don't think of me as your tormentor," said Stephanie. "More as a reminder of what you can't have."

"Ha!" Bill laughed bitterly.

"That's right," said Stephanie. "Laugh at your problems. After all, everyone else does."

"You never did have much time for anyone except yourself," he said. "Not even your own child."

"Darling," she said, "I was a mere child myself when I had Ben. I was barely 21. I had my career to pursue."

"Not many kids are brought up with two nannies. One for daytime, the other at night."

"That child," she said, "was always a black hole of need. And it's not as if you did anything to help."

"I was 38," he said. "At the pinnacle of my career."

"Not much of a pinnacle, was it?" she asked. "Investigative reporting for a downmarket rag, now happily defunct."

"Excuse me," I said. "A thought just crossed my mind."

"That," replied Stephanie, "must have been a long and lonely journey."

"Why don't you go and talk to someone you actually

like?" I asked Stephanie Sharp. "Or do you dislike absolutely everyone?"

"Of course she does," said Bill. "Can't you see she's just a bitter old hag? Those who can, do. Those who can't, bitch."

"Why don't you slip into something more comfortable?" said Stephanie to Bill. "Such as a coma."

"I'm sorry, mate," Bill told me, "but I don't think I can stay. I'm off back to London."

"Please don't go on my account," said Stephanie.

"You know, Stephanie," said Bill, "a lot of people think your bitchiness is just an act, but I know why you are the way you are. You just hate to see other people being happy. You envy wealth, you envy talent, you envy success of any kind."

"I certainly don't envy you," retorted his ex-wife. "Did you enjoy your time in prison with your fellow perverts?"

"I was never guilty of that crime," said Bill.

"What a pity you couldn't prove it in court," said Stephanie.

"Leave me alone, you poisonous old reptile," said Bill.

Stephanie ignored him and addressed Marion instead.

"A lot of people ask me why women can't tell jokes," said Stephanie. "My reply is that we don't tell jokes, we marry them."

"That's it," said Bill. "I'm sorry, Charlie, I've got to go. I'll see you tomorrow."

The last thing I saw of him that evening, Bill was talking to our host and shaking his hands. In the time-honoured tradition of *News of the World* journalists, he made his excuses and left.

Over dinner, I hoped to sit somewhere in the vicinity of Marion Brooke. Instead, I found myself next to Edward Killingfield.

"Hello, Handsome," he said, breathily.

"Hi," I said.

"You must be pleased you're sitting next to me," he said, "and not that awful journo bitch."

"Stephanie Sharp?" I said.

"Alias the Wicked Witch of the West End," he said. "Why she's so popular, I can't imagine."

"Well, Simon Cowell's very successful," I said. "And Anne Robinson."

"I know, dear," he said. "It's a good job some of us have style and taste, isn't it?"

I pondered on this for a moment. Somehow, I didn't fancy discussing the nature of style or taste with an overweight transvestite who enjoyed cooking the kind of food that made me throw up.

"It's hot in here, isn't it?" I said.

"Yes," he said. "Humid. It's like the calm before some tropical storm."

We chomped our way through our lamb cutlets in silence.

"Good, these," I said.

"If you like that sort of thing," he said. "If you ask me, the cooking leaves something to be desired, and as for the ingredients."

He gave a theatrical shudder. I could see that he was not the kind of chef who would find it easy to give another chef a compliment. It was over pudding that I made another attempt at conversation, this time about our mutual friend Joseph Gildenstern.

"I gather Joseph was called away to London," I said.

"Oh, that's what you heard, was it?" he said, with elaborate disdain.

"Isn't it true?"

"I really wouldn't know," he replied, with more than a hint of huffiness.

"Have you and he had an argument?" I asked.

"Is it that obvious?" he asked.

"Well, it is, a bit."

"Didn't you see the way he looked at that film star?" he said.

"You mean Jean-Paul De Mode?" I asked.

"Who else?" he said. "Couldn't keep his eyes off him. Joseph practically drooled."

"Well, De Mode is very good looking," I said. "Though shorter than he looks on screen."

"That's what I said to Joseph," said Killingfield. "He told me I was being a jealous old queen. As if I would be jealous of Jean-Paul De Mode!"

"Didn't the two of them drive off together?" I asked.

"Did they?"

"Marion told me they had."

"Oh, that's his wife, isn't it," said Killingfield. "That rather conventionally good-looking woman at the other end of the table."

"Yes."

"And was she upset at all?"

"No. On the contrary, she seemed perfectly okay about it," I said.

Killingfield appeared mollified.

"Perhaps it was platonic, and Joseph was trying to impress him. You know, with his car. It's the latest Merc."

"I'm sure you're right. Anyway, I can't believe that you have anything to worry about," I said. "I mean, look at Marion Brooke. Who would want to cheat on someone like that?"

"You have a point," admitted Killingfield. "She does have a certain superficial allure."

"I think she's wonderful."

There must have been something in my voice that made the corpulent chef smile lasciviously.

"Ha! Don't even think about it," said Killingfield. "She's way out of your league."

"Why does everyone keep telling me that?" I said

"Probably because it's true," remarked the chef.

Before I went to sleep, I phoned my sister.

"Where are you?" I asked.

"Outside a house in Mayfair," she said.

"What are you doing there?"

"I've been following De Mode," she said. "Now he's inside the house. So I'm waiting for him."

"He must be with Gildenstern," I said.

"I thought I recognised him," she said. "Isn't he a footballer?"

"Used to be," I said. "Now he's an arms dealer."

"I don't think it's arms they've gone in there to discuss," she said. "First they went to Killingfield's and had a meal. Then they came back here, and they were all over each other."

"Have they gone upstairs?" I asked.

"No," she said. "It looks as though they're downstairs. The lights are on in the basement."

"That's the dungeon," I said.

"Christ," said Tracey. "What do you think they're doing to each other?"

"I'd rather not conjecture," I said. "Do you want to go home?"

"To Gareth?" she said. "This looks far more interesting."

I couldn't get to sleep, partly because of that phone call and partly because of the humidity. It was a relief that after midnight the storm finally broke. The thunder and lightning were frighteningly loud, and so close together that the storm must have been virtually overhead.

It was around one o'clock that the door to my bedroom opened. There, silhouetted in the doorway, was a woman. For a moment or two, I wasn't sure who it was, or whether I was dreaming.

At first, I thought it was Stephanie Sharp, come to haunt my nightmares. But the voice that spoke was not hers. It was Marion Brooke's.

"Do you mind?" she asked. "I've always been frightened of storms."

"What? No," I said. "Do come in."

She came over to the bed. I could tell she was barefoot.

"Move over," she said.

She didn't sound particularly frightened. I felt the warmth of her body press against mine. The consequence was predictable.

"You are pleased to see me, aren't you?" she laughed, climbing on top of me.

This is not one of those kiss and tell books, so I won't go into detail about everything that happened next. I don't want to be in the running for one of those 'bad sex' prizes for dodgy literature. Suffice it to say that I didn't get a lot of sleep that night. And it was absolutely bloody fantastic.

When I awoke, Marion was gone, and I wondered for a few moments if I had been dreaming. But I could still smell her scent.

Oh, Charlie, what have you done? I thought. But I reassured myself that, even if I had committed adultery with one of my own clients, thus breaking Bill Slope's Rule Number One, at least we had had an amazingly pleasurable time doing it. I even fantasised that, were she to ditch her handsome, gym-honed, wealthy film star husband, she might come running to me for more than professional advice.

I showered and went down to breakfast. Marion was already downstairs and greeted me with a wicked smile.

"Sleep well?" she asked.

"Fantastically well," I said. "You?"

"I had an incredibly vivid dream," she said. "You were in it."

I could tell from her giggle that I had blushed again. Any further conversation was hindered by the arrival of Edward Killingfield, never a pretty sight and even less so first thing in the morning, without his makeup.

"Morning, all," he said. "Has anyone got anything for a headache? I seem to have the most awful hangover."

"Greetings, guests," said Bernhard Spritzer, entering with a spring in his step. "You're the last ones to rise. I've already been out riding with my fiancée. I hope you're all ready for a cooked breakfast. You'll find it in the silver salvers over there, on the sideboard, next to the newspapers."

It was Edward Killingfield who saw the headlines first.

"Heavens," he said, "there's been even more rioting. All over West London – Notting Hill, Brent and Ealing."

"And in the south," said Marion. "Clapham, Merton, Southwark, Greenwich, Croydon…"

"And the east," I said. "Newham, Stratford and Hackney. That's where my sister lives. I'd better ring her to make sure she's okay."

But before I could do so, she rang me.

"Hi, Trace, are you okay?"

"Not really," she said.

"Were you caught up in the riots?"

"What are you talking about?" she said. "I've been stuck in Mayfair all night. I fell asleep in the car."

"So where are you now?" I asked.

"That's the thing," she said. "I'm in a spot of trouble. I'm in a dungeon with two dead men. One of them's that ex-footballer."

"Gildenstern?" I asked.

The mention of his name made Edward Killingfield look across at me inquiringly.

"Christ," I said. "And I suppose…?"

"Yeah. The other one's De Mode."

"That's terrible," I said.

"It gets worse," she said. "The police are just arriving. Someone must have tipped them off."

"I suppose it saves you having to ring them."

"You don't understand, bruv. It doesn't look too good. I think I may be holding the murder weapon. Sorry, got to go."

I looked down at the mobile phone.

"What's the matter?" asked Marion. "You look as though there's been a death in the family."

"In a way, there has," I said. "But not my family. Yours."

"What?" she asked.

"I'm afraid it's Jean-Paul," I said.

"What do you mean?" asked Marion.

"But Joseph took him back to London," said Edward Killingfield.

"I know," I said. "That was my sister just now. She was watching them."

"Why?" asked Marion.

"You asked me to keep Jean-Paul under surveillance," I said. "She says they went to your restaurant and then back to Gildenstern's place. Where they've been found in the basement. I'm afraid they're both dead."

"Dead?" gasped Killingfield.

"No!" said Marion.

"Murdered," I said.

"Who by?" asked Marion.

"I only wish I knew," I said.

Bill Slope was the next person to ring me.

"Where are you, mate?" he asked.

"On my way back to London," I said. "Bernie Spritzer's lent me his chauffeur."

"Are you coming back to Soho Square?" Slope asked.

"I was planning to," I said.

"That might not be such a great idea," he said. "The news about De Mode and Gildenstern has just hit the internet, and there's a lot of reporters outside. They seem to have got wind that we're involved."

"Is Tracey okay?"

"She's helping the police with their inquiries," said Bill. "it doesn't look too good. They found her with blood all over her, and a machete in her hand."

"What a mess," I said.

"That's not all," he replied.

"Not another murder," I said.

"Not exactly," he said. "But it is quite weird. Guess who's been trying to contact you."

"Who?"

"Lorenzo Fettucini."

"I wish he'd make up his mind," I said. "He keeps telling me he has nothing to say to me."

"He sounds like he has plenty to say to you, right now," said Bill. "In fact, he sounds scared. No, not scared. Terrified."

"He's been ringing the office?" I asked.

"He says he doesn't have your mobile number, so I told him I'd ring you, and that if you were interested you'd call him back."

"Okay," I said.

Lorenzo had obviously been expecting my call, because he picked up the phone before I could hear it ring.

"Charlie," he said. "Thank God you called. I am all on my own here, and I don't like it."

"What about your family?" I asked.

"They still in Italia," he said. "Charlie, I need your help. You're the only one I can trust."

"I can't believe that's true," I said. "What about your agent?"

"Spritzer tell him he know all about the betting scam. Now he no answer my calls."

"So what are you afraid of?" I asked.

"I no tell you before, but a man is out to get me."

"What kind of man?" I asked.

"I think maybe he want to kill me."

"Lorenzo, you're not making any sense," I said.

"I need protection," he said.

"Why don't you call the police?"

"What am I going to say?" Fettucini demanded. "He no try and kill me yet."

"Are you sure you're not over-dramatising?"

"I see on the news," said Fettucini. "About the film star and Gildenstern. I could be the next!"

And he told me where he lived, in a very swanky area of Kensington.

"Okay," I said, "Stay where you are. I'll be right over."

And I was. But when I got there, it wasn't a pretty sight.

25

PSYCHO

"So here we are again," said Frank Drake companionably. "I'm sure you remember Sergeant Patel."

We were in the conference room at Soho Square. I was relieved to see that Bill Slope had tidied away his sleeping bag and belongings. I assumed they were behind the couch.

"Of course," I said. "I must say these murders have shaken me up a bit."

"Not only you," said Drake. "They're causing quite a stir down at the Yard. Though you'll understand we do have other things on our mind right now."

"You mean the riots?" I asked.

Drake nodded.

"But that doesn't mean we're not giving these murders our full attention," he said. "It's not every day we find two well-known public figures hacked to death with a machete as they are engaged in a homosexual act."

"This killer must be a total psycho," I said.

"You think so?" asked Drake.

"I presume you're linking these three murders," I said, "to the deaths of O'Riordan and Parente?"

"We're keeping an open mind," said Drake. "Contrary to rumour, serial killers are uncommon in this country. But it looks as if we might have one here, wouldn't you say?"

Something about the way he looked at me made me squirm in my seat.

"A pattern," Drake continued, "is certainly emerging. And the curious thing is, everything seems to be centred on you."

"Me? I had nothing to do with it," I said.

"It's too bad, then, that you were found at the scene of one crime, and your sister at another," said Drake. "And you seem to have been involved with every single one of the deceased over the last seven days."

"Couldn't that just be a coincidence?" I said.

"I don't believe in coincidences," said Drake.

"You told me that before."

"It remains true."

"So why haven't you arrested me?" I asked.

"What makes you think we're not about to do so?" inquired Drake.

"Perhaps I should have my solicitor present," I said.

"I'm not sure that's necessary," said Drake. "The person we're looking for appears to be a highly intelligent, devious serial killer. Nothing I know about you fits that profile."

"Thanks," I said. "I think."

"I don't intend to be offensive," continued Drake with a smile he presumably intended to be encouraging, "but your conduct seems to me not so much highly intelligent as weirdly incompetent bordering on imbecilic."

"Oh?"

"You're meant to be finding a runaway Russian heiress, are you not?" he asked.

"That's correct."

"But you don't know where she is," he pointed out.

"Not yet," I admitted. "I thought she was having an affair with Jean-Paul De Mode, but under the circumstances in which you found him, that seems, ah, improbable."

"So you no longer think she was impelled to leave home for love of Mr de Mode," said Drake.

"Even before the events in the dungeon," I said, "I had my doubts."

"Oh, really?" drawled Drake. "And why was that?"

"I found out that Mr De Mode had taken out an injunction."

"Against anyone in particular?"

"A woman named Stephanie Sharp," I said, "who coincidentally used to be married to my associate, Bill Slope."

"I told you before," said Drake. "I don't believe in coincidences."

"But this case is riddled with them," I pointed out.

"And doesn't that strike you as peculiar?" asked Drake.

"Now you mention it, yes," I admitted.

"And, by another of these extraordinary coincidences," continued Drake, "I believe you were investigating Mr De Mode."

"Oh," I said, "you know about that."

"His wife has told us everything."

"Everything?"

"About her hiring you. She also mentioned your night of passion."

"In fact, you owe her some gratitude," continued Patel. "Because of that, we know you can't have been in a dungeon thirty miles away, murdering her husband."

"Not unless she's in league with you," said Drake, "and your sister. Perhaps the three of you conspired together to murder De Mode."

"Tracey wouldn't do a thing like that," I said. "Nor would I. Nor would Marion."

"Just how well do you know Marion Brooke?" asked Drake.

"Well enough to know she's not a murderess," I said.

"That's your opinion, is it?" said Drake. "Interesting."

"Anything more to tell us about De Mode?" inquired Sergeant Patel.

"Well, I had my doubts about the story about him having an affair with Olga," I said. "Especially when I discovered he had a background in gay porn."

"Oh?" Drake looked interested, as if for the first time I was telling him something he didn't know.

I looked across at Patel. I seemed to have aroused his interest, too.

"And how did you discover that?" asked Patel.

I thought for a moment about concealing my source, then decided I had no reason not to tell the truth.

"It was Bernie – I mean, Bernhard Spritzer."

"And Mr Spritzer had first-hand knowledge?" asked Drake.

"I'm pretty sure he financed the films in question," I replied. "Besides, it made sense. I knew De Mode had taken out an injunction to conceal something. And Bernie boasted that he used his knowledge of De Mode's past to make him come to his parties and give them a touch of celebrity glitter."

"Did Mr Spritzer mention which porn films De Mode was in?" asked Patel.

"Yes, he did," I said. "I can't remember the titles. Quite a few of them were like Spielberg films, but not quite."

"*Raiders of the Lost Arse?*" asked Patel.

"I think that was one of them, yes," I said.

"That is most interesting and possibly significant," said Patel. "Mr De Mode was discovered in a dungeon."

"Yes, I know," I said.

"What you may not know is that he was, so to speak, conjoined with Mr Gildenstern."

"Conjoined?" I asked.

"Mr Gildenstern perished," continued Patel, "with a part of his anatomy inside Mr De Mode."

"You mean?"

"No," said Drake. "It's not the part you're thinking. It was his arm. Up to the elbow."

"And now I know what they were doing," said Sergeant Patel, excitedly. "They were re-enacting a scene from one of Mr De Mode's old porn films."

"You mean you know them?" asked Drake.

"I know this one," said Sergeant Patel. "Did Mr Spritzer ever tell you of the movie *Schindler's Fist*?"

There was a silence, as Drake looked first at me, then at his sergeant, clearly unsure whether to be grateful or repelled at the range of his expertise.

"No," I said. "I'm pretty sure I'd have remembered that one."

"Another thing," said Drake. "I gather you were professionally involved with the deceased Mr Gildenstern."

"Yes," I said. "He approached me on behalf of Bernie Spritzer. They wanted to know why Bernie's principal striker at Southern Athletic wasn't scoring any goals."

"I take it you're talking about the other deceased gentleman," said Patel.

"I am," I said.

"I suppose your finding his corpse," remarked Drake drily, "was another coincidence?

"They do seem to be piling up," I acknowledged.

"And were your investigations into Mr Fettucini bearing fruit?" asked Drake.

"Yes, we pretty much solved the mystery," I said.

"We?"

"Me and Bill Slope," I said.

"Mr Slope works for you?" asked Drake.

"In an informal capacity," I said. "I don't pay him anything, just give him board and lodging."

"Where?"

"In here," I said. "He sleeps on that couch."

Drake looked across at the couch with barely concealed distaste.

"Isn't Mr Slope a convicted paedophile?" said Patel.

"He is," I said, "but I have reason to believe he may have been the victim of a miscarriage of justice."

"Oh?" Drake raised one eyebrow.

"I'm not sure it has any relevance to this case," I said.

"Let me be the judge of that," said Drake.

"You'll have to talk to Bill," I said. "I think he just wants to put that whole business behind him."

"Hmm," said Drake. "So what was the solution?"

"Excuse me?"

"You say you solved the mystery, but you didn't tell us what you found out."

"To cut a long story short," I said. "Fettucini had got himself involved with a betting scam, which meant he had to avoid scoring a goal during his first thirty games for Southland Athletic."

"He admitted this?" asked Drake.

"Pretty much," I said.

"And then you told Gildenstern and Spritzer what he was up to?"

"Yes," I said.

"Has it occurred to you that revelation might have contributed to Mr Fettucini's demise?"

"I suppose it might have," I admitted. "But Gildenstern seemed to have other things on his mind, such as taking Mr De Mode home with him. And didn't he die several hours before Fettucini?"

"What about Bernie Spritzer?" inquired Drake.

"Well, Mr Drake, you probably know him better than I do," I said. "You were at his party."

Patel shot a curious glance at his boss.

"Go on," said Drake, impassively.

"I simply don't think Bernie Spritzer works like that," he said. "He's more into firing people than having them put to death ritualistically."

"Possibly," said Drake, starting to look distracted.

He got up and paced around the room. Then he shook his head.

"I'm sorry," he muttered. "One of the many things I'm trying to get my head round is why Mr Fettucini asked you, of all people, to protect him."

"That's right," said Patel. "Hadn't you just signed his professional death warrant when you shopped him to Gildenstern and Spritzer?"

"Yes," I said. "But he didn't know that. And I had looked after him when he was in trouble before. I think in a funny way he still trusted me."

"He must have been incredibly thick," said Drake.

"He was, yes," I said.

"Even for a footballer," said Drake.

I decided not to rise to the insult.

"So why did you go to his house?" asked Drake.

"He told me someone was going to kill him."

"But he didn't say who."

"No."

"And when you reached him, it was too late," said Patel.

"I rang on his door, but there was no reply. The door was open. I walked straight in. And there he was. In his living room. Or rather on the living room wall."

"Describe the state in which you found him."

"What, again?"

"Yes, again."

"He was crucified," I said. "Nailed to the wall. With, you know, bits missing."

"And those were?"

"Fingers and toes."

"That is part of what intrigues me," said Drake. "Virtually all these deaths have involved missing body parts."

"Well, you can search my premises any time you like," I said. "I'm not hoarding them."

"You think someone is?" asked Drake.

"How should I know?" I said. "Isn't that what some soldiers do? Keep the ears of their enemies?"

"Except it isn't the ears he's interested in," said Drake.

"Is it always the fingers and toes?" I asked.

"No," said Drake. "But he seems to be extremely handy with a knife."

"You mean, like Jack the Ripper?" I said.

"There are similarities, yes," said Drake.

"Down at the Yard, we have a nickname for him," said Patel.

"Just a little gallows humour," said Drake. "They're calling him Jack the Snipper."

"Or the Trophy Hunter," added Patel.

The two men chuckled. I was a bit shocked at their flippancy.

"You mean," I said, "he cuts off body parts and keeps them as trophies?"

"That would seem to be the case, yes," said Sergeant Patel.

"And that's true of all his victims?"

"Except Mr Parente," said Patel. "But we're working on the assumption that the killer may have been interrupted before he could start mutilating him."

"Does he always take the same bits?"

"No," said Drake. "But I don't wish to go into detail."

"You say he," I said. "Couldn't be it a she?"

"It would take someone fairly strong to pick up Fettucini and nail him to a wall," said Drake.

"So you don't suspect my sister?"

"Despite her attempt to incriminate herself by being found with a machete and leaving fingerprints all over one crime scene," said Drake, "she could hardly have murdered Mr Fettucini, since she was at that very moment helping us with our inquiries."

"Was she any good as a witness?" I asked.

"She never saw the killer, unfortunately," said Drake. "All she heard were screams from the dungeon, which made her go and investigate."

"But by the time she got in, the assailant had gone," said Patel.

"No trace of him," said Drake. "We think they died around 1 a.m."

"Along with body parts from the victims?" I asked.

"As no doubt your sister will tell you, Mr De Mode was missing his tongue, and both men were minus various other parts, including their pancreas."

"Their sweetbreads," I said.

"Sorry?"

"In restaurants they call them the sweetbreads," I said.

"Are you suggesting our killer may be a cannibal?" asked Drake.

"I have absolutely no idea," I said. "I was just thinking aloud."

"So perhaps, as the 21st century answer to Sherlock Holmes, you have formed an opinion as to the killer's identity?" asked Drake. "You know, as one investigator to another."

He said this with a straight face, but I had a feeling that inwardly he was laughing at me.

"Sorry," I admitted. "I haven't a clue."

"You haven't even formed a view as to his motive?" asked Drake.

"I imagine he enjoys killing people and cutting them up," I said. "Is that enough?"

"Not really," said Drake. "There is a pattern to these deaths. Perhaps we're all too close to them to work out how they are inter-related."

"So I take it you're not arresting me?" I asked.

"Good heavens, no," said Drake. "If we'd wanted to do that,

we'd have hauled you down to the station. I've already said you don't strike me as serial-killer material."

"I don't?" I didn't know whether to feel relieved, or aggrieved.

"No," said Drake. "You're the sort of person who blushes when he's guilty of bedding a world-famous film star. I hardly think you've got the guts to murder her husband and four others."

"Added to which," said Sergeant Patel regretfully, "she's given you an excellent alibi."

"Don't you think Marion and I might be covering up for each other?" I asked. "Couldn't it be some kind of crime of passion, like in *Double Indemnity*?"

"To be perfectly honest," said Drake, "I don't think Marion Brooke feels that strongly about you. In fact, with regard to last night's escapade, I'm fairly sure she already regrets it."

"Besides," added Patel, "Mr Spritzer is kindly supplying us with all his surveillance tapes for the relevant period."

"That's right," said Drake, "so we can check that all his guests including you, Miss Brooke and Mr Killingfield, were where they say they were, and didn't slip out of his compound for a spot of gratuitous serial-killing. And now perhaps you would ask Mr Slope to come in? I have a few questions I'd like to ask him."

Around an hour later, Bill Slope came out of being interviewed by the two policemen. He walked into my office and slumped into the chair on the opposite side of his desk.

"Bloody hell," he said. "What are you doing?"

"I'm playing the FA Cup Final," I said. "Arsenal versus Manchester United. We're two up in extra time."

"Aren't you a bit old for computer games?" he asked.

"Probably," I said. "But this one helps me to relax."

"You don't want to get dependent on them," he said. "My son did, to those shoot-em-up games, and look what happened to him."

"You mentioned he joined the army," I said.

"Precisely. Ben joined up and got blown up twice. Once in a helicopter accident and once by a roadside bomb."

"Unlucky."

"I blame myself," said Bill.

"Why?"

"I wasn't the world's best father," he said. "And Stephanie was a bloody awful mother. Maybe we should have been more supportive, I don't know."

"Do you think Tom and I get on all right?" I asked.

"Yeah, mate. Obviously he thinks you're a silly old sod, but nowadays that's par for the course."

I looked back at my computer screen.

"He doesn't approve of my wasting my time on Football Manager," I said.

"Yeah, well, at least he cares," said Bill. "Would you like me to leave you in peace?"

"I'll be with you in a moment," I said. "Yay! We've won!"

"Congratulations," he said.

"Sorry about that," I said.

"No worries," said Bill.

"You okay?" I asked. "You were in there a long time."

"They wanted to know if I had an alibi," he said.

"What, for last night?"

"For all the crimes," he said. "And of course I didn't."

"You were up in Norfolk for the first two, weren't you?" I asked.

"Yeah, but that's not much of an alibi," he said. "You saw my cottage, it was miles from anywhere."

"As for the other murders, you were with me last night," I pointed out.

"But after my little spat with Stephanie, I came back here and had an early night."

"No witnesses?"

"None," he said.

306

"But why would you want to kill five people?"

"That's the really weird thing about it, mate," he said. "I'm glad they're all dead."

"That doesn't mean you killed them," I pointed out.

"No, but they're all people I've done work on," he said. "And I know they're all scumbags."

"Sure, but for you the biggest scumbag of them all is Igor Molotovski, and he's still alive."

"Maybe the killer hasn't got round to dealing with him yet."

"What are you saying?" I asked.

"I dunno. It's kind of spooky," he said. "It's almost as though my thoughts about people – that they didn't deserve to live – have somehow transformed themselves into actions."

"I know what you mean," I said. "They pretty much accused me of being like Typhoid Mary. You know, killing everyone I came into contact with."

"Yeah," said Bill. "That's the way I feel."

"But you're not responsible for these murders," I said.

Bill shifted in his chair, and looked me full in the face.

"It's almost like I've willed it," he said. "Perhaps I just don't *know* that I'm responsible."

26

SABOTEUR

Wednesday, 10th August

I was settling in for an evening in front of a good DVD – I'd put in disc one of a Danish TV series called *The Killing*, which seemed appropriate – when the doorbell rang. I looked through the spyhole. The person outside looked like Marion Brooke, in a dark wig. I opened the door. The welcoming smile must have frozen on my face.

"Sorry," said the woman. "Is this a bad time?"

"Oh, you again," I said. "I spent a good part of today talking to your dad."

"Socially?" said Detective Inspector Smith.

"No," I said. "Assisting him with his inquiries. Into this string of murders."

"I've been reading about them. Were you able to help?" she asked.

"I'm not sure," I said. "I don't think I was, really."

"So you didn't crumble," she said, "make a full confession."

"Obviously I was tempted," I said. "But there was this minor problem. I wasn't guilty."

"That's good," she said.

"To what do I owe the pleasure of this visit?" I asked.

"I'm bringing back your computer hardware," she said. "And your son's. And the rest of your stuff. It's all in cardboard boxes."

"I take it you didn't find anything incriminating."

"No," she said. "We didn't. Sorry about that."

"I'm not."

"I don't mean I'm sorry you're innocent. I meant I'm sorry about the raid. And your door. Though I see you've had it fixed."

"Yes," I said. "Where's our stuff?"

"It's there," she said. "In my car. I only live nearby. So I said I'd bring it round."

"That's good of you."

After we had brought in the Charlesworth treasures, she hesitated.

"Can I have a word?" she asked.

"About what?" I asked.

"I'm concerned," she said, "about who gave us false information about you."

"Yes," I said. "I'm concerned about that too."

"Do you have any idea who that might be?"

I paused.

"Would you like to have a drink?"

"I'm officially on duty. Do you have anything soft?"

"I think we may have some fizzy water."

"That would be perfect."

When I returned, she was studying my pride and joy, a 1954 Wurlitzer jukebox.

"You seem to like Tamla Motown," she observed. "You must have most of their hits on here. What's your favourite?"

"Probably 'I Heard It On The Grapevine'," I said. "It's the story of my life."

"The Marvin Gaye version?"

"Of course."

"I like 'Ain't No Mountain High Enough'," she said.

"It's the same band," I said.

"No," she said. "It's Marvin Gaye and Tammi Terrell."

"Same backing band," I said. "The Funk Brothers."

"Who are they?" she asked.

"Great musicians like James Jamerson, Earl van Dyke, Joe Messina," I said. "None of them got any recognition until 1971. Officially, there were thirteen of them."

"What do you mean, officially?"

"Thirteen of them were honoured at the Grammys, but if you include every session man who played on a Motown hit, you'd have upwards of 84."

"And I expect you could name them, couldn't you?"

"Oddly enough, I probably could."

"That's a bit obsessional," she said. "You do know that, don't you?"

"I've never claimed to be normal," I said.

"What made you memorise their names?"

"It's something I did when I was in my twenties," I said. "I noticed that it's the big names who get the fame, but the real talent is often behind the scenes. It's true in football as well."

"There's more to you than meets the eye," she said.

"Thanks," I said, "I hope so."

After we had sat down, she took a sip of water and sat on the edge of the sofa. She seemed as though she was going to tell me something.

"By the way," she said, "I'm sorry if I was short with you at the party yesterday."

"Not at all," I said. "I can see it must have been embarrassing to run into one of your suspects at a social event."

"It wasn't that," she said. "By then I knew that you were pretty much innocent. I was just in a bad mood. Nothing to do with the job. It was more a personal thing. That's why my father took me to the party, I think. To take me out of myself."

"And did it work?"

"Not really," she said. "In fact, I found it pretty depressing. Seeing a silly little man bragging about how great it was to be a pornographer. It made me feel a bit sick, actually."

"I felt the same way," I said. "Though it's probably not politically correct to say so."

"If you don't mind my saying," she continued, "you seem a decent bloke."

"I hope I am."

"I mean, that's your nickname, isn't it?" she continued. "Proper Charlie."

"I'm never sure if that's a tribute," I said, "or an insult. I think a few people reckon I'm thick."

"I don't think you're thick," she said. "Well, not that thick. Specially not for a footballer."

"Thanks," I said.

"Anyway," she said, "I wanted to check out who you think might have been trying to set you up."

"As a paedophile?" I said. "I haven't a clue. Or rather I do have one clue. Which is that someone tried to do exactly the same thing to a bloke I know, and succeeded."

"And he was?"

"A bloke named Bill Slope," I said. "He's a former *News of the World* reporter and not above a bit of skulduggery, but I've got to know him a bit recently, and I'm a hundred percent sure he isn't a paedophile."

"Didn't he get sent to prison?"

"He did," I said. And a few days ago, he had his house burnt down, along with his belongings. All his books, records, even photos of his son."

"That's dreadful," she said. "Especially if he was innocent."

"And now he's living on a couch in my office," I said, "while he tries to put his life back together again."

"Nice of you to do him a good turn," she said.

"He's a bloody good investigator, actually," I said. "Miles better than me. I'm too trusting."

"Trusting is good," she said, with an encouraging smile.

"Not in my line of business, it isn't," I replied. "I'm pretty sure your father thinks I'm an imbecile."

"And you think he's right?"

"Not completely," I said. "I may not be that quick on the uptake, but I do tend to get there in the end."

"Like the tortoise and the hare?" she asked.

"Exactly."

"But you don't know who our serial killer is," she said.

"I'm working on it," I said. "Or rather my subconscious is. Whirring away in the background, while I do other things."

"Such as play Football Manager?" she asked.

"Yikes," I said. "You saw that on my hard disk."

"Yes," she said. "I play it too."

"Your father mentioned that," I said. "Which club?"

"Arsenal, of course."

"Me too," I said.

"How are you doing?" she asked. "I keep getting fired."

"That happened to me at first," I said.

"But then you learned how to cheat," she said.

I blushed.

"You saw that, did you?" I said.

"Actually, I did," she said.

"How embarrassing," I said.

"Not really," she said. "It's not as if you're subverting the entire game. It's just that before the really big matches, you save so that if you lose you can reload and try again."

"You know all that from studying my hard disk?"

She nodded.

"To tell you the truth," she said, "I do the same thing. I was relieved to find a fellow offender. I thought it was only me. My husband thought I was mental."

"Husband?"

"Ex-husband. We broke up around a year ago," she said. "Irreconcilable differences. One of which was my addiction to computer games."

"Football Manager?"

"That's just one of them," she said. "The one I'm really addicted to is called The Seven Deadly Sins. Do you know it?"

"Unfortunately, yes," I said.

"You should play it," she said. "It's really, really sick. You know, killing people and all that. But seriously addictive."

Maybe I really am thick, or I'd have taken what she said and come to the right conclusion a whole lot earlier than I did. But at that point, I was more interested in pumping her for information.

"So, er – sorry, I've forgotten your name."

"Carol."

"Carol, do you have any clues?" I asked. "Do you know who gave you the tip-off about me?"

"It was my sergeant who took the call," she said.

"Ah yes, Sergeant Karp," I said.

"He said it was a female," she said.

"Any accent?" I asked.

"No," she said. "Just normal, received pronunciation. But he did say one other thing."

"What's that?"

"Karp says she didn't sound very old. He said she sounded like a teenager. Eighteen or nineteen was his guess, but she could have been younger. And she had a stutter."

"Ah," I said.

"Does that sound like anyone you've met?"

"It sounds like someone I've never met."

"What do you mean?"

"Olga Molotovski."

"She stutters?"

"So I'm told."

"Isn't she that girl who's disappeared?"

"Yeah," I said. "And I'm one of the people looking for her."

"You think she might have been using us to try and sabotage your inquiries?"

I nodded.

"Well, if you do find her," continued DI Carol Smith, "it sounds like she might have some explaining to do."

"You're not wrong," I said. "Thanks for coming round personally. It was really nice of you."

"That's okay," she said. "It was the least I could do for a fellow Arsenal supporter."

All at once, there was a noise outside. Two people were shouting, one of whom I recognised. Before I could investigate, there was the sound of a key turning in the front door. Tom walked in, with the youth with green hair. The latter was carrying a can of spray paint.

"Look who I caught, spray-painting the front door," said Tom.

"I refuse to say anything," said the youth, before fastening me with a savage look. "Because you are a killer!"

"Look no further for our dyslexic loon," said Tom. "He thinks Killer starts with a C."

"What makes you say Mr Charlesworth's a killer?" asked Carol.

"Who are you?" asked Tom.

"I'm the copper who took away your computer," she replied. "Carol Smith."

"She's been returning our property," I said.

The youth with green hair seemed indignant that he was no longer the centre of attention.

"Why do I call him killer?" asked the youth. "Because he murdered my boss."

"He's referring to Mr Parente," I explained to Carol. "This kid was his receptionist."

"I'm not a kid," retorted the youth. "I am thirty-three years old."

314

"You look amazingly youthful," I said.

"Thank you," he said.

"But why do you think I murdered your boss?" I asked. "I can assure you I didn't."

"Did you see him after you have visited our office?" asked the youth, or rather youngish man. "I thought he was going to die then. He told me to follow you. And when I reported back that you had gone to see Jack O'Riordan, it was as though he had lost the will to live."

"Did he say anything?"

"He said that you were after him, and the authorities would not rest until they had him behind bars. So I took him home, cooked him a meal, and when I took it into him, he was dead."

"Dead?"

"He had taken a lot of pills, and with his heart he had many of them. He took his own life."

"But you said my dad killed him," Tom objected.

"He pursued Mr Parente into an early grave," he said.

"That's not the same thing as murdering him," I said.

"Look, did you tell the police any of this?" asked Tom. "I'm pretty sure they think Mr Parente was the victim of a serial killer."

"I could not be involved," said the youth. "I am not here legally. So I threw away the dinner I had cooked, disposed of his suicide note."

"You disposed of his suicide note?" asked Carol.

"The note just said they were out to get him, and he had decided to end it all."

"Why didn't you leave it where it was?" I `asked.

"Where I come from, in Singapore, aiding and abetting a suicide is a capital offence."

"It isn't here."

"No, but I told you I am here illegally. If the British authorities had known of my involvement, they might have sent me home, and then where would I be?"

"You don't by any chance have a history of mental problems?" I asked.

"How did you know that?" he demanded. "Have you been investigating me?"

"No," I said. "I just had this crazy hunch."

"You don't have any idea of the trouble you've caused, do you?" Tom asked the Singaporean non-youth.

"Look, matey," said Carol. "I'm a policewoman and I'm going to take you down to the station. And if I were you I'd do two things. One is stop accusing Mr Charlesworth here of a murder he didn't commit. And two is, you need to tell the police all about how you found Mr Parente, so they're no longer under the impression that he was attacked by a serial killer. Right?"

The man struggled to assimilate this information.

"Will they send me back to Singapore?" he asked.

"With the Human Rights Act the way it is," said Carol Smith, "that is amazingly unlikely."

27

SHADOW OF A DOUBT

Thursday, 11th August

I passed a restless night. Various suspicions were forming in my head, and I didn't like what they were telling me. I was drinking my first morning coffee in the kitchen when Tom came in.

"Fancy another coffee?" he asked. "What do you think, instant or espresso?"

"No thanks, son," I said.

"Anything wrong, Dad?" he asked. "You're looking peaky."

"I've been thinking."

"About what?"

"About who might have set us up over that paedophile thing."

"Any conclusions?"

"Yes, and I don't like them one bit."

"Want to share them with me?"

"The girl who tipped off the police was Olga."

"How do you know that?"

"You saw Carol Smith came round last night."

"So?"

"She told me the tip-off to the police had been by a young woman."

"She saw her?"

"No her sergeant answered the phone. He said it was a young female voice. And she stuttered."

"That does sound like Olga," said Tom. "But why would she do that?"

"And if it was her, why did she do it to Bill Slope?" I said. "Added to which, I'm sure she had help."

"Why?"

"Because she must have had someone who came to our office and downloaded stuff on to my computer."

"When could that have happened?" asked Tom. "Do you think someone broke in?"

"There's only one person I can think of who might have done it," I said.

"Who?"

"I'd like you to find out all you can about Marion Brooke."

"You think it was her?"

"I don't see how it could have been anyone else."

"How come?"

"Remember the first time I was interviewed by the police?"

"In the conference room? Yeah."

"Marti showed Marion into my office," I said, "and she was in there for a long time on her own. A good twenty minutes. I'm pretty sure my credit card was on my computer."

"Wouldn't she have needed your password?"

"They're not hard to access. They're in a folder on my desktop, called Passwords."

"That's not very bright," said Tom.

"I know it isn't," I said. "But I hardly need to tell you that I allow you and Marti to use my credit card when you're ordering stuff for the office off the internet."

"True," said Tom.

"So she could have downloaded porn on to my computer."

"Yeah, she had the opportunity. But why would she do it?"

"I can't imagine," I said. "Unless…"

"What?"

"I'm just thinking out loud here," I said. "But couldn't she be the woman Harry Crouch saw collecting Olga from Jack O'Riordan's place?"

"Could be," said Tom. "So what we're looking for is some link between Olga Molotovski and Marion Brooke. You think they might be working together."

"It's the only hypothesis I can come up with."

"Okay," said Tom. "I'm on to it."

28

BLACKMAIL

Thursday, 11th August

I spent an enjoyable hour at home, buying and selling players. By the time I arrived at the office, Tom was looking pleased with himself.

"Any luck?" I asked.

"He raised one hand to acknowledge my presence, but did not move his eyes from the screen.

"You could say that," he said.

"What have you found?" I asked.

"A few things. One is a connection between Marion Brooke and Olga Molotovski."

"And that is?"

"They went to the same school."

He said that as if it was a big deal. I felt disappointed.

"Is that all?"

"There's more. Marion Brooke went back to her old school to deliver a speech. And guess who delivered the vote of thanks?"

"Olga?"

"The same," he said. "Look at this picture of them together. It was in the local paper."

"Okay, but what does that prove?" I asked.

"Wait," he said. "I told you there's more. Much more. I've spoken to Aunt Tracey this morning. You know she's keeping Chalcot Grove under surveillance?"

"I meant to call her off, now that De Mode is dead."

"It's just as well you didn't," said Tom. "She's seen a girl's face at an upstairs window."

"Not Marion Brooke?" I asked.

"Not Marion Brooke," said Tom. "Aunt Tracey took a photo on her phone. I'll put it up on the screen. Look, I'll zoom in on it."

I looked at it. Blurred though it was, and partly concealed by the reflection of a tree, the face was unmistakable."

"Bloody hell," I said. "It's Olga."

"It certainly looks like her to me."

"But what's she doing there?" I asked. "Wasn't she having an affair with De Mode?"

"Think about it," said Tom. "The person who told us that was Fairycakes. Would you say she's a reliable witness?"

"She said she saw De Mode kissing the girl, and he was stripped to the waist."

"And what do we now know about him?" asked Tom.

"He was gay, or at any rate bisexual."

"And he and Marion had a lavender marriage," said Tom.

"Looks like it," I agreed. "But what was in it for Marion?"

"It helped dispel those rumours that she was gay."

"So what was the sense of her hiring me to check on her husband?" I asked.

"To distract us," said Tom. "Olga must have heard from O'Riordan that we were hunting for her."

"And she'd have told Marion," I said. "That's assuming she was the woman who collected her from O'Riordan's house."

"And the two of them feared we were getting too close, " said Tom. "So they worked out a plan to infiltrate our office."

"And when she was in there, she saw a chance to kybosh our investigation, once and for all."

"Exactly," said Tom. "Pull off the same trick on us that had worked before on poor old Bill. I mean, all's fair in love and war."

"I can't believe she'd do that to me," I said. "She seemed so… nice."

"Dad," said Tom wearily, "the woman's an actress."

Chalcot Grove was an upmarket terrace of four-storey houses in pastel shades of blue, yellow and pink. It was easy to spot number 17, because it was besieged by several dozen members of the world's media. Any pushing and shoving had long since subsided, and they were keeping themselves busy by doing 'to camera' pieces in a multitude of languages, recounting the tragic and still mysterious death of Jean-Paul De Mode, saying that this was his London address, and that his grieving wife, film star Marion Brooke, was somewhere inside but showing no inclination to come out.

Some police were holding the crowd away from the door, and they were reluctant at first to let us through.

Tom and I walked up the front steps and knocked. After a few moments, Marion peered round the door. Although she took care not to venture out far enough for the cameras to take photos of her, I could see that she looked puffy-eyed, as though she had been crying.

"Charlie?" she said. "it's sweet of you to drop by, but I need to be on my own right now."

"I'm here with Tom," I said. "There are some questions we need to ask you."

"And they need answering. Now," said Tom, with a firmness I'd never heard in him before.

"Please," I said.

"Okay. You may as well come in," she said.

We sat down in the living room. The curtains were drawn, to prevent anyone looking in.

"It's like being under siege," said Marion. "Would you like a coffee? I only have instant, I'm afraid."

"That would be great," I said.

"Milk and no sugar," said Tom. "And would you like to ask Olga to come down?"

"Olga?" she said.

"We know she's staying here," I said.

"Why on earth do you think she's here?"

"My sister took a photo of her looking out of an upstairs window," I said.

"You've had me under surveillance?" she asked. "How could you?"

"How could you try and get me arrested for being a paedophile?" I asked.

She paused and looked stricken.

"Why… why would you think I'd do a thing like that?" she asked.

"I notice you don't deny it," I said.

"You may as well own up," said Tom. "You're the only person who could have done it."

"Don't worry. I'm not going to take it any further," I said. "With the police or anything. As far as I'm concerned, it's water under the bridge. Nothing happened. They never found anything on my computer."

"We had to throw it away, though," said Tim. "A perfectly good one."

"If you don't object," I told Marion, "I might add that to your bill."

She agonised for a few more moments, then decided to come clean.

"Oh God, you must think I'm horrible," she said. "I'm sorry. It wasn't my idea."

"I know," said Tom. "It was Olga's, wasn't it? That's why we need to speak to her."

"Shit," said Marion. "Okay, I'll fetch her."

A few moments later, a thin, pale-faced girl joined us. She looked older than in the photos Jack O'Riordan had taken of her. In fact, she seemed old and careworn beyond her years. I rose and shook her by the hand.

"Olga Molotovski, I presume," I said. "I'm Charlie Charlesworth. And this is my son, Tom. And now perhaps you'd like to tell me what's been going on?"

"M-m-my m-m-m-mother asked you to find me, didn't she?" said Olga.

"Yes," I said.

"I suppose O'Riordan told you that?" asked Tom.

"Yeah," said Olga. "I was s-s-staying with Jack when you came round."

"We knew that much from the police," said Tom. "Would you please start telling us things we don't know?"

"Go easy on her, Tom," I said. "She looks traumatised."

"She has been," said Marion. "Have you any idea what her parents have done to her?"

"I do, actually," I said. "Bill Slope gave me a pretty good idea."

"They sold her body from the age of six," said Marion.

"Really?" I asked Olga.

She nodded.

"For a long time I thought it was n-n-normal," she said. "M-my m-mother said she had done it as a child, and m-my f-father said I was helping him in his business. Which I suppose I was."

"Did they abuse you in any other way?" I asked.

"N-not really," she said. "In most other ways, they were good parents. They gave m-me everything, materially, and an education. I c-can't c-complain, really."

"Even now, it hasn't sunk in how people have been exploiting her," said Marion, kissing her hair. "Poor baby."

"So," I asked Olga, "what made you run away?"

"I got this letter," said Olga. "From B-bernhard Spritzer. You know, the b-b-billionaire?"

"Yes," I said. "I know him. He said he wrote you a letter."

"This dwarf came to the door with it. It was really creepy, saying how much Spritzer loved m-me and how he wanted m-m-me to inherit all his wealth. He even said he was my f-f-father. It kinda f-f-f-freaked me out."

"Why?"

"It was b-bad enough having parents who had used me as a p-p-p-prostitute, but here was this p-pornographer writing m-me a love letter, and he didn't even know that he'd had sex with m-m-m-me."

"He had sex with his own daughter?"

"Yes," she said, "when I was eleven. He didn't even remember. Which upset m-m-me a good deal."

"So you ran off to O'Riordan."

"For a time. B-but then I looked on his computer and found all these photos of Marion, and I d-discovered he'd b-been b-b-lackmailing her with them for years."

"Is this true?" I asked Marion.

"Yes," said Marion. "O'Riordan was one of the few people who knew about my past. I was paying him a few thousand a year, just to shut him up."

"So, Olga, you called up Marion and she came round and collected you?" asked Tom.

"How d-did you know that?" asked Olga.

"The dwarf told us," I said.

"I'm n-not with you," said Olga.

"It doesn't matter," said Tom. "All that matters is did the two of you murder O'Riordan?"

"Of course not," said Marion. "It m-must have happened just after we left."

"It sounds as if there was no shortage of people who wished him dead," I said.

"The police think he was a blackmailer," said Tom.

"I know he was," said Olga. "I found pictures of m-me and other children with several other people. I'm pretty sure Jack was b-blackmailing them all."

"Was one of them Joseph Gildenstern?" I asked.

Olga nodded.

"And Loco Parente?" I asked.

"He was one of the worst. He abused m-me from the age of five," said Olga. "Until I told m-my f-f-father I wouldn't do it any more. But Parente had sex with almost all his m-m-models. He called it his commission."

"Weren't you one of his models?" I asked Marion.

"Yes," said Marion.

"Did he...?" I asked. "Did you....?"

Marion nodded. She put one hand round Olga's waist, and hugged her closer to her.

"And O'Riordan was one of his photographers," sad Tom.

"Yes," said Marion. "He did a lot of the hardcore. Here, and in the States. That's how I first met Jean-Paul. He was doing porno, and I was an escort."

"You were a prostitute?" I asked.

"You sound as if you're shocked," said Marion. "Surely you know lots of Hollywood actresses start out that way? You must know about Joan Crawford, Marilyn Monroe, Grace Kelly."

"Grace Kelly?" I said, remembering how much Marion reminded of her. "I can't believe it."

"Charlie, you're so gorgeously naïve," she said. "I could reel off the names of a dozen movie stars working today who came up the same way."

"American or British?"

"Both," she said. "Not to mention the odd Mexican and Italian."

"So how did you two meet each other?" I asked.

"That was years ago at Loco Parente's," said Marion. "He used to make us have sex together."

"I really got into that. It was okay. But he used to watch," said Olga. "I d-didn't like that."

"And then I met her again," said Marion, "when I went back to my old school to give the girls an expurgated account of how to become an actress."

"Leaving out the callgirl years," said Tom.

"I don't think that part would have gone down well with the headmistress," replied Marion.

"And we hit it off right away," said Olga. "I m-m-mean, by the time I was sixteen I knew I was t-t-totally gay."

"Thanks to your friend Fairycakes," said Tom.

"M-mainly her," said Olga. "But she wasn't exclusively gay, and I was. Ours was m-more like an open relationship."

"She was jealous enough to follow you here," I said. "She saw you kissing Jean-Paul and thought you were having an affair with him."

"Per-lease!" said Olga. "Jean-Paul would n-never be interested in me!"

"He was interested in Marion," I said.

"Not in that way," said Marion. "I mean, we rubbed along okay, when he wasn't drunk or stoned or aggressive. But it was never a sexual thing."

"So yours was what they call a lavender marriage," said Tom.

"Sure," said Marion. "I mean, it worked for both of us. They're nothing new. Rock Hudson, Rudolph Valentino, Robert Taylor, they all had them. Barbara Stanwyck, Janet Gaynor, Mary Martin…"

"Judy Garland and Vincente M-m-minnelli," said Olga.

"Okay, I get the picture," I said. "So Marion, why did you come to me with your story about super-injunctions?"

"To set you up, of course," said Marion. "Olga knew you were after her, and she wanted you out of the way."

"So you came to my office, found my computer and downloaded child pornography on to it?"

"Yes," said Marion. "It was ridiculously easy. You shouldn't have left your credit card hanging around. And your passwords are on your desktop."

"I know," I said.

"I'm sorry," said Marion. "But it was too good an opportunity to miss."

"So you were willing to have me sent to prison," I said, "in order to protect Olga."

"I was," said Marion. "I'm sorry."

"I'm s-s-sorry too," said Olga.

"I still don't understand," I said. "Because, Marion, you've done this before, haven't you? To Bill Slope?"

"That was nothing to do with M-marion," said Olga. "That was m-me."

"You?" I asked. "What had poor old Bill ever done to you?"

"You've m-m-met him, haven't you?" said Olga.

"Yes," I said.

"You know he's an investigative reporter."

"Of course."

"And he writes b-b-books."

"Sure."

"Well, he's writing a b-book about m-me," said Olga. "Or rather, not centrally about m-me. It's about my f-f-father."

"Which father are we talking about?" asked Tom. "Bernhard Spritzer or Igor Molotovski?"

"Igor," said Olga. "Bill had been investigating him for some time, examining his b-business dealings and so on, and he found out how Igor had used m-me, you know, to get what he wanted."

"And you helped Bill, didn't you?" asked Tom. "I mean, he was your Facebook friend."

"I told him way too m-m-m-much," said Olga. "But then I realised I shouldn't have."

"So what did you do?"

"I told Igor what I'd done. And he said that B-bill would have to be k-k-k-killed."

"And was Igor angry with you?"

"In a weird sort of way, he wasn't. He told me I'd been young and foolish, and that I'd have to make it up to him."

"How?"

"He said there were only two ways to deal with Slope. One was to murder him. The other was to d-d-discredit him."

"So you framed him as a paedophile."

"It wasn't my idea initially," said Olga. "It was Igor's. It amused him a good deal. You see, one of the things B-bill has against Igor is that he's actually proud of being an evil influence on the young. So it appealed to Igor that he was going to m-make B-bill look even worse."

"So you did the dirty on Bill."

"Yes," said Olga. "I know it was an awful thing to do. But if I hadn't done it, Igor would have had B-bill k-killed. In a way, I was d-d-doing him a f-favour."

"I see," I said.

I had a sinking feeling in my stomach. Not for the first time in my life, I felt betrayed. From the way Marion was stroking Olga's hair, I saw that Marion was in love – not with me but with Olga.

"You never really cared for me at all, did you?" I asked Marion.

"Of course I fancied you," said Marion. "But it was never going to work in the long term. It's Olga I love."

"So you two intend to stay together?" I asked.

"Today's my eighteenth b-b-birthday," said Olga.

"Many happy returns," I said.

"Which m-m-m-means that as of today my parents don't have legal control over me."

"It seems to me," I said, "that they haven't had that much control over you for some time."

"Well," said Olga, "you've heard what happened when they d-d-d-did."

"Fair point," I said. "I presume, by the way, that you genuinely have no idea who killed Jack, Jean-Paul, Gildenstern and Fettucini?"

"None at all," said Olga.

"Me neither," said Marion. "I know Jean-Paul could be a vicious little swine, but he didn't deserve what happened to him."

"Nor did Joseph Gildenstern," said Olga. "He may have been a d-d-dirty old perve, but he was always a gentleman."

"High praise indeed," I remarked. "They should have that put on their tombstones."

"So now you know the sordid truth," said Marion, "what do you intend to do about it? Go to the press? Spread it all over the internet?"

"I'm not sure," I said. "I presume that you'd prefer to keep your private life private?"

Marion and Olga nodded.

"In that case," I said, "I think the proper thing for me to do is pay a visit to Mr and Mrs Igor Molotovski. After all, we have finally found you."

"Do you want me to come too, Dad?" asked Tom.

"You know something?" I said. "I'd prefer to leave you out of this. I get the impression that Mr Molotovski might be a little bit, what's the word, volatile when he doesn't get what he wants. If anything does happen to me, I'd like to feel the business is being left in safe hands."

"Are you sure, Dad?"

"Yes," I said. "I think it's for the best."

"Thank you, Mr Charlesworth," said Olga. "I'm genuinely s-s-s-sorry."

"You're a lovely man," said Marion. "Really."

"We'd better go," I said. "Maybe I'll see you again."

"Are you going to the big opening?" she asked.

"The what?"

"The opening of Edward Killingfield's new restaurant, at the top of The Pyramid. It's tomorrow night."

"Won't he be putting that off?" I asked. "It doesn't seem very tasteful, under the circumstances."

"I went online to see if it had been cancelled," said Marion. "And there was a banner saying 'The show must go on'."

"And you're intending to go?" I asked. "Won't people find that odd, so soon after the death of your husband?"

"I've talked about that with the creepster."

"Sorry. Who?" I asked.

"That's what Jean-Paul and I used to call Rex Crawley," she said. "He says he can spin it so that I come across as heroic. Stiff upper lip and all that. I won't be able to take Olga, of course. Not if I'm playing the grieving widow."

"It's important to keep up appearances," said Olga. "That's why Marion is still going to be on Stephanie Sharp's show, on Saturday n-n-n-night."

"Aren't you worried about these murders?" I asked. "I mean, you could be next."

"I don't see why," said Marion. "Besides, Stephanie Sharp's vengeance would be terrible were I to break my contract."

"Incidentally," I said, "for the record I did find out that Jean-Paul put an injunction on her."

"Oh, I knew all about that," she said dismissively. "Jean-Paul was always terrified people would find out about his career in gay porn."

"Stephanie Sharp found out about it?"

"I think Bernie Spritzer must have told her. He really is amazingly indiscreet. It's a wonder no one's tried to murder him."

"I imagine there's no shortage of people who'd like to string up Stephanie Sharp."

"Anyone who did that would be doing everyone a favour," Marion agreed. "She's everywhere at the moment."

"Plugging her new chat show," I said. "With you and that fat Mexican director."

"Yes," said Marion. "I gather they're both going to be at the Killingfield banquet too. Stephanie Sharp must love the idea of a restaurant in the sky. You know how she likes to look down on people."

"What's the name of the restaurant?" I asked.

"Vertigo," said Marion.

"Oh," I said. "Like the Hitchcock film."

"What Hitchcock film?" asked Marion. "Oh, wasn't he the man who directed Lawrence of Arabia?"

I realised there and then that she and I could never have been a serious item.

29

ROPE

Friday, 12th August

I should have rung the Molotovskis that evening, but I couldn't face it. I wasn't looking forward to telling them what I knew. I was just about to ring Katasha Molotovski the next morning when my mobile rang. It was Tracey.

"Hey, bruv," she said. "You doing anything tonight?"

"No," I said.

"Well, you are now," she said. "I'm having a knees-up."

"What are you celebrating?"

"The departure of my mother-in-law, for a start," she said. "And our finding the missing heiress. So I'm organising an impromptu Friday night dinner party. There's someone I want you to meet."

"Who?"

"It's a surprise," she said.

"Male or female?"

"Female," she said. "And I know you're going to like her."

"Oh yes?"

Perhaps the weariness in my voice alerted her to my feelings about other people match-making for me.

"I know what you're thinking," she said. "There's Tracey interfering in my love life again. But it's high time you met someone nice. Especially now Tom's found someone."

"You think it's serious?" I asked.

"Yeah, I do, actually," she said. "You've seen the way Tom and Marti look at each other. It's sickening. Gareth and me haven't looked at each other like that for years."

"Okay," I said. "What time do you want me?"

"Prompt at eight and don't be late," she said. "I've asked Marti to pick you and Tom up in her car."

"You've got it all organised, haven't you?"

"I have," said Tracey. "It's quite sad really, innit? I mean, it's not as if I haven't got plenty of other things to do. Ta-ra!"

After this, I couldn't put the moment off any longer. I dialled Katasha Molotovski on her mobile, and she picked it up after a couple of rings.

"Mrs Molotovski?"

"Yes," she said.

"I've found your daughter," I said.

"That is good," she said.

"But I'm afraid there's some bad news."

"Oh?"

"She won't be coming home," I said.

"Why not?"

"She doesn't want to, and I can't really make her. Nor can you."

"Why not?"

"She's just turned eighteen, and she's entitled to go where she wants."

"And where is that?"

"She's staying at the house of a woman named Marion Brooke."

334

"The film star?"

"Yes."

"How does she know a film star?"

"They are… I'm sorry, there's no other way to say this. They are lovers."

"I thought this Marion Brooke was married."

"Yes. But now her husband's dead, and she wants to make a new life with your daughter."

There was a long pause. So long that I wondered if the line had gone dead.

"Are you still there, Mrs Molotovski?"

"Yes."

"Do you want me to come and see you?"

"That will not be necessary," she said. "I will make sure you get rest of your money."

"Thank you," I said. "Would you like me to talk to your husband?"

"That is not possible," she said.

"I'm sure he'd like to know where his daughter is," I said.

"He will never know," she said.

"You're not going to tell him?"

"I am not able to tell him."

"Why not?"

"I am looking at him now," she said, "and he is dead."

"Dead?"

"For more than year, he not well man," she said. "And now he is dead. I am here in his conservatory. But he is not alive."

"Are you sure?"

"Big, hairy spider, it just crawl out his mouth. He is dead. Most definite."

"I'm sorry," I said. "I had no idea. This is a bad time."

"Is as good a time as any," she said. "Anyway, Igor not Olga's real father."

"Yes," I said. "I found that out too."

335

"Then you know her real father is Bernhard Spritzer?"

"I did, yes."

"I knew him before he had an H in his name. He put it in because he think it make him look better."

"I see."

"He used to see me before I was married."

"Yes."

"And afterwards," she said. "He much better in bed than Igor. I can say that now. Igor not hear. He dead."

"Yes," I said. "You mentioned that."

"Did Olga say anything about me and Igor?" she asked. "You know, as loving parents?"

"Yes," I said. "She did. She mentioned that you, er…"

"I teach her everything I know," said Katasha, "about how to please a man. I start myself when very young, and it stood me in good stead. I very rich woman."

"Yes, I know."

"And now you tell me she is lesbian."

"Yes," I said. "I suppose she is."

"Is terrible shock."

"I suppose it must be," I said.

"I wish I knew where we went wrong."

There was no easy or succinct answer to this, so I made a non-committal grunt.

"Okay," she said, in a curiously flat voice. "I go now."

It was two days later that I discovered she went upstairs soon after our conversation. She made a few calls to regularise her affairs, including one to have me paid the rest of my money, and hanged herself. The coroner said it was suicide out of grief at her husband's death. I didn't consider it worth my while to contradict him.

30

STRANGERS ON A TRAIN

Friday, 12th August

I should have seen them coming.

For some reason, I thought they wouldn't bother me after Fettucini was dead. But I should have anticipated that gangsters like to punish people who disobey them. They have a nasty habit of trying to take revenge. Chin Sun Fong's heavies burst into our office, and they looked in a mood to create some damage. Maybe even take a life or two.

Muscle, the bigger of the two goons, gave Tom a nasty wallop with a cosh, and the smaller, who I'd mentally named Brains, threatened to cut Marti's tongue out if she didn't stop screaming. As soon as they broke in, I was sorry Bill Slope wasn't about. He'd asked for an afternoon off to get himself kitted out for some social event that night. So the only other proper grown-up around was me.

The smaller of the two goons acted as spokesman.

"Mr Fong isn't pleased with you," said Brains. "And neither am I."

"Sorry to hear it," I said.

"He doesn't like being, how do you people say it, out of pocket."

"I imagine he's also sorry that one of his highest-earning clients has been crucified," I replied. "But that's nothing to do with me. I only found Lorenzo's body."

"Didn't Mr Fong warn you to stay away from him?"

"Yes," I said. "But afterwards Lorenzo asked me to look after him. It was all very confusing."

"Did you know that the police have ordered Mr Fong to leave the country," said Brains. "And make his home elsewhere?"

I decided to refrain from saying that this sounded an extremely good idea.

"Can they do that?" I asked.

"And a Mr Bernhard Spritzer has told him his presence in London is no longer acceptable."

"I'm sure Mr Fong has excellent lawyers."

"Mr Fong is at present in hospital," said the goon, "after a shooting incident."

"Blimey," I said. "What happened?"

"He was attacked by a small child in a sailor suit."

"Really?"

The bigger goon pulled on the smaller one's sleeve and whispered in his ear.

"My colleague says it might have been a dwarf."

I nodded. I suddenly had a pretty good idea who that might be.

"It can't be very nice to be shot by a child, or a dwarf," I said. "Do pass on my condolences."

"So Mr Fong's badly in need of some news to cheer him up," said the talkative goon. "Such as your office going up in flames, with you inside it."

"You think that's likely?"

"Very, very likely," said the goon. "You shouldn't be keeping paraffin in these offices."

Right on cue, the bigger goon disappeared into the hall and came back with two large cans of paraffin, which he proceeded to empty all over our suite.

"Look at all this paper," said the goon. "This whole place is going up in flames."

"I'm sure it will make Mr Fong feel better when we're burned to a crisp," I said. "But isn't this just an act of senseless violence?"

"You're crazy, you are," said Marti. "All it's going to do is make the police reckon it's you lot responsible for all these murders."

The two goons looked at each other. Evidently they hadn't examined this possibility.

"Yeah, well we're out of here on the next train," said Brains.

"Don't you mean plane?" asked Marti.

"No we're going on the Eurostar," said Brains. "It's very good. That will get us to Paris, and from there you can go anywhere in the world."

"What's wrong with Heathrow?" asked Marti.

"Look, lady," said Brains, "I'm not interested in discussing my travel arrangements with you. Light!."

Muscle fumbled in his pocket and brought out his cigarette lighter in the shape of a gun. He pulled the trigger, and there was the unmistakable clicking of a lighter that wouldn't light. Brains sighed.

"Haven't you bought a new lighter yet?"

The big goon whispered in the smaller one's ear.

"Okay," said the talkative one. "Anyone here got matches?"

"That's not very bright, is it?" I asked. "Trying to commit an act of arson and not bringing a light. Doesn't either of you smoke?"

Both goons shook their heads. For the first time, I saw a ray of hope in the situation.

"It's a good job Bill Slope does," I said. "He hangs out in our conference room. I'll fetch his lighter."

"What are you doing, boss?" said Marti. "They're going to kill us."

"No, they're not," I called out from the conference room, trying to sound calmer than I felt.

"Oh yes we are," said Brains, following me into the conference room.

"Oh no, you're not," I said, pulling Bill Slope's service revolver out of his holdall.

Muscle looked oddly pleased as his colleague backed out into the reception area with his hands in the air – as if he was glad that it wasn't only him who made mistakes.

"You're going to get on the next plane out of this country," I said, "and never come back."

"Will a train do?" asked Muscle. "I like trains."

"So you do speak," I said.

"He's bluffing," said Brains, lowering his hands. "That's one of those cigarette lighters that looks like a gun."

"No," I said, "it's a gun that looks like a gun. It's loaded like a gun. It fires bullets like a gun. And right now this gun is aimed at your head."

"What's happening?" asked Tom, coming round.

"Don't worry, son," I said. "Everything's under control. These two gentlemen are going to apologise for hitting you, and then they're going to leave."

Which is pretty much what happened.

"Bloody hell, Dad," said Tom. "Why does this place reek of paraffin?"

"Our visitors were planning to incinerate us," I said.

"Why?"

"I'm not sure they'd really thought it through," I said. "But I think revenge for Fettucini's death, the collapse of their boss's betting scam, and his getting hospitalised by a dwarf in a sailor suit all came into the equation."

"Harry Crouch?" asked Tom.

"I wouldn't bet against it," I said.

"I always thought he had a ruthless side," said Tom.

"And now I would suggest we grant ourselves the afternoon off," I said. "I need some thinking time, and you're going to come by later and pick me up."

"Oh yeah," said Marti. "Tracey's dinner party. I'd almost forgotten. We must pong of paraffin."

"I could certainly do with a bath," I said. "How's your head, son?"

"Not too bad, thanks," said Tom. "But I think there's going to be a lump."

"Let me see," said Marti. "Come round to my place and I'll kiss it better."

"What about the office?" Tom asked me.

"Leave it for now," I said. "I'll get some professional cleaners in. They're long overdue anyway."

31

MR AND MRS SMITH

Friday, 12th August

Tracey and Gareth's house is on London Fields, just round the corner from the house in Hackney where we had once hoped to find Fairycakes Parks. It's a terraced Victorian house with lots of stripped pine, and most of the walls ripped out for open-plan living. A bad mistake, as it meant that when the children are up it's impossible to hear yourself think.

"Hi, Aunt Tracey," said Tom.

"Blimey," said Tracey. "What's that big lump on your head? It's like an extra bollock."

"I was attacked," said Tom. "But I don't think there's any permanent damage. You remember Marti?"

"From the premiere of that awful film," said Tracey. "Love the outfit!"

"Thanks," said Marti. "You don't think this skirt is too short?"

"Not with your legs," said Tracey.

I explained to Tracey about the attack on the office, and she seemed duly impressed.

"Wow!" she said. "Sounds like you three need a drink!"

"It seems ominously quiet round here," I said. "Where are the kids? What have you done with them?"

"Oh, they're in bed," said Tracey.

"At this time?" I asked. "That's not like them."

"I know," said Tracey. "I gave them each a slug of Night Nurse."

"Oh, dear. Have they got colds?" asked Marti.

"Gawd no," said Tracey. "But it slows them down. Sends them off to sleep. I didn't want them yelling, climbing over furniture, bouncing off the walls. They're like a pair of Jack Russells, only bigger and not quite as vicious, bless 'em."

"Shall I go up and see them?" I asked.

"Better not," said Tracey. "It'll only excite them. And you know what they're like when they're excited."

I nodded. I did, indeed. Loud. Very loud. And active. Incredibly active.

"Are we the last?" I asked.

"Not at all," said Tracey. "Come through to the living room."

Gareth was serving drinks to the guest who had already arrived – clearly, not that much earlier. I recognised him, but thought I'd better address the host first.

"Hallo, Gareth," I said. "Long time no see."

"It has been a long time," he said, in his lugubrious Welsh accent. "I was starting to think you were avoiding me."

"Of course not," I lied. "I'm always fascinated to hear your views. They're always so... original."

"Thank you," he said. "I always try to see things from a different perspective. Not merely the conventional one."

"You certainly do, that," I said.

"In my opinion," said Gareth, "the cosmic carrot is always preferable to the celestial stick."

"Oh yes?" I said.

"That's right," he said with the solemnity of a great thinker.

"When you feel as if nothing makes sense, there is only one thing you can do. Nothing!"

"Is that right?" I asked.

"Yes!" Gareth said. "Nothing is the only thing that makes sense. And then, of course, there are times when you may as well do anything, because anything makes sense if you think about it long enough. And nothing."

I nodded, as though I knew what the hell he was talking about.

"Right now, though," said Gareth, "one thing makes more sense than all the ideas in the world put together."

"What's that, Gareth?" I asked.

"And that's the thing you need to be doing," said Gareth.

"What thing is that, Gareth?"

"If you can't see a way to do it, look harder," said Gareth, earnestly. "It's there in front of you, just waiting to be recognised. And nothing is more important!"

"Hello, Uncle Gareth," said Tom. "Been at the magic mushrooms again?"

"Hello, Tom," said Gareth. "You've grown. Has someone hit you on the head?"

"Just a bit," said Tom. "This is Marti."

"Oh yes," said Gareth, "I've heard a lot about you."

"Nothing bad, I hope," said Marti, nervously.

"Let me think now," Gareth pondered for longer than most normal people would have considered polite. "No, I don't think so."

Tracey came in.

"Gareth," she said, "have you done the introductions?"

"Not really," said Gareth. "Charlie, Tom and Marti, this is Oliver Avery-Castle. He only lives round the corner, and we're both on the Neighbourhood Watch committee."

"I bet those meetings are a lot of fun," I said.

"Gareth is always most loquacious," said Oliver Avery-Castle, through gritted teeth.

"But Oliver always brings me sailing back down to earth," said Gareth, "with the force, the range, the majesty of his intellect. Oliver is a professor."

"Yes," I said. "Modern cultural studies, isn't it?"

"You know my work?" said Avery-Castle, who plainly had not recognised us. He was wearing a different t-shirt from the one I had originally seen him wearing. This one carried the message: "I like to party hard."

"No, we have actually met," I said.

"Oliver here often accuses me of being away with the fairies," said Gareth. "But what I want to know is: why is this such a bad place to be? Might this world not be a better place if we were all to spend a little more time in fairyland?"

He paused, impressively. I could see that Marti was transfixed, in much the same way I had been on first meeting Gareth. It was hard to imagine that he was not sending himself up, or possibly even the whole Welsh nation. In full flow, Gareth was, and is, the windbag's windbag.

"We all have a choice," he continued. "We can resolve to be more sensible or we can listen to our intuition and trust our judgment. We face a difficult, delicate scenario, do you see? Even if one were a rocket scientist, it would be impossible to sort things out with logic alone. So why not sprinkle a little fairy dust?"

There was a long pause.

"Yes," I said. "Thanks for that, Gareth."

"The professor here helped us track down a missing person," said Tom hurriedly, before Gareth could start another stream of consciousness.

"Oh, did I?" said Avery-Castle.

"Well, this is all very nice," said Gareth, in a mournful voice that could have been used to announce that the world was shortly about to end. "Is white wine all right for everyone?"

"Could I have sparking water?" asked Marti. "I'm the designated driver for these two reprobates."

"No," said Gareth, as though sparkling water was impossibly exotic. "We only have tap."

"That will be all right," said Marti brightly.

"Why don't you crack open some champagne?" Tracey asked her husband. "We should be celebrating. Charlie's solved a couple of cases, one of them with my help."

"You should have warned me," said Gareth. "I'm not sure we have any chilled."

"I put a couple of bottles in the fridge this afternoon," said Tracey. "They're bound to be cold by now."

We all sat down, and I thought I'd better kick off some conversation.

"So you and Gareth are on the Neighbourhood Watch," I said to Avery-Castle. "I gather there was quite a lot of trouble here in Hackney, earlier in the week."

"We were the second area to be hit," said the professor.

"Yes," said Gareth, with surprising brevity. "The rioting began in Tottenham but spread to round here."

"It's hardly surprising," said the professor. "So many are victims of an uncaring society. A massive vacuum is now very apparent between the haves and have-nots. I work with young people, and there is a sense that they feel that they are not being listened to, especially not about the cuts by this beastly Coalition."

"So let me get this right," said Marti. "You're blaming the government?"

"I would have thought that you, of all people," replied the professor, "would be the first to appreciate alienation and exclusion."

"Alienated? Excluded? From what?" asked Marti. "We've got it cushy in Britain. Education is free, up to university. Health is free. Housing is free. What isn't free is your designer clothes, your flash footwear, your spanking new iPad. That stuff, you're meant to work for."

"Marti does have a point," I said. "The youth of the Middle

East are rising up for basic freedoms. But what do the youth of England rise up for? HD-ready 42-inch plasma TVs."

The professor sniffed, disparagingly. There was a momentary lull in the conversation, as everyone decided to drink at exactly the same time.

"Look who's here!" said Tracey, with the special kind of brightness hostesses have when they fear the evening is not going as well as she had hoped.

"Sorry I'm late," said a female voice I instantly recognised.

"Carol," I said. "What an unexpected pleasure."

Carol Smith was wearing a floral dress that was infinitely more feminine than anything I had seen her in before. I noticed for the first time that she had a figure. Rather a nice one. With a waist, and everything.

"Carol, this is Professor Avery-Castle, Marti Vane. You know Gareth, and this is my brother Charlie and his son Tom."

"Yes," said Carol, "we three have met."

Her eyes met mine, and I was surprised to find myself thinking how blue they were, and intelligent. She was scarcely recognisable as the person who had demolished my front door less than a fortnight ago.

"I hate to be the bearer of bad news," said Carol. "But the reason I'm a bit late is that they've blocked off the next street. There seems to be some kind of riot going on, and a whole lot of buildings are on fire."

"Oh, no!" said Tracey. "Where?"

"Round there," Carol indicated. "The shops are in flames, and the house next to them. It looks pretty bad."

"That could be me!" said Professor Avery-Castle.

We all rushed round the corner. Sure enough, the professor's house was on fire, along with the row of shops next to it. From the look of it, the fire had spread from the shops to the house. Firefighters were vainly trying to put out the flames, and in return were being pelted with bricks and rocks by rioters.

Some were white and some were black. Most were young, though one or two seemed older and bulkier. All wore hoodies or scarfs to cover their faces. Even so, I immediately recognised one of them.

"Fairycakes!" I said. "Is that you?"

"You!" said the professor. "Why are you burning down my house?"

"We didn't mean to," said Fairycakes. "The fire spread from these Paki shops."

"They're not Pakistani," I said. "They're Turkish, Indian, Bangla Deshi…"

"Whatever," said Fairycakes. "Don't you understand, we're rioting? You're all fascist wankers!"

Later, we sat round Tracey and Gareth's dining table, enjoying Tracey's main course.

"It's a shame Oliver can't be here," said Tracey.

"It's understandable he's lost his appetite," I said.

"It's great that you're still able to be here, Carol," said Tracey.

"The duty police seemed to be gaining control of the situation," said Carol. "I wouldn't miss your dinner party for the world."

"It's only roast chicken," said Tracey. "So, Charlie, how do you know Carol?"

"I, er…"

Carol looked across at me and grinned.

"Charlie and I met under unfortunate circumstances," she said. "I thought he was a pervert, and he was a bit miffed that I'd smashed his door down."

"Oh, no! I had no idea!" said Tracey.

"Evidently not," said Carol.

"It wasn't the ideal introduction," I said. "But we've made it up since then. In fact, Carol has been extremely helpful in the solving of one particular case."

"I have?"

"Yes," I said. "Thanks to you, I've managed to track down quite an important missing person."

"Really?" asked Carol. "Who?"

"Olga Molotovski," said Tom.

"The missing heiress? How fascinating!" exclaimed Carol. "Where was she?"

"Staying with a friend of hers," I said. "Marion Brooke."

"The film star?" asked Carol. "You are moving in glamorous circles."

"Oh she's not that glamorous," I said. "In fact, I think you're better looking than she is."

"You old smoothie," said Carol. "That might be the nicest thing anyone's ever said to me."

I caught sight of Tom and Marti casting meaningful glances at each other, but decided to ignore them.

"Isn't Marion married to that actor who was murdered?" said Carol. "My dad's on that case."

"I know he is," I said. "He interrogated me about it. Remember?"

"Not having much luck with my family, are you?" asked Carol.

"It could be worse," I said. "At least he hasn't arrested me for anything yet."

"So how do you and Aunt Trace know each other?" asked Tom.

"Oh, we studied together at police college," said Carol. "Entered the force together, in fact. But then Tracey met Gareth here and started a family, and I got married and didn't start a family, thank God."

"You don't want children?" I asked.

"It's not that," she said. "You know Gary Smith, the goalkeeper?"

"Played for Fulham, didn't he?" I asked.

"She's always had this thing for footballers," said Tracey, with a grin.

"Tracey!" Carol scolded her.

"So you married Gary, and that's why you're not Carol Drake," I said.

"I was old-fashioned and took the name of my husband. Also, I didn't want to let anyone think I'd joined the force because of my father," said Carol. "Mr and Mrs Smith had a nice, anonymous feel about it."

"But you and Gary didn't work out?" I asked.

"No," she said. "I spent most of my life working, and he spent more and more of his time womanising. It wasn't an ideal combination."

"And how long have you been apart?"

"A year now," said Carol. "During which I've been burying myself in work and computer games. I think that's why Tracey here thinks I should be looking around."

"Maybe you should," I said.

There was an awkward silence.

"Shall we have pudding first, or cheese?" asked Tracey brightly.

It was over coffee that I felt like sharing my thoughts with the others.

"I've been thinking," I said.

"Not again, bruv!" exclaimed Tracey. "Don't strain yourself!"

"About this video game," I said.

"Not Football Manager again," said Tom. "No one's interested, Dad."

"I am," said Carol.

I smiled at her, gratefully.

"I don't mean Football Manager," I said. "I've been thinking about the murders."

"I'm going to bed," said Gareth. "I'm not feeling too well."

"Yeah," I said, taking the hint, "maybe it's time we all went."

"Not before we've heard what you have to say," insisted Tracey.

"Spit it out, Dad," said Tom.

"Well, it's like real life is following this game."

"What do you mean?" asked Marti.

"It's like a copycat crime," I said.

"Go on," said Tom.

"Are you okay?" Carol asked me.

"Don't worry," Tom told her. "Dad always looks like that when he's going into Sherlock mode."

"So, bruv, what's on your mind?" asked Tracey.

"Well, who was the first bloke to get killed?" I asked.

"Jack O'Riordan," said Tom.

"What do we know about him?" I asked.

"That he was involved in pornography," said Tom, "and then turned to blackmail."

"So what would you say about his character?"

"He was a shit."

"No, I mean more specifically. What adjective would you use about him?"

"Well, I suppose I'd say he was greedy, avaricious," Tom said.

"Right," I said. "And who was the second victim?"

"Wasn't that the bloke who ran the fashion agency?" asked Tracey.

"No," said Carol. "He turned out to be a red herring. He committed suicide."

"So who was the second victim?"

"One of two people," said Tom. "Either Jean-Paul De Mode or Joseph Gildenstern."

"Let's take Jean-Paul first," I said. "What was wrong with him?"

"He kept hitting people," said Marti. "Paparazzi. Those sort of people."

"He even took a swing at me," said Tom.

"So," I said, "what was his problem?"

"Anger management?" suggested Carol.

"So he was angry," I said.

"Oh, I get it," said Tom. "I see what you're driving at."

"I don't," said Marti.

"Me neither," said Tracey.

"That's because none of you have played it," said Tom. "It's The Seven Deadly Sins!"

"It's as if someone has been applying the game to real life," I said, "and bumping off people in order to earn points."

"But that's insane," said Tom.

"No one earns points in real life," said Carol. "That's just weird."

"But we're talking about a serial killer," I said. "Who said a serial killer has to be rational?"

"I'm still not sure where that German ex-footballer comes into all this," said Marti.

"You knew him better than any of us," Tracey told me. "How would you describe him?"

"Good footballer," I said, "but sneaky. International businessman. Arms salesman. Football admin."

"He doesn't seem to fit the pattern," said Tom. "He doesn't seem to have had a deadly sin."

"Except," I said.

"Except what?" came a chorus from around the room.

"He *was* the greediest man I've ever met," I said.

"We've already had greed," pointed out Tom, "with Jack O'Riordan. In the game, you're not allowed to double up on the same deadly sin."

"I don't mean greed in the sense of avarice," I said. "I meant, he really loves his food. He dines at Killingfield's all the time."

"Gluttony!" said Tom, his eyes shining. "Of course!"

"Which leaves us with Fettucini," said Tracey.

"And what was wrong with him?" I asked.

"Well, he gambled," said Tom, "and lost money."

"No," I persisted, "what's wrong with him character-wise?"

"Well," said Tom. "From what you've told me, he fancied himself as a ladies' man. He was cocky about being a Premiership footballer. He boasted a lot about money."

"So if you had to choose an adjective about him," I said, "which one would sum him up?"

"Stupid," said Tom.

Everyone laughed.

"No, that's not it," I said. "His fault, or deadly sin, was pride."

"Oh wow," said Carol. "You realise what this means?"

"Of course," said Tom. "This serial killer's completely bonkers."

"No," I said. "I see what Carol's driving at."

"So do I," said Marti. "It means that if this bloke's playing out a video game in real life, he hasn't finished yet. How many people has he killed?"

"Four," said Tracey.

"Which means he has three more to go," said Marti.

"So what deadly sins hasn't he done?" asked Tom.

"Which ones are there?" I asked. "I keep getting them muddled up with the seven dwarfs."

"I know," said Tracey. "They'll be on the box. The kids play with it all the time."

"Where is it?" asked Tom.

"It's normally by the telly," said Tracey. "Except I must have cleared it up."

"There it is," said Marti, pointing. "Isn't that it under the sofa?"

"That's it," I said, recognising it from Olga's bedroom and Bill Slope's cottage.

I pulled it out from under the sofa, and started to read.

"Oh my God," I said. "He's even doing them in the right order."

"Of course," said Tom. "He's trying to win maximum points."

"He started with Avarice, moved on to Gluttony, then Anger…"

"So he must have killed Gildenstern before De Mode," said Tom.

"And his fourth victim was Pride."

"Fettucini," said Tracey.

"Dad, you're a genius," said Tom.

"So who's next?" asked Carol.

I read from the back of the box.

"The fifth victim has to represent Sloth. The sixth is Lust. And the seventh is Envy."

"That's all very well," said Carol, "but they could be anyone."

"That's not strictly true," said Tom.

"What do you mean?"

"The weird thing is," said Tom, "that there's something all these victims had in common."

"And what's that?" asked Carol.

"Dad," said Tom. "He knew all of them, so there's got to be a good chance he'll know the next three victims."

"I can see your logic," said Carol, "but I still don't know why."

"This is doing my head in," said Tracey.

"Hang on a moment," I said. "There is one other possible scenario."

"There is?" asked Tom.

"What if the linking factor isn't me at all," I said. "What if it's Bill Slope?"

"How do you mean?"

"Think about it for a minute," I said. "You remember when we went up to see Bill?"

"Of course," replied Tom. "It was only a week ago."

"He knew who Jack O'Riordan was, didn't he?"

"Yes," said Tom. "But that doesn't mean he wanted to murder him."

"Let's leave motives aside for the moment," I said. "The point is, Bill knew who he was. The next question is: did he have the opportunity to murder him?"

"Not really," said Tom. "At that point Bill was living in deepest Norfolk."

"A-ha!" I said.

"What do you mean 'A-ha'?" asked Tom.

"Do you remember going to that garage with him?"

"Where we bought that paper with him on the front page? Of course I do. I thought that woman behind the counter was going to send for the police."

"But why did we have to go to the garage?" I asked Tom.

"Because he was running out of petrol."

"But," I said, "he'd only been in there for petrol the day before. He told us that. So, somehow or other, he'd managed to get through an entire tank of petrol over the course of 24 hours."

"You mean he could have gone down to London," said Tom, "murdered Jack O'Riordan, then come all the way up again in time for his appointment with us?"

"Exactly."

"I suppose it's possible," said Tom.

"And what about this tie-in with the video game?" asked Tracey.

"I remember seeing The Seven Deadly Sins at his cottage," I said. "It didn't seem like the kind of thing a person his age would be into."

"Oh my God!" exclaimed Tom. "Do you remember the videos he was watching?"

"Not really," I said.

"I do," replied Tom. "There was *Taken*, with Liam Neeson. And *Rambo*, starring Sylvester Stallone."

"And a couple of Jason Statham movies," I said.

"That's right," said Tom. "*Death Race* and *The Mechanic*."

"Do you remember any other titles?" I asked him.

"Only one," he said. "*I Spit On Your Grave.*"

"So he has dodgy taste and enjoys action movies," said Carol. "That doesn't make him a serial killer."

"You're missing the point," said Tom. "Those aren't just action movies. They all have one crucial thing in common. They're all about revenge."

"One thing I don't understand is why Bill would think O'Riordan was avaricious," I said.

"Don't you remember, Dad?" asked Tom. "It was Bill who told us that Jack worked for Loco Parente and went in for a bit of blackmail on the side."

"What about the next three victims?" asked Carol. "Gildenstern, De Mode and Fettucini."

"Bill knew them all," I said.

"And where was he the night they were murdered?" asked Carol.

"He was in London," I said. "He was with me at Bernie Spritzer's party. But he went back to London because his ex-wife turned up. He couldn't stand all her bitching."

"Or she gave him a good excuse to leave," said Tom.

"That's all very well," said Carol. "But what about motive?"

"Bill once threatened to kill De Mode," I said. "At the time, I thought he was being funny."

"Maybe you should have taken him more seriously, bruv," said Tracey.

"What about Gildenstern?" asked Carol.

"Bill reckoned he was one of the most corrupt people at FIFA," I said.

"Is that really enough to make Bill kill him?"

"FIFA have been trying to get Bill for years. Maybe Bill blamed them for this paedophile framing thing, and flipped."

"And Fettucini?" asked Carol.

"That's easy," I said. "Bill was the person who tipped me off about Fettucini's gambling debts. He once told me that of all the footballers he'd met, Fettucini was the most corrupt, and also the most full of himself."

"So who is he going to go for next?" asked Tom. "Who would

Bill regard as the most slothful, lustful and envious people he knew?"

"Well, I know who he thinks is the most envious person in the world," I said. "It's his ex-wife."

"Stephanie Sharp!" exclaimed Tom. "What about lust?"

"Oh my God," I said. "He tried to put me off Marion Brooke by telling me she was a nymphomaniac."

"He did, did he?" asked Carol. "And why was that?"

"Dad had a thing about her," said Tom. "But I have a feeling that's all over now."

"Indeed," I said. "She's shacked up with our missing Russian heiress."

"No!" said Marti, Carol and Tracey in unison.

"But Lust and Envy are sixth and seventh on the list," said Tom, "The fifth person he's out to kill should be Sloth."

I pondered for a moment.

"Any ideas?" asked Tracey.

I shook my head.

"I haven't a clue – unless… Oh no!"

"What's the matter, dad?"

"What's the name of that Mexican director guy?"

"Alfredo Di Cojones?" asked Tom.

"He's famous for his laziness. He's only made a tiny number of films—"

"And they're not exactly noted for their paciness or intellectual rigour," said Tom. "Yeah, Alfredo could be our man."

"But why would Bill Slope harbour a grudge against him?" asked Tracey.

"Maybe he's seen one of his films," said Tom.

"Now there, I have to admit," I said, "I haven't the foggiest idea."

"I'm not convinced, either," said Tom. "I mean, Bill Slope, serial killer? Seriously?"

"They don't all look like Hannibal Lecter," said Carol. "Harold

Shipman was just like any normal family doctor, except he killed over 200 people."

"At the very least, we should warn these people," said Carol. "In case Charlie's hunch is correct. Any idea how we can contact them?"

"Right now," I said, looking at my watch, "I reckon they're all in the same place. At the top of The Pyramid, at a banquet."

"And where's Bill Slope?" asked Carol.

"I bet he's there too," I said. "He said he was off to a social event."

"So? He's hardly going to be able to overpower three people at the same time," said Tom.

"Tom's right," said Tracey. "And they're hardly going to stand around and let him kill them one at a time."

"Doesn't anyone here think we should call the police?" asked Marti.

"I am the police," said Carol. "And it's too late for that. It will take too long to explain what we're on about. By the time we get through to anyone important, Slope could have committed his last three murders. Only we can stop him."

"How soon can we get to The Pyramid?" Tom asked me.

"Oh God," I said. "I'm over the limit."

"Don't worry," said Marti. "I'll drive."

"How are we going to stop him?" I asked.

"Come off it," said Tom. "He's not exactly Mike Tyson."

"I do have this," said Carol, producing something from her pocket.

"What's that?" I asked.

"It's a taser," she said. "I carry it for self-protection."

"Tracey, you stay here," I said.

"Why?" she asked. "I'm not your little sister, you know!"

"Yes you are," said Carol. "And Charlie's right. We need you to contact my dad. I'll give you his home phone number. You fill him in and bring him up to speed. Tell him where we've gone. He'll know what to do."

"Okay," said Tracey. "Shall I get Gareth to go with you?"

"No," came four voices in unison.

"Let him sleep," I said. "There's four of us. We should be able to handle one crazed journo knocking 70."

"That's what I'm saying," said Tom. "How hard can it be?"

If only we'd known.

32

VERTIGO

Friday, 12th August

The Pyramid is the second-tallest skyscraper in the City of London and the sixth tallest in the country. It's marvellous, the things you can find out from the internet. Not that any of this was of the slightest importance to us as we burst through its doors and tried to get past the commissionaire.

"Not so fast, ladies and gents! Not so fast!" he remonstrated. "Where do you think you're going?"

"Top floor!" I gasped.

"Police!" gasped Carol, showing him her badge.

"The fortieth floor is closed for a private function," he said.

"We know," said Carol.

"Are you all police?" asked the commissionaire. He seemed particularly unconvinced by Marti.

"There's more coming," said Carol. "We're the advance guard."

We took the nearest of the sixteen high-speed passenger lifts. The doors opened, and we walked into the restaurant, past a protesting front-of-house manager. The room was strangely silent except for the clatter of cutlery.

"Look, there's Bill," said Tom. "Why on earth is he at the top table?"

"Marion Brooke's on the top table too," said Tom. "At least she's still alive."

"Where's Stephanie Sharp?" I asked.

"I can't see her," said Tom.

"What about Di Cojones?" I asked. "Marion thought he would be here."

"Maybe he didn't show," said Carol.

"I must say Bill Slope doesn't look like a crazed serial killer," said Tom. "In fact, he's waving at us to come over."

"Hang on a moment," I said. "I think I may have got the wrong person."

"What do you mean?" asked Carol.

I picked up a menu. Something I remembered Stephanie Sharp saying at the film premiere had suddenly come back to haunt me. Something I should have raised with Bill Slope before now, except that it had slipped my mind.

"Oh no!" I said.

Across the top was a logo reading DRIES HELLING'S VERTIGO. Under it was a menu, preceded with the words:

"This menu is the first to have been inspired by a video game. Each course has been dedicated to one of the seven deadly sins. To preserve a sense of mystery, we would like you to guess the ingredients, all of which have been foraged from within thirty miles of the restaurant."

Below that were printed the names of the seven deadly sins.

AVARICE

GLUTTONY

ANGER

PRIDE

SLOTH
LUST
ENVY

"Tom," I said, "have you still got The Seven Deadly Sins on your mobile?"

"Yes," he said. "A cut-down version of it. It's an app."

"Can you find me the avatar page?"

"*Avatar* page?" asked Carol. "What's *Avatar* got to do with this?"

"Not the film," I said. "This is the page where you choose a gameplaying identity?"

"Sure," said Tom.

After a few moments, he handed his phone to me.

"All you do is put your real name in that box there," said Tom. "Then choose the language you're in, and the one you want it changed into."

"I tapped the words 'Dries Helling' into the name box, 'Dutch' into the nationality and ordered an English translation.

The name I half-expected showed up.

"Okay," I said. "Now I know who the killer is."

I turned to the nearest diner, whom I recognised as a food critic who'd been one of the judges on *Masterchef*.

"Excuse me," I said. "What course are you on?"

"The seventh," he said. "And I must say it was the culinary experience of a lifetime."

"Absolutely," agreed the gaunt woman beside him. "And it's so ecological, isn't it! To think he foraged all his ingredients from within a few miles of here!"

"I don't suppose you know what the ingredients were?" I asked.

"No," said the food critic. "But here's the man who's going to tell us. Bravo!"

This last word was aimed at the small, unassuming man who

was walking through the dining room, accepting the plaudits of the diners.

"Bloody hell!" said Tom.

"It's Jason Statham!" exclaimed Marti.

"No, it isn't," I said, for I had seen the man before, though never in a chef's outfit. "He's Dries Helling, but that's not his real name. His real name is Ben Slope."

Hearing his name, the man turned round.

"Oh it's you, Charlie," he said. "Glad you could show up after all."

"I'm here to bring you to justice," I said. "Sorry about that, Ben."

"Don't be," he said. "I was planning to come clean about everything in due course. Now's as good a time as any. I'd be obliged if you'd let me say my piece."

"I'm not sure we can do that," said Carol.

"And who are you?" said Ben Slope.

"I'm Detective Inspector Carol Smith," said Carol.

"Blimey," said Ben Slope. "The pigs really are looking younger and younger these days. Must be a sign I'm getting old!"

"You know what they call you down at Scotland Yard?" asked Carol. "The Trophy Hunter."

"Oh, yeah?" said Ben Slope. "That shows how little the police know about me."

"He wasn't collecting trophies," I told Carol. "He was foraging for ingredients."

"I was trying to put together a truly memorable meal," said Slope, "and rid the world of some of its most appalling scumbags at the same time."

"But why?" asked Carol.

"Why does anyone do anything?" he asked. "Why did you go into the police?"

"To be of service to the public," said Carol. "And, I suppose, to make my father proud."

"The same with me!" exclaimed the chef. "I've always wanted to do something to leave the world a better place, and make my dad proud. He taught me everything I know about foraging for food."

"Bill Slope?" asked Carol.

"Look, Charlie," said Dries, or rather Ben. "I was planning to make a speech to the assembled multitude. Make a clean breast of my sins. Why don't we do this as a question and answer thing? Make it a bit less formal?"

It was the most bizarre proposal I had ever had in my life.

"Okay," I said. "I'll do it."

"Let's go," he said. "The mike stand is over by the window."

As we walked over to the mike stand, Dries Helling – alias Ben Slope – acknowledged the congratulations of the diners. I spotted Des Mullarky, accompanied by a buxom woman who was presumably Berthe from Belgium. In a prominent position at the top table were Bernie Spritzer and his new fiancée. I even recognised I.P. Blood and Fairycakes Bonanza Parks, both looking surprisingly respectable as representatives, presumably, of the nation's trendiest, most rebellious youth.

"Thank you so much," said Ben.

"No, thank *you*!" called out someone, at which there was laughter and more applause.

"Unaccustomed as I am to public speaking," said Slope, "I've had all the doors locked, so none of you can escape!"

There was nervous laughter from his audience. Ben Slope continued to smile pleasantly as he introduced me.

"I've got a bloke here who you probably all remember from his footballing days. He's Charlie Charlesworth, formerly of Arsenal and England but now one of London's finest private investigators, and he's going to help me tell you what this evening is really all about."

"Great food!" called out somebody.

"Foraging!" said another.

"Thanks," said Slope, raising a hand in salutation. "You're very kind."

"I'm not sure how we're going to do this," I whispered in Ben Slope's ear.

"How about if you start," he said softly, "by asking who the serial killer is who's been terrorising London the last week or so."

"But I know the answer," I said.

"I know you know, Charlie," muttered Slope. "But the punters here don't."

"Okay, er, Dries, who's been murdering all these people we've been reading about in the papers?"

"Well, Charlie," said Slope, "I'm very much afraid that would be me."

There was an appalled hush, as the diners wondered if this was some joke, in dreadful taste. The last time I heard a hush like that, Ricky Gervais was presenting at the Golden Globes.

"And that's not a joke, is it?" I asked him.

"Indeed it isn't, Charlie," said Slope.

"I believe you started off your killing spree with Avarice."

"Yes," he said. "In the form of Jack O'Riordan."

"Why him?"

"He was a pornographer and a blackmailer."

"And how did you know that?"

"From my dad," said Ben Slope. "O'Riordan was blackmailing him. Dad tried to reason with him, but he wanted more and more money. My dad couldn't keep paying him, so in the end I thought I'd cut the geezer's head off."

"Why did you put it on a platter?"

"It was kind of a post-modernist joke. After all, I was about to turn the guy into food. I was feeling a bit peckish, so I ate his eyes," he said.

Various people said "Oo," and I.P. Blood fell off his chair.

"No, they're really tasty," said Ben Slope. "Quite salty. A bit like scallops."

"Did you cut anything else off?"

"I cut out some of his organs and took his fingers. They were just something to gnaw on. For the long drive back to Norfolk."

"Norfolk?"

"I was staying overnight with my dad," he said. "He didn't know my plans. He just thought I needed his car to go back to London, which I did and returned it to him. I was still there when you and your son dropped by. It's a good job you didn't come upstairs."

"So the violent videos were all yours?" I said. "All those movies about revenge?"

"I wouldn't say they were that violent," he said. "But I used them to psych me up to do what I knew I had to do. What is they say about revenge? That it's a dish best served cold. I've often wondered if that's literally true, and tonight I think I've proved some of it can be served hot and still taste good."

There was a rumble of disgust from the audience, mingled with – for the first time – an element of fear. What was Slope about to do to them? He winked at me encouragingly.

"Go on," he said. "We haven't got all night. And I certainly haven't."

"Your next act was, I think, a double murder."

"That's right," he said. "One was Gluttony in the form of Joseph Gildenstern, followed seconds later by Anger, personified by Jean-Paul De Mode."

"Perhaps you could enlighten us," I suggested, "about why you selected them?"

"I have to admit there was a personal element involved," said Ben. "Well, you knew Gildenstern. He was a nasty little shit who constantly cheated on his wife and kids."

"That doesn't normally incur a death sentence," I said.

"You're right," he said. "Anyway, I had a much more personal reason than that to kill him. Do you know what really got up my nose about him?"

"Is it to do with his business?" I asked.

"You're good," he said, encouragingly. "I expect you even know why he moved it from Germany to South Korea?"

"Is it something to do with land mines?" I asked. "I know his company make more of them than anyone else."

"You see, ladies and gentlemen, Charlie's not as thick as he looks!" said Slope. "Most countries including Germany and this one have signed up to ban land mines. South Korea is one of the few nations not to ban them."

"Why do you feel so strongly?" I asked.

"I was blown up by one, out in Afghanistan. Sold by Herr Gildenstern's company to the Taliban."

"Then how come you're still here?" I asked.

"Because a couple of other guys were nearer it than I was," said Slope. "Even so, the mine took most of my face off. I had to have plastic surgery."

"So that's why you look like that," I said. "But why Jason Statham? Johnny Depp or George Clooney, I could understand, but Jason Statham!"

"I happen to think he's a very underrated actor," said Slope. "Did you see him in *Snatch*? *The Bank Job*? He was really good!"

"What about *Death Race*?" called out one of the diners.

"*The Transporter 3*!" yelled another.

"*Revolver*!" cried out a third.

"Shit," said Slope, "these days everyone's a fucking critic. Do you want to hear my confession or not? Charlie, help me out here."

"Why did you murder De Mode?" I asked.

"What a tosser!" he said. "Come on, say he didn't deserve it!"

"But you didn't have to kill him."

"Why not? He nearly killed me. We were at film school together, and we had an argument. I can't remember what it was about, but he lost his temper and stabbed me, and then his wealthy family helped him escape the consequences."

"But that must have been years ago," I said.

"So?" he asked. "You don't forget these things. Especially not when he marries the girl you love."

"Marion Brooke," I said.

"Yeah," he replied. "She was just starting out in the industry, and I had her in my student film."

I looked across at Marion. She was squirming in her seat.

"When you say 'had her'," I said. "You mean...?"

"You know what I mean," said Slope. "But she wasn't interested in settling down with me. She had bigger fish to fry. And then she goes off and marries that vicious little poof."

"Okay," I said. "Then there was Pride."

"Ah yes," he said. "Lorenzo Fettucini. He put the final nail into the coffin of my career."

"As a restaurateur?"

"As a film director," he said, addressing the audience. "As Charlie here knows, I've always been a football fan, and he struck me as a fascinating character – you know, charismatic, as well as a great footballer."

"But you went off him?"

"I saved up for years to do a film about him, with him putting up half the money and me the other half."

"And he gambled all the money away," I said.

"How do you know that?"

"I heard about it from a bloke I met in Belgium, though I didn't take much notice of it at the time. In fact, he's here this evening. Desmond Mullarky."

Des Mullarky stood up. There was even a tiny ripple of applause. The diners seemed relieved that they hadn't yet heard anything to turn their stomachs. I was fairly certain that they soon would, but pressed on with the narrative.

"And then we have Sloth," I said.

"And who better to personify Sloth than Alfredo Di Cojones?" said Slope. "God rest his soul."

"I didn't know he was dead," I said.

"I slaughtered him this afternoon."

A wave of shock and revulsion swept through the room. Evidently the fact that four other people had died had already lost its shock value. I continued.

"So why did he have to die?" I asked.

"First, he's a terrible director. Pretentious, sanctimonious and slow."

I made a non-committal grunt. I've always made it a rule not to speak ill of the dead, especially not publicly. But I had to admit Slope had a point.

"And he ruined my career," he said.

"In food?" I said.

"No," he said. "I told you I trained to be a director. I wanted to be the new Hitchcock. But this old fart slept through my end-of-year movie. What's worse, he then gave it a Fail, saying that sleep was the purest form of criticism."

"And that's why you murdered him?" I asked.

"Let's just say I felt his life, like his films, needed editing."

"Which brings us to killing number six – Lust."

"I felt a bit guilty about this one," said Slope. "But I needed another big guy if I was going to cope with a whole banquet. So I chose Edward Killingfield."

"You murdered your mentor?"

"Yeah," he said. "I'm not proud of it. But when it comes to poofs, I have to say I'm with my old mate Des Mullarky."

I looked over at Mullarky. He hadn't minded when I'd mentioned his name, but he didn't look too chuffed at being mentioned as a friend by a serial killer.

"Cheers, Des," said Slope, acknowledging him with a wave. "There are just too many of them about. So I thought a judicious cull was in order. Edward has been making a real nuisance of himself, trying to chat me up. He just wouldn't take no for an answer. So I strung him up this afternoon when he came to wish me good luck."

Another murmur of fear and revulsion ran through the room.

"Which brings us on to your final victim," I said. "Envy."

"Well, here I owe all of you an apology," said Slope. "The last course was meant to be more substantial than coffee and petit fours. But my seventh victim got away. Or, to be accurate, she never showed up."

"And she was?"

"She still is," said Slope. "Stephanie Sharp. Over there in the corner. She was meant to be interviewing me this morning as an insert for her new chat show. But she never turned up. Told me someone better had turned up. More of a celebrity. It turned out to be Jedward."

"Bad luck!" I said. "From the memory of my one and only film premiere, I could remember how bad it had felt to be looked upon as a lower life form than the Tintin-quiffed, non-singing, non-dancers."

"I don't know why I was surprised," said Slope. "All my life, she's let me down. She's never been much of a mother."

"So she was meant to be your seventh victim," I said. "Why envy?"

"My dad always told me she was the meanest, most envious woman he'd ever met, and he was right. She only thought of herself from the moment I was born."

"So you were planning to give your mother her just desserts," I said.

"I thought it would be a challenge," replied Slope, "turning someone that sour into a sweet."

I looked across at Stephanie Sharp. For possibly the first time in her life, she seemed lost for words. She looked very old and tired. All the colour had drained from her face, leaving only a slash of red lipstick. I almost felt sorry for her.

"Which means, of course, that Bill Slope is your father," I said.

"He is," said Slope, turning towards Bill. "Dad, I realise

that not everything I've done has been strictly ethical, even by journalistic standards. But believe me, all I ever wanted to do was impress you, make you see I could accomplish something. I've always wanted to put together a great meal, forage for my own food, and tonight it feels as though everything has come together."

"So why did you use a different name?" I asked. "And pretend to be Dutch?"

"That's down to Seven Deadly Sins," he replied. "The computer game, you know? It's a great game. Inspirational."

"I'm more of a Football Manager man myself," I confessed.

"I'm not saying that isn't good too," said Ben Slope. "But I prefer something with a bit more action, know what I mean? I played Seven Deadly Sins all through my convalescence, after my face was blown off. Dries Helling was the name of my avatar. I always played the game as him, and when I took the game on into real life, he seemed a good fit."

"And what does Dries Helling mean?" I asked.

"Can't you tell me that?" he asked.

"I can, actually," I said. "It's Dutch for Warrior Slope. Why Warrior Slope?"

"Because, Charlie, that's what I've become – an eco-warrior serving fresh, foraged food."

"Wait a minute," I said. "Another thing you've done is turn all these good people into cannibals."

At this point, various people tried to run retching from the room. Someone on the food critics' table appeared to suffer a coronary. I was surprised this kind of reaction hadn't happened before. Either they were slow on the uptake, or up to now the diners had thought this was all some kind of elaborate joke.

"Working with Edward Killingfield," said Ben Slope, "I learned to look beyond bourgeois taboos."

"You think murder's a bourgeois taboo?" I asked.

"Everyone in here asked me to murder," said Ben, "on behalf

of Queen and Country. But now I choose to murder in a wider, more noble cause. To cause the death of bad people and to serve the best kind of food."

"I take it you're a cannibal," I said.

"Every great cook tastes his own food," he said.

"But Ben," I said.

"Call me Dries," said Ben. "I prefer to be called Dries, when I'm on duty."

"Dries, I kind of understand why you've done the killing," I said, "but why the cannibalism?"

"Oh, that," he said, as if it were the most natural thing in the world. "I just got a taste for it. My helicopter was shot down in the Iraqi desert, and you do what you have to do."

"You ate human flesh?"

"I had to," he said. "I needed to survive. The other guys around me were all dead, or dying. When the medics found me, they were surprised at how healthy I was. To be honest, I'd never felt better."

"Charlie," said Carol, advancing on us with her taser. "I think this man has said more than enough."

"Oh?" said Ben. "What are you going to do to me? What is that thing?"

"It's a taser," said Carol, "And I am arresting you on suspicion of six counts of murder. And cannibalism."

"I'm not sure if cannibalism is against the law," said Ben. "Though I think it is in Germany."

"Look, does it matter?" I said. "Let Carol finish what she's got to say."

"You do not have to say anything," Carol told the unrepentant serial killer. "But it may harm your defence if you do not mention when questioned something which you later rely on in court. Anything you do say may be given in evidence."

"A simple 'You're nicked' would have sufficed," said Ben. "But that's enough gabbing. I have unfinished business."

Before anyone could stop him, he ran to the nearest window, opened it and stood for a moment on the ledge outside.

"Goodbye, Charlie," he said. "Did I mention I was always your biggest fan?"

Under normal circumstances, it would have been encouraging to receive that kind of acclaim. However, it didn't sound quite as good, coming from the lips of a self-confessed serial killer.

He raised his arms into a crucified pose and launched himself backwards. He plummeted downwards for approximately 200 metres, if Wikipedia is to be trusted.

In a funny way, I felt a bit sorry for Ben. Life had been tough on him. He'd had a rotten childhood. He'd had his dreams of being a director smashed at film college. Survived a helicopter crash. Been disfigured. If you cared to look at the world from his perspective, he'd turned his life around. Thanks to his crimes, he'd achieved celebrity status in his own lifetime, though not quite as much as Jedward. Now he was dead, he'd be remembered as the most gruesome British serial killer since Jack the Ripper. And, even the toughest food critics seemed agreed that he had cooked a memorable last supper. I was glad that I hadn't been there to eat it, though. Give me roast chicken, any day.

33

THE LODGER

Saturday, 13th August

Under the circumstances, Carol provided great moral support. She stayed all night at my place, and in the same bed, though we didn't do much more than cuddle. She said she didn't feel much like sex, what with thinking about all that senseless killing. I said that was okay. I was feeling a bit knackered myself.

Mind you, we made up for that in the morning. When I went downstairs, I was surprised to find Bill Slope asleep on our couch.

"What are you doing here?" I asked.

"You said I should come home with you," he said. "You said I shouldn't be alone. And the office stinks of paraffin."

"Bloody hell," I said. "So I did. How are you feeling?"

"Not great," he said. "And after last night I'm not expecting to win any awards as Father of the Year."

"Never mind," I said. "Fancy a coffee?"

"Great," he said. "I see you've got one of those new fangled coffee machines. Will you show me how to use it?"

After not much of a breakfast, Carol and I went with Tom

to talk to her father. We left Bill on our couch. He'd fallen asleep again, despite the caffeine, and it seemed a shame to disturb him.

The police took it all rather well. I think they were pleasantly surprised that the case had been solved so quickly. The riots were clearly foremost in their minds, with a crazed cannibal serial killer significantly lower down their list of concerns. Frank Drake was drily complimentary, though I could see he kept wondering what the connection was between me and his daughter. I knew that he knew about me and Marion Brooke, and that it was only a matter of time before he raised this with Carol. I'd have to talk to her about Marion before he did.

"I think dad likes you," said Carol, when we emerged from Scotland Yard and waited to hail a taxi.

"Really?" I asked. "If that's how Frank Drake is when he likes you, I'd hate to see him when he's tetchy."

"I think he may be a little bit jealous," said Carol. "After all, you found the serial killer before he did."

"Yes, he did call it impressive detective work," I admitted.

"And I thought you were brilliant," she said. "I felt like Dr Watson must have felt, watching Sherlock Holmes in action."

"Now you're taking the piss," I said.

"No, seriously," she said. "I'm impressed."

"Come back to my place?" I asked.

"Yes, please,' she said.

"Can I come too?" asked Tom.

"I'd forgotten you were with us," I said.

"Don't mind me," said Tom.

When the three of us got back, Bill Slope was watching the television. He didn't even ask how the meeting with the police had gone.

"It's a really good picture, this high-def," he said. "I can see why those looters stole so many of them."

"How's England doing?" asked Tom.

"It's a massacre," he said. "Jimmy Anderson's swinging the ball both ways, and the Indians don't have any answers. It'll be all over by tea. You lot will be number one in the World."

"Really?" I asked. "Higher than the Australians?"

"We're down to number four or five," he said. "Too many of our best players retired at the same time. Some of our younger players would struggle against Zimbabwe."

"So you'd fail the Tebbit test on immigrants," I said.

"What test?"

"Tebbit. Norman Tebbit. Former cabinet minister."

"Oh, him. What about him?"

"He said you could tell the loyalty of a British subject when you found out what team they supported at cricket."

"Did he?" he asked. "What if they only watched football?"

"I'm not sure," I said. "Maybe that would be proof of integration."

"Not if you're an Arsenal supporter," said Bill. "Hardly any of them are British."

"We've got Wilshere and Ramsay," I said. "And the Ox, Walcott and Gibbs, when they aren't injured."

"Isn't today the start of the football season?"

"Yes," I said. "It seems to start earlier each season. And already the Arsenal are in disarray. We're about to lose two of our best players."

"Oh yeah," said Slope. "Fabregas and Nasri."

"And we're away to Newcastle."

"Didn't you throw away a four-goal lead against them last season?"

"Thanks, Bill," I said. "You really know how to hurt."

"Look, Bill," said Carol, evidently feeling there were bigger issues to discuss than football. Women are like that. "I'm really, really sorry about your son."

"No worries," said Bill, amiably. "He kinda brought it on himself, didn't he?"

He turned off the telly with the remote control.

"Hey, I was watching that," said Tom.

"Tom!" I said.

"Sorry," he said.

"That's right," said Bill. "You listen to your father. I only wish Ben had done a bit more listening to me."

"You mustn't blame yourself," said Carol. "It wasn't you that turned Ben into a serial killer."

"You're right," said Bill, nodding. "Mostly I blame his mother."

"Why didn't you ever mention he was alive?" I asked. "Until last night, I thought he was dead."

"I didn't mean to mislead you," said Bill. "The subject simply never came up."

"You told us he'd been blown up on active service," said Tom. "Remember? In your cottage?"

"Be fair," said Bill. " I didn't say the bomb had killed him."

"True," I admitted. "By the way, Bill, I owe you an apology. At one point I thought you were the killer."

"You did?" asked Bill. "Strewth, mate. Why?"

"I thought you'd used your car to drive down to London and back the night of O'Riordan's murder," I told him.

"That wasn't me," said Bill. "You heard. I lent the car to Ben. He said he had a party to go to."

"And I noticed you had that video game, The Seven Deadly Sins," I said. "So I put two and two together, and made five."

"There was an innocent explanation," he said. "I told you, I was writing a book about Igor Molotovski. The game was just research material. At least it was as far as I was concerned. It was Ben who couldn't stop playing it. I think he may have had what you might call an addictive personality."

"And I saw those violent videos by your telly, and they were all about revenge."

"They weren't mine," said Bill. "They all belonged to Ben."

"I thought they'd given you the idea to murder all those people," said Tom. "Sorry."

"Yeah, well, I'm not really the murdering kind," said Bill. "Never had the time or inclination."

"So you accept Ben's explanation of why he did it?" I asked.

"Well, it makes a kind of sense," said Bill. "He didn't have much luck studying film. His tutor slept through his one and only movie. His nympho girlfriend threw him over for a woofta. Who also happened to be the classmate who stabbed him at college, and got away with it because of his wealthy family."

"Did he speak to you about any of that?" asked Carol. "I mean, before last night?"

"Yeah," said Bill, "and I did what most dads would do. Told him to turn the other cheek, get on with his life, that sort of thing. And, for a time he did. He became a soldier. Good at it, too."

"But then he got shot down in Iraq," I said.

"He was never the same after that," said Ben.

"Did you know he was a cannibal?" asked Tom.

"No way. But he did say that in the helicopter crash he'd had a bad knock on the head, and he saw things differently now."

"They say Fred West's personality changed when he had a blow to the head," I said. "I think he had a bicycle accident."

"Fred West?" said Bill.

"You know, Fred and Rosemary West. The serial killers."

"Oh yeah," said Bill. "Sorry, I was still thinking about Ben. You know, I think losing his face was the final straw."

"Getting blown up in Afghanistan?"

"Yeah," he said. "He was in a terrible mess. And I didn't think a lot of his new face. Maybe I shouldn't have let that show."

"Oh?"

"Yeah. I told him he should have gone for a more heroic look. Russell Crowe, in *Gladiator*. Or Shane Warne."

"Shane Warne?" I asked.

"Yeah," he said. "Of course, that's Shane Warne before he got made over by this Hurley woman and turned into some kind of metrosexual waxwork."

"Bill," said Carol. "May I call you Bill?"

"Sure," said Bill.

"Ben said one thing last night that I didn't understand," said Carol. "I hope you won't mind my asking about it."

"No," said Bill. "Go ahead. What was it?"

"He said the reason he killed Jack O'Riordan was that O'Riordan had been blackmailing you."

"Oh yeah?"

"I was just wondering, why was he blackmailing you?"

"It's a bit embarrassing," said Bill. "Especially in mixed company."

"Don't think of me as a woman," said Carol. "Think of me as a police officer."

"Yeah? Well, I can see Charlie thinks of you as a woman," said Bill, "and I don't blame him. You're a looker."

"Thanks," said Carol. "And?"

"Look," said Bill after a lengthy pause, "If you really want to know, it's to do with Loco Parente."

"The model agency man?" asked Carol.

"Yes," I said, "but the agency was a cover for a lot of things, among them prostitution."

"The thing is I was investigating Parente," said Bill, "for a piece I was writing, about corruption in football, how FIFA gets influenced to award the World Cup to one country and not another, and… I got myself compromised."

"Compromised?" I asked.

"Yeah," he said. "I was in this bar in Singapore, and I may have had a bit too much to drink. And this sheila comes on to me, and she's a pretty little thing, and though I'm drunk I'm not too drunk to… you know, get aroused."

"And?"

"So I go with her to her hotel room, and she takes off her clothes, and blow me down she ain't a sheila, she's a bruce."

"A transsexual?"

"Yeah, but by this time we'd gone pretty far, so I got on with it. And a few weeks later, I get this DVD in the post, and it's me getting it on with this shemale. There must have been hidden cameras all over the room. Professionally edited, too. And there's a note saying that it will be all over the internet if I don't stop my investigation into Parente and pay this guy who made the video for his trouble."

"And the guy who made the video was O'Riordan?"

"Yeah," said Bill. "He didn't say who he was, but I knew, because I'd come across him before. He'd done a lot of dirty work for Parente."

"So you paid him off?" asked Carol.

"Course I did," said Bill. "This all happened when I still had a reputation, before the paedophile thing."

"But O'Riordan kept coming back for more?" I asked.

"Yeah," said Bill. "He was quite shrewd, only asking for as much money as I could afford. But I did mention his name to Ben, and I suppose he decided to take care of him for me."

"But you didn't ask him to?" asked Carol.

"Of course not," said Bill. "Why would I want to get my son into that kind of trouble? As far as I knew, he had a promising future as a chef."

"Why didn't you suspect Ben when the news came of O'Riordan's death?" Carol asked.

"Why should I?" asked Bill. "I told you, he said he'd gone to a party. I thought his interests lay in finding new, exotic foods."

"Well, in a way, they did," said Tom.

"Yeah," said Bill. "Every time I think about what I ate last night, I feel a bit churned up."

Carol looked up at me and squeezed my hand.

"Fancy a spot of lunch?" she asked.

"Not really," I said. "I seem to have lost my appetite."

"Me too," she said. "At least for food. Fancy coming upstairs?"

"Mind if I stay down here? The cricket will be back on in a moment," said Bill.

"Sure, Bill," I said. "What about you, Tom?"

"Don't mind me," said Tom. "I'm just going to change my shirt, and then I'm off out."

"Where?"

"Not sure," he said.

"On your own?"

"No," he said. "With Marti."

"Oh?"

"We were planning to watch Spurs versus Everton, but the police have called it off because of the rioting."

"You're not telling me…" I said.

"Yes, Dad, I'm afraid it's true," said Tom, ruefully. "Marti's a Tottenham supporter. We've tried to keep it from you, but it was bound to come out in the end."

I tried not to let my stricken feelings show.

"Are you absolutely sure she's right for you?" I asked.

"Yeah," said Tom. "And there's more. We're going to get married. We were just choosing the right moment to tell you. I suppose now is as good a time as any."

"Congratulations!" said Carol.

"Yeah, cheers, mate," said Bill.

"You couldn't find a better girl," I said, giving him a hug and adding as a selfish afterthought "I hope she'll continue working."

"Of course she will, Dad," he said.

"Good," I said, "because we're moving offices next month. Upstairs to the bigger of those two vacant suites. I've had a word with the landlord."

"Why, Dad?" asked Tom.

"It struck me that our lodger here is too valuable a member of our team to continue sleeping on the floor of our conference room. He's going to need his own office if he's going to join the team. What do you say, Bill?"

"Well," he said, "I was planning to retire, but if you really need me…"

"A man with your talents and experience?" I said. "I'd be a fool to let you slip through my fingers."

"Okay then," he said. "So you don't mind if I carry on watching the cricket while you two go upstairs?"

"Not at all," I said.

In my bedroom, Carol pressed herself against me and stroked the back of my neck. It was a good feeling.

"I bet you never thought this was going to happen," she said, "when we first met."

"No," I said. "But I like a story with a happy ending."

"You old softie," she said, giggling.

"I'm not that soft," I said.

"Mm," she said.

"Why are you laughing?" I asked. "I'm trying to be serious."

"Sorry," she said. "I was thinking."

"You know something, Charlie?"

"What?"

"I'm really, really happy you're not a paedophile."

"No, but…"

"But what?" she said sharply.

"About Marion Brooke," I said. "She and I… well…"

"You slept with her?"

"We, er, didn't get much sleep."

"I thought she was a lesbian."

"Not exclusively."

"And you still hanker after her?"

"God no," I said. "I don't think we're very compatible."

"And we are?"

"Yes," I said. "At least I hope so. What do you think?"

"You are a proper Charlie, aren't you?" she said, unbuttoning my shirt.

"I suppose you'll be wanting your own key next," I said.

"Absolutely," she said, unbuttoning her blouse. "You wouldn't want me to have to break down your front door again, would you?"

We climbed into bed.

"Blimey, Carol, I just thought of something," I said.

"What?"

"I forgot to ring this shrink in Harley Street."

"Charlie, have you anything really bad to tell me?"

"Not really," I said. "It's just that Tom keeps saying I'm addicted, and I don't think I am."

"Oh, Charlie, you're not a sex addict, are you?" she said, climbing in beside me.

"Not yet," I said. "No, it's computer games. One in particular."

"Oh," she said, "Yes. Football Manager. It is compulsive, isn't it?"

"But that's the thing," I said, surprised. "Do you know, I haven't played Football Manager for hours. Days, even. I haven't even thought about playing it."

"Me neither," she said. "I suppose we've both been too busy."

We looked at each other and spoke in perfect unison:

"Maybe we're cured."